Praise for

DAVID FENNELL

'A truly extraordinary crime novel ... a gritty, dark thriller with a
serial killer of frightening proportions'
LYNDA LA PLANTE

'I flew through it ... Tense, gripping and brilliantly inventive'
SIMON LELIC

'You couldn't ask for a more assured, if startlingly graphic and
gory, debut'
IRISH INDEPENDENT

'Unsettling, fast-paced, suspenseful and gripping ... Excellent'
WILL DEAN

'A tense-as-hell, high-body count page turner, but a rarer thing too –
one that's also full of genuine warmth and humanity'
WILLIAM SHAW

'A hair-raisingly dark thriller ... you won't be able to put it down'
ARAMINTA HALL

'A blend of Lynda La Plante and Thomas Harris'
CRIME TIME

'A stunning start to what promises to be a fantastic new series ...
layered, twisty and so deliciously dark'
M. W. CRAVEN

'David Fennell more than earns his place at the crime fiction table with
this superb exploration of a psychopath with the creepiest modus
operandi I've read in a long time'
FIONA CUMMINS

'A serial killer classic in the making ... hooks you in and holds you tight,
right up to the extremely satisfying final page'
SUSI HOLLIDAY

David Fennell was born and raised in Belfast. He left for London at the age of eighteen and jobbed as a chef, waiter and bartender for several years before starting a career in writing for the software industry. David has played rugby for Brighton and studied Creative Writing at the University of Sussex. He is married and lives in Brighton.

To find out more, visit his website: www.davidfennell.co.uk

Follow him on Twitter: @davyfennell

Also by David Fennell

The Art of Death
See No Evil

The Silent Man

DAVID FENNELL

ZAFFRE

First published in the UK in 2023 by
ZAFFRE
An imprint of Bonnier Books UK
4th Floor, Victoria House, Bloomsbury Square, London, WC1B 4DA
Owned by Bonnier Books
Sveavägen 56, Stockholm, Sweden

A CIP catalogue record for this book is
available from the British Library.

ISBN: 978-1-80418-173-7
Trade paperback ISBN: 978-1-80418-174-4

Also available as an ebook and an audiobook

1 3 5 7 9 10 8 6 4 2

Typeset by IDSUK (Data Connection) Ltd
Printed and bound in Great Britain by Clays Ltd, Elcograf S.p.A.

Zaffre is an imprint of Bonnier Books UK
www.bonnierbooks.co.uk

For Ethna

I fear a Man of frugal Speech
I fear a Silent Man
Haranguer I can overtake
Or Babbler entertain

But He who weigheth While the Rest
Expend their furthest pound
Of this Man I am wary
I fear that He is Grand

Emily Dickinson

Part 1

Chapter 1

Sunday, 13 March

H E RETREATS BEHIND THE FOLIAGE with his back to the wall and becomes one with the shadows in the shared garden of Albany Mansions in Battersea. An earthy perfume fills his nostrils. He shudders, and for a moment, is transported back to his childhood. A different time. A different place.

Pushing the memory from his mind, he watches the lighted windows of the two-bedroom ground-floor flat. Double doors lead into a dimly lit modern white kitchen. A stack of dirty dishes from the evening's meal lies on the worktop above a partially opened dishwasher. A flat archway leads through to the living room where the green of an expansive television broadcasting *Match of the Day* silhouettes Jason Todd's head. He's half watching the football and half focused on the screen of his mobile phone.

The evening is close and muggy. The forecast predicts a downpour. He must be quick and hopes the rain holds out for now.

His eyes slide past the dark empty bathroom, the main bedroom, and stop at the second bedroom where Lucas Todd, dressed in pyjamas, his arm in a blue cast, sits at his desk. School books lie open and ignored on the surface. Bulbous headphones, too big for his small head, cover his ears. He is pointing a pistol at a computer monitor depicting an unending influx of bloodthirsty undead hurling themselves at the screen. Lucas has a talent for conquering them.

He turns his attention back to Jason Todd. He is talking on his mobile. Todd's arm reaches up and across and strokes his bald head. His shoulders shake. He is laughing. The call ends, Todd switches off the television, stands, yawns and stretches his limbs. Plunging the living room into darkness, he walks into the kitchen, carrying two empty beer bottles. He is barefoot, wearing grey jogging bottoms and a white T-shirt. He stops and peers down the hallway. 'Lucas, time for bed,' he calls.

Lucas is still in the world of the undead. He does not hear his father's voice.

The kitchen lights flicker brightly into life.

Todd sets the bottles by the kitchen sink, washes his hands and looks at the window in front of him. They could almost be looking at each other, eye to eye, but Todd is looking at his reflection. Lifting his head, he turns it from side to side and presses the soft flesh under his chin. Frowning, he dries his hands and crosses the kitchen to fill the dishwasher. He looks back towards the hallway. 'Lucas!' he calls once more. He waits, but the boy does not respond.

Todd leaves the dishwasher, walks down the hallway and enters Lucas's room without knocking. He taps him on the shoulder. The boy jolts in fright.

He cannot hear the conversation but gets the gist from Todd's angry face. The man points his fingers at the video screen and at the boy's homework. Lucas shrugs, switches off the monitor and gets up from his chair. He leaves the room without looking at his father.

The bathroom light switches on. Through the frosted glass he can make out Lucas brushing his teeth.

4

A purring sound grabs his attention. At his feet is a cat, black as night. It peers up at him with a curious expression, taking in the stranger. Crouching down, he slides his hand underneath its belly and picks it up. He strokes it with his gloved hand. The creature is unafraid and allows itself to be caressed.

A woman's voice comes from the rear of the block, 'Charcoal. Hey, kitty. Come to Mama.'

The cat wriggles to free itself. His grip tightens, his eyes narrowing at the creature's scrawny neck. He pictures snapping it in two. A hot sensation surges through him.

The cat hisses, sensing danger.

'Charcoal!' the woman calls in a sing-song voice that grates on him.

Its claws sink into his coat. He lifts it up and leans across, facing it, his eyes flared. The cat hisses and pushes itself away. He loosens his grip and lets it go, stamping his foot on the ground. The creature lets out a sharp meow and darts to the safety of its owner.

'There you are,' she says. 'Let's get you inside.'

He hears the neighbour's door closing and turns his attention back to Todd's flat. Lucas is back in his room, sitting on his bed. Despite his father's warning he gets up, places the headphones back on and returns to the world of the undead. Fortune favours the brave, he thinks.

Jason Todd is in the toilet pissing, judging by the downpour he hears. Todd leaves the bathroom, returns to the kitchen and finishes loading the dishwasher. Pulling on a pair of trainers, he picks up the two beer bottles, unlocks the back door and carries them to the recycling bin at the rear of the block.

He takes his moment, emerges from the shadows with the stealth of a snake and shoots across the pathway, a shadow flitting inside the Todd house. Making his way to the living room he crouches in front of the sofa and peers over the top at Jason Todd, hovering outside, 'Who's there?' he calls into the communal garden.

No one. I was there. But now I'm here, inside your home.

After a moment, Todd shrugs, steps inside, locks the kitchen door and turns out the light. He makes his way down the hallway.

He hears water running, the sound of teeth being brushed and spitting. He glides across the living room, down the hallway and hovers outside the main bedroom. Shooting a look towards Lucas's room, he sees the faint glow of the video monitor through the gap at the bottom of the door. The water stops running. Todd gargles and spits one final time before pulling on the bathroom cord and extinguishing the light.

He's in Jason Todd's bedroom. A soft chugging sound followed by a hiss. He hesitates. A lemony fragrance fills the air. Todd is approaching. He retreats into the darkness, hand sliding into his pocket firmly gripping the taser.

Todd enters the bedroom, walks to the window and pulls the curtains across. For a moment the darkness is absolute. He hears the man yawn, and as his eyes adjust, he sees him pull his T-shirt off.

He activates the taser. It crackles into life, the blue charge lighting up Todd's shocked face. He shoves it hard into the man's neck. Todd drops to the floor, paralysed and shaking, the taser pressed for five, ten, fifteen seconds.

From his coat pocket he removes a roll of duct tape and swiftly wraps several layers tightly around the man's neck, face and head. Todd lets out a muffled groan; his trembling increases as he struggles for breath. The tape clings to his face as the last of the air dissipates. Todd tries to batter him with his fists, but his strength is diminishing. In moments, he stops moving and lies limp.

He slides the duct tape back into his pocket and takes out a black marker. Pressing the taser button once more, he holds the small light close to Todd's head and draws on the tape.

The padding of feet in the hallway startles him. He climbs off the body and pushes the door closed. Lucas's footsteps stop outside his father's bedroom.

He can hear the boy breathing through the gap in the door. A moment passes. 'Dad?' says Lucas.

He holds his breath and waits. The boy must have heard Todd fall to the floor. He imagines him wondering if it's worth waking his father and risking another telling-off. But the boy chooses wisely and walks on. He hears the click of the bathroom cord light. Lucas is peeing.

Moving swiftly, he heaves the dead man's body onto the bed and covers it with the duvet.

The toilet flushes. The tap is running.

Lucas is outside his father's room once more. The door creaks slowly open.

He retreats into the shadows.

Light from the hallway slices through the darkness.

The silence is interrupted by the soft chugging, a hiss and the scent of lemon.

'Goodnight, Dad. Sorry about earlier.' When no response comes, he says, 'Love you.'

He is relieved when Lucas eventually pulls the door shut and pads down the hall to his room.

Chapter 2

A STORM IS EXPECTED. A BANK of grey clouds billow across the morning sky, ten minutes into her run. Droplets fall, splashing her hot face. She welcomes them, preferring to run when the weather is tempestuous. The wilder the better, she considers, hungry for a battle with a tornado or monsoon, which is unlikely in Central London.

She smiles as the droplets mutate into a downpour pounding the rough concrete surface of Queen's Walk. Cold water prickles her skin like needles. She laughs, increases her pace, tearing through the rainstorm as fellow runners head for cover and wait for the bombardment to pass.

The Thames, a long shimmering black mirror dividing the north and south of the capital, is shattered into a million pieces. Grace Archer hurtles under the spirals of the Millennium Bridge and joins Bankside. Across the river, peering over the skyline and Broken Wharf, she catches the imperial dome of St Paul's Cathedral. Focusing her attention ahead, she narrowly misses a runner coming in the opposite direction.

'Watch where you're going!' he shouts.

Archer waves an apology and keeps going, enjoying every moment of the storm as she passes a row of smart Georgian townhouses. Wiping her eyes, she squints ahead through a bank of trees and sees the Globe Theatre. The Elizabethan-style white mortar walls and supporting black timbers give it a soft cake-like appearance that seems on the verge of disintegration from the siege of arrowhead rain.

She feels a sudden deep thudding on her ribs and is knocked off her feet, falling onto the hard, wet ground.

'Oomph!'

Winded and confused, she clutches her side and gasps for air. 'What the hell!'

Archer looks up to see a thickset man with shorn hair looking down at her with little in the way of an apology. Pushing herself up to a sitting position, she winces at the pain in her ribs. 'Don't mind me,' she snaps, taking stock of him. He's wearing jeans and a leather jacket. Clearly, not a runner. She narrows her gaze. There's something familiar about him.

He crouches down beside her. 'Bet that hurt,' he says, in a mocking tone.

Archer feels the hairs on her neck rising. This was no accident. She's injured, and in this position, he has the upper hand. She realises where she has seen him before. He's one of Frankie White's stooges.

It'd be an understatement to suggest that London gangster, Frankie 'Snow' White, is Archer's nemesis. The phrase is absurd and laughable, but how else could she describe him. Although never proven, everyone knew White had ordered the execution of her father, DI Sam Archer, more than twenty years back. He'd been leading an investigation that was on the brink of shutting down White's drug cartel. For his trouble, he'd been shot and executed with a single bullet to the temple. Sam Archer had been left dead, bleeding and alone on a cold, deserted London street. She had never gotten over his murder. Archer wanted to finish what her father could not. She was determined to see the bastard go down.

Shielding her eyes from the rain, Archer holds his gaze. 'Did Frankie send you? There's a surprise. So which one of his vertically challenged brown-nosers are you? Judging from your humourless mug you must be *Grumpy*, or from your build, *Dumpy*?'

'I have a message,' he tells her.

'*Plumpy?*'

Archer notices his fists curling. She's riling him and thinks maybe she should rein it in. He could do her some damage. Despite this, she feels a surge of courage. 'Tell Frankie to go fuck himself.'

For a man of his build, he is swift. Archer barely registers his hand as it slices through the air, slapping her hard across the face. She gasps in shock and feels her cheek go hot. His hand is on her neck, squeezing firmly. She tries to disengage but his grip tightens.

'Oi!' comes a woman's voice. 'What the hell you playin' at? Get off her!'

Relief surges through her. She's not alone.

The man leans in closer. 'Today is a very bad day for Mr White, as you are well aware, Detective Inspector Archer. He blames you. And you will pay the price.'

'Get off her or I'm calling the police!' shouts the woman. Her voice is loud, she is nearby, but Archer cannot see her.

'Your day is coming,' he tells her. Releasing her neck, he shoves her, stands up and hurries away, disappearing through the trees and into the rain.

Archer pushes herself up, helped by the woman. 'I saw everything. That bully,' she says.

Archer is trying to see where he has gone. She has a mind to follow him, perhaps get a number plate if he's in a car, but the woman guides her to a bench and forces her to sit down.

'Are you OK?' the woman asks.

'I have to find him,' Archer insists.

'You're in no fit state. Sit down, gather yourself and tell me all about it.'

'I'm fine.' Archer is grateful for the woman's intervention but at the same time can't help feeling irritated. She hurries in the direction of the man, searching for him but it seems he has disappeared somewhere up New Globe Walk.

'Fuck,' she whispers.

'Come on, dear. Sit down.'

'I need to make a call,' Archer says, regretting that she never brought her phone.

'Just take a moment.'

Archer sighs and allows the woman to guide her to a bench. 'Do you have a phone?' she asks.

'Happens, I do,' she says, reaching into her handbag.

She's a slim woman, with lank, sodden, bleached hair that hangs over a thin face. Even through the rain, Archer can smell the bitter stench of cigarettes. She does not seem concerned about the downpour. Removing a mobile phone from her bag, she presses the device's screen. 'Oh typical,' she says, 'No battery.'

Archer rubs her ribs and wipes the rain from her face. 'That's OK. I should go home.' Archer stands.

The woman stands with her and regards Archer for a moment. 'Such a pretty face. Shame what Mr White is going to do to it.'

Archer's stomach clenches. 'What did you say?'

'You heard me. This is a sad day for Mr White and his family. A particularly sad day for Janine, wouldn't you agree?'

Archer says nothing.

'Janine would like to be here herself to pass this message on, but as you can imagine, she has a lot on her plate today. She wants you to remember what happened to her dear sweet boy. You remember him, don't you?'

12

Archer turns to leave, but the woman grabs her arm and squeezes it with a vice-like grip.

'Once Mr White has had his way, and your face is cut to ribbons, and you is somewhat dead, then Janine will visit your grave and dance on it under the silvery light of the moon.'

Archer yanks the woman's grip from her arm and leans towards her. 'I'm not sure she'll get that opportunity.'

The woman's thin lips contort into an icy smile. After a moment, she turns to walk away and then stops. 'One last thing,' she says. 'How's Jake?'

Archer flinches. 'What does that mean?'

'He's alone right now in that charming little house in Roupell Street. So . . . very alone.'

Archer feels her heart sinking. Her head spins. *Grandad.*

'Hurry. You may just make it in time,' the woman tells her.

Archer backs away, and ignoring the pain in her ribs, turns on her heels and bolts back down Bankside. An old woman is standing under a shelter. Archer hurries towards her.

'Please, do you have a phone I can borrow? I need to call the police.'

Chapter 3

ARCHER BARELY NOTICES THE RAIN easing by the time she arrives back at Roupell Street, sprinting up the middle of the road, breathless, heart pounding like a hammer in her chest, ribs throbbing. She dives at the front door of number fifty-two and raps the door knocker loudly.

'Grandad!' she calls, her voice cracking. 'Grandad!'

She fishes the key from the pocket of her jogging bottoms, pushes it into the lock, turns it and shoves the door open. Holding her breath, she scans the hallway. The inane chatter of a breakfast television show drifts from the living room. There are no signs of a struggle. The umbrella stand, the photographs on the walls, the coats hanging on the hatstand. Everything is in its place. Reaching down to the umbrella stand, she cautiously removes a concealed extendable police baton. She eases the living room door open. The big hand of the old ticking clock on the wall above the television is approaching 7.30 a.m. The French mirror above the marble fireplace shows an empty room. The sofa and armchair are vacant. No sign of Grandad.

Archer feels her stomach twisting. Is she too late?

A banging noise comes from the kitchen.

She hurries up the hallway and darts into the kitchen, baton ready. But no one is there. The back door handle is flapping up and down, the door is creaking as if someone is trying to push it open. The door is bolted. With one hand firmly on the weapon, she slides the bolt across and pulls open the door.

Grandad, dressed in his pyjamas and bathrobe, tumbles inside. 'Oh Lord!' he says, as Archer catches him. His white hair, his clothing, are drenched.

Relief washes over her.

In the distance, she hears a siren.

He laughs. 'Well, that was a lucky escape.'

She eases his thin, bony body up. 'What were you doing out there?'

'I was pruning the bushes and it started to rain. I tried to get back inside but appear to have locked myself out.' He laughs. 'I'm absolutely dripping.'

Archer feels a lump in her throat. She does not want to ask why he's pruning at this time of the morning in his pyjamas and robe. He's in the early stages of dementia and sometimes his memory and comprehension of the simplest things is a challenge. But there is no way Grandad could have locked himself out. The kitchen door is bolted from inside. Archer looks at the well-kept garden, thirty feet long, walled and private. The only access is from the kitchen. The walls lead over to neighbouring properties.

'Has anyone been here this morning?' she asks.

He takes a moment to consider this and replies, 'I don't think so.'

'The door was bolted from the inside, Grandad.'

His bushy grey eyebrows fold in together like a couple of confused caterpillars, 'That's very strange.' He wrings his hands together and thinks. His gaze slides to her baton. He frowns a confused expression as if trying to figure out a complex puzzle.

Outside, the heavens open once more, and sheets of rain fall from the sky. Archer closes the back door, locks it and sets the

16

weapon on the worktop. 'I'm sure it's nothing,' she tells him in soft tones. 'Why don't you change out of those wet clothes, and I'll make us some breakfast.'

His face pales. He's clearly unsure about how he got locked out. She gives him a reassuring smile.

'I'll get changed,' he says.

'If you bring those clothes back down, I'll wash them for you,' she says, trying to sound upbeat and normal.

Grandad nods solemnly and makes his way upstairs.

'Fuck!' Archer says under her breath.

It's then that she notices what she feared most. Sitting on the weathered pine kitchen table is a blank white business card. She catches her breath. It's embossed with a symbol and letters. Archer leans in for a closer look. In the centre is what looks like a bullet hole. Above it is the name, Jake Archer.

Archer feels her stomach turning. She thinks she might be sick, hurries to the kitchen sink and gags as bile comes up, burning her throat. She runs the cold water tap and drinks a tall glass of water. Her phone is charging in the living room. She leaves the kitchen, grabs it from the side table and calls DS Harry Quinn, her partner and close friend. Through the window, she sees two uniformed Met officers get out of a response vehicle.

'The weather's shite this morning,' are Quinn's first words, his wipers swiping furiously in the background.

'How fast can you get here?' she asks.

'By here, do you mean ...'

'I'm at home.'

'Is everything OK?' he asks in a concerned voice.

'Just get here as quick as you can.'

'I'll be there in twenty minutes max.'

She opens the door, introduces herself to the two officers and shows her ID. She explains what happened and asks them to question the neighbours and establish if they saw anyone they didn't recognise entering the house.

Archer closes the door and returns to the kitchen. She looks at Frankie White's calling card. The 'Death Card', his associates call it. If your name is on it, then you're a dead man, or woman, walking. Her father had been left for dead on a street in London; lying on his chest was his Death Card. It was the first time White had used one. Back then there was no connection back to gang leader, so it could not be used as evidence against him, despite it being known that White had ordered the hit. Everyone knew. White's people, his friends, his enemies, even the Met. But nothing could be proven.

Through the kitchen window, Archer checks the garden again. There is no sign of anything or anyone. In the living room she peers through the curtains at Roupell Street, but all is quiet. She hurries upstairs to get a better look. Everything seems normal. She breathes a sigh of relief and feels safer now the uniforms are here talking to neighbours.

She hears the shower running and Grandad whistling an unrecognisable tune. This is a good sign. An indication of a better mood. With dementia sometimes there are small mercies. Perhaps he's forgotten his confusion at being locked out from the inside. She hopes so. The truth is she has more to deal with now. Grandad has become a target for Frankie White. He wants Grandad dead before he eventually finishes her off. Like her father before her, she has been a pain in White's bony, corrupt arse, and she knows he has it in for her, especially after what happened to his grandson, Ethan. Archer never anticipated Grandad would become a target. He's just a sweet innocent man, who has had his fair share of heartache over the years, all due directly to Frankie White. She feels a crippling guilt at not anticipating this. This is an eye for an eye situation. Despite the painful and infuriating fact that Frankie White had sanctioned the murder of her father, it seems that is just not enough. Grandad's murder is revenge for the life of someone else. Someone important to White.

Six weeks back, during the investigation into the Aaron Cronin murders, Archer had arrested White's grandson, Ethan, for the murder of his girlfriend. The troubled and fragile Ethan was later found to be innocent, however, before he was released Ethan hung himself in his cell. White blames Archer for his death, and will have his revenge by killing Grandad. Her mind is racing. First things first, she has to get Grandad out of London to a safe house fast.

Chapter 4

ARCHER WATCHES QUINN ARRIVE AND get out of the unmarked Volvo. He looks up, holds her gaze for a moment and nods. As she makes her way downstairs, she hears Grandad in his bedroom getting dressed.

Quinn steps inside. 'Why are the pigs here?' he asks.

Archer ignores his humour, closes the door behind him, locks it and glances up the stairs. There's no sign of Grandad. She leads Quinn into the kitchen, gestures at the Death Card and switches on the radio to drown out their voices.

Quinn looks at the card with a curious expression. He reaches for it.

'Don't touch it. I'll need to bring it in for prints.'

He leans over and takes a closer look. Archer can see him tensing.

'How'd you come by this?'

'Someone has been here. Inside this house. While Grandad was here.'

'When?'

'This morning.'

'How'd they get in?'

'I don't know. Either they have a key or Grandad left the front door open. Wouldn't be the first time. He said no one's been here. But perhaps he just doesn't remember.'

'Is his memory that bad?'

Archer considers this. 'He has good and bad days.'

'Let's say today was a bad day. One of White's meatheads gets lucky, gets inside and drops the card with Jake none the wiser.'

Archer folds her arms. The thought makes her ill.

'Why not kill him?' Quinn asks. 'There and then.'

The question stuns her. Hearing Grandad's potential execution spoken out loud is like a punch in the gut.

'Sorry. I didn't mean to be so blunt,' Quinn apologises.

Archer shakes her head. 'You're right to ask. Who knows? White will assume I'll be out of my head with worry. And he's right. He'll want to prolong the torture for as long as he can.'

'Has Jake seen it?'

'No. And I didn't bring it up. During my run this morning, I had the great misfortune to bump into two of his people. One of them warned me about Jake. I came running back as quick as I could . . . ' Archer's stomach turns again.

'You're white as a sheet, so you are. Sit down. I'll make us a hot drink.'

Archer sits at the table as Quinn fills the kettle. Elbows resting on the surface, she bites her thumb. 'We have to get Grandad to a safe house.'

'I'll make the arrangements. You should call the boss, let her know.'

Archer bites her lip. 'She may ask me to take time off and I'm not going to do that.'

'Your call. Did these people you bumped into say anything else? Did they threaten you or make any other promises?'

'Other than my time is coming, nothing much.'

In the background, the radio DJ announces the 8 a.m. news.

'White holds you responsible for his grandson's untimely murder.'

Archer frowns at him. 'What do you mean, "murder"?'

Quinn rinses the teapot with hot steamy water and adds three tea bags to it. 'Oh, I received some news this morning. A grass, from inside. Apparently, Ethan didn't kill himself. He was murdered in response to White screwing someone over on a deal.'

Archer lets this sink in. She is shocked but at the same time, not. Since his release from prison, White has been playing hard with some of the big players in town.

The local news finishes with Ethan White being mentioned. 'Speak of the devil,' says Quinn.

'*And finally, today is the funeral of a local man, Ethan White. White had been charged with the murder of his girlfriend, Elizabeth Harper. Awaiting trial, he was vindicated after a teenage boy, whose name cannot be revealed, was charged with the murder. However, while in custody, White took his own life before his release date. He is survived by his mother, Janice White, and grandfather, Francis White . . .*'

Archer stands and switches off the radio. In a cupboard she finds a clear plastic sealable freezer bag and from a drawer she takes out a dinner knife which she uses to slide the Death Card into the bag. 'I need to talk to Grandad this morning. Taking him away from his home is going to stress him out.'

'Maybe you should be upfront with him.'

Archer sits back down and rubs her temples.

'Upfront, you say,' says Grandad.

Archer turns to see him standing at the kitchen door, his brow furrowed. How long has he been there and how much did he hear?

'Oh, Grandad. Harry's here. He's just making tea. Would you like a cup?'

'Two sugars, easy on the milk, Jake?' says Quinn.

23

Grandad's eyes slide from Archer to Quinn and back to Archer. He sits at the table. 'Yes, please.'

'Comin' up.'

'I've been following the news. I knew that lad was being buried today.'

'Grandad . . .' says Archer.

'Sad to die at such a young age. But when you're related to *him*. That piece of dirt. When you're part of his world. What can you expect?'

Quinn places two mugs on the table. One for Grandad. One for Archer. He pulls up a chair opposite her and sips his tea. Archer takes a drink of the hot liquid. Grandad stares into his mug. His cheeks are flushed, his fists are balled. 'You and this house are all I have. I'm not leaving my home. Not for him. Not for anyone. The coward can send his heavies. They can come. I'll be here, ready for them. You watch. I may be old. I may be losing my marbles. But I still have some fight in me.'

Archer feels herself tearing up but keeps it together. She glances at Quinn. He shrugs and takes another mouthful of tea.

'Don't do it for him, Grandad,' says Archer, 'do it for me.'

'If I leave here. If leave everything I know, then he's defeated us again. Don't forget, he had your father killed, never mind what he did to you when you were just a girl.' His voice cracks with emotion. 'After that, your grandma just gave up. I can't think about any of that any more or I will lose my mind. I'm not going anywhere. The answer is no, Grace. I'm staying put.'

'But Grandad . . .'

He frowns and pushes himself up from the table. 'I've made up my mind and said my piece. And that's that.'

Archer sighs heavily as Grandad leaves the kitchen.

'That went well,' says Quinn.

'I need to talk to the boss. See if she has budget enough for someone to watch over him.'

'Pierce may want you to take some time out. Go to a safe house until this blows over.'

'This will never blow over, Harry. Not as long as White is a free man. Going into hiding is not an option.'

Quinn nods. 'I thought you might say that.'

A crash from the living room startles them both. They hurry from the kitchen.

Grandad has fallen over a side table. Shattered ornaments lie on the carpet. He is lying among the pieces, deathly pale, body trembling.

Quinn pulls out his mobile. 'I'll phone an ambulance.'

Terrified, Archer kneels beside Grandad and takes his hand. It's cold and dry. 'Grandad, it's Grace. Can you hear me?'

There is no response. It's like he's having some sort of seizure.

Quinn speaks into the phone, 'Ambulance. I need an ambulance.'

Archer chokes back tears.

Quinn is talking. 'An elderly gentleman. I'm not sure of his age.'

'Eighty-one,' says Archer.

'Eighty-one,' repeats Quinn. 'What's wrong with him? . . . I think he's having a stroke.'

Chapter 5

ARCHER SITS ALONE IN THE waiting room of St Thomas's, her muscles knotted with anxiety. She has been waiting for two hours with no update on Grandad's condition. A nurse – a round blonde woman dressed in washed-out blue scrubs – enters and scans the occupants, a sombre, diverse mix of people, heads down, eyes fixed on their smartphones. Some read books, others, tabloids.

Archer sits up, hopeful for news.

'Mrs Khan?' asks the nurse.

Archer sinks back into her chair.

No one responds to the nurse's call.

'Is there a Mrs Khan in the room?'

Still no response.

The nurse leaves and looks up and down the corridor, searching for the elusive Mrs Khan. Archer decides she can't wait anymore and hurries after her.

'Excuse me,' she asks.

The nurse turns and smiles. 'Yes.'

'Hello. Jake Archer came in this morning with a suspected stroke. I was wondering if there's any news.'

'Are you a relative?'

'His granddaughter.'

'Jake Archer, you say?'

'Yes.'

'I'll see what I can find out,' she says, with a practised, reassuring smile. 'Please take a seat in the waiting room.'

'Thank you.'

Archer sighs, leans against the wall, arms folded, thinking about Grandad. He must have heard the entire conversation with Quinn. The suggestion of taking him away from his home in Roupell Street to an isolated soulless safe house must have tipped him over the edge. How fragile he is, which she stupidly seems to forget sometimes. She swears under her breath, berating herself.

'Hey,' comes a voice.

Archer looks up to see Quinn holding two plastic bottles of water. 'Vending machine was a bit limited.'

She is parched from her run and takes a bottle. 'Thank you. I need this.'

'Have you eaten?'

She shakes her head.

From the jacket of his suede bomber jacket, he pulls out a Snickers bar and offers it. She has no appetite.

'No, thank you.'

From another pocket, he retrieves a bag of salted peanuts, but she declines again.

'You should eat something,' he says, opening the Snickers and taking a bite.

'Maybe later.' Archer takes two large gulps of water. 'Didn't think I'd see you so soon.'

'Wanted to check in and make sure you're both OK. Any news?' Quinn asks.

'Nothing, yet.'

'I caught up with Pierce. She sends her best and said call her when you can.'

Archer nods.

'What about you? Have you thought about what you'll do?'

'I'm fine.'

'No, I mean you can't go back to Roupell Street, can you? Not yet anyway.'

'I don't have much choice.'

'There's always choices. Is there anywhere else you can stay – with your mother maybe?'

'We haven't spoken in twenty years. And the answer is no. Besides she moved away from London a long time ago.'

'No friends?'

'Yes, but I'm not going to load myself on to anyone when I'm in Frankie White's cross hairs. Seems a little ... unfair.'

'Aye. I suppose. There's only one thing for it. You'll have to stay with me.'

'I don't think so.'

'Wise up! You know it makes sense. We're working together anyway. Just think of it as a temporary solution until Pierce sorts something out.'

'What exactly is Pierce sorting out?'

'I recall the term she used was "safe house".'

Archer shakes her head. 'No, absolutely not.'

'Grace, seriously, you have to stay clear of Roupell Street.'

Archer sighs and nods her head. She knows Quinn is right.

They say nothing for a moment.

'So, if Jake gets through this ... '

'He *will* get through it.'

'Sorry. Wrong choice of words.'

Archer says nothing.

'Pierce is going to make sure he has his own room with a twenty-four-hour police guard.'

'That's nice,' she says, quietly. She is of course grateful but just doesn't know how to communicate it or feel it right now. Her world is collapsing in on her and there's nothing she can do about it. She's lost control and the consequence is Grandad is fighting for his life. How the hell did she get to here? An image of Frankie White flashes in her mind. A blistering-hot rage begins to pulse in her chest.

'So how about it?'

'What?'

'Stay at mine for a few days. I'll take the sofa. You can have my room. I'll even change the sheets.'

'That's so considerate of you.'

'I'm that kinda guy.'

Archer smiles for the first time.

Quinn continues, lightening his tone, 'Well look, in other news, Pierce wants us to look into a killing in south London. A thirty-five-year-old man, murdered last night in his flat.'

'OK, let's go there when we're done here. I really need to get out of these clothes.'

'Grace,' comes a voice. 'Grace Archer?'

'Yes, that's us!' calls Quinn, as if he's just won at bingo.

A casually dressed young Asian man carrying a clipboard and wearing a lanyard approaches.

'I'm Grace Archer,' she tells him.

'Doctor Prasad. I'm one of the neurologists at St Thomas's. I've been—'

'Is he alive?' Archer interrupts.

Prasad smiles patiently. 'He is stable.'

Relief ripples through her.

'Your grandfather has suffered a stroke. A small one, thankfully, but a stroke, nevertheless. It's too early to determine the impact. However, we will know more later.'

'Do you have any sense of how serious it is?'

'I wouldn't like to say. I can tell you that he was awake for a few moments. He was able to lift his arms and talk, although we couldn't understand what he was saying. That could be down to exhaustion as a result of the stroke.'

'Oh . . . '

'Has he been overdoing it recently or been subject to stress?'

Archer hesitates before answering, 'It's been a difficult few months.'

'I understand. Please rest assured your grandfather is in good hands for now. We're looking after him.'

'Can I see him?'

'He's sedated and sleeping. He needs to rest. Perhaps you can come tomorrow?'

'Yes . . . I can do that.'

'Are there any other questions?'

'How long do you think he'll be here for?'

'Difficult to say at this stage. He will certainly need to spend weeks perhaps longer under care. I would also say be prepared. He might be different.'

Archer feels a quiver in her stomach. 'Different?'

'There's a possibility his speech might be affected. His cognitive abilities, too. We will know more soon.'

'He already has early onset dementia.'

'I'm aware. Let's take things one step at a time. Please feel free to call the neurology ward, if you have any concerns.'

'Thank you, Doctor Prasad.'

'You're welcome.' Prasad hurries off.

'He sounds positive,' says Quinn.

Archer is not so sure. 'Thanks for being here, Harry.'

'No worries.'

Archer finishes the last of the water and drops the bottle in the waste bin. 'We should get back to work. Let's follow up on this murder in south London.'

Chapter 6

ARCHER HAD DECIDED TO RISK going home to Roupell Street. She showered quickly, packed a fresh supply of clothes for the week ahead and grabbed some of Grandad's things: pills, spectacles, his phone.

She calls Cosmo, Grandad's close friend, and breaks the news. He is shocked and promises to visit.

Downstairs, Quinn is standing at the bay window watching the street outside.

'Are we under siege?' she asks.

'Not unless they're over the age of sixty-five.'

'Nothing would surprise me with White.'

They go straight to the crime scene at Albany Mansions, a vast Victorian mansion block, on the Albert Bridge Road. Two uniforms guard the perimeter, the front entrance is sealed off with police tape much to the consternation of the residents milling around outside.

Marian Phillips, a Charing Cross DC, emerges from the front entrance.

'Hi, Marian,' says Archer.

DC Phillips is a slight woman with a thin face and bobbed hair. She's wearing a forensic suit with the hood pulled back.

'Hey, Grace. Harry.'

'What have we got?' Archer asks.

'A weird one. Jason Todd, thirty-five. Murdered last night at home with his son, Lucas, in the bedroom next door. No signs of forced entry. Nothing appears to be stolen as far as we can see. Looks like the killing happened in the bedroom.'

'How did he die?' Archer asks.

'Suffocation. Duct tape wrapped around his neck, face and head. Take a look at this.' Phillips reaches inside her protective suit and takes out a Samsung phone. Swiping through the security, she opens a picture from the photos folder. The picture shows half of Jason Todd's face peeking out from behind torn duct tape. 'Lucas ripped at the tape when he found his dad.' She flicks to another picture. 'I placed the pieces together.'

'Shit,' says Quinn.

'It's like the killer mummified the head and drew this silly face,' says Phillips.

The 'silly face' is two round black eyes, a teardrop and a frowning mouth.

'It's like an emoji,' says Archer.

Phillips looks back at her phone. 'I suppose it is.'

'His son didn't hear a thing?' asks Quinn.

'We didn't get much time with him. He said he thought he heard something at bedtime and checked in on his dad, who was under the covers, sleeping. This morning at breakfast there was no sign of him, which the boy thought unusual. He went to wake him, pulled back the covers and discovered his body.'

'Grim,' says Quinn.

'Was he killed in bed?' Archer asks.

'We don't know yet.'

'Where's the boy now?'

'With his mother, Penny. She and the victim are separated.'

34

'Divorced?'

'Planning to. An amicable split from what I understand. Do you want to take a look around? I can get you suited up.'

'Thanks.'

With their forensic suits on, Phillips leads them into the living room. 'There's no sign of a struggle in here but you can see there are small traces of mud and grass on the living room floor and kitchen.'

'It's quite a clean and tidy place for a bloke's flat,' says Quinn.

Stepping across the forensic floor plates, Archer makes her way into the kitchen and looks out at the garden.

'We found footprints in the bushes,' says Marian. 'The killer must have been hiding there.'

'Have you spoken to any of the neighbours?' asks Quinn.

'We've done a door to door. No one heard or saw anything.'

'They never do,' adds Quinn.

'His computer and phone?' asks Archer.

'I've bagged them up.'

'Good. Bring them to Charing Cross. Klara can speed up the analysis.'

'Shouldn't we give them to Lambeth Digital Forensics?' asks Phillips.

'We could be waiting a long time. Klara has the skills and can expedite it.'

'Fair enough.'

Archer opens the kitchen door, steps outside, crosses the narrow grass verge and looks back at the flat. All the rooms are visible. The curtains in both bedrooms are drawn. Quinn and Phillips are watching her.

'Were the curtains on the kitchen door open when you arrived?' Archer asks Phillips.

'Yes.'

Archer retreats into the bushes. 'In the dark this is an easy place to hide,' she says. 'Far enough from the main road and the rear of the block, concealed. The killer has the perfect view of a Sunday evening in the Todd household.'

'A targeted kill?' Phillips asks.

'Perhaps. You said Lucas is with his mother?'

'Yes. They're a five-minute drive south of here. Holden Street.'

Chapter 7

PENNY TODD'S HOUSE IS A Victorian mid terrace in a well-kept residential Battersea street. Each house has two upstairs sash windows and one downstairs sash. The front doors are uniformly framed in a quaint white church style arch.

The blinds are closed in all of Penny Todd's windows.

'Might not be home,' says Quinn.

'Or she wants privacy.'

Archer crosses the short path of worn black and white tiles to the door and rings the bell. A moment later the door cracks open. A woman with shoulder-length fair hair peeks through a chain-locked gap. Her eyes are red raw.

'What is it?' she asks.

'Mrs Todd, I'm Detective Inspector Grace Archer and this is Detective Sergeant Harry Quinn.'

'I've already spoken to the police.'

'Mrs Todd, we're leading the investigation. We'd like to ask you some more questions.'

The woman is clearly distressed and seems confused.

'We'll be as quick as we can,' Quinn says softly.

She nods her head, unlocks the chain and opens the door. 'Come in.'

The door opens into the living room, a cluttered space in contrast to her ex-husband's pristine flat. It's around twenty feet long with a stairwell leading up to the next floor. At the foot of the stairs is a discarded pair of boy's trainers. There are magazine stacks and novels heaped untidily on shelves and schoolbooks littered on top of a dining table at the rear of the room. The TV is broadcasting a vapid daytime chat show. The radiators are blasting out an oppressive heat. The air is stale.

She shoos a cat from the sofa, gestures for them to sit and perches on the armchair opposite, wringing her hands.

'Mrs Todd, we're so sorry for your loss,' says Archer.

She's wearing a long wool cardigan that she pulls across her chest. 'I . . . I just can't believe he's gone. Who would do that? Who would kill a man, a father, in that horrid way?'

'That's what we intend to find out. When did you last speak to Jason?'

'Two days ago, when he came to pick up Lucas.'

'How did he seem to you?'

'What do you mean?'

'Did he seem stressed or upset?'

She frowns as she considers her answer. 'No, he was just normal. Just like he always was.'

'What kind of person was he?' asks Quinn.

'He was . . . Jason . . . just Jason . . . no one special. He was decent, kind, generous. Funny . . . sometimes. Lucas adored him and Jason adored Lucas; he's so devastated.' She pulls a crumpled paper hanky from her cardigan pocket and blows her nose. 'What are we going to do?'

'Mrs Todd, do you know of anyone who might want to hurt your ex-husband?'

She unfolds and refolds her hanky as she thinks this over. 'No one. There isn't anyone I can think of. Everyone liked him.'

'Did he have any money problems?' asks Quinn.

'Not that I'm aware.'

'He earns ... earned ... a good salary. He pays for Lucas and me and this house too.' She palms her cheek. 'Oh God, are we going to lose the house now?'

'I'm sure that won't happen,' Quinn tries to reassure her.

'Where does he work?' Archer asks.

'He's an area manager for Mercedes dealerships.'

'A responsible job.'

'He has ... had ... a lot on his plate.'

'Where is his office?'

'He's based mostly in Milton Keynes. But he travelled around a lot. Around the south-east. Sometimes he'd have to go to Germany on business.'

'Sounds intense.'

Penny Todd nods her head.

'You and Jason were on good terms?' Archer asks.

'Yeah, we've known each other a long time. Since before we were teenagers. We grew up together, started dating in our teens and then broke up when we went to different universities. We got together again after uni, got a place and then I got pregnant.'

'How long were you married?'

'Five years.'

'Could I ask why you separated?'

'Different reasons. We got bored.'

'Both of you?'

She shrugs. 'If I'm honest, it was mostly me. He was working all the time, constantly stressed and drinking a lot. He'd get angry at the slightest things sometimes. We'd argue all the time. It was ruining our marriage, our family. In the end I just told him to leave. For both our sanities. And Lucas's too. But we remained friends and even joked about getting back together again.'

The doorbell rings. 'That'll be Oliver.' Penny Todd stands, crosses the living room and peers through the peephole. She opens the door and a tall man with thinning brown hair steps inside and embraces her. 'I'm so sorry, Penny.'

Penny sobs into his chest. He kisses the top of her head.

'The police are here,' she says.

The man called Oliver looks across at them with a hard expression. He pulls away from Penny and crosses to the living room. 'You could have given her some time,' he says.

'They're just asking some questions.'

'You should have called me. Don't speak to these people without me present.' He looks towards Archer and Quinn. 'I'm a solicitor, you know.'

Archer gives him a half-smile. 'Detective Inspector Archer and my colleague, Detective Sergeant Quinn.'

'Shouldn't you be out looking for whoever did this?'

'And you are?' Quinn asks, levelling his gaze with the new arrival.

The man flinches at Quinn's tone. 'Stocker . . . Oliver Stocker.'

Penny says, 'He's my . . . erm . . . Oliver and I have been seeing each other.'

'Where's Lucas? Is he OK?' Stocker asks.

A creak on the stairs pulls their attention. Lucas Todd is sitting midway, watching and listening. He's a blond-haired kid, around twelve years old, dressed in a grey sweatshirt and jeans. His arm is wrapped in a blue cast covered in names and schoolboy graffiti.

'Lucas, are you OK, darling?' says Penny.

The boy's eyes slide from Archer's to Quinn's.

'Hi, Lucas, my name's Grace and this is Harry.'

'Hey, buddy,' says Quinn.

The boy wraps his arms around his knees and looks down at his feet.

'You should go rest in your room, Lucas,' says Stocker.

'Mrs Todd, could we please speak to your son?' Archer asks.

'I don't think so!' says Stocker.

Penny seems uncertain. 'He's not talking much at the moment. Perhaps we could do another time.'

'It could really help.'

'He can't talk to the police without an appropriate adult present,' says Stocker.

'Can't get more appropriate than his mother,' says Quinn.

'I can talk to them, Mum,' says Lucas.

Mrs Todd sighs, closes her eyes and nods. She perches herself on the side of the armchair. 'OK. Come sit beside me.'

Lucas sits. His mum tries to take his hand, but he pulls it away.

'I broke my arm once,' Quinn says. 'It was the worst pain I ever experienced.'

'You had a little accident, didn't you, Lucas?' says Mrs Todd.

'Best not go into that one,' says Stocker, rolling his eyes.

'We're so sorry, Lucas,' says Archer.

A flicker of pain crosses his small face, but he holds it together.

'Lucas, do you mind if we ask a few questions about last night?'

He shakes his head.

'They may seem dumb and obvious but anything you can remember, no matter how small, could help us find who did this to your dad.'

He nods his understanding.

'I was on my PlayStation and Dad came into my room and told me to stop and got to bed.'

'What time was this?'

'Around ten thirty. He normally lets me stay up on Sundays. Usually, we'd watch a movie or the football, but I wanted some time on my PlayStation. I was at an important stage of the game. Dad was upset cause it was too late so I switched off the monitor and pretended I was done.'

'What game were you playing?' asks Quinn.

'The Last of Us.'

'Nice. Did you go straight to bed?'

'No, I brushed my teeth then said goodnight.'

'Where was he?'

'In the bathroom.'

'What did you do then?' asks Archer. 'Tell us everything, no matter how small the detail.'

'I closed my door, sat on the bed and listened. I couldn't hear him so thought he must be in bed, so I put my headphones back on and finished the game.'

'How many zombies did you take out?' Quinn asks.

'They're not zombies.'

'Apologies. They're the *infected*?'

A ghost of a smile crosses Lucas's face. 'I took out thirty. Maybe more.'

'Impressive.'

Archer notices a shift in Lucas, as if he's slowly coming out of his shell.

'How long did that take?'

'About three minutes.'

'Then what?'

'I switched off the PlayStation and closed the curtains. That's when I heard the noise.'

'What did it sound like?'

'Like a thudding sound. I thought maybe Dad dropped something. I stopped outside his room but didn't hear anything. I called for him, but he didn't reply. I peed and washed my hands and thought I heard something again. I thought maybe he'd pretended to be sleeping because he was upset with me. So, I went into his room and apologised and told him I loved him.'

Mrs Todd lets out a sob.

'Did you turn the light on?'

Lucas shakes his head. 'He was under the covers. I thought he was sleeping, I really did.' Tears fill the boy's eyes. 'But he wasn't sleeping. He was dead, wasn't he? Whoever killed him covered his head in tape and left him under the duvet.' Lucas is trembling. His mother takes him in her arms and squeezes him.

Archer looks at Quinn and mouths, 'We should go.'

He nods his agreement.

'Once again, we're so sorry. We'll leave you both. Thank you, Mrs Todd, and thank you, Lucas.'

Lucas's face is red, and wet with tears and snot. 'Promise me you'll find whoever did this,' he says.

'We'll do our best.'

'Promise!'

Archer can relate to the boy's pain. She knows that feeling all too well. Her father had been murdered when she was not much older than Lucas.

'I promise,' she says.

As they leave, Archer asks, 'Was Jason seeing anyone?'

Penny looks to Oliver Stocker. 'Could you take Lucas into the kitchen. There's some ice cream in the freezer.'

Stocker nods and guides the boy away.

Penny folds her arms and waits until they are out of earshot. 'He was seeing a woman called Katie Fox. She's a parent of one of Lucas's friends. They met at the school gates, apparently, shortly after we split up.'

'Do you have her contact details?'

'She's on my parents' WhatsApp group.' Penny takes out her phone and shows her a number. 'This is hers.'

Archer takes a picture of the number. 'Thank you. Just one more thing. Even though Lucas confirmed with the officers the body was his father, we will need an adult identification. Do you think you could do that for us?'

'Oh God.'

'I'm so sorry.'

'No. It has to be me.'

'I'll be in touch with the details. Goodbye for now, Mrs Todd.'

Chapter 8

ON THEIR RETURN TO CHARING Cross, Archer had phoned ahead and asked Klara, Os and DC Phillips to meet her and Quinn in the incident room.

She drops off the Death Card for priority fingerprint analysis before joining the team. They're bantering and joking as she enters the room. Os Pike, a young black man with a talent for computers and digital analysis, is holding court and making them laugh. Klara Clark is an old colleague and friend of Archer's from her years working at the National Crime Agency. She had first met Klara when she was Keegan Clark, a gangly computer geek who didn't really fit in with the blokey NCA dynamic. Archer, and her boss at the time, Charlie Bates, had seen in Keegan a rare genius that became invaluable to their investigations of organised crime. But Keegan had always seemed so unhappy and Archer didn't know why. Five years back, Keegan revealed to her that he planned to transition. Keegan became Klara and with that came a confidence and happiness that Archer had never witnessed in Keegan.

Klara catches her eye and smiles. Archer smiles back. Klara looks different today. Androgynous in a double-breasted navy suit, her hair chopped into a buzz cut and dyed a burnt orange colour.

'Hey, everyone.'

'Hi, Grace, I heard about Jake,' says Klara. 'How's he doing?'

'We still don't know. Too early to say. The doctors seem confident though.'

'Well, that's something. How're you holding up?'

'I'm doing OK, thanks.'

'If you need anything, you know where I am.'

'Thanks, Klara.'

'Yeah, same,' adds Os.

'Hope he makes a fast recovery, Grace,' says Phillips.

'He's a fighter,' says Quinn.

Archer takes a seat. Quinn too.

'Marian, assume you've briefed Klara and Os?'

'I have indeed. I think we're all on the same page.'

'Good. Any developments after we left?' Archer asks.

'Nothing. CSI have everything to start building a report. I've given Klara and Os Jason Todd's computer and phone, as requested.'

A knock on the door. DCI Pierce enters. Behind her is a young mixed-race woman. Archer has met her before.

'Excuse me for interrupting. I wanted to introduce . . .'

'Mel, isn't it?' says Archer.

Mel smiles. 'You remembered.'

'I'm good with faces.'

'You were with Linda Bailey after her husband was murdered in Battersea Park,' says Quinn.

'The Cronin case?' says Pierce.

'Yes, that's right. Small world . . . '

'Then Grace and Harry need no introduction. Everyone, this is our newly appointed DC, Melanie Anderson.' Pierce introduces the rest of the team. 'Marian, I'd like Mel to shadow you. She's talented so use her well.'

'Yes, ma'am.'

'We could do with an extra pair of hands,' says Archer. 'Welcome, Mel, and congratulations.'

'Thank you.'

'I'll leave you to get on,' says Pierce. 'Oh, Grace, a quick word outside.'

Mel joins them at the table. Archer exits as Quinn brings Mel up to date on the case.

'I'm so sorry about Jake. Any word?'

'He's stable. I should find out more later today or perhaps tomorrow.'

'He should be in a room by himself with a guard. I'll organise that.'

'Thank you.'

'We should discuss your safety and the next steps. Come and see me after your meeting. I'll catch up with you later.'

Archer rejoins the team. Marian is laying out printed photos from the scene.

'Marian, could you take us through these, please,' Archer asks.

'This first picture is the communal garden outside the flat. We found faint footprints behind the foliage here. Probably no DNA because of last night's downpour. The footprints were pointing towards the flat. Safe to assume the killer was watching them from this spot.' She points to another set of pictures. 'These depict the view from the garden. As you can see, the killer can see pretty much all that was going on.'

'Lucas Todd confirmed that the curtains were open last night.'

Phillips continues, 'There are traces of mud on the carpet. Unlikely to be the victim's. We understand he was fastidious about cleanliness. Therefore, walking on damp mud and grass and stepping onto your nice cream carpets was not Jason Todd's thing. These are various shots from inside the flat and these are the victim. Murdered in his bedroom. Likely died from suffocation.'

The pictures of Jason Todd's half-naked body are grim. His head is framed by the torn duct tape that surrounds his face like a balaclava. His eyes are wide and bloodshot.

'The morning after, Lucas Todd found his father in bed and unresponsive. He clawed the tape from his face, thinking he could save him.'

'It's like a mask,' says Klara. 'A weird smiley mask.'

'We know that nothing was taken. Unless Jason Todd owned something very valuable that we don't yet know about. So, if this was a robbery, why leave the mask on his head?'

Quinn interjects, 'Let's say he was involved in something. The killer gets access to his flat. Kills him. Gets whatever he was looking for and leaves the mask as a signature. Or even a warning to others.'

Like a Death Card, Archer thinks.

Archer catches Quinn looking her way and knows he's thinking the same as she is.

'It's possible. So, we can assume this was no ordinary kill. It was targeted. What relevance this mask has we don't know yet,' says Archer. 'Klara, could you do some digging and find out if there are any similar murders recently or in the past?'

'I'll get on to that.'

'Poor kid. He must have been terrified when he saw that,' says Os.

'Marian, could you arrange a DNA test for Lucas,' says Archer. 'We may be able to salvage something from the duct tape.'

'Will do,' she replies. 'Oh, and Krish said he will do his best to get his report back this week.'

Krish Anand leads one of the Central London CSI teams.

'Good to know. Thanks.' Archer addresses the team, 'So, Harry and I interviewed Jason's ex-wife, Penny, and Lucas too. Jason had a senior job working for Mercedes. Penny said he was under pressure at work. She hinted he had a drink problem, suffered from stress and could fly off the handle at times, which is part of the reason they split up. We should talk to his work colleagues and find out a bit more about him. Klara, Os, make the computer and phone a priority. Mel, could you look at Jason Todd's social media and find out who his friends are?'

'Of course.'

Archer looks at Quinn. 'We can hotfoot it to the mortuary, see what Doctor Kapur has.'

'Always a fun place to visit,' says Quinn.

Glancing towards Pierce's office she can see the DCI deep in a meeting. Pierce had wanted to talk to her but that would have to wait.

Through the windows of the swing doors leading into the Horseferry Road mortuary theatre, Archer can see the dour-faced Doctor Kapur, a slight man dressed in grey scrubs, standing at a stainless-steel sink, washing his hands. Pushing open the door, her nose wrinkles at the cloying chemical lavender scent that struggles to disguise the fetid odour of decomposition.

'How do you work here with that smell?' she asks Doctor Kapur.

His bushy grey eyebrows knit together. 'I like lavender,' he replies in his monotone voice. 'It has a tranquil quality that calms the mind.' He smiles and adds, 'If you're referring to the smell of death, well, I just don't notice it anymore.' He dries his hands meticulously with two paper towels.

'Wish I could say the same,' says Quinn.

In the harsh light, Kapur's complexion appears waxy not unlike the prostrate clients he spends his working hours with. A bank of four stainless steel tables are lined in a row in the centre of the room. Three are unused. Draped in a white sheet, Jason Todd's naked corpse lies on the end table closest to the sink.

'Shall we?' Kapur gestures to the table where Jason Todd's body lies. 'His eyes are bloodshot, which would indicate he died from suffocation. There is nothing to suggest a struggle took place.' Kapur points to the right side of Jason Todd's neck. 'However, there are these.'

They circle the table and stand beside the pathologist and follow the direction of his long, gnarly finger. There are two blotches criss-crossing each other, both with parallel puncture marks.

'He was tasered,' says Archer.

'It would seem so.'

'Twice by the look of it,' says Quinn.

'Well observed, Harry,' Kapur says, drily.

'Tasered once so that he could not put up a fight as the killer covered his head with duct tape. Tasered a second time as he comes round and his body goes into panic mode,' says Archer.

'From the moment that first taser hit his skin, he was toast.'

Kapur arches his eyebrows at Quinn. 'Toast?'

'It's an expression.'

Kapur considers this for a moment with a perplexed look on his long face.

'It means he was scuppered. A goner.'

'If you say so,' says Kapur.

Archer takes a photo of the taser marks. 'Thank you, Dr Kapur,' she says. 'We really appreciate you expediting this.'

The doctor nods.

Chapter 9

THE RAIN IS TORRENTIAL. UNDER the cover of a black umbrella, Frankie White stands over the six-foot-deep rectangular hole looking down at the solid oak coffin housing the remains of his grandson, Ethan. Clutching on to his arm, trembling and sobbing, is his daughter, Janine, Ethan's mother. Around them, the mourners dressed in black, comprise Ethan's friends, Janine's friends, Frankie's associates, employees, hangers-on. All watch on quietly with sad expressions, as if they really care.

Frankie slides his eyes across the graveyard where Archer and her lackey take shelter under a tree. He feels an ache in his jaw and realises he's been grinding his teeth. The fucking nerve of her to come here.

'Mr White,' says the vicar, urging him on.

Frankie fires him a filthy look. The vicar flinches.

'Dad, please,' says Janine, softly.

Frankie tries to relax and catches a breath. Crouching down, he digs a hand into the mound of sodden earth and closes his fist tightly over it. His eyes focus back on the coffin and the saints, angels and cherubs carved into burnished oak sprinkled with gobs of rain. Rolling the dirt through his fingers, he sprinkles it liberally over the coffin. His blood had run in Ethan's veins, yet he had never much warmed to his grandson. Janine had spoiled him from the get-go and he, in truth, became a demanding little snot-rag. Then Frankie had gone to prison and when he came out, Ethan was all grown up yet, somehow, he was still pushing high on the snot-rag scale. With Frankie being inside, they had never bonded, and to his disappointment, Ethan had also turned out to be feckless and weak. He could blame himself. But what could he expect from the offspring of a halfwit *Mick* who'd had the brass neck to fuck his Janine and get her pregnant. Ironically, Frankie had buried him too. In a basement grave of concrete, much to Janine's horror. She had begged him to keep her baby. He had refused at first, but she got around him as she always did. Anyway, with the child on the way she soon forgot about the *Mick* and they moved on, as they would with Ethan's passing. But to do that, Frankie had two debts to pay back. The first one would be tomorrow night. The second would be to remove that one fucking fly in his ointment. The bitch responsible for the wrongful arrest, imprisonment and eventual death of his hopeless grandson. He looks across the graveyard once more.

Grace fucking Archer.

Her time was coming.

Frankie and Janine step to the side to make way for the queue of mourners. One by one, they toss a handful of soil and pay their final respects. They greet Frankie obsequiously, shake his grubby hand with their own, murmur their sentiments and hug Janine. Despite being bored of this entire event, he goes through the motions, nodding his thanks and praying, not for the soul of his grandson, but for this to be over soon.

A young man, around Ethan's age, is embracing Janine and speaking softly to her. He is tall and broad-shouldered with short, wiry dark hair. She sobs and pulls him closer. Releasing him, she smiles up at him and caresses his cheeks. 'Thank you for coming, Toby.'

'I still can't believe it,' he says to her.

Janine holds his hands, closes her eyes and nods. 'I know,' she says, tears streaming.

Janine turns to Frankie. 'Dad, you remember Toby, don't ya?'

Frankie regards him suspiciously. He's mixed race with a chiselled jaw and seems to have captured the furtive attention of the women at the funeral. He tries to place him but can't.

Frankie sniffs and frowns at Janine.

'Toby was Ethan's best friend at school,' says Janine. 'He came with us once when we visited you inside. Don't you remember?'

Frankie tries to think back and has the vague memory of Ethan and some other kid many years back.

'It was a long time ago, sir,' says Toby. 'Good to see you again, Mr White.'

Frankie shakes his hand. The lad has manners and a firm, confident grip.

Over his shoulder Frankie notices a large black shiny Land Rover park up. Two tall, suited men step out from the front. One opens the rear door, the other opens an umbrella. A medium-sized man with a neatly trimmed beard, a Mediterranean tan and an Armani suit gets out and looks Frankie's way. The Russian. Andrei Brodsky.

Frankie feels the pain in his jaw once more.

'Toby works for you now, Dad. At the warehouse,' says Janine. 'Jack of all trades, he is.'

Frankie takes a breath. Distracted by the arrival of the Russians, it takes a moment for him to come back to the conversation.

'I look after distribution and imports, sir. A bit of enforcement too,' says the lad.

Frankie takes stock of him. He looks like he can take care of himself.

'Come with me, son,' he says.

'Dad?' says Janine.

'Follow me . . . what's your name?'

'Toby. Toby Cullen.'

Frankie turns to his two dim-witted minders. Both called Kevin. For some unfathomable reason they have the same shorn haircuts and are wearing matching black leather jackets. He rolls his eyes. *Why?* 'This way,' he tells them.

'Dad?' Janine asks again.

'Meet me at the car, Janine.'

Frankie leaves the graveside and makes his way down the path. Archer and the lackey are watching on with interest. Frankie focuses his attention on the Russian. 'You have a fucking nerve showing up at my grandson's funeral.'

The Russian regards Frankie with his trademark smug look. 'Nice to see you too, Frankie.'

'Take your monkeys and piss the fuck off. You're not welcome here.'

'We come to pay respects to your dear, departed . . .' Brodsky turns to his monkeys. 'What was his name?' They shrug.

Frankie's teeth feel like they're grinding to powder. Toby stands beside him.

'You heard, Mr White. Take your monkeys and piss the fuck off,' he says with a calm, confident tone.

Brodsky ignores him. 'Remember what you did, Frankie. Everything could have been so different.'

Frankie feels his pulse racing. He looks straight into Brodsky's pale blue eyes and imagines gouging them out with his thumbs. It takes all his strength to hold himself back.

'Leave,' commands Toby.

Brodsky smiles. 'Let's go,' he says. As he climbs into the car, he turns to Frankie and says, 'See you soon.'

'Not before I see you,' White mutters.

They leave and Toby says, 'Are you OK, Mr White?'

Frankie is rattled.

'Fine, son,' he says. 'Are you coming to the wake?'

'I have some business to take care of at the warehouse.'

'No business today. Come to the wake.'

'Yes, sir.'

'Good lad.'

Frankie summons his driver as Janine approaches. 'Time to go, Janine.'

He helps her into the car and climbs in, pulling the sides of his coat over his knees.

'Ready, sir,' says the driver.

'Get us the fuck out of here.'

Frankie pushes any thoughts about Brodsky from his head and looks through the window. Archer is standing under the tree watching him with an arrogant look on her face as he passes. 'Full of herself, she is. Climbing the shit-stained career pole of the Metropolitan Police, the Keystone fucking Kops. Cunt!' he mutters.

'Dad?' says Janine.

He turns to look at her and blinks. He'd forgotten she's in the car. Placing his hand on her knee, he squeezes it gently. 'Nothing, sweetheart. Nothing.'

Janine seems not to hear. She dabs her eyes and looks out the window on the other side.

Frankie smiles to himself. *Archer's time is coming. Her time is coming and coming soon.*

Chapter 10

ARCHER WATCHES FRANKIE WHITE'S LIMOUSINE cruise by. Her eyes lock with White's briefly. She holds her breath but keeps her expression fixed and cold as the car exits the graveyard.

Quinn is making a call. 'Hey, Klara, it's Harry ... I'm good. How're you? Grand. Listen, Grace and I are on our way in. I'm just sending some pics of a Land Rover and three dapper dudes. Could you find out who the Land Rover is registered to and run a face rec on the blokes, if possible. The quality's not great but see what you can do ... Aye OK, thanks. See you later ... Bye ... bye.'

They begin to make their way out of the graveyard and back to the car.

'There's something familiar about the beard in the expensive suit,' Archer says. 'I know him.'

'From your days of kicking the ass of organised crime at the National Crime Agency?'

'Obviously.' She scours the folds of her memory, searching for a name to match the face. 'He's definitely Eastern European.'

'His tête-à-tête with White was as frosty as a gipsy's riddle in a Siberian snowstorm,' says Quinn.

'He didn't come here to pay his respects. He came here to make a point.'

'I can think of one reason. A stab in the dark . . . '

'Frankie reneged on a deal with the bloke in the graveyard and as a consequence he murdered Ethan to teach the old boy a lesson.'

'Took the words outta my mouth.'

A call comes through on Archer's phone.

'Grace Archer,' she answers.

'Hi, Grace, it's Lizzie here from Charing Cross.'

'Hi, Lizzie. Do you have news for me?'

Archer had left Grandad's Death Card with Lizzie for finger-print analysis.

'I wish I had better. I've examined the business card you gave me and unfortunately have found no prints.'

Archer sighs. 'It was a long shot. Thanks for letting me know.'

'You're welcome. Anytime.'

'Have a good day.'

'Sorry about that,' says Quinn.

'My expectations were low, to be honest.'

They check in at the Charing Cross Police Station thirty minutes later.

DCI Pierce is sitting in her glass cube office and sees them entering. She beckons to Archer.

'I'm being summoned,' Archer says to Quinn.

'I'll be in the incident room.'

Archer makes her way to Pierce's office and spots Klara Clark's bright orange hair sitting like a sunset over a raised bank of monitors. Klara looks up, smiles and waves. Archer waves back.

'Close the door behind you,' says Pierce. 'Take a seat.'

Archer sits at the small meeting table opposite the DCI.

'The threat against you and Jake must not be taken lightly.'

'I'm taking it very seriously.'

'In an ideal world we would put you on leave until we figure this out.'

Archer remains tight-lipped, cautious about what Pierce might want her to do.

'If you continue to work as you are then not only are you in danger, but Harry is too.' Pierce drums her fingers on the table, levelling her gaze at Archer.

'I don't want to put him, or anyone else, in danger,' Archer replies.

'Then we're on the same page?'

'I'm not sure if we are.'

'These are unusual circumstances and we must take preventative action, Grace.'

'Is that another way of asking me to take time off?'

'Not at all. I want you to keep a low profile. You should base yourself out of Charing Cross ... '

'Absolutely not!'

Pierce rolls her eyes. 'I thought you might say that. You should at least move from your house.'

'That's already arranged.'

'Good.'

'Is that all?'

'If it's any consolation, White is being watched by the National Crime Agency. Perhaps Charlie mentioned something?'

Charlie Bates was Archer's old governor during her years at the NCA.

'But Charlie's retired.'

'Semi. I think he's helping out. In what capacity I don't know.'

'I haven't heard from him in a while.'

'Give him my best, if you do.'

Archer stands. 'Sure.'

'How is the Todd investigation progressing?'

'We worked late yesterday evening compiling info. We're waiting on Forensics, which could take forever. Harry and I are going to start digging deeper this afternoon.'

Pierce nods. 'Any conclusions?'

'Too early to say.'

'OK. Good luck with it. Keep me posted.'

'Will do.'

'And take care.'

'Thanks.' Archer opens the office door.

'Oh, one last thing. Rod Hicks called in earlier. He's not returning anytime soon.'

'OK . . . ' Archer tries to disguise her indifferent tone.

'You don't sound impressed.'

Archer's history with DI Rod Hicks has not been an easy one. During her time at the National Crime Agency, she had been involved in a sting operation that resulted in the arrest of Andy Rees, a corrupt Met DI and close friend to Hicks. To add salt to the wound, Archer shifted from the NCA to the Met and took over the vacant position left by the incarcerated DI Rees. Archer and Hicks's relationship had never really developed yet they had come to tolerate each other. Over time, Archer had noticed a subtle shift in his attitude. Maybe, just maybe, he was getting used to her being around. That said, he was still not the easiest of people to get on with.

'I don't rate him.'

'We could do with his experience right now.'

Archer folds her arms. All help is welcome but she'd rather work extra hours than endure Hicks's snide remarks and general laziness.

'You underestimate him,' says Pierce.

Archer bites her tongue. After a moment, she says, 'Was there anything else?'

Pierce shakes her head.

Archer joins Quinn in the incident room.

'So, I'm assuming your quick chat with the boss was on the matter of your personal safety,' he asks.

'She's concerned. Not just about me. About you too.'

Quinn considers this.

'Listen, Harry, on reflection, I don't want to put you in danger.'

'Let's just stick with our plan for the time being,' Quinn says.

Archer is conflicted. It's bad enough Grandad was threatened but putting Harry at risk too was selfish.

'I can see the doubt on your face, Grace. Don't—'

Her phone rings. She recognises the number. 'The hospital,' she tells him and answers the call. 'Hello, this is Grace Archer.'

A female voice replies, 'Hello, this is Jenna Williams. I'm a nurse at St Thomas's Neurology ward.'

'Hello.'

'I just wanted to let you know your grandad's sleeping. He's comfortable and it's entirely possible he'll sleep through the night. The stroke may have taken it out of him.'

'Did he wake up at any stage?' Archer can hear the tremor in her voice and feels Quinn looking her way.

'For a little while. He was able to move his arms and feet. He didn't say much. That may be because he is so tired. Rest assured, we're watching over him.'

'Should I come and see him?'

'Tomorrow would be best.'

'Tomorrow ... Yes ... OK, thank you. I will.'

'If there's any change, we'll call you.'

'I would appreciate that.'

'Don't worry too much.'

No news is good news, Archer hopes, ending the call.

'Anything?' Quinn asks.

Archer shakes her head.

'He's in good hands, Grace.'

'I know,' she replies, quietly.

'Hey,' says Klara, stepping into the room. 'How's Jake doing?'

'The hospital just rang. He was awake but has gone back to sleep. They don't know much else yet.'

Klara steps forward and embraces her. 'He might be a ripe old age but he's as strong as an ox.'

Archer chuckles. 'I hope so.'

'I'm here for you if you need anything.'

'I know. Thank you.'

'Any update on the Land Rover, Klara?' Quinn asks.

'I got the registration details. It belongs to Andrei Brodsky. Mean anything to you?'

'Shit,' says Archer.

'That'd be a yes,' says Quinn.

'I remember him from years back. He was a small operator with fiercely loyal muscle behind him. He's ruthless and ambitious. Judging by his flashy car, well-dressed bodyguards and expensive suit, he's doing well for himself.'

'The pictures are a bit hazy for a face rec. I can keep at it if you want me to, though.'

'No. That'd be a waste of your time. Brodsky's name is all we need. The question is why is he facing off against Frankie White at his grandson's funeral?'

'Saying sorry for murdering his grandson?' says Quinn.

'Or sticking the knife in where it hurts.'

'Whatever the reason, the outcome ain't going to be pretty.'

Chapter 11

ARCHER WAKES TO A LOUD motorised whirring noise. She blinks her eyes and briefly wonders where she is. The room is gloomy with just a sliver of light slicing through a crack in the curtains. She remembers she's in Quinn's flat, in his bed. Archer had wanted to sleep on the sofa, but Quinn had insisted she be comfortable. It was after 9 p.m. by the time they had finished making up the incident room and left Charing Cross Police Station. It was almost ten o'clock when they arrived at Quinn's. Archer had crashed immediately, borrowing one of his old Clash T-shirts to sleep in. It feels weirdly intimate, but a necessity considering the night had been cold and Quinn's duvet low on the tog count.

She slides out of bed, steps onto the cold vinyl flooring and opens the bedroom door. The whirring noise is the electric shower, judging by the splashing sound in the bathroom. Quinn's flat has not changed much since he moved in. He'd told her it had not been decorated for almost forty years, which some might say is an understatement. The entire apartment is a museum of 1970s working-class chic. Patterned orange wallpaper covers the hallway walls; the floral carpet is woven in threadbare shades of brown, blue and red. For anyone 'under the influence' time spent within these walls could be a trip.

She peers into the living room. Quinn's clothes and an empty sleeping bag lie across the brown Chesterfield sofa.

A knock at the front door startles her. She feels a knot in her stomach. Her first thought is Frankie White's men have tracked them down. *Shit!* Logic kicks in and she figures if they had the smarts to follow her and Quinn home, they would have made the hit in the middle of the night, when they were sleeping.

She feels a hand on her shoulder and turns quickly. A wet, soapy Quinn, wearing nothing but a thin towel round his waist, raises a finger to his lips. He pads barefoot down the hallway, stops at a built-in storage cupboard and removes a baseball bat. Archer feels her heartbeat quicken. Quinn glances back at her with a reassuring look. She can see the tension in his taut back muscles as he peers through the peephole. To her relief, he looks her way, relaxes and gives her a thumbs-up.

He opens the door. 'Morning, Zel,' he says.

Zelda Frutkoff is Quinn's neighbour, an inquisitive woman of indeterminable age, who had befriended and latched onto him when he moved in three years back. According to Quinn, Zelda knows everything about everyone in the block. Yet, she has a heart of gold, and is a feeder, forever bringing him meals, despite never seeming to eat anything herself. Quinn had once told Archer, Zelda's only 'nourishment' is cigarettes and gin, which had made them both laugh. Archer cannot work out whether Zelda has a crush on Quinn or just wants to mother him. Perhaps both. Zelda swans into the hallway uninvited, all five foot five of her, smoking like a Victorian chimney, arms folded.

'Betty woke me with a text saying you brought a woman home last night,' she says.

'Betty hanging out the window with her binoculars again?' says Quinn, as he places the baseball bat behind the door, out of sight.

Zelda takes a long drag on her cigarette. 'You know what she's like. Just can't mind her own business.' She exhales a plume of smoke through her nose and notices Archer.

'Hi, Zelda,' Archer says.

Zelda blinks, inhales another long drag, as she takes in Quinn's Clash T-shirt and Archer's bare legs. Her eyes light up. She exhales a cloud of smoke and waves her cigarette at Archer. 'I knew it was you. Betty described you in great detail. That's his "colleague", Bets, I told her. Grace whatshername.'

'That's me,' says Archer.

'It's not what you think, Zel,' says Quinn. 'Grace is just staying for a few days.'

'Uh-huh.'

'We're just heading out, Zel,' says Quinn. 'Big case.'

Zelda winks at Archer. 'Understood. I must talk to Betty. You kids have fun. Call in later if you're passing.'

'Bye, Zel,' says Quinn, closing the door shut behind her.

Archer and Quinn stand in an awkward silence.

'Don't mind her. She's bonkers.'

'I'll just get a shower.'

'Sure. There's clean towels on the radiator.'

'Thanks.'

Chapter 12

'SIT DOWN, ROD. RELAX. LET'S enjoy the day,' says Tanya Hicks.

Detective Inspector Rod Hicks and his wife, Tanya Hicks, are in Walpole Park with their twin boys, Daniel and Dylan. Hicks looks up at the grey skies with a glum expression.

'It's gonna rain again,' he says.

'It might not,' Tanya replies, cheerily.

Hicks feels a twinge of irritation but holds his tongue.

'Nice to get out at last. All of us together,' Tanya says.

Hicks shrugs and thrusts his hands into his anorak pockets.

Tanya takes a small towel from her tote bag and wipes the morning rain from a bench outside the sand-covered natural play area. She smiles and gestures for him to sit down. He sighs, plants himself on the bench and idly watches his two sons giggling as they swing on a tyre suspended on rope.

'I was thinking ... ' says Tanya.

'Here we go.'

'Don't be like that. I'm just worried about you is all.'

A moment of awkward silence hangs in the air between them. He feels a kick of guilt but can't bring himself to apologise. Not because he doesn't want to. He just doesn't know how to. He has just spent four weeks locked up at his Ealing home on sick leave. He'd been signed off with stress-related mental health issues. He's not proud about it. Feeling this way is for weak people not blokes like him, but the truth is, he's crumbling inside and has never felt so alone.

'I just don't think it's good for you to be stuck at home every day. It's not you, Rod. You . . . you . . . should go back to work. For your own well-being and . . . well, they need you.'

Hicks sighs heavily. He's aware Charing Cross Police Station is stretched. Fuck, the entire UK force is thin on the ground. He understands that as much as the next copper. Since 2010, Tory cuts had seen a reduction of 23,500 police staff in England and Wales. Of those, 9,300 were London coppers alone. Crime was spiralling and the country was in crisis. He feels shit about not being there to do his bit. But something's eating away at him and no one could understand what's going through his head. No one! The truth is he's in deep shit and is aware his time of keeping his head in the sand is drawing to an end.

'Have you taken your tablets today?' Tanya asks.

'Which ones?' he replies in a petulant tone, which he instantly regrets.

'All of 'em. Aspirin. Statin. Ramipril . . . '

'Yes. Took them all this morning, after breakfast.'

She is looking at him, but he watches his twin boys, Daniel and Dylan, and draws from their happiness, their freedom, their innocence. How lucky they are.

'The Diazepam?' Tanya asks.

Hicks feels his mood darken. He bites his tongue, looks away, his signal for her to stop pressing him.

'I know you don't like me bringing it up, but I'm worried about you and that drug. You shouldn't be on it if you're taking Ramipril. That article said the combination of Ramipril and Diazepam causes depression in men.'

'You shouldn't believe everything you read in *Take a Break*, Tan!' he snaps.

She flinches, turns away and rubs her hands together. A nervous habit that has always irritated him. A mousy pale woman, with dyed brown hair, Tanya Hicks was once a good-looking and spirited woman. Sometimes he wonders what happened to her. How did she change so much over the years? He supposes she's a good mother, and a good enough wife. There's always food on the table, the kids are looked after, and she will 'put out' when he wants her to. Even when she doesn't want to.

'It wasn't *Take a Break*,' says Tanya. 'It was an article on the NHS website, for your information.'

Hicks says nothing to this.

They sit in silence, watching the boys clamber across a tall wooden climbing frame without a care.

'There's going to be tears,' says Tanya, standing abruptly.

'They'll be fine. They're just doing what boys do.'

'Daniel! Dylan! Be careful, please,' she hollers.

The boys look up, wave and then continue their boisterous race across the climbing frame, their mum's words disappearing in the breeze.

'I thought it was you two,' comes a voice from behind them.

Hicks's muscles seize and he feels a sudden urge to flee.

Tanya spins round and smiles. 'Hi, Jimmy. How are you? Long time,' she shrills.

Hicks's colleague, DS Jimmy Barnes, smiles, walks into view and embraces Tanya. 'Good to see you, Tan,' says Barnes, his smile fading when he locks eyes with Hicks.

A thickset fit man with the build of a rugby prop, Barnes is handsome with olive skin and salt and pepper hair. He can turn on the charm like the flick of a switch. The ladies,

Tanya included, all seem to adore him. If only they knew the real Barnes.

'You too, Jimmy.' Smiling and flustered, she extracts herself from him, but not too far as his thick arm rests on her shoulder. For a moment Hicks despises her.

'How're you doing, Rod?' asks Barnes.

His tone is friendly but at the same time cold. Tanya's expression tells him she detects something is not right.

Hicks shrugs and is about to speak but Tanya answers for him. 'He's still not a hundred per cent, Jimmy. He won't mind me saying but he's been prescribed Diazepam, which I don't think is right . . . '

'For Chrissakes, shut it, Tan!'

'Diazepam, is it?' says Barnes. 'That sounds rough, Rod.'

Hicks shrugs and does not look at his colleague. He can feel Barnes's questioning gaze asking, *why the fuck have you been ignoring my calls and texts for the past four weeks?*

'Hope they're working, mate.'

Mate? Fuck off, he thinks. He knows why Barnes is here. It was only a matter of time. Despite the cool afternoon temperature, Hicks feels a sweat coming on.

Barnes looks across at the play area. 'Boys seem to be having a good time.'

'Yes. We thought we'd have a nice family day out. Didn't we, Rod?'

'Such healthy, happy kids. You're lucky to have them,' says Barnes.

His tone is icy. Was that a warning? His hands clench into fists in the pockets of his anorak. With a punch of courage he asks, 'What're you doing here, Jimmy?'

'Thought you'd never ask. Tan, do you mind if Rod and I have a quick word? Five minutes tops.'

70

She lets out a short nervous laugh and shoots a concerned look at her husband. 'No, of course not. I'll go see to the boys.'

'You do that,' says Barnes.

When Tanya is out of earshot, Barnes says, 'We have some catching up to do.'

Hicks shifts uneasily on the bench as Barnes sits next to him.

'Mr White is very disappointed with you, Rod. He asked me to visit you in person because you've been keeping your distance.'

'I haven't been well.'

'Have you been in a coma?'

Hicks frowns. 'No.'

'Are your fingers broken?'

'No.'

'Lost your voice?'

Hicks's jaw tightens. He does not respond.

'Then why can't you answer the fucking phone?'

'I'm stressed. PTSD.'

Barnes snorts. 'From what exactly? You're the laziest cunt I know. The thing about you, Rodders, is that you let everyone else do the work and then you take the glory when it's dished out. PTSD, my arse!'

'That's not true.'

'We both know it's true. So does your old mate DI Andy Rees. Serving time for our mutual employer, and you know I'm not talking about the Met.'

'Andy and I are mates.'

'That's not what he thinks. You've abandoned him as much as you've abandoned Mr White.'

'No, I've been . . . '

'Sick, I know. Spare me the bullshit.'

'You wouldn't understand.'

'It's you that doesn't understand.'

71

Hicks is sodden underneath his clothes. 'I want out! I can't do this anymore. I have a family for fuck's sake.'

'Mr White had a family. His brothers. His wife. His grandson. All gone. Just him and Janine left. That's sad, don't you think?'

'That's rich coming from you. You don't have one bit of empathy in your body. You can fool Tanya, the other wives, Pierce, Quinn, Archer, everyone. But you don't fool me. I know what you are.'

'Good. Then you'll understand this is not a negotiation.'

'I don't care. I've done my bit.'

'Which is what exactly?'

Hicks has no answer to that.

'Mr White believes you view him as some sort of cash cow. You take money every month, but you give nothing in return.'

'That's bollocks and you know it!' retorts Hicks, his voice raised.

He catches Tanya watching them. She quickly looks away.

'OK,' says Barnes, 'You've overseen a few operations and ensured Mr White's people avoid arrest. Terrific.' Barnes scrunches his face. 'Trouble is, it's just not enough. How much have you earned in the last five years?'

'I don't know.'

'I checked in with the accountant this morning. It's upwards of £150k. Nice for you, Tanya and the kids.'

'I've worked for it.'

'You're nowhere close to earning your salary.'

Hicks looks back at Tanya and the boys and feels his world caving in. He's failed them. He's in the shit and knows this will not end well. His true feelings for Tanya unfurl as if they've been buried under soil for years. Oh God. He'd be lost without her and the boys. He wishes more than anything he had the foresight to use that money and take them somewhere far away from London, from White, from Barnes, from Charing Cross. Oh Jesus. What can he do?

Barnes continues, 'All that said, Mr White remains a generous man. You can redeem yourself by taking one last job.'

'What job?'

'An important job.'

'An important job' for Mr White is never a good thing. Hicks feels the urge to flee again. 'What if I say no?'

'Like I said, this is not a negotiation.'

'I can give the money back.'

'Nope.'

'I'll go see Mr White myself. He'll understand.'

'I thought you might say that. So, I want you to consider this. Have you seen the movie, *Sophie's Choice*?'

Hicks frowns. 'No.'

'I didn't think so. If it doesn't have Vin Diesel and cars, you're not interested. Am I right?'

Hicks says nothing.

'It's based on a book. Could be a true story, I suppose. It's set in Auschwitz, during the Second World War and stars Meryl Streep as Sophie, a Polish mother of two kids. Just before they enter the camp, the doctor makes Sophie choose which of her children should enter the camp and which one should be gassed. I think they were short on beds.' Barnes's eyes slide briefly to Dylan and Daniel. 'See where I'm going here?'

Hicks can feel himself going cold inside.

'After much deliberation, Sophie has to make her choice. I won't spoil it by telling you who she chooses in case you want to watch it later.'

Barnes winks at Hicks. He quivers inside and at the same time imagines sticking a knife in Barnes's throat.

73

'Sophie makes that whopper of a decision. One kid is taken to the gas chambers and dies a horrible death. The other lives.' Barnes shifts on the bench and leans towards him in a faux friendly way. 'So here's the plan. We're going to do our own updated version and call it *Tanya's Choice*. If you decline Mr White's request, then we will take you and your family somewhere remote. While you and the kiddies watch, I will ask Tanya to make the decision on whether Dylan or Daniel gets a bullet in the head. If the lovely Tan does not comply, then both boys die. Tan too, and you live with the guilt.'

Hicks feels the blood drain from his face. He looks towards his boys. His perfect boys, so innocent, so happy, the only good thing in his lousy fucking life.

'Don't worry though. I'll make it quick, I'm not a monster.'

Hicks feels his head spinning. How could this be happening? How has his life turned to crap so spectacularly?

'So, what's your answer?'

It takes a moment to answer. 'I'll do it. Just promise to leave my family out of this. Please.'

'We'll see. If you deliver, you're off the hook. Scout's honour.'

Hicks knows Barnes's promises are not worth shit.

'What does he want me to do?'

'First things first. Later, when you get home, you contact Pierce and tell her you're ready to return to work tomorrow. Mr White needs you on the inside.'

'I already told her I wasn't coming back just yet.'

'Then tell her you changed your mind.'

Hicks sighs.

'Then, go upstairs to yours and Tan's bedroom.'

'Excuse me?'

'You'll find a box underneath your bed.'

'What box? What the fuck were you doing inside my house?'

'I like what you've done with the place. Very nice. Looks expensive. No surprise considering you've been raking in the cash.'

Hicks looks away.

'The box contains a loaded Glock 17. I left it on Tanya's side just for the hell of it.'

Hicks's heart sinks. 'A fucking gun?'

'Mr White wants you to perform a very special hit for him.'

He swallows.

Barnes looks at Tanya. 'At certain angles, Tan could pass for Meryl Streep. Don't you think?'

Tanya is looking back at Hicks with a concerned expression. He smiles weakly at her. 'Who's the target?' he asks.

'Should be an easy one for you. It's someone you already have a difficult relationship with. I know what you're thinking. People that fall into that category are most of the Met, most of your mates, even Tanya. Your kids too.'

'Fuck you!'

'That's the spirit. When the deed is done and the police catch you, you will tell them you were motivated by hate and jealousy.'

'What do you mean, when the police catch me?'

'You'll go down for the murder. That way, the scent will be taken from our employer.'

'No fucking way!'

'Remember *Tanya's Choice*? If you do this your family lives and even gets to keep the money you took from Mr White. Can't say fairer than that, can we?'

Barnes stands. Hicks feels defeated.

'Who's the target?'

'Do you really need to ask that?'

Hicks closes his eyes and sighs heavily. White has had it in for her since the arrest and subsequent death of his grandson. 'Archer.'

'Not so dumb, after all. You have one week. Don't fuck it up.' Barnes turns to leave and waves at the family. 'Bye, Tan. Bye, Dylan, Daniel.'

They smile back at him and wave.

The world around him seems to spin. Hicks can almost feel himself shrinking and disappearing. How he wishes he could.

Chapter 13

THE TRAIN CRAWLS THROUGH LONDON like an old clunky snake. The carriage is stale and damp and crammed with grim-faced commuters returning home from a long day working in the city.

Brynn Hughes sits squeezed between two blokes in wet trench coats. His school uniform is soaking wet, his shoulder-length dark hair is dripping and lies flat against his skull. Leaning forward, he glances at his reflection in the window and swears under his breath. His large ears are sticking out. Sitting back, he furtively uses his fingers to comb through the wet tufts and fix them over his ears, concealing them out of sight. He had got caught in a downpour after spending two hours in detention for fighting with an English boy, Garret Brown, in school. Garret had approached Brynn in the hallway, pulled his ears, mimicked his accent and called him a 'queer'. Brynn did not like it one bit and surprised himself by twatting him. A fight kicked off, with Garret getting the better of him. To Brynn's relief, a teacher broke up the fight. Unfortunately, they had both been given detention, but Garret had been allowed to leave early because he didn't feel well. Lying little shit, he is.

Brynn and his parents had moved to London from Swansea eleven months back, looking for better job opportunities. That's the story Mam told him anyway. The move had come out of the blue and happened so quickly that Brynn suspected something was not right. He'd asked his parents, but they wouldn't give him a straight answer, or any answer for that matter. They barely spoke to each other at the time, but he continued to press them. Mam'd say: 'Just finish your tea, Brynn,' or 'Have you no reading to catch up on?', or, 'Mind your beeswax, Brynn.' His dad ignored him or growled some rude word. And then one day, Dad had enough of his questions, and it all came to light that Mam had been seeing some bloke in Swansea. Dad had put the bloke in hospital, hurt him bad, which was why they had to skip town. He recalls Mam having a black eye and a busted lip at the time. His dad's payback obviously. Brynn hated him sometimes. He's a bad-tempered, punchy drunk. It wasn't unusual for Mam to be bruised and battered. Same for Brynn, who suffered similar beatings when Mam left them for some other bloke she met at work. It was just him and his dad now.

The train pulls up at his stop. Abbey Wood Station. He slides across the seat, pushes open the door and steps onto the platform. Using all his strength, he hauls the door back and slams it shut.

Brynn exits the concourse, relieved to see the rain has eased. He makes his way to Holstein Way in the Erith Estate and his home, a run-down three-storey social housing property that looks more like a concrete box than a house. Brynn hates it. It's the opposite of their cosy, comfortable semi back in Swansea. Life had been so much better there.

With Mam gone, Brynn was spending a lot of time on his own. Dad worked most evenings and nights too, so he hardly saw him. He had heard a saying on some telly programme: 'Every cloud has a silver lining'. He supposes that applies in this situation.

Brynn makes his way up Alsike Road and takes a short cut left through a back alley. He hears rapid footsteps behind.

'Oi, freak!' someone shouts.

Brynn turns to see a fist flying towards his face. A blinding pain tremors through his head. His school bag slides from his shoulder and falls to the ground. Brynn tries to get a grip but stumbles over his bag and falls on all fours.

'Payback, you fucking Welsh fag!' says Garret Brown.

Brynn's head is spinning, his eye throbbing.

'Kick him, Stevo!' Garret says.

Stevo is Garret's twin brother.

They begin kicking the shit out of Brynn. He curls into a ball and covers his head with his arms as their trainers pound his back.

'Pull his trousers down, Stevo.'

'What? No!'

'Just fucking do it!'

'Why?'

'I'm going to teach him a lesson.'

Terror swallows Brynn and he tries to wriggle away. A kick to the ribs soon stops that.

'I'll fucking do it then!' says Garret.

He feels his hands tugging at the waistband of his trousers. The front button pops. His underwear is next. 'No!' he cries, tears tripping from his eyes, as he feels the cold air on his bottom.

Garret laughs. 'Look at his tiny bare white ass. Don't shit yourself, fag! Give me that stick.'

Brynn peeks from behind his elbow and sees Stevo handing Garret a grubby broken broomstick. Garret raises it in the air and begins beating it on Brynn's bottom.

Brynn screams.

'Piss on him, Stevo.'

'What?'

'You said you needed to go. So go.'

Brynn hears the sound of a zipper.

'No please,' says Brynn.

'No please!' Garret mimics in a mock Welsh accent.

Brynn's heart sinks as warm piss spills onto his bottom.

Garret and Stevo laugh.

'Someone's coming,' says Garret.

Brynn hears the stick drop to the ground and their feet hurrying away. He pushes himself up. He's hot, sweating and in pain. Looking towards the entrance to the alleyway, he sees a tall, gangly girl with long dark hair, covered in a weird, padded helmet. He has seen her occasionally at Mrs Toolan's house. She is looking his way, her eyes wide, mouth open. Pulling up his trousers and pants, he turns away, hiding his face. He glances back at the twins. They are pointing and laughing at the girl.

'It's Epi-Iris. Show us one of your turns, Epi-Iris! We need a laugh.'

Brynn is not hanging around. Clutching the front of his trousers, he legs it down the alley, pushing past Epi-Iris. His heart racing, he runs for his life up Holstein Way. Arriving at his house, he fumbles for his key in his blazer pocket and preys it hasn't fallen out. To his relief he finds it, inserts it into the lock, ignoring the goading voices as they draw closer.

An empty beer can hits the wall to the side of the door. He turns to see the twins pulling waste from the dustbins and hurling it his way. He pushes the door but it's stiff. He feels something bump the back of his head. A mouldy sandwich.

'Got him!' laughs Stevo.

A woman's voice shouts from a window next door. Mrs Toolan, their neighbour. 'Oi, you lot! Piss off and leave him alone.'

'Fuck you, lard-ass!'

'You little shit! Don't think I won't come down there and kick your arse,' she hollers.

80

'Come on then. Bring some doughnuts while you're at it. We're starving!'

Through the corner of his eye, he sees something flapping through the air from Mrs Toolan's window. Glancing around, he sees a paperback book crash like a dead bird at the feet of the brothers.

'Hahaha! Is that the best you can do?' Garret calls.

He hears Mrs Toolan shout, 'Bastards!' as she slams her window shut.

Panting, he pushes open the door, tumbles inside and shoves it closed. Relief washes over him. He is safe. Their laughter fades. Brynn drops to his knees and collapses on the floor, curling into himself. He's been defiled and humiliated. Tears trip from his eyes. Tears that turn to sobs that evolve into a wracking cry that comes from somewhere deep in his soul.

Part 2

Chapter 14

JASON TODD'S MURDER HAS MADE the news. A brief
mention on BBC London, the local radio stations and a
column in the local papers. Interest is minimal. Todd is
just another victim of rising crime in the capital. People are
immune to these headlines. A dead man, killed by someone
who broke into his home. What's new about that? Shit happens.
Break-ins happen every day. People get hurt. People die. That's
the world we live in. He'll be forgotten tomorrow. But not by
his family. Not by his friends.

Archer is relieved there is little fuss. She had made it clear
that the details of the mask and the lack of evidence of a
robbery be omitted from the press communication. The mask
would generate too much speculation and attention that would
spiral into lunatic conspiracy theories. As for the robbery, the
truth is they still did not know if Jason Todd was killed because
he had something someone wanted. She has her doubts though.
There was something about his death. Something just too
calculating and sinister that made her think this killer had
it in for his victim.

Archer had called Todd's lover, Katie Fox, and arranged to
meet at her home in Honeybrook Road, Clapham, first thing
this morning. Fox is an attractive blonde woman in her late

thirties. She wears a flowing white blouse and greets them with a fixed smile, in a cloud of Issey Miyake.

'Please come in,' she says, her voice is gravelly, her tone confident. 'Do wipe your feet. Filthy weather, we're having.'

Her living room is a masterclass in minimalistic decor. Everything is white or bone-pale: the walls, the floorboards, the two sofas, the coffee table, the television. Despite having one twelve-year-old child, there is no evidence of children ever occupying this space.

'Please sit.'

'Thank you for seeing us so early.'

'Would either of you like a drink?' she asks.

'Nothing for me,' says Archer.

'I'll pass, thanks.'

Fox sits on the sofa opposite, 'So awful about poor Jason.'

'Just you at home today?' asks Archer.

'Arthur, my son, is at school and my husband, Derek, is at work.'

'Jason's son, Lucas, and Arthur, go to the same school?'

'Yes.'

'Are they friends?'

'Yes.'

'Close friends?'

'I suppose. As much as twelve-year-olds can be.'

'What does Derek do?' Quinn asks.

'He's a finance director. For a start-up in Farringdon.'

'Must have been a shock for you all – Jason's death.'

'For Arthur and me, certainly.'

'Not Derek?'

'Derek didn't know Jason.'

'How well did you know Jason?' Archer asks.

'Not very well. We met through our boys.'

'When did you last see him?'

Fox knots her fingers together and looks across the room. 'Let me think . . . Around two weeks back.'

She looks at Archer, who holds her gaze. 'What was your relationship with Jason?'

Fox straightens her posture. 'Relationship? None per se. We were friends. We saw each other at the school gates. Chatted and had coffee in Clapham occasionally. We had some things in common. We're both fastidious about clutter and hygiene. Jason's place was always immaculate—' She stops abruptly and begins tugging at the sleeves of her blouse.

Bingo. Archer parks that thought for now.

'It was a blossoming friendship,' says Quinn.

'I suppose it was.'

'How long have you known each other?'

'About a year or more.'

'Did you ever notice anything about Jason that would cause you concern?' asks Archer.

'Like what?'

'Was he stressed, worried, frightened even?'

'No . . . no . . . nothing like that. He was always so . . . sweet. Oh God, are you suggesting someone set out to murder him? The news said it was a burglary gone wrong.'

'We don't know anything for sure yet.'

Fox nods her understanding. 'I can't believe what's happened. It's just so awful.'

'It really is. We're doing our utmost to find out who did this, so we are,' says Quinn. 'Whatever you can give us will help. Anything at all.'

She smiles, quickly, and insincerely, and rests her hands on her lap.

'Did you spend much time at Jason's flat?' Archer asks.

Her face tightens as her eyes slide from Archer to Quinn. 'Excuse me?'

'You mentioned earlier Jason's flat was immaculate. I presumed you'd been there.'

She clears her throat and looks away. 'No . . . '

'Were you and Mr Todd intimate?'

'I'm a married woman.'

'Jason Todd was married also.'

'He was separated!' Fox snaps. She turns from them, her face flushing pink, almost lighting the pale room in a warm glow.

Silence hangs between them. Archer and Quinn let it run its course.

Fox sighs and shakes her head. 'I suppose the tongues have been wagging.'

'Maybe you can tell us,' says Archer.

'You didn't say how you got my number. I suppose Penny gave it to you.' She rolls her eyes. 'That woman is so jealous.'

Archer keeps a level, considerate tone to her questions. 'Why would Penny be jealous of you and Jason?'

'You'd have to ask her.'

'Mrs Fox, we'll be doing a full DNA search of Jason's flat. Is it possible we would find your DNA there?'

Fox's face drops. She stands abruptly and walks to the white fireplace. After a moment she says, 'Is this going to go any further?'

'We don't know yet. We just need to establish some facts and understand what was going on in Jason's life. Any inform-ation you give us could lead to finding out who killed him.'

'Oh God. I knew it was a mistake.'

She fidgets and hesitates before answering. 'It was only twice. Maybe three times. I can't remember. We weren't having an affair. We were just "friends with benefits".'

'Where did you and Jason meet?'

'We had a coffee sometimes, as I mentioned, and then we'd meet at his flat.'

'Do you recall the dates and times?'

'Some, possibly.'

'If you could write them down, that would be helpful.'

'I'll check my diary and email them to you.'

'Thank you. Does anyone else know about you and Jason?'

'Obviously, Penny and her gossiping women friends, I should imagine.'

'Your husband?'

She shakes her head. 'And he mustn't find out.'

Archer reaches into her coat pocket and takes out a card with her contact details. 'My phone and email. If there is something else you think might be important, please get in touch.'

Fox takes the card.

'Thank you for your time, Mrs Fox. Have a good day.'

A rattled Katie Fox sees them out and closes the door without so much as a goodbye.

As they make their way to the car, Quinn says, 'An easy nut to crack.'

'It wasn't difficult. We should also investigate Derek Fox.'

'Are you thinking murderous jealous husband?'

'I'm not discounting anything at the moment.'

Chapter 15

GRANDAD IS SMILING AND CHATTING to a nurse who is taking his blood pressure, when Archer shows the police guard her ID and steps into the private room.

He looks across at her and smiles. 'Here she is. My girl.'

Archer swallows at the slight slur she hears in his voice and forces a smile.

The nurse, a sturdy Asian woman, says, 'Just relax now, Mr Archer, while I finish up.'

'Call me Jake, dear.'

'Jake dear, it is,' she replies.

Grandad's gaze lingers on Archer, reading her expression. He smiles and shoots a sideways glance at the nurse. 'Can't keep her hands off me, this one.'

The nurse gently pulls the Velcro from the blood pressure cuff and slides it from his thin arm. 'How can any woman say no to you? You're irresistible, Jake dear.'

'It's a burden I've had to come to terms with.'

'How're you doing, Jake?' Quinn asks from behind.

Grandad raises an arm and gives a thumbs-up. 'Doing good, son.'

'You're certainly looking better than you did yesterday.'

'Could we have a quick word outside?' Archer asks the nurse.

The nurse nods an affirmation.

Archer leans over the bed and kisses Grandad on his rough, grey, unshaven cheek, 'I'll be back in one moment.'

Quinn strikes up a conversation about football as Archer and the nurse step into the hallway.

'How's he doing?' Archer asks.

'He's better. Awake, eating and drinking. Flirting, too.'

'He's slurring,' Archer says.

'Yes. That might be temporary.'

'Might?'

'As you know, your grandfather has had a stroke. Not a serious one, but a stroke all the same. He's lucky to have pulled through the way he has. We will keep an eye on his speech.'

Archer takes a moment to process this.

The nurse continues, 'Also, at times he seems a little confused. At other times he seems fine. But you know we see that a lot in patients with early dementia. This could be just a symptom of that horrible disease.'

'Yes, I suppose it could be.'

'When you talk to him you will be able to gauge if there is a difference in his speech and cognitive abilities.'

Archer nods, 'What happens next?'

'He'll stay here for a few days. We'll monitor him, make sure he's OK. Then the doctors will make a decision.'

'A decision?'

'They'll decide if he needs therapy or further rest.'

'I see.'

The nurse smiles warmly at her. 'He's in good spirits, as you saw. We don't always see that with stroke victims.'

Archer feels a deep relief. 'Thank you ... for everything.'

'You're welcome.'

Back in the room, Grandad and Quinn are chatting away. Grandad turns his attention to her. 'So, what's the verdict?'

Archer sits on the side of the bed and places the holdall beside her. 'She says you're doing well.'

He says nothing for a moment.

'My mind feels slow.'

Archer reaches for his hand and takes it in hers. 'You had a stroke.'

'So I understand.'

'She says you're doing OK, and I believe her.'

Grandad looks at her with hollow eyes. After a moment, he says, 'I'm scared.'

Archer feels her throat tightening. She squeezes his hand gently. 'Do you remember what happened?'

'No. But unless I'm hallucinating, there's been a police guard outside my room since I woke up. Did I rob a bank or something?'

Archer does not want to stress him out any further. Yet, she cannot lie to him, especially as he is assessing her face for any sign of an untruth.

'There's a threat against me. From Frankie White. A threat that extends to you too.'

Grandad turns his gaze to the ceiling. His face darkens. 'And that's why I'm here.'

'You're safe here. The nurses will look after you and there is a guard, twenty-four hours a day.'

He turns to look at her. 'What about you?'

'I'll be fine. Don't worry about me.'

'How can I not?'

'I'm not alone, Grandad. I have the support of the Met, the NCA and Harry, as always.'

Grandad's eyes begin to water. He slides them to where Quinn is standing. 'I'm begging you, Harry, please don't let anything happen to her.'

'As long as there's breath in my body, I'll do everything I can.'

A voice from outside the room speaks, 'Hello. Can I get you a tea or a coffee?' A thin male catering assistant wearing a faded blue uniform is looking in.

'A tea, please,' Grandad replies. 'A biscuit would be nice. Need all the strength I can muster.'

Archer opens the holdall. 'Brought you some clean underwear, pyjamas, glasses, pills, et cetera.' She reaches into the bag and takes out his mobile phone and the charger. 'Keep this by your bed at all times. Call me if you need anything. I will check in on you as often as I can.'

Grandad takes the phone from her. 'I will.'

'Promise?'

'Promise.'

'We need to go, Grandad.'

He grips her hand. 'Be careful, Grace.'

She leans across and kisses his forehead. 'Get some rest. I'll come and see you tomorrow.'

'See ya, Jake,' says Quinn.

They walk in silence, Archer lost in her thoughts, consumed with guilt, as they navigate the labyrinthine hospital corridors and make their way to the car park.

'That must have been tough,' Quinn says as they get into the car.

'He's alive and is in good enough form. That's all that matters for now.'

'Where to now?'

'Let's head back to Charing Cross. I'd like to review Todd's files and see if there's anything we missed.'

The rain has not eased on the trip back to Central London. As a consequence, the journey takes almost one hour with traffic backed up not helped by ongoing roadworks in the most random of places.

After parking up and hurrying through the rain to the rear of the station, Archer sees Jimmy Barnes hurrying down the stairs, two at a time.

'Hi, Jimmy,' says Archer, shaking the rain from her coat.

'Grace. Harry. How're you guys doing?' says Barnes.

'Fine, thanks,' says Archer.

'Lovin' life, Jimbo,' says Quinn.

Barnes gestures behind him. 'Look who's returned to the fold.'

Holding back behind Barnes, at the top of the stairs, is a familiar face. One she has not seen in four weeks.

'Hi, Rod. I wasn't expecting you back so soon.'

'He's feeling much better,' says Barnes.

Hicks doesn't meet her gaze.

'Nice to have you back though. Glad you're feeling better.'

Hicks nods an acknowledgement, thrusts his hands into his coat pocket and makes his way down the stairs.

Barnes says, 'Let's hit the road, Rod.'

Archer stands aside to let them pass.

'See you two later,' says Barnes, as he heads into the rain. Hicks follows him, trailing behind in his wake.

'What's that about?' asks Archer.

'God knows. I don't get the dynamic between those two. I mean, Hicks is not the sharpest tool in the box but at least he could hold his own with his partners. Not so with Jimmy. Before he went out on the sick, he seemed to be barely functioning under Jimmy's shadow.'

'Do you think that's why he went on the sick?'

'Who knows? Jimmy is a no-nonsense guy. He wouldn't stand for any of Hicks's bullshit.'

'He can learn a lot from Jimmy. It'll do him good.'

'Aye. I'd suppose he could.'

Chapter 16

IN HIS DRAUGHTY OFFICE AT the rear of the Isle of Dogs warehouse, Frankie White gestures for the Albanian to take a seat.

'Thank you.' A short, bearded man called Bes Tola, he sits and places a small sports bag on the floor.

In the back-room kitchen attached to the office, Frankie hears the kettle boiling.

'One minute,' he says.

Stubbing out the last of his fag, he enters the kitchen and closes the door behind him. It's a grubby rectangular space, ten by twenty, used as a place to make tea, and when the need arises, a room to hold and fuck over undesirables. Frankie pours steaming water from the kettle into a mug containing a tea bag, milk and four sugar lumps. He stirs the mixture with a tea-stained spoon and regards the steel table bolted to the floor. The manacles chained to the table are caked in dried blood. He tuts his disapproval. Someone needs to clean this shit up. Frankie returns to the office and sits at his desk without looking at the Albanian, whose name he has already forgotten.

'This is an impressive place you have here, Mr White.'

Frankie glances through the windows and into the warehouse. A recent shipment had arrived safely and was sitting in storage. Rows of crates containing over two hundred weapons: Scorpion submachine guns; G9A automatic pistols; AK47s; Kalashnikovs. And explosives. Lots of explosives.

'Yes, it is.' Frankie takes a slurp of hot sweet tea and lights up. 'It's been a right fuck-up since I've been inside, Mr . . . ?'

'Tola.'

'That's it, Tola. I don't know you but I'm going to confide in you and perhaps you can pass this on to your colleagues. During my incarceration at Her Majesty's pleasure, my businesses have suffered. Some of my allies have set up on their own or have aligned themselves with my rivals, taking large parts of my business away from me. That's not reasonable. I'm sure you'd agree?' Frankie exhales two plumes of smoke through his nose, enjoying the squirming Tola.

'No, Mr White. You are correct. It is not reasonable.'

'Not just my allies have let me down. My family too. Most of them dead now though. Just my daughter Janine left, but she hasn't got the smarts or the balls. As for my grandson, Ethan, God rest his soul. He was just useless. Most of the leadership that remained during my time inside betrayed me on what we would call in the country, Mr Tola, "a fucking Shakespearean level".' Frankie smiles and taps the side of his head. 'But they didn't know I was smarter than them. I paid my way out of jail and have returned to reclaim what's owed me. I'm glad you've got to see my armoury. I'd like you to tell all your pals that I'm back, and I have big plans.'

The Albanian pales and shifts in his chair. 'Mr Kadare . . . '

'Is not fucking here. Yes, I can see that.'

'Mr Kadare sends his deepest apologies. He has some pressing business.'

'Pressing business? What could be more pressing than a ten million pound deal?'

'He has some private matters to take care of.'

Frankie frowns, 'Is there a problem with our arrangement?'

Tola shifts in the seat. 'No, no, none at all, Mr White. I can assure you.'

Frankie scratches his chin. 'It's just a bit fucking rude, don't you think?'

Tola lets out a nervous laugh and dips his head. 'I understand. I will convey that back to Mr Kadare.'

'You do that.'

Tola lifts the bag onto the table, 'As an apology, Mr Kadare sends this gift.'

A knock on the door.

'What is it?'

One of the Kevin's ugly mugs looks inside. 'Toby's here.'

Frankie looks across the warehouse and sees Toby talking to the staff and giving them direction. There are thirteen people in total, all different ages, each of them obediently doing what Toby asks of them. Impressive. How has he not noticed Toby before? Is he getting sloppy in his old age?

'Mr White,' says Tola.

'One minute.'

Toby looks towards the office and catches Frankie's eye. Frankie beckons him inside.

'You were saying,' Frankie says to Tola.

Tola opens the bag, revealing two brick-shaped blocks wrapped in silver duct tape.

Toby enters.

'Toby, this is an associate of Merkush Kadare. Merkush is having problems with our arrangement and has sent his monkey to butter us up with some free crack.'

Toby folds his arms and leans on the wall by the back room, watching Tola.

'No, no, not so, Mr White. He just needs some more time.'

'Time is something I'm not in the mood to give.'

'Please, Mr White. Try it.' Tola leans across, takes out a small knife and slices open one of the blocks. 'It's pure like the first snows of winter but with a kick . . . ' He offers a small pile on the blade of his knife.

Frankie takes the knife and tips the contents onto his desk. With a credit card he divides the coke into five perfect lines. From his pocket he takes out a small silver pipe. Leaning over the desk, he snorts two lines, one in each nostril. He feels a tingling rush as the coke begins to work its magic. He hands the pipe to Toby, who also snorts two lines.

Frankie feels like he's on fire. 'Not bad,' he says.

Tola looks at Toby. Toby gives him a non-committal shrug. Tola seems disappointed.

'We have a proposition,' says Tola.

'And what would that be?' asks Frankie.

Tola gestures at the bag. 'Yes. This is a gift but so is a stake in our county lines, as a down payment.'

'A down payment?' Frankie says, puzzled but also euphoric.

'Yes, until we honour our side of the bargain.'

Frankie exchanges a look with Toby.

'How much of a stake?' asks Toby.

'Fifteen per cent.'

Toby frowns. 'You're going to have to do better than that.'

'That's the best I can do. Please . . . '

Frankie says, 'You must be up shit creek if you're coming here with an apology and this paltry gift.'

Tola's eyes widen as if he's been slapped.

'Forty per cent,' says Toby.

Tola shakes his head. 'No. Not possible.'

'Then leave.'

Tola looks from Frankie to Toby and back to Frankie.

'Go on. Fuck off and take your party gear with you,' Frankie says.

Tola remains rooted to the chair. After a moment he reaches into his jacket pocket. 'I must make a call.'

Tola dials a number and talks quietly in Albanian before looking up. 'Twenty per cent.'

Frankie looks at Toby. Toby shakes his head.

Outside the office a crate has been opened and two men are checking over two Kalashnikov assault rifles. The heavy metal clicking sound causes Tola to turn and look. He whispers in Albanian to the contact and turns back to Frankie, his face pale.

Frankie says, 'As a gesture of goodwill and trust, I'll take thirty per cent. I'm also giving you an extra forty-eight hours to complete our arrangement.'

Tola consults with his contact. After a moment he ends the call. 'We accept,' he says.

Chapter 17

'So, you and my grandson was good mates?' Frankie White asks Toby Cullen.

It's early evening and Toby is driving Frankie's Jag, navigating through the neon streets of Central London, wipers on full. Frankie is watching him thoughtfully from the back of the car.

'Ethan and I were thick as thieves at school. Always up to no good. Bunking off. Nicking shit from shops. Drinking. Smoking.'

'Sounds like Ethan, all right,' Frankie muses as he pushes his horn-rimmed glasses up his nose. He turns his gaze to the window. Outside, people are running to shelter from the downpour.

'We made a pact when we were twelve.' Toby chuckles to himself. 'We were so dumb . . . '

Frankie turns his gaze back to Toby and studies his expressive eyes, or what he can make of them from the narrow reflection in the rear-view mirror. He is intrigued by Toby. He has a confidence that none of his other people have. Everyone who works for Frankie – psychopaths, sycophants, morons – walk on eggshells around him, even Janine for Christ's sake. Yet Toby is different. He takes everything in his stride. He isn't afraid of anyone. Not the Kevins, for instance. They have a fearsome reputation not helped by the fact both their faces resemble a well-scalped badger's arse. The fact that they have a combined IQ total lurking somewhere around the mid-twenties, and that's being generous, may be more than a contributing factor to Toby's lack of interest or fear in the two bodyguards. *Fuck me. How have I managed to survive this long with those two halfwits*, he thinks. No, Toby doesn't fear them or Frankie for that matter. If anything, he talks to Frankie as if he has known and respected him all his life, which is more than Ethan ever did. Yeah, Frankie is intrigued. Unlike Ethan, Toby is ambitious, and ruthless too. He sees in him a younger version of himself. He sees in him the grandson he wanted but never had.

Toby continues, 'We were hiding out in my mum's flat. She was at work. We took a knife from the kitchen. One of the sharp ones. "Brothers in blood," I said to him. "Brothers in blood," he replied. I drew the knife down my right palm and made a cut. Not too big. There was some blood. Ethan's face turned white as a ghost, man. So, he hesitated. "Brothers in blood," I said again and handed him the knife. He looked at it with uncertainty. "Remember who you are, Ethan," I said. He nodded, but I could see he didn't want to do it. The knife hovered over his hand. After a few moments he said, "Fuck it!" and drew it across his palm, cutting it open. I could see he was sweating. I grabbed his hand with mine. Our blood mixed. "Brothers in blood," I said.' Toby laughs, seemingly lost in the memory.

He glances at Frankie in the rear-view mirror and smiles.

'And?' Frankie asks.

'Everything turned to shit. Ethan went too deep with the cut. There was a lot of blood. His eyes rolled back in his head, and he passed out.'

'I don't remember any of this.'

'You were inside, Mr White. I imagine Janine chose not to tell you.'

Frankie rolls his eyes, 'So, what happened?'

'I wrapped Ethan's wound with a tea towel and took him to the hospital. They gave him six stitches! Man, did we get into trouble. Janine went apeshit. My mum flipped her lid. We got our arses well and truly kicked,' laughs Toby.

Frankie feels something like a hiccup from the bottom of his stomach. But it's not a hiccup. It's something he has not done in a long time. Years perhaps. Another one comes and his shoulders start jerking. He's laughing and can't seem to stop. His eyes water and he doubles over. Toby is laughing at him laughing. Frankie's laugh becomes a coughing fit; inside he is still giggling. He loves that story. His idiot grandson slicing open his hand. Janine losing it.

'We're close to Q-Park in Westminster. It's about a twenty-minute walk to Westminster Bridge.'

'Looks like the rain is easing. Park there, son. The walk'll do us good.'

'Yes, sir.'

There's something else about the story that resonates with him. Ethan's blood, which is also Frankie's blood, is in some way within Toby. He lets that process for a few moments.

After a moment Toby asks, 'Everything OK, Mr White, sir?'

'Everything is good, son. Are those two meatheads still behind us?'

Toby checks the rear mirror.

'Yes, they are. Kevin One and Kevin Two are following you like devoted puppies.'

Frankie snorts.

Toby finds a parking space. Frankie struggles to get out of the car. His leg muscles are stiff and seize up. Toby offers to help. Normally, Frankie would tell anyone else to fuck off. Not Toby, though. He allows Toby to ease him out of the car.

'There's an umbrella in the boot. Just in case,' says Frankie.

Toby grabs it. They leave the park, walking side by side, in silence for a few moments. Frankie breaks it. 'I liked that story you told.'

'I'm sure if I put my mind to it I could remember a few others.'

Frankie chuckles. 'I bet you could.'

They walk for twenty minutes through Westminster with the Kevins keeping a safe distance behind them. They turn right onto Bridge Street and begin the walk across Westminster Bridge. Frankie stops about halfway and looks across the river towards the giant Ferris wheel of the London Eye, illuminated purple, a striking and odd addition to the skyline that wasn't there when he was last a free man. *How much can change over time*, he wonders.

'This'll do. Right here,' he says.

Frankie's eyes take in the glittering lights on the other side of the river. This is his city. This is where he was born, raised and he has no doubt it's where he will die. He inhales the river air and feels emotional.

'I love this city,' he says.

'Me too,' Toby replies quietly.

'I have big plans for it. I'd like you to be part of those plans, Toby.'

'That would be my honour, Mr White. Thank you.'

'I need people I can trust. Smart people.'

'You can trust me, sir.'

Frankie checks his watch and sniffs. 'Should be here soon.' He looks over the other side of bridge and then down at the water. 'I can hear them coming now.'

'What are we waiting for, sir?'

Frankie looks at Toby and smiles, 'Fireworks, Toby. Fireworks.'

Chapter 18

THE MURDER WALL IN THE incident room has expanded since yesterday but remains light on suspects. Archer has pinned a headshot of Jason Todd she had printed from his Instagram page. He is smiling and seems content and happy, a suitable picture she thinks to infuse empathy from the team. Below it is DC Phillips' shot of Todd's face staring blankly out from the torn duct tape mask. She has printed other shots she acquired from social media: Lucas Todd, Penny Todd, Oliver Stocker, Katie Fox and Derek Fox. She expects the suspect list to grow in the coming days. For now, it remains a small circle of middle-class Battersea and Clapham residents.

Archer steps back and takes in the view of the entire wall.

Quinn says, 'Jesus! Wives, husbands, exes and lovers. It's like we've stepped into an episode of *Midsomer Murders* set in south London.'

It's the end of the day and Archer has asked the team to join them for a meeting. Klara, Os, DC Phillips and DC Anderson begin filing in. Archer glances across the office. DCI Pierce is on the phone and looking her way. She puts her index finger in the air and mouths, '*One minute.*' Archer nods a confirmation.

'I'll get Krish on the phone,' says Quinn, reaching across to the conference phone and dialling the CSI's number. After a few moments the call is picked up.

'It's Krish.'

'Hi, Krish, it's Harry.'

'Hey, man.'

'Hey. In the room we have Grace, Klara, Os, Marian and our new DC, Mel Anderson.'

'Hi, everyone, and welcome, Mel.'

A murmur of greetings is interrupted by Quinn, who adds, 'And just joining us is DCI Pierce.' Quinn looks at Archer. 'We're good to go.'

Archer begins, 'OK, let's make a start. We'll go round the table and see what everyone has. Krish, I know you have to be elsewhere. Could you kick us off?'

'Absolutely. It's only been two days and we're still compiling everything. We have a backlog of other jobs that we're struggling to get through so apologies for not having much to report. The tape wrapped over the victim's neck and head is bog standard duct tape, and the ink is from a whiteboard marker; all accessible materials to get hold of. I'm pushing for the DNA and should have the results next week, hopefully.'

'OK. Understood. Anything you can do to move this along will be much appreciated, Krish,' says Archer.

'I'll do my best. If something comes up, I'll be in touch straightaway.'

'Thanks.'

'Bye for now.'

Archer turns to Quinn. 'Harry, could you run us through where we're up to?'

'Sure. Yesterday we met with the mortician. The killer tasered Jason in the neck twice with a stun gun before smothering him.

110

Pictures showing the marks are on the wall. This clearly gave him a strong advantage. Perhaps the killer is smaller or female. We don't know yet, obviously. Our conclusion, they wanted to get in and complete the job quickly and without fuss.'

'Do we know what type of taser?' asks Phillips.

'Not yet. Judging by the bruises and the puncture marks we think it could be a hand-held device that you press directly to the skin, rather than what the Met uses, for example. This morning we met with Katie Fox, Jason's "friend with benefits". Her term not mine. They've known each for a year or so and have met for the occasional coffee and rolls in the hay that no one else knows about, except for Penny Todd and her circle of friends, apparently. Katie says her husband is not aware of her infidelity.'

'He knew,' interrupts Klara. 'I found an email from Derek Fox to Jason Todd.'

'Good stuff. We'll come to that in a moment. According to Katie, her and Jason's coition has always taken place at his Albany Mansions flat. She has just sent through the time and dates of those rendezvous. The days vary. However, they usually meet on a morning, after the school run when Jason was working from home.' Quinn looks to the murder wall. 'For reference, Derek and Katie's mugshots have been added to the wall. Any questions?'

There are none.

'Mel, you were profiling Jason Todd?' says Archer.

'Yeah, I checked over his social media. Nothing stands out. There's lots of pictures of his son and him, his ex-wife too. They were still friends by the look of it despite the separation. There are other shots of nights out with the lads and business trips to Germany with Mercedes. He just seems like a regular guy.'

'OK. Keep digging. Look at friends and family pages and see if there's a nugget of something. Anything related to that mask.'

'I'll get on it.'

Phillips chips in, 'We also visited his head office in Milton Keynes. Jason was one of their top performers in line for a position as senior director. He had a good salary, company car, all the benefits. We spoke to a few of his colleagues. They seem to think he was an all-round sound bloke.'

'Thanks, Marian. Klara, how did you get on with the search for similar murders?'

'I'm still searching. So far, I've yielded nothing. I'll keep at it. However, Os and I have been ploughing through Jason Todd's data and have some interesting updates from his emails and texts. First up, let's talk about Oliver Stocker. There are several polite warnings to Jason demanding he stay away from Penny. Here's an example of one. Stocker's very cross, but also very polite: "Dear Jason, I understand from Penny that last night that you told her you 'cared for her and missed her'. I thought you and I agreed this was all over. She has moved on. She doesn't need you hanging around and telling her this nonsense. Penny is with me now. I am helping her rebuild her life. Please, please for her sake, and Lucas's too, move on with your life and find someone new."'

Klara looks up. 'And that's not the half of it. Jason's response to Oliver is colourful. Os can take over here.'

'As Klara says, Jason's responses are colourful as is the language. I'm embarrassed to read them out loud.'

'Don't hold back, Os. We're all adults here,' says Pierce.

'Yes, ma'am . . . here goes. In response to the text Klara just read out, Jason replied: "Fuck you, fucknuts! Who do you think you are, telling me how and when to speak to my wife? Fuck right off! We may be separated but that could change tomorrow.

She still loves me – don't you get it? She doesn't care about you. You're just a convenience. Also, stay the fuck away from my son. He's not comfortable with you hanging around the house all the time. What he means by that I don't know but if I find out you've laid one of your filthy fingers on him I will not be responsible for my actions."'

'It gets worse,' says Klara. 'Coming back to Derek Fox. Here's that email from him: "I know what's going on between you and Katie. Stay away from her. You are poison. You're a drunk and an abuser. We all saw what you did at Lucas's party. You should be ashamed of yourself. Stay AWAY from my family!"'

'Do we know what he did at Lucas's party?'

'Don't know the details but according to these exchanges Jason broke his son's arm.'

Chapter 19

MADDY WATSON STANDS ALONE ON the bow of *The Pride of Elizabeth* smoking a Marlboro Light and enjoying the gentle rhythm of the cruiser as it makes the approach towards Westminster Bridge.

The rain has mercifully stopped, a break in the clouds reveals a gorgeous canvas tinted with the darkest of oils. She is tempted to close her eyes, stretch out her arms and say, 'I'm flying, Jack!' just like Kate Winslet in *Titanic* but decides against it. Wouldn't do to get caught by her boss, Andrei, or one of his new business partners. That would be mortifying.

A chilly river breeze pierces her thin business suit and makes her shiver. After tossing the cigarette into the dark waters, she rubs heat into her arms and turns to make her way back to the party. She stops when she hears footsteps. She looks in the direction from where they came. Through the gloom, she sees the white jacket and white gloves of the waiter-for-hire as he closes the front glass doors of the party room. He was a last-minute show after their usual waiter had phoned in sick. She has to admit she's less than impressed with this one. For a start, he lacks people skills. There was no smiling or banter despite Maddy insisting that he make more of an effort with Andrei's clients. She makes a mental note to tell the agency not to send him back. Maddy watches him for a moment, and wonders why he's outside and not tending to their guests.

Her eyes slide to the meeting room, where she sees Andrei stand in preparation for his speech. She is about to make her way back when her phone vibrates. A message from Sofia.

Hey, Maddy. How's it going?

Maddy bites her thumb and wonders whether she should respond. Relations between Andrei and his sister are strained and pressing ahead with this new partner meeting without her has only made things worse. As usual, Maddy, the humble, obliging PA, is stuck between them both. After a moment's consideration she composes a response; something generic and positive, concluding with a promise for them all to meet first thing tomorrow. She presses send and pockets her phone.

Maddy makes her way back to the conference room and pulls at the sliding glass doors, but they don't budge. They're locked. Had the waiter just locked them? Why would he do that?

Fuck!

She grins an apologetic smile inside at anyone who might be looking her way and searches for Andrei, but he's already making his speech. She hurries around the side of the boat to the rear doors, still holding her phone and is surprised to see the waiter standing at the doors, looking in at the conference room. He shakes the door handles. It seems they are also locked.

'What's going on?' Maddy asks.

His head swings around to look at her. He frowns but says nothing.

'Are the doors locked?' she asks, confused.

The waiter pulls away from the door and edges a few feet behind her. Maddy tries the doors: they don't budge.

116

She turns to look at the waiter and frowns. He's undressing. Underneath his uniform is a wet suit of all things. 'What the hell?'

Looking in at Andrei, Maddy waves to him, but he is giving his speech and has the attention of the room.

A cold sensation runs up her spine like the blade of a dagger. This isn't right. She knows Andrei does business with some strange and dangerous people. She had told him she preferred not to know about that stuff. Maddy composes herself. 'Just stay where you are,' she says to him in a firm tone. 'I need to consult with Mr Brodsky.' Using her phone, she calls Andrei's number. Eyes wide and fixed on her boss, she waits for the line to connect. The boat falls into shadow as it cruises under Westminster Bridge. It's then that the clock strikes and the Great Bell rings the first of eight sombre chimes.

'He won't hear you,' says the waiter from behind.

Maddy is about to speak but something flashes past her face and locks around her throat, squeezing tighter and tighter. She can't breathe. Dropping the phone, she reaches for her neck, her fingers feeling what feels like a chain. She kicks at the doors twice with all her strength. Inside the conference room, the guests turn to look her way. Andrei too. They frown and run to the doors. Maddy wants to scream but it's impossible. She cannot get purchase and feels herself being dragged across the boat. She kicks, a shoe flies from her foot. And then she tips over backward, falling, falling. She plunges into ice-cold water, and he is with her, pulling, tightening and squeezing the life from her. Above her the skies flash in a ball of flame. Water floods her mouth and nostrils and in moments darkness consumes her.

Chapter 20

ARCHER SITS AT A PLASTIC table for two under the glaring white lights of Covent Garden's Five Guys burger restaurant. She has just finished on a call to the hospital and spoken to Grandad. He had sounded tired and veered off topic twice before eventually drifting off mid-conversation. Despite that, it had been good to hear his voice.

She opens Instagram, finds Penny Todd's account and searches through her posts. She finds a group of pictures from Lucas's birthday, taken in the garden of her home. It was a sunny day, bunting hangs from a tree and adorns a table of food and presents. Lucas is grinning ear to ear at the camera with an assortment of smiling and laughing friends. Scrolling across to the next shot is another picture depicting the children peering up at a man with a painted face, wearing a bowler hat, a double-breasted coat and brandishing a magician's wand in one hand and flowers in the other. The next shot shows Penny, Jason and Lucas smiling together. The party table contains beer and wine bottles. In the background, among the adults she doesn't recognise, she picks out Oliver Stocker, Katie Fox and, surprise, surprise, Derek Fox. None of them look like they're enjoying themselves. But then again, do adults really enjoy kids' parties?

Through the corner of her eye, she sees Quinn approaching, carrying a tray crammed with enough food to feed a family.

'Someone's hungry,' she comments, her brows knitted.

'Starvin'...' Quinn plops himself down, hungry eyes focused on the spread. He lifts a tall drink and a straw from the tray and places them on the table in front of her. 'One vanilla milkshake for you ... everything else, for me.'

'How can you eat all that and remain so ... lean?'

'I have the metabolism of an Olympic athlete, Grace. Surely you must have clocked that by now.' Quinn leans into the burger, tears a huge chunk from it and chews awkwardly with his mouth thankfully closed.

Over his shoulder, she notices a man with a tattooed neck and cropped hair enter the restaurant. She feels her stomach tighten. Steve Barry. One of Frankie White's men. His eyes search the clientele and stop at Archer. He watches her, his thin lips twisting into a dark smile. Unflinching, she holds his gaze.

Quinn's voice jolts her. 'Grace, you're white as sheet. Are you OK?'

'I'm fine,' she lies, peeling the paper from her straw.

Quinn narrows his eyes and looks around. He sees Barry. Quinn takes a second chunk from his burger and turns back to Archer.

'How's your delicate little sandwich?' she asks.

Quinn stops chewing, smiles, points at the burger and gives it the thumbs-up and glances behind him before going in for a third bite. Barry has joined a long queue for food, his eyes remaining steadfast on Archer.

Archer inserts the straw into the thick shake and lifts it to her mouth but decides she can't drink. 'We should go,' she says, not wanting to be in the same place as Barry.

'Aye.'

'Bring your dinner.'

'Lost my appetite,' he replies.

Quinn swallows the last of his burger.

They stand. Archer leaves her milkshake but Quinn picks his up. They walk past the queue, Archer ignoring Barry's stare. As she steps outside, she hears Quinn's voice: 'Oops! Sorry about that.'

'What the fuck!' someone says, among the giggles of the clientele.

Turning back, she sees a furious Barry, arms wide, face and jacket covered in strawberry milkshake. His fist flies at Quinn but he's quick and grabs it, kicking Barry's legs from under him. Barry lands with a thud on the tiled floor and gasps as Quinn places his boot on the man's neck.

'Harry, no . . . ' says Archer as she hurries back inside.

Quinn squats down, his face close to Barry's ear. 'Take your ugly face back to White's sewer and lodge it firmly up his ass, where it belongs. I don't want to see it again.'

'Harry, enough!' cries Archer.

Quinn ignores her as he twists Barry's arms and applies more pressure to his neck. 'Understood?' he growls.

Barry's pink milkshake-coated face twists. He groans in pain.

'I didn't quite get that.'

Barry nods his head. 'Yesh! Yesh!'

Quinn lifts his boot and lets go of his arm. Barry scrambles across the floor, lies against a trashcan, panting and cradling his arm.

Archer is about to speak but Quinn, his expression stony, says, 'Leave it, Grace.' He stalks out of the restaurant.

Outside, Archer grabs his arm. 'What was that about?'

Quinn takes a breath and casually wipes away speckles of milkshake. 'He was getting on my nerves.'

Archer points inside the restaurant. 'That's not how we do things, Harry!'

'Sorry. Not sorry!'

Archer's anger melds into dread. She thrusts her hands into her coat pockets and looks away. 'You don't get it, do you? By asserting yourself as my knight in shining armour – which, by the way, I never asked you to do – you've now just upgraded yourself to White's kill list.'

'I'm not afraid of him.'

'Great! I'm so happy for you.'

'Well, that's OK then!' retorts Quinn.

'And what good is that to me, Harry? Don't you understand? I need you. I can't do this without you. White will take out Grandad. Then you. Without both of you . . . I'm done, if not dead.'

A heavy silence hangs in the air between them.

She hears Quinn sigh. 'I'm sorry.'

'We should go,' she replies.

'Yeah, we should.'

They sit in silence on the way back to Quinn's flat. Archer gets a news alert on her phone.

Explosion erupts on Thames River Cruiser

'Shit,' says Archer, reading the brief summary.

'What is it?' asks Quinn.

'A river cruiser exploded on the Thames earlier. About thirty minutes back. No sign of any survivors yet.'

'Jesus.'

In Quinn's flat, Archer and Quinn sit silently on the Chesterfield, watching the rolling news coverage of *The Pride of Elizabeth*. There is phone footage showing a clip of the cruise ship emerge from Westminster Bridge, explode in a ball of flame, float across the water and collide with a tourist cruiser before crashing against the Embankment walls. In another video the fire brigade and the marine police unit struggle to tether the now smouldering cruiser like fishermen of old subduing a restless whale.

Quinn is half looking at his phone. 'According to this report, it's not a tourist cruiser. Someone hired it for the evening. Must have been a party or something.'

'Horrible,' says Archer. 'Those poor people. And their families too.'

'I wonder what caused it,' Quinn muses.

'We'll find out soon enough.' Archer yawns. 'I'm going to go to bed.'

'No worries. Goodnight.'

''Night, Harry.' Archer gets up and makes her way across the living room.

'Grace ... listen, about earlier.'

She gives him a tired smile. 'It's fine, don't worry about it. G'night.'

Chapter 21

ARCHER WAKES TO THE MURMUR of voices the following morning, which she assumes is Quinn's television. Blinking, she reaches for her phone, but the screen is dark. She had forgotten to charge it.

'Shit.'

She squints at the digital alarm clock. It's 8.15. Late. She slides out of bed and plugs her phone into the mains. It had rained overnight. She had fallen asleep listening to it pound the windows of Quinn's bedroom. She opens the curtains and pauses at the view of Kennington Park. The morning is grey and misty. Pools of water like black mirrors are dotted across the estate.

She realises the voices are not coming from the television. It's Quinn talking with someone. A second voice she knows well. A moment of panic grips her and she fears the worst. Archer exits the bedroom and is greeted with the nutty aroma of fresh coffee. A half-dressed Quinn is in the kitchen, sipping from a chipped mug. To her surprise, Charlie Bates is there too.

'Charlie, what are you doing here? Is it Grandad?'

'Morning, Grace,' says Charlie. 'Nothing like that. I phoned the hospital and he's doing fine. Don't worry about him.' He sets down his mug and embraces her. His overcoat still carries the cold, damp moisture from outside. 'I tried to call but your phone kept going to voicemail.'

'The battery died.'

'Coffee, tea?' asks Quinn.

Relief surges through her. 'The coffee smells good.'

'You might need a few strong coffees today,' says Charlie.

Quinn hands her a mug. 'Charlie brings news.'

Archer grips the hot mug, takes a sip and looks to Charlie. 'What might that be?'

'It's about *The Pride of Elizabeth* incident on the Thames last night. It was no accident.'

'Arson?'

'Worse. The boat was packed with explosives. Possibly set to a timer. Everyone on board was killed. That everyone includes Andrei Brodsky.'

'Are you serious?'

'As serious as – if you'll forgive the pun – a dead man.'

'Why was Brodsky on the boat?'

'He'd hired it to celebrate a new business deal.'

'So, it was a hit?'

'Yes.'

'White?'

'It's looking that way.'

Archer's mind processes Charlie's news. Could this mean a swift arrest of Frankie White and an end to the threat against her and Grandad?

'Brodsky killed Ethan, didn't he?' she says.

'During White's incarceration, Brodsky had muscled in on White's territory with a network of county lines and minors trafficking drugs. Earned him a lot of cash, it did. Cash that White believes is his. Since his release, White has taken back control, eradicated Brodsky's county lines and set up his own. Essentially, a turf war with White as the victor.'

'Has this intel come from your mole?'

126

'Mostly.'

'So, he's taken out Brodsky to end the turf war?'

'That's one reason,' Charlie replies. 'Brodsky is – was – brutal. He wasn't going to sit back and let White get away scot-free. So, to answer your previous question, he orders a hit on White's grandson.'

'And makes it look like a suicide,' says Quinn.

'That's right. From what I understand, once Ethan's conviction was dropped, he became a different person. To him it seemed he'd been given a second chance. He was eager to get out and restart his life. Killing himself was the last thing on his mind. Poor kid. Everyone knew Ethan was fragile, so no one asked any questions. Brodsky made sure Frankie knew though.'

'So, White comes back at him like a savage.'

'And fries Brodsky, his team, and a bunch of people he was going into business with.'

'Who were they?' asks Quinn.

'Believe it or not, Brodsky had a few legit businesses along-side his nefarious ones. On board were foreign investors he had brought in to bolster a property deal in Canary Wharf.'

'Does your contact have proof of all this?' asks Archer.

'We're working on that and I'm confident we'll get it. Soon.'

'How soon?'

Charlie rolls his shoulders and hesitates before answering, 'I don't know, Grace. I'm pushing hard.'

Despondency sweeps through her. For a moment it seemed the threat against her and Grandad would disappear. 'So the status quo remains,' she says, more a statement than a question.

'I'm afraid so. Sorry, Grace.'

'No worries,' she says, placing the mug down on the cracked Formica worktop.

'Grace, I need you to promise me you will not engage with White or his people, unless of course you find yourself in an impossible situation.'

Archer shrugs her shoulders.

Charlie continues, 'We're on this and will do everything we can.'

She meets his gaze. 'I know you will.'

'Obviously, don't mention any of this to anyone. Especially your colleagues in Charing Cross or any station for that matter.'

'Why?' asks Archer.

'Someone in Charing Cross is on White's payroll.'

'This is from your mole, too?'

'Yes.'

'Hicks,' says Quinn.

'Seems too obvious,' says Charlie. 'But you never know. Both of you need to watch your backs.'

'We're good at that,' says Quinn. 'Have a lot of experience.'

'I gotta go,' says Charlie. He stops for a moment and takes stock of Quinn's decor. 'Bloody hell. You need to get the decorators in. This place is like a seventies museum.'

Quinn smirks. 'Aye, you're not wrong there, Charlie. It has a certain retro charm.'

'Each to their own, I suppose. All right. Take care, you two. I'll check in with you later if I know any more.'

'Bye, Charlie,' says Archer.

Quinn sees him to the door. She watches them talk privately for a moment before Charlie leaves and Quinn locks up.

'What was that about?'

Quinn shrugs and doesn't meet her gaze. 'Just stuff.'

'What stuff?'

Quinn coughs, 'You know . . . '

'No, I don't.'

128

'Bloke talk.'

'Bloke talk?'

Quinn shrugs. 'Bloke talk.'

'Which is what exactly?'

Quinn levels his gaze at her and smiles. 'No flies on you. Ever thought of becoming a detective?'

'I've known Charlie a long time.'

Quinn rubs his neck as he considers his answer. 'He has something. For me.'

'Is it a bloke thing?'

He looks away. She waits for his answer.

'A gun. He wants me to keep a gun.'

'Fuck! No way, Harry. This isn't New York or LA for that matter.'

He raises his hands in a placating gesture. 'I know.'

'What did you say?'

'I said no. Absolutely not. Out of the question.'

Archer narrows her gaze at him.

'He's only looking out for you.'

'We're detectives in the Met, Harry. We don't carry weapons, we're not allowed to. If anyone found out, we'd be finished.'

'In fairness to Charlie, these are unusual circumstances. In his opinion, your life, our lives, are more important than our careers.'

Archer shakes her head. 'Ridiculous idea.' She turns and heads to the bathroom. 'I need a shower.'

'I'll put another pot of coffee on and call Derek Fox. Tell him to expect us today.'

'You do that.'

Archer closes the door behind her and sits on the edge of the bath. Her fists are bunched. She takes several deep breaths through her nose. She's angry. Not at Harry. Nor Charlie.

They are risking everything for her. Everything. She's angry with Frankie White as she has been all her life. The thought of a gun is tempting. It always has been. She imagines, as she has many times in her life, holding a pistol to White's temple and blowing out his brains. Just like her father had suffered. It's a vicious fantasy. Not one she would ever enact. But still. The temptation is strong.

Chapter 22

'STRAIGHT OUT OF A DICKENS book, this place is,' Quinn comments as they walk up Saffron Hill – a narrow, dark thoroughfare with looming Victorian blocks on either side.

'It's all about the gentrification now,' says Archer.

'Aye. I noticed the lack of barefoot grubby street urchins and came to the same conclusion.'

'Here it is,' says Archer. She stops at a mirrored glass door and presses a buzzer labelled 'Secure Camz Ltd'.

'Hello,' comes a woman's voice.

'Hello, we're here to see Derek Fox.'

'Is he expecting you?'

'Yes.'

'OK, I'll let him know. Come in, we're on the second floor.' The door buzzes and unlocks.

Archer and Quinn step inside and make their way up a steel staircase.

Derek Fox greets them at the top of the stairs. 'Very good to meet you,' he says, shaking their hands firmly as if they are business associates. 'Come through here. There's a private room we can talk in without disturbing the office. Busy time for us right now.' He leads them into a small reception area. Photographs of slick security cameras decorate the walls.

A woman sits behind a desk wearing a phone headset, her eyes half on the screen, half on the new visitors.

'You're in the big brother business?' Quinn asks.

'In a manner of speaking. We create high-tech CCTV that provide safe, secure solutions to protect businesses and the home. This is our sales office.' He gestures to the chairs at a white conference table. 'Please take a seat.' He sits at the head of the table and knots his fingers together. 'How may I help?' he says.

'As mentioned by DS Quinn, we'd like to talk about Jason Todd.'

Fox affects a sad expression. 'It's just so awful. Who would do such a thing?'

'We intend to find out,' says Archer.

'I'll do what I can, but I'm not sure if it will be of any help. I didn't really know him.'

'How many times did you meet him?' Archer asks.

'Three or four . . . I can't be sure. We never really had much to do with each other. I'd sometimes see him during the school run but that was all.'

'When was the last time you saw him?'

'That would be at Lucas's birthday party. His son and mine are friends.'

'How was he that day?' Archer asks.

'What do you mean?'

'How was his mood?' Quinn asks.

'He seemed chipper.'

'Chipper?' says Quinn.

'Yes. Happy. He was with his family.'

'Were there any arguments?'

Fox's expression is fixed, unreadable. 'None that I recall.'

'He'd had a few though, hadn't he?'

'He'd been drinking.'

'Was he drunk?'

'Hard to tell with him.'

'How would you know that if you didn't know him that well?'

Fox shrugs. 'He seemed sober but often people with serious drink problems do.'

'He had a serious drink problem?'

'That was the rumour.'

'And you witnessed it at Lucas's party?'

'I witnessed a man drinking at his son's birthday party.'

'How did Lucas break his arm?'

'You heard about that, did you?' Fox looks down at his hands. 'Well, as I mentioned he seemed sober, but was possibly not as composed as we'd imagined. Anyway, the adults had gathered in the kitchen to escape the madness in the garden. Jason was upstairs with Lucas. We heard some sort of altercation and Lucas crying out. We came out of the kitchen and found Lucas lying at the bottom of the stairs, cradling his arm and screaming. Jason was at the top of the stairs, looking down at his son. He just stood there, apologising. He kept saying it was an accident.'

'Do you think it was?'

'If he said it was.'

'But what do you think?'

'I don't think he meant to break the boy's arm. He was just drunk and careless and shouldn't have been near his son or any of the kids for that matter. That's all.'

'What were the circumstances of the accident?'

'No one knows exactly. Jason left quickly. Lucas was whisked off to hospital. Penny didn't say much about the incident, which was odd.'

'Do you think she has something to hide?'

Fox shrugs. 'She still loved Jason and wouldn't have a bad word said against him.'

'So, the last time you saw Jason was at the party. That was four weeks back.'

'That's correct.'

'Have you had any communication with him since then?'

He lifts his chin. 'What sort of communication?'

'An email, text, letter. Something like that.'

Fox's eyes slide from Archer's to Quinn's. 'What are you implying?'

'Would you say your wife, Katie, knew Jason better than you did?'

His jaw tightens. A flicker of irritation passes over his face. 'Who told you?'

'We have a string of heated emails and texts from you and Jason.'

Fox rolls his eyes and shakes his head. 'Jason isn't my wife's first. Nor likely to be her last. I knew something was going on. She was being secretive with her texts and phone calls. She thinks I don't notice but it's just so obvious. I followed her one morning when she was doing the school run. She met him at the school gates then brazenly got into his car and went to his flat in Albany Mansions. I parked outside and walked to the side of the block. I could hear them at it in his bedroom. It was devastating. I was going to confront them but . . . I couldn't. I left, hurried away back to my car.'

'Why didn't you mention it to your wife?'

'Because I don't blame her. You see my wife has appetites that I am no longer able to keep up with. I still love her and know she loves me, in her own way. After her first lover, I confronted her. She wanted to leave me, and I begged her not to. Her lover subsequently dumped her. We then came to a special arrangement. I told her never in the house and never put our family at risk. She agreed.'

'Why did you write that text to Jason if you didn't mind Katie being with other men?'

'I didn't like him. He was a drunk. After what he did to Lucas, Lord knows what could have happened to Katie.'

A knock on the door. The receptionist peeks her head through, 'Your ten o'clock is here.'

'Thanks, Lily. I'll be there shortly.'

Fox turns back to Archer and Quinn. 'Is there anything else?'

'That's all for now, Mr Fox. We appreciate your time. We may need to talk to you again.'

'You can book an appointment with Lily.'

Archer takes out her contact card. 'If you think of anything else, do let me know.'

Fox takes the card. 'Of course.'

Archer and Quinn make their way down Saffron Hill and back to the car.

'Thoughts?' asks Quinn.

'He's arrogant.'

'Yep.'

'He had no problem being economical with the truth when it came to his connection to Jason.'

'I get the impression he's a man to whom lying comes easy.'

'His poker face was impressive.'

'Do you think he killed Jason?'

'He's definitely a suspect. Don't you think?'

'No question. I wonder what happened on the stairs when Lucas took his tumble. Want to talk to him and his mum again?'

'Maybe another time. I'm not so worried about that for the moment. It's happened and we know Jason was somehow responsible.' Archer stops as they pass The One Tun pub. 'I get the sense everything is there, but something is just out of reach.'

'You think one of these people killed Jason – or had him killed?'

'I'm keeping an open mind.'

Chapter 23

A LARGE SQUARE WHITE TENT HAS been erected on the South Bank with a corridor leading up the smouldering ruin of *The Pride of Elizabeth*. The air is choked with the bitter smell of charred wood, and from a gap in the tent, DI Rodney Hicks catches a whiff of stale barbecued flesh. He feels his stomach rolling and turns away, pressing a handkerchief to his face. He almost hurls but manages to keep his breakfast where it belongs.

'This is all his doing,' Hicks says to DS Jimmy Barnes, pocketing his handkerchief.

'Is it?' Barnes replies casually.

'You and I both know it is. This is payback for Ethan White.'

'I don't know anything about that.' Barnes inches closer to Hicks. 'I'm not sure Mr White would appreciate you stating that out loud for everyone to hear.'

'It's true then.'

'Take note of what has happened here,' replies Barnes. 'And remember your promise to your employer.'

Hicks feels his posture sagging. He hears voices from the tent and turns to see a sealed black body bag on a stretcher being carried to one of the ambulances parked nearby. A second follows, then a third and a fourth. The reality hits him like a sucker punch. He pictures his twin boys on their knees and

Barnes with a pistol swinging back and forth at their heads as Tanya makes her choice on which one of their precious kids lives and which one dies. Tanya's choice, like the film. He can't remember the character's name. He'd tried to block it out and pretend the threat was all in his imagination but he knows better than that. Oh Jesus! His boys. His beautiful boys. He feels dizzy, his stomach churning again and this time he cannot hold anything down. Up it comes, spilling from his mouth and splattering on the ground at Barnes's feet.

'Oh, for fuck sake!' says Barnes.

Hicks's throat burns with acid as he pulls the handkerchief from his pocket and wipes his mouth.

'I can't do it,' he says, his voice hoarse.

Barnes's jaw tightens. 'Then you know what'll happen.' Furtively, he makes a pistol shape with his hand and mouths, 'Tanya's Choice.'

Hicks feels his pulse increasing. He rubs his neck and trembles. 'Jimmy, please!' He reaches across and grabs Barnes's arm, tears welling in his eyes, 'Jimmy, Jimmy ... we go way back. We're old friends. You've got to help me. Get me out of this. I'll give you whatever I can. Money. I still have some. Take our house! It's almost paid off. Please talk to Mr White. Tell him you'll kill her. You're better suited to this. You've killed before. I've never killed anyone. I can't. I don't want to. Please, please, please, Jimmy, help me!'

Barnes snatches his arm away. 'You're fucking pathetic.'

'No, Jimmy ... '

'You don't get it, do you? Mr White is on the warpath. He's taking no prisoners.' Barnes's face is red. He's pointing his finger at Hicks. 'If you fuck this up and don't kill Archer, then we both lose. The boys die. Tanya dies. You die. I die. Your fuck-up is my fuck-up.'

'Then you do it. You kill her. I'll give you the gun. I'll help you. Mr White doesn't need to know. I won't tell him. I promise. On my kids' lives. On Tan's life. I swear to God, Jimmy.'

'You have been warned so man the fuck up and do what's expected of you!'

'Rod, Jimmy,' comes a familiar voice, interrupting their exchange. It's DCI Pierce.

'Fuck,' whispers Hicks.

'She's coming in under the tape. She hasn't heard anything so don't panic,' hisses Barnes. He turns to greet the DCI. 'Ma'am.' Barnes smiles. 'Good morning.'

Hicks takes a deep breath and wipes his sweaty brow. He turns to face her. 'Hi, Clare.'

Pierce's eyes slide from Hicks to Barnes and back to Hicks. 'Is everything OK?'

Hicks's heart is pounding. He thinks for a moment he might have a heart attack.

'Fine, ma'am,' replies Barnes. 'We're . . . '

Hicks puts the handkerchief back into his pocket. 'Yes, ma'am,' he says, asserting what little authority he can muster.

The DCI looks down at the pool of yellow vomit.

'Rod's feeling a bit delicate today, ma'am,' says Barnes with unconvincing humour.

'Are you feeling OK, Rod?' she asks.

Hicks doesn't respond, he just looks beyond her and feels himself zoning out. He can't seem to stop. Her voice and Barnes's voice are like insects buzzing around his head. He wills them to go away. He's breathing through his nose. Rapidly. The voices continue. He ignores them. A hand grips his arm. He feels a fire in his belly spreading outwards, consuming his chest, head, shoulders, arms and legs. It's cleansing and brings with it a clarity, and an anger, a deep-rooted fury that he has never felt before. Clarity, yes. He understands now what he must do to protect his family. He thinks of the gun. The Glock 17 Barnes had concealed in his and Tanya's bedroom. The fucking nerve. It's hidden in a different place now. Yes, he understands what he must do. It's time.

'Rod, Rod, take this,' says DCI Pierce, holding out a small plastic bottle of Evian.

'Sorry, ma'am. I ate something bad last night.'

'Curries don't agree with you, do they, Rod?' snorts Barnes.

Hicks ignores him and takes the water. 'Thank you.' He unscrews the lid and swallows the bottle in two gulps.

'Are you sure you're feeling all right?' asks Pierce. 'You can go home if you're not a hundred per cent.'

He meets her eyes and smiles. 'That won't be necessary. I feel much better now.'

'Well, that's a relief. You were so pale,' she replies. 'For a moment I thought you were going to pass out.'

'Just a little dizzy. I'm doing fine now.'

'So, what's been happening here? Do you have an update?'

'The first batch of bodies has been removed. The rest will be leaving within the hour.'

'Do we have a list of the passenger names?'

'Andrei Brodsky's sister, Sofia, is providing that list this morning, ma'am.'

'Very good. The cause of the explosion remains undetermined. That said, I have a meeting with the National Crime Agency this afternoon. They have some intel on who is responsible.'

'I'd be interested to know what they think,' says Barnes.

'We'll see what they have. Listen, I'm heading back to Charing Cross. Catch up with you both later.'

'Bye, ma'am,' they say in unison.

They watch her leave, and when she disappears through the onlookers, Hicks turns to Barnes. 'You're acting SIO for the time being.'

Barnes frowns. 'Excuse me?'

'Are you fucking deaf?'

Barnes laughs. 'Don't tell me you're pulling rank?'

Hicks turns and walks away.

'Where are you going?' asks Barnes.

'I have a promise to keep. Remember?'

'Good. Don't fuck it up.'

Hicks slips under the police tape and takes two Diazepam from the packet in his pocket. Barnes's words reverberate in his head as he shuffles through the crowd, crunching down on the bitter pills.

Chapter 24

SCHOOL IS OVER FOR THE day. It's almost five o'clock and Brynn Hughes is shuffling past the ugly concrete block houses of Holstein Way, trailing his school bag behind him. Sitting on Mrs Toolan's wall reading a book and wearing her soft helmet is Epi-Iris. Her large eyes rise from behind the novel and appraise him as he approaches. She is dressed in a blue puffer jacket, a red tartan skirt and has a flowery scent about her, mixed with cigarette smoke. She had recently witnessed his humiliation at the hands of Garret and his brother. He cannot bring himself to look at her. He feels his face flushing and casts his gaze downwards. Despite that, he is sure her eyes remain fixed on him. He feels his muscles stiffen as he increases his pace. He is in front of her. To his surprise, she stretches her leg in front of him, blocking his path. He stops, eyes focusing on the pale smooth skin of her shin. He swallows.

'Halt. Who goes there?' she says, closing her book and placing it on the wall.

Brynn doesn't know what to say.

'I know your name,' she begins and doesn't stop for a breath. 'It's Brynn. That's a pretty name. My aunt told me it's Welsh. She's your neighbour. Lives here.' She nods at the book. 'I borrowed this book from her. It's a bonkbuster.' She winks at him. 'Do you know what that is?'

Brynn shakes his head.

'It's a book about people having sex, more sex and even more sex. Anyway, it's too early for us to be talking about that kind of stuff. We hardly know each other and I'm not that kind of girl. Anyway, I'm staying with her for a bit. My parents have "problems".' She uses her fingers to make quote marks. 'Are you from Wales? I suppose you are. I'm from London. Obvs. But not from here. South London. Streatham. How long have you lived in London?'

'Erm . . . '

'My name's Iris. Iris Pond, thanks for asking.'

Brynn blinks and turns to look at her. Her head is cocked to the side. She is smiling warmly at him with teeth as large and as white as a cluster of mint crumbles. He opens his mouth to speak but she starts laughing, her face lighting up. 'My parents say I talk a lot. My aunt too. I say, life is too short for silences. My parents don't talk much. Our house is quiet. When they're not arguing, that is. They barely talk to each other. They hardly talk to me too. They're both unhappy people. I think they hate each other, or they're just bored. Marriage does that apparently. They had me when they were quite old. How old were your parents when they had you? Bet they're not as old as mine. My dad is sixty-five. My mum is fifty-seven. She had me when she was forty-three, which is quite old to carry a baby, don't you think?'

Brynn realises his mouth is still open. He closes it.

She continues, 'They've been fighting a lot recently. Shouting all the time. Proper fist fights and smashing up the house. Years of misery and bottling emotions. That's my conclusion. I saw a couple like that on daytime TV once and someone said it was down to decades of bottling emotions and not expressing what needs to be expressed. Or something like that.' She shrugs.

144

'Anyway, I've been sent here to live with my aunt until they sort it out. It was getting too much. They were doing my head in, literally. I blooped out. Been blooping out since. That's why I have to wear this.' She points to the helmet on her head.

'What's it for?' Brynn asks.

'I have seizures. Big ones. They say it's my hormones making them worse but I think it's my parents. I'll say it again, they were doing my head in.' Iris points to her head, rolls her eyes, sticks out her tongue and pretends to shake.

'Does it stop you having them?'

'No, silly. It stops my head getting bashed when I topple over and hit the concrete.' She points at the pavement to highlight the point.

'Oh . . . '

She sighs. 'They call me "Epi-Iris". I hate that name. It's so mean.'

Brynn recalls Garret and Stevo throwing the name at her.

After a moment she asks, 'Why were those boys picking on you?'

His face burns and he looks away.

'I shouldn't have asked. Sorry. They're dickheads. Neanderthals,' says Iris.

'I should go. My dad'll be back soon,' he says, stepping around Iris's leg eager to get home, but she pushes herself off the wall and falls against him. 'Oops!' She giggles. 'Would you mind doing do me an ickle favour? Please,' she says.

He hesitates and surprises himself by saying, 'Erm . . . OK.'

She turns away from him and brushes the back of her skirt with her hands. 'Could you check if there is any dust on my skirt?'

Brynn shifts on his feet. Hesitating, he glances at her skirt and long legs. 'There's nothing I can see.'

'Look again.'

Brynn narrows his gaze. 'It looks OK to me, it does.'

She sighs and leans forward against the wall.

'One more time.'

'No, it looks fine. Honestly, I wouldn't lie to you.'

She turns to look at him, smiling. 'You're so checking out my ass,' she says.

'I wasn't! I wouldn't do that.'

She turns round, folds her arms, leans on the wall and looks him up and down. 'I wouldn't mind if you did. I like your accent. It makes me go a bit funny,' she says, blinking her lashes.

Brynn swallows, uncertain of what to say.

'You're a quiet one, aren't you? You know what they say about the quiet ones?'

Despite his embarrassment, Brynn feels himself thawing. 'No. What do they say?'

Iris leans into his ear. 'They're demons in bed.'

Brynn feels a surge of excitement he's never felt before.

'I hate this thing,' says Iris, unstrapping the helmet from her head. She tosses it behind the wall and combs her long dark hair out with her fingers. 'That's better. I feel a new woman now. How do I look?' she asks, placing her hands on her hips and pushing out her chest. Brynn's mouth dries, he looks away, utterly lost for words.

'I think we should be friends, or something,' says Iris.

Or something?

'Do you fancy a cigarette? I nicked sixty from my mum's stash.'

'OK.'

Iris smiles. She loops her arm into his. 'Not here though. Don't want my aunt to see. She'll go off on one. Let's go round the corner. I know a spot where we can be alone, just the two of us.'

146

Something flickers from the upstairs window of his house. Iris follows his gaze.

The silhouette of his father is framed in the window, watching them from behind the net curtains. *He's home already*, he thinks.

'Is that your old man?' Iris asks.

Brynn feels the hairs on his neck rising. 'Let's go,' he says.

Chapter 25

ARCHER IS IN THE INCIDENT room with Quinn, combing through Jason Todd's various email and text exchanges with Oliver Stocker, Derek Fox, Katie Fox and Penny Todd.

'Who knew so much was going on that small circle of mums, dads and one wannabe dad,' says Archer.

Quinn sits back and stretches. 'So, in today's episode of *Murder in the Suburbs* aggrieved ex-wife, Penny Todd, confronts femme fatale, Katie Fox, and holds her responsible for the break-up of her marriage to local self-styled stud and lothario, Jason Todd. Meanwhile, jealous husband of femme fatale and fuming shag-piece of aggrieved ex-wife are cranking up the attack on lover boy, who is about to meet a grisly death at the hands of a maniac.'

'Are you reading that from your report summary?'

Quinn chuckles. 'Wordsmithing is one of my many talents.'

Klara enters the room holding several sheets of paper. 'I printed these off. Thought we could add some of them to the board.' She lays out Penny Todd's Instagram pictures of Lucas's birthday on the table. There are two pictures with the children, one of which shows them being entertained. There are two of the adults, one in particular with the poker faces of Derek Fox, Katie Fox and Oliver Stocker looking across at a smiling

Jason and Penny. Archer points to it. 'This is probably all we need,' she says.

'OK. I'll pin it up and discard the others.'

'The whole mask thing is weird, don't you think?' asks Quinn. 'I mean, kill a man, fine. I get people do that. But drawing a smiley face on what's essentially a death mask is fucked up.'

'Fucked-up murders are our domain, don't forget.'

'They seem to seek us out.'

Klara finishes pinning the party picture to the wall. 'This murder seems tame compared some of the humdingers you've investigated,' she says.

'What do you think the killer was trying to say with the mask?'

Klara joins them at the table. 'He's leaving a message maybe? That said, still no luck with finding any similar murders. Also, slim pickings from the CCTV collected that night.'

'Nothing at all? Not even one shady character?'

'A couple, but nothing discernible. The night was dark and picture quality poor.'

'Thanks for trying.'

'Don't look up,' Quinn mumbles, taking them off topic. 'Someone's been eyeballing the room for a little longer than he should.'

Archer turns and looks across to see DI Hicks standing in the middle of the office, staring in at her. He has one hand in his coat pocket, the other hanging limply by his side. He is pale, gaunt, his hair dishevelled. He seems lost.

'He doesn't look well,' says Klara.

Archer pushes her chair back and stands.

'Ignore him,' says Quinn. 'He probably wants a few coins for a tin of Special Brew.'

Archer exits the incident room and walks towards Hicks.

Hicks flinches as if suddenly noticing her.

'Rod, are you feeling OK?' Archer asks.

He doesn't respond. He just stares at her, his face blank, expressionless.

'Can I get you anything – tea, coffee or water?'

Still no response. His arm twitches in his coat pocket.

'What's up, Rod?' Quinn appears by her side. 'You OK, mate?'

Hicks's mouth opens and closes. He tries to say something but can't seem to find the words.

'Has something happened? Are Tanya and the boys OK?' Archer asks.

A pained expression flashes on Hicks's face.

Archer had never met Hicks's family, but she had overheard him talking fondly about them. It had always intrigued her hearing this other side of Hicks, the devoted father, husband and family man. This was not the Hicks she knew. He hated Archer and had done so since she had taken over from his best friend, the corrupt DI Andy Rees. It didn't seem to matter to Hicks that Rees had been bent. Rees was still a serving police officer, and you don't screw over other coppers, regardless of their crimes.

'Come sit down, Rod,' she says. 'Harry can get you a glass of water.'

'Sure,' Quinn replies as he heads to the office kitchen.

Hicks's face begins to crumple, and he looks at the floor. Archer reaches across and touches his shoulder. He flinches again and steps back quickly.

'Sit down, Rod. You don't look well.'

He pauses and then shakes his head. Without saying a word, he turns quickly and hurries across the office, colliding with Quinn and knocking the plastic cup of water over his jumper and jeans. Hicks disappears down the stairs. Quinn lifts the cup, drops it in a waste basket and approaches Archer, shaking the excess from his hand. 'What was that about?'

'No idea. I'm worried about him. Something is going on there. Maybe it's too early for him to be back at work.'

'We should talk to Clare.'

'Maybe we should have a quiet word with Jimmy.'

'Good idea. We can take him for a beer or something.'

'Listen, I'm going to go see Grandad.'

'I'll drive you.'

'You don't have to.'

'Nothing's changed, Grace, I do have to.'

Archer nods, gratefully. 'Thank you.'

Archer grabs her peacoat and Quinn his black suede bomber. They hurry down the stairs.

'Maybe we can stop at a supermarket and grab him some supplies.'

'No probs.'

Quinn presses the remote lock on his key fob, unlocking the doors of the car.

She hears the beep of a horn and looks across to see Jimmy Barnes smiling out at them from the driver-side window of his car. Archer smiles back.

'Grace,' Harry says, 'stand still. Don't move.'

'What?' Looking up, she sees Quinn standing in front of her with his hands raised.

Almost two feet in front of him is Hicks, his eyes wide, a terrified expression haunting his face. Archer feels her stomach turning. Hicks's arm is outstretched. In his hand is a Glock pistol.

'Get out of the way!' he says to Quinn.

'Don't do this, Rod,' Quinn says.

'Shut up!' His arm is trembling, his finger closes in on the trigger. 'Get out of the way, Harry. Don't make me shoot you too.'

'You don't have to shoot anyone, Rod. What's that going to achieve?'

'I said shut up!'

A ripple of terror runs through Archer. Quinn is in the firing line. She cannot allow this to happen. She stands beside him.

Hicks swings the pistol at her chest.

Archer swallows. 'White put you up to this, Rod, am I right?'

Hicks's face creases.

'Don't do this, Rod. Don't give in to White. Don't give him the satisfaction.'

Hicks shakes his head. 'You don't understand.'

A crowd has gathered across the way, mostly hiding for safety behind cars. Hicks is clearly not in his right mind doing this here outside Charing Cross. The place will be swarming with armed police in minutes.

'Make us understand,' says Archer. 'We can help you.'

His face contorts. Tears pool in his eyes. Snot runs down his nose.

'What about Tanya, Dylan and Daniel? What are they going to think?' says Quinn.

'I'm doing this for them!' he cries.

'What do you mean?' Archer asks. 'Does White have your family?'

'Fuck,' whispers Quinn.

Quinn sidesteps forward, blocking Archer from Hicks's view. 'Rod, give me the gun,' he says, gently.

'Stay back!'

'Rod,' says Quinn, inching forward.

'Harry, no,' says Archer.

'Stop!' Hicks cries.

'We can help you,' Quinn says, gently.

Archer feels her heart pounding. She reaches for Quinn. This is her problem. Not his. Before her hand can reach his shoulder it's too late. The gunshot shatters the quiet. A streak of warm blood splashes her face. A scream from the crowd. Archer trembles as Quinn drops to the ground at her feet. She swallows and looks at Hicks. He is staring down at Quinn, his eyes wide, his lip quivering.

Quinn's blood rolls down her cheek and onto her lips. She can taste its coppery tang. The shot still rings in her ears and is overlaid with controlled deep breaths through her nose.

Harry.

Confused, she reaches into her jacket pocket and takes out her phone. Hicks's Glock is still pointing her way, his hand is trembling, but she is not afraid. She dials 999 and looks into Hicks's terrified eyes. The wail of police sirens comes from all directions.

'What's your emergency?' says the operator.

'Ambulance. A police officer has been shot.'

'Is the officer dead or alive?'

'I don't know,' she replies, quietly.

'I . . . I'm sorry,' Hicks croaks.

'Drop the gun,' comes a voice.

Hicks turns and swings the pistol at two unarmed uniforms. The officers step back and raise their arms. He looks back at Archer. His face contorted. He's a broken man. He backs away slowly before picking up his pace and running up Chandos Place, disappearing among the dispersing, screaming onlookers.

Quinn is lying in pool of blood seeping from his head. His eyes are closed, his complexion bone white.

Archer kneels beside him and takes his hand, squeezing it gently. 'Harry, the ambulance is almost here. Stay with me. Please.'

He does not respond.

'Harry, can you hear me? ... Harry? ... Stay with me. The ambulance is close.' Archer can hear the croak in her voice.

A crowd has gathered around them. She hears Klara's voice, DCI Pierce's, Os's too. They are assembled around Quinn, talking, but she does not take in what they're saying. The wound on his head is severe. She can see bone. Behind her is the sound of police officers herding the public off the road to make way for the ambulance. The paramedics are out in seconds. She releases his hand and stands. Klara is at her side, crying, her arm wrapped around her shoulder.

Pierce is talking. 'Grace, are you hurt? What on earth happened?'

Quinn is being lifted into the ambulance.

Archer takes a breath to compose herself. 'Hicks did this.'

'What?'

'I need to go,' she replies. 'I need to be with Harry. He mustn't be alone.' She turns to the paramedic. 'I'm with him.'

'Please come in,' he says.

'Grace, I'll see you at the hospital,' says Pierce. 'Which hospital are you going to?' she asks the paramedic.

'The nearest is St Thomas's,' he replies.

Archer climbs inside and sits on the seat opposite Quinn.

The paramedic closes the doors and shouts to his colleague to drive. The sirens wail as the ambulance takes off and gathers speed.

'What's his name?' the paramedic asks.

'Harry.'

'I'm Joe. What's your name?'

'Grace.'

'Are you injured, Grace?'

She shakes her head.

155

'Let me give you something for your face,' he says, removing two wet wipes from a packet.

'Thank you.' Archer wipes her face.

The paramedic tends to Quinn. 'Harry, my name's Joe. I'm a medic. We're taking you St Thomas's Hospital. Can you hear me?'

Quinn doesn't respond.

Chapter 26

GRANDAD IS SITTING UP IN his bed, chessboard on his lap, mid-game with Cosmo. Squeezing his chin, his eyes scan the pieces as he tries to figure out his move. Archer hangs back, watches them and feels her heart bounce after what has been a tragic day. Cosmo is playing white. To her surprise, Grandad seems to have the advantage and is close to checkmate with his knight, rook and bishop.

She steps into the room, but he doesn't register her.

Cosmo turns and smiles. 'Hello, Grace.'

'Hi, Cosmo. Hi, Grandad.'

Grandad looks up and beams. 'Hello, my girl.' His eyes are red, and he looks tired.

Archer crosses the room, bends over and kisses him on the forehead. 'How're you doing?'

'Much better,' he replies.

There is still a slight slur in his voice.

'So I see. Can't believe you're playing chess already.'

'Me neither, although I must admit Cosmo's been helping me with some of the moves.'

'I wouldn't say that was the case, Jake. The old grey matter is still working. You've been doing pretty good. If you ask me, that stroke has improved your game.' Cosmo chuckles.

Grandad looks at Archer. 'Grace, could you call the nurse and ask her to take this crazy person back to his cell?'

Cosmo leans back on his chair and lets out a chesty laugh that pushes him into a coughing fit that won't ease.

'Cosmo, are you OK?' Archer asks.

Doubling over, Cosmo raises his hand with a thumbs-up.

'You might want to summon the undertaker,' says Grandad, casually.

Archer takes the plastic jug of water from Grandad's tray table, fills a beaker and hands it to Cosmo.

Gripping it with two hands, Cosmo tips the water into his mouth and slugs it down, spilling half of it onto his grey beard.

'Thank you,' he says, handing back the beaker. 'That old fool will be the death of me.'

'Are you sure you're OK?' says Archer.

'Fine, fine.' Cosmo turns to Grandad. 'OK, old man. Do you want to make your move so that I can leave you and Grace in peace.'

'Victory awaits,' says Grandad. Blinking his tired eyes, he focuses his attention back on the game.

Archer looks at Cosmo and mouths a thank you.

He smiles back at her.

Grandad reaches across the board. He has only one move to take out the white king. There is something weirdly symbolic about this moment. The 'white' king. Archer crosses her fingers. All he has to do is move his black knight forward. All other options are covered by his bishop and the rook. She wills him to do it. To have a victory that he so deserves. *Come on, Grandad.*

She notices his eyelids are drooping. He's sleepy.

'You've got me,' Cosmo says, a gentle urging.

Grandad perks up. 'Indeed, I do.'

158

Reaching across, he lifts one of Cosmo's pawns and pushes it forward. 'Take that!' he says.

Archer's heart sinks.

'No, no, old man,' Cosmo says, placing the pawn back in its place. He points to the black knight. 'If you move this fellow to here, you'll have me in checkmate. See ...'

Grandad frowns at the board. Closing his eyes, he pushes it to the side. 'I don't want to play anymore.' Some of the pieces fall to the floor. Cosmo picks them up. 'No problem, Jake. No problem.'

'I'm tired.'

Archer sits on the edge of the bed and takes his hand. 'Of course you are.'

He looks across at Cosmo. 'Sorry, old man.'

'No worries, you old fool. I'll come back tomorrow and kick your bony ass.'

'Have you seen a doctor today?' Archer asks.

Grandad looks at her with a lost expression. 'I ... I really don't know.'

'There was a doctor here earlier,' says Cosmo. 'Can't remember her name. She said he's doing well, didn't she, Jake?'

'That's great,' says Archer.

'And listen to this, Grace. Remember what she said to me, Jake.' Cosmo starts to chuckle.

'How would I know if I don't even remember she was here!' Grandad snaps.

'She said to me ... no, she asked me if I was Jake's partner ... his partner, Grace. Me? We laughed at that, didn't we, Jake?'

Grandad rolls his eyes. 'If you say so.'

Grandad's white hair is untidy. She reaches across and combs it with her fingers. 'Can't really see you two as a couple,' she says.

159

'I'd rather shoot myself.'

Cosmo laughs. 'That would be some hard times if we ended up together. Listen, I'll go and leave you both. Nice to see you, Grace.'

'You too, Cosmo.'

'Do you want me to bring anything tomorrow, old man?'

'Some Werther's.'

'I'll get you some Werther's. Anything else? A rainbow flag maybe?' Cosmo giggles as he leaves the room. 'See you tomorrow, old man.'

'He's an idiot,' says Grandad.

'You're looking well,' Archer says.

'I'm tired all the time. I think they're drugging me with something to make me drowsy.'

'The doctor said the stroke will make you tired. Also, it's warm in here and you're not active. That won't help.'

'I hate it here.'

'Hospitals are never fun places.'

'I want to go home.'

'You'll be home soon.'

'Why is that policeman always hanging around?'

Archer glances at the guard in the corridor outside.

'Don't you remember?'

Grandad sighs and leans back, resting on his upright pillow. He looks across the room at nothing in particular. 'I don't really remember how I came to be here. Or how long I've been here.'

Archer feels an ache in her chest. She squeezes his hand gently.

He turns his gaze back to her and cocks his head. 'Have you cut yourself?' he asks.

'What? No.'

He points to the right side of her neck. 'Is that blood?'

160

'No, of course not,' she lies. 'Excuse me one moment.' Archer crosses to the en suite and closes the door behind her. Lifting her head, she examines her neck. There is a thumb-sized splotch of Quinn's blood on her neck. Turning on the tap, she grabs a paper towel, dampens it and wipes the blood away.

Her phone rings. It's Pierce. She swipes the screen and answers. 'Clare.'

'Where are you?'

'With Grandad.'

'Oh. How is he?'

'OK.'

'I'm in A & E.'

'Harry?'

'It's not good. Can you come down?'

Archer feels her stomach turn. 'I'll be straight there.'

Exiting the bathroom, she enters Grandad's room. His eyes are closed, he is quietly snoring. She approaches the bed, gently lifts the covers, places them over his shoulders and hurries out of the room.

Chapter 27

'THAT MOTHERFUCKER!' QUINN CROAKS.

Archer is in an A & E bay closed off with blue curtains. She can't quite believe what she's looking at. Quinn is alive. She stares at him in disbelief, unsure if she's dreaming. He's lying on a cot with a bandage taped to the side of his head. His face is pale, his neck and shirt caked in dried blood.

'I knew he was bent! Motherfucker!'

'I can't believe it. I really just can't believe it,' says Pierce.

'You're alive,' Archer says, finding the words at last.

'I think so . . . they've pumped me full of painkillers yet my head's poundin' like an Orangeman's drum. I feel like I have the worst hangover in the history of hangovers. Fuuuuck!'

'As long as that's all you have,' says Pierce. 'Thank God you're OK.'

'Clare, you said it wasn't looking good,' says Archer.

'Look at the state of him.'

Archer says, 'But I thought . . . I really thought . . . '

'The important thing is he's OK, Grace. However, we will need to reconfigure the team. Quinn could be out of work for weeks. Perhaps more. That's so inconvenient.'

'You're all heart, Clare. Fuuuck!' cries Quinn, as he tries to push himself up. 'Give me a few days. I'll be fine.'

'I don't think you should sit up,' says Archer, placing one hand behind his back to support him.

'I'm fine,' he says, slumping forward and taking several deep breaths. His eyes are closed, his face buckled with pain.

'He has nine stitches,' says Pierce. 'The bullet skimmed his temple. He's lucky. Very lucky.'

Pierce's phone rings. She looks at the screen. 'It's Jimmy. I need to take this. One moment,' she says, leaving the bay.

'I thought I'd lost you.'

'I'm not going anywhere,' he replies, quietly.

'What the hell did you think you were doing?'

Quinn keeps his eyes closed and does not answer.

'Harry, you knew he was going to shoot yet you stood in the way. Why would you do that?'

'A moment of madness.'

'You could have been killed.'

'Yet here I am. Alive to fight another day.'

The curtain opens and Pierce steps in. 'We've launched an official manhunt for Rod,' she says, pocketing her phone. 'For Chrissakes, the press are going to fucking love this! I really, really cannot believe it. Rod! Of all people working for Frankie White.'

Archer meets Quinn's gaze. Charlie had warned them someone in Charing Cross was on White's payroll.

'Is it really that much of a surprise?' Archer says. 'He was a close friend of Andy Rees after all.'

Pierce bristles at the mention of the ex-DI, Rees. As well as being his governor, she had been his lover, all the time he had been moonlighting for White. Pierce's reputation had suffered but she had managed to claw back some respect, which was mostly due to the results Archer and Quinn had with their murder investigations.

'How did he get away so easily?' asks Archer. 'The place was swarming.'

'He's a desperate man with a gun,' replies Pierce. 'They followed him but lost him in the crowd in Covent Garden. We're checking CCTV where we can. We'll find him.'

'He was being blackmailed,' says Archer.

Pierce frowns. 'How do you know that?'

'He said he was doing it for his family,' adds Quinn.

'Which means Frankie has threatened them. Or worse, has them,' says Archer.

'He has been acting weird recently,' says Quinn.

'Has anyone been to his house?' Archer asks.

'I sent Jimmy and a team,' says Pierce. 'They had to break in. No one was at home. Jimmy said it looks like there's been no one living there for days. The neighbours backed that up.'

Folding her arms, Pierce says, 'So, just to get this into my head. Frankie White ordered Rod to kill you while holding his family to ransom. Is that the sum of it?'

'We have no proof, but that sounds about right.'

'Clare, we need to put the pressure on Frankie White. Hicks's family is in danger.'

'I'm not sure what we can do about Frankie White. We just can't march over there, point the finger and shout, "*J'accuse!*"'

'We have to do something.'

'I could get Jimmy to do it. He's a no-nonsense copper, he won't take any shit from White.'

'Then send him. He can make something up about an accusation. Perhaps one of his people was seen hanging around Hicks's house. These are desperate times. A bluff won't do any harm.'

Pierce nods her head. 'Agreed. I'll take over the manhunt. Jimmy can work with me on White. The search for Rod is a priority though.'

'Of course,' replies Archer. 'There is a contact that might be able to help us?'

'Who?'

'I don't know their name. Someone working undercover.'

'On whose authority?'

'Charlie Bates.'

'OK, I'll talk to Charlie. He might be able to help us out.'

'Thanks, Clare.'

'Also, I may have to move some resources around. We're two men down. With Harry and Rod out of the picture, I may need to beg, borrow or steal. Grace, how about I assign Marian to you until Harry comes back?'

'That'd work. She's doing good work on the Todd case.'

'That's what I thought. I can assign Mel to work with Jimmy.'

'We're forgetting something here,' Quinn says.

'Oh. What would that be?' asks Pierce.

'It's not safe for Grace. White has failed. Hicks is still out there, he'll try again.'

Pierce sighs and closes her eyes. 'Fuck,' she mutters. She looks at Archer. 'He's right.'

Archer is conflicted. There is still much work to do but is she really helping herself or anyone else by remaining on duty? Shouldn't she disappear until White is nailed?

'Where are you staying at the moment?'

'At Harry's.'

'Who knows you're staying there?'

Archer looks at Quinn. 'Just Charlie. We deliberately kept it under wraps.'

'Is it safe?' Pierce asks.

'As safe as anywhere,' says Quinn. 'One advantage is that White does not have a presence there. The local thugs have no love for him. Also, it has a network of elderly curtain twitchers.

They know everyone in the block who comes and goes. I could ask them to keep an eye out for undesirables.'

'Is that what we've come to?' asks Pierce. 'The Met relying on the elderly, the people we serve, to look out for our own?'

'I'd rather not but I could find somewhere else,' says Archer. 'One of our safe houses, perhaps.'

'They're all out of town. I'd prefer to keep you close. Stay at Harry's for now.' Pierce reaches into her coat pocket and takes out a car key. 'Take my car, go straight to Harry's. Keep a low profile. Work from his until I find somewhere else.'

'Understood.'

Quinn reaches into his pocket. 'Here's my keys.'

Archer takes them.

'I'll grab a taxi back to Charing Cross,' says Pierce. She looks from Archer to Quinn. 'Take care. Both of you.' As she leaves, she looks back. 'Grace, I'll get Jimmy to check in on you later.'

Chapter 28

THE SOUND OF A WHIPLIKE crack and Daddy's voice crying out shakes Uma Whitmore from the deepest of sleeps. She bolts upwards, breathing in short, rapid bursts, small hands tightening on the edges of the warm duvet.

Her bedroom is a blur of pink, a warm glow from the baby penguin nightlight on the bedside table. She rubs her sleepy eyes and waits for her vision to focus. Collecting her thoughts, she tries to figure out what made that noise and why Daddy would cry out in that way.

'Daddy,' she calls in a tired, tiny voice, her throat dry and tickly.

The house is as quiet as a graveyard. Daddy does not respond.

She senses something in the air and furrows her brow.

After a moment, she realises there's a smell, a sour damp odour that reminds her of an old black street cat that she had once bent down to pet. It had hissed at her, scratched her hand with a grubby claw, and drawn blood. The pain had felt icy and had shocked her. Tears had filled her eyes. They were not tears of hurt, or pity. They were tears of anger. She had hissed back at the creature and stomped her foot. The mangy thing had run off, scooting over dustbins and the neighbours' fence. Uma had always thought of herself as a girl who loved pretty much all animals. However, since the cat incident, she had always kept her distance from them.

She wonders if the cat has returned, maybe climbed through a window to seek her out and scratch her again. Perhaps it had scratched Daddy, and that's why he'd cried out. She dismisses this thought. There's no way a cat could get inside the house. Daddy locks the doors and windows every night.

She scans the room, uncertain of what she might find. The doors to the pink rattan wardrobe with the love hearts are closed and there is no scowling cat watching her from the shadows on top. Her eyes move to the white wooden desk. School books and novels litter the surface. 'Ordered chaos', Daddy calls it. On the floor are her dollies. Disney heroines Lilo, Moana, Merida and Elsa line the walls in more 'ordered chaos'. Cautiously, she peers over her bed at the teddies who form a ring around her bed, her soldiers protecting her from the bogeyman. It's gloomy on the floor and something is out of place. Something is different. She inches forward and narrows her gaze, but jolts at the sound of a floorboard creaking in the hallway outside her room. The bedroom door is wide open, yawning into a swirling darkness. The sour cat smell seems stronger now as if it's occupying the black hole into the hallway. Uma's nose wrinkles.

'Who's there?' she says, trying not to sound scared.

When there is no response, Uma stiffens and shrinks like a mouse back under the duvet.

A moment passes and the floorboard creaks again, slowly, as the weight eases off it. In seconds, she hears feet padding down the stairs. Peeking from the top of the duvet, she feels her skin tingling.

Uma hesitates but steals the courage to jump from her bed, crossing over the protective ring of teddies. She takes a calming breath and with her body secure in the safety of the baby penguin pink glow, she stretches her arm up and into the darkness of the hallway and switches on the light. She squints up the hallway at Daddy's bedroom and sees him lying quiet and still under the covers.

She hurries up to his bedroom, stands at the foot of the bed, grabs his feet and shakes them. He doesn't wake.

'Daddy, there's someone in the house,' she says, shaking him harder. But still he sleeps.

She turns on the light, squints at the brightness and rubs her eyes.

As her vision adjusts, she can see him. She gasps and clutches her hands to her chest, 'Daddy, you're scaring me . . . '

A clicking sound, downstairs. The familiar sound of the back door, closing.

Uma gasps and feels her heart pounding.

She leaps into Daddy's bed. Huddling beside him, she pulls at the mask on his face. 'Daddy, wake up! Someone's in the house.'

But still, he does not reply.

The mask is taped to his neck and taped around where his mouth is. She tries to pull at it but she's not strong enough. 'Daddy, wake up,' she cries. She pounds his chest, but he just lies still. Tears fill her eyes. Something is not right. Something is wrong. Her breath catches and then she screams.

Chapter 29

BRYNN STIRS FROM HIS SLEEP to the sound of stumbling feet and glass smashing at close to two o'clock in the morning. His heart in his mouth, he sits up and wonders if someone is breaking into the house. And then he hears Dad's voice. As his mind wakes, the truth becomes clear: Dad has returned home late from a night of boozing and is drunk. This is becoming a habit.

It has gone quiet downstairs and Brynn worries he might have fallen over and hurt himself. Dressed in his pyjamas, Brynn tiptoes barefoot to the midway point of the stairs, stopping when he hears the low hum of Dad's voice. There are no other voices. Just his. He is talking to himself, muttering incomprehensibly. Brynn can make out the occasional swear word, slurred and laced with vitriol. There was a time, after Mum had left them, when Brynn would have asked Dad if everything was all right. The first time Dad ignored him. The second time he swore at him. Any time after that, Dad would frown, his eyes bloodshot, his teeth gritted, and swipe at him with a slap across the face or a punch in the stomach. Brynn would cower from him, and Dad would always glare back with that confused and angry expression. Brynn knew Dad could see Mam in his face. People always said how much he looked like his mam. For that reason, Brynn had come to understand that Dad despised him.

Mam had left six months ago, shortly after they had moved to London. She had met another man, someone she worked with. Dad had found out about them and got so angry he tried to drown her in the bath. He had made Brynn watch. Iris's aunt, Mrs Toolan, heard the noise and called the police. Mam was taken away in an ambulance. She was OK but never returned. Dad was in custody and Brynn stayed with Mrs Toolan until Dad returned home the next day. Mam had gone and moved in with her new boyfriend. She told Brynn it was only a one-bedroom flat and that they would look for something bigger so he could come live with her and Kevin. That was six months ago. How long does it take to get a two-bedroom flat? There's lots of them around for renting. He knew cause he'd been checking the papers every night. He was hearing less and less from her and his despair had grown by the day. She had sent him a card at Christmas with a fiver inside. She didn't even call him for Christmas Day. Brynn's heart was broken; sometimes he wondered if she had actually drowned in the bath that night and someone was playing a cruel trick on him by making him think she was still alive.

'Fuggin' hoor!' Dad cries suddenly.

Brynn flinches. The floorboards creak under his feet. He pads softly but quickly back to his room, locking the door behind him. Dad's boots are stomping up the stairs. Brynn slips under the covers, pulling them over his head.

'Brynn!' he calls, his voice dry, raspy. 'Come out here!'

Brynn's heart pounds in his chest.

The door handle is shaking. He's trying to get inside.

No, please!

'Brynn, get out here, ya fuggin' faggot!' he shouts, pounding the door.

Brynn curls into himself and wishes he was far away. Somewhere else. Maybe with Mam and Kevin. Anywhere but here.

Moments pass and the pounding stops. Dad has started talking to himself again. To Brynn's relief, he hears him shuffle up the hallway away from his door. He hears him stumbling down the stairs and then rattling around the kitchen, slamming cupboard doors, probably looking for something to drink. And then he hears his voice roar angrily once again coupled with the sound of more glass and crockery smashing. Within minutes everything is quiet. Brynn lies like a hibernating mouse under the covers. Outside the rain is pouring. The sound relaxes him. He loses himself in its rhythm and pretends he is somewhere else. Eventually, he pushes Dad from his mind and drifts into a restless sleep.

Brynn's alarm clock rings at 7.30 the following morning. His arm flops out from under the covers and shuts the shitting thing off. He blinks his eyes open. They're dry. Rubbing the sleep from them, he slides out of the warm bed and into the cold air of his small bedroom. He shivers as his mind rouses; the events of the small hours hurl back at him like a volley of broken masonry. Wringing his hands, he thinks of the mess that waits downstairs. He'd better clean it up or he'd get the blame. Anything broken in the house is always his fault.

Unlocking the door, he peers up and down the hallway. It's clear. He hurries to the bathroom for a pee and a quick wash. Back in the bedroom, he pulls on his school uniform and piles his books into his school bag. In his stockinged feet, he creeps quietly up the hallway, stopping briefly outside Dad's bedroom. The door is closed. It's quiet inside. He must still be sleeping.

Padding down the stairs, he enters the kitchen. The cupboard doors are open, there is broken glass and smashed crockery everywhere. He'd have to go the charity shop and replenish everything. Again! It's not safe to walk on the floor. Where are his trainers? He steals across the hallway, eyes searching, and sees them lying outside the living room. Leaning on the door frame, he pulls them on one at a time. He realises there's a strong smell coming from the room. It's beer. The blinds are closed inside, the room is gloomy. Brynn reaches for the switch and flicks it, but the light doesn't come on. He tries a second time and a third.

'The light's broken,' Dad rasps.

Brynn's heart leaps to his mouth. As his eyes adjust to the gloom, he sees the figure of his dad sitting on the armchair by the window. He can also see the shape of a beer can resting on top of the arm.

'I ... I ... thought you was sleeping, Dad.'

'You ... you ... thought I was sleeping,' Dad replies, mimicking his voice.

'Yes,' Brynn whispers.

Dad exhales a long breath.

'I better get going. I 'ave school ... '

''Ave you seen the state of this place? It's a shithole.'

'Uhm ... I'll 'elp clean up.'

'You'll "'elp clean up"?'

'Yes.'

'But what did you do here?'

'Nothing. I ... '

'Did you 'ave a party?'

'No, Dad. I wouldn't do that. I was 'ere by myself. I swear, Dad. It was just me, it was.'

Dad rises slowly from the chair.

Brynn shrinks into the hallway. He jumps at a sudden movement and sees the beer can fly across the room, hitting the hallway wall to his left. Warm foamy beer splashes his face and blazer. It stinks.

'Dad . . . please.'

'Did you have your mates here in my house last night?' His voice is a dog-like growl.

'No . . . I . . . I don't have any friends, Dad. None.'

'You 'ad that hooer here!'

'What?!'

And then Dad is charging across the room like a bull. Fight or flight, they say. But there is no fight. Not today. Only flight. Brynn gasps, spins on his feet and runs as fast as he can for the front door. Yanking it open, he rushes out, the tips of Dad's fingers grazing his neck, but Brynn is fast and legs it, running like Forrest Gump.

'Come back 'ere, you cunt!'

But Brynn just keeps running and running.

Chapter 30

ARCHER HAS KEPT THE LIGHTS off in Quinn's flat. She is sitting on the Chesterfield sofa, in the glow of her laptop, unaware where the time has gone. She finishes her final report and stretches. It's quarter past ten in the evening. Picking up the TV remote, she flicks on the news and catches the tail end of a press conference led by DCI Pierce.

'Investigations are ongoing for the explosion on *The Pride of Elizabeth* . . .That's correct. No arrests have been made yet . . . Yes, we are following up on leads . . . We always maintain a close working relationship with our colleagues at the National Crime Agency . . . We do not know if this explosion was related to organised crime . . . There is no link between the officer shot on duty and the incident with *The Pride of Elizabeth* . . .'

Archer's phone rings. Klara. She switches off the television, swipes her phone and answers. 'Hey.'

'Hey, Grace. How're you doing?'

'I'm fine. Just watching Clare.'

'They're kicking her ass.'

'Nothing she can't handle.'

'She's a tough bird.'

Archer stifles a yawn.

'You sound tired.'

'I'm OK.'

'Are you sure? Do you need company?'

'Not with all this hanging over my head. It's too dangerous.'

'I can't believe you're on your own.'

'Clare said Jimmy might pop by. I'm fine though. Honestly.'

'I hate the fact you're all by yourself at this time.'

'I've been through worse.'

'I suppose you have. Hey, I popped in to see Harry earlier.'

'How was he?'

'Grumpy. Drowsy. Sweary. They doubled his painkillers. I left him because he couldn't keep his eyes open.'

Archer squeezes the phone, a wave of emotion hitting her. Tears threaten to come but she holds them back. 'Harry and Grandad . . . They're both in hospital because of White.'

'Why Jake?'

'He overheard Harry and I talking about the threat from White. It was too much for him.'

'Oh no. Poor Jake. I'm so sorry, Grace.'

A second call comes through on Archer's phone. It's Zelda, Quinn's neighbour. 'Klara, thanks for checking in. I need to take this call.'

'No worries. If you need anything, you know where I am.'

'Thank you. Bye. Talk tomorrow.'

'Take care.'

Archer takes the second call. 'Hi, Zelda.'

'Detective Archer, this is Zelda calling. Over.'

Archer frowns. 'What's going on, Zelda – and why are you whispering?'

'We may have an intruder in the building. Maureen saw a hooded figure approaching from the park. He was walking slowly, suspiciously, in her opinion. She pinged Betty. Betty caught him with her binoculars and confirmed

180

the sighting. She pinged me and now I'm calling you. He's on his way up. Over.'

Aside from thinking she has landed in an episode of *Murder, She Wrote*, Archer feels a knot in her stomach. 'How long ago was this?'

'Three minutes. Over.'

'Zelda, you don't need to keep saying "over".'

'Oh . . . '

Archer hops off the Chesterfield, hurries to the window and side peeks through the blinds. It's wet outside. Kennington Park is a void of darkness in the distance. There's no sign of anyone.

Zelda is whispering again. 'Fortunately the lift is out so he has to walk up the stairs.'

A knock on the flat door startles her.

'That's just me,' says Zelda.

'Zelda, go back inside.'

'I'm not leaving without you. Those were my instructions in case we crime busters saw something. "Sweep in and pick up," Harry said. I was to drag you kicking and screaming, if I had to. So come quick, he'll be here soon.'

Archer bites her thumb. 'Wait for me at your place. I'll be straight there,' she says, ending the call. Hurrying to Quinn's hallway, she grabs the baseball bat from the cupboard and peeks through the spyhole. She sees Zelda's shadow flit across the open space and into her flat. There's no one else there.

Archer opens the door, steps into the hallway and closes the door behind her. She hears footsteps climbing the concrete steps and darts across the hallway. Slipping into Zelda's flat, she pushes the door softly closed. She could ring this in, but if it's a false alarm then it'll be a waste of valuable police time. Besides, no one knows she's here. Only Quinn, Klara and Pierce. And Jimmy too. She hopes it's Jimmy.

Resting the baseball bat against the door, she feels Zelda beside her. She whispers something incomprehensible. Archer places her finger to her mouth, hushing her and reaches across to switch off the light in Zelda's hall. She peers through the peephole and sees the profile of a hooded figure looking at Quinn's flat.

Zelda tugs at Archer's sleeve. 'Detective Archer.'

Archer ignores her. There's something familiar about the hooded man, his posture, that she recognises.

'Detective Archer, Betty and Maureen are on their way,' says Zelda.

'What? No! Tell them go back. It's too dangerous,' Archer says. But it's too late. She can hear voices approaching. Two women talking loudly and quickly.

'Oh, hello. Can we help you?' one of them asks.

'That's Betty,' whispers Zelda.

Outside, the hooded man is flanked by two women in their sixties wearing bathrobes. One is stocky with short, bleached hair, the other has a tight white perm and is smoking a cigarette.

'Who ya looking for?' says the woman with the bleached hair.

'That's Maureen. She's tough as old boots, she'll give him what for.'

The man turns from them and leaves, hurrying down the steps.

'Well, that's nice, that is,' says Maureen.

'Learn some manners,' calls Betty.

Archer opens Zelda's door and ushers the women inside.

'That was exciting,' says Betty. 'We chased him off.'

'Please stay here,' says Archer as she exits the flat and hurries after the hooded man, being careful to keep her distance. She hears voices above her and sees Zelda, Maureen and Betty on her tail peering over the banister. Betty is holding a kitchen knife. Maureen is brandishing Quinn's baseball bat. Zelda is carrying a wooden spoon. Archer blinks. Was Zelda planning to give cooking lessons?

'There he is!' Maureen calls at the top of her voice. 'Oi, you, stop! We're Old Bill.'

'Shit!' says Archer. She looks down and sees the hooded man peering up. Her heart races. It's Hicks. She almost didn't recognise him. His face is gaunt and grey. He stares back at her with a haunted expression.

'Rod, stop. Don't go. Let me help you.'

Their eyes lock.

'Come back with me. We can talk. I know you don't want this.'

He hesitates, his hand gripping the steel banister.

'Please,' says Archer. 'We can finish White together.'

He hesitates. In his eyes, she can tell he's considering it.

Hicks jumps at the scream of police sirens approaching. They break the spell, the dream of freedom that for a second seemed so attainable. His jaw tightens, he turns and runs down the steps.

'Rod, wait!'

Archer jumps down two steps at a time. At the front of Quinn's block a response car and an unmarked car pull up. The latter contains Jimmy Barnes. But there's no sign of Hicks. He has disappeared into the night.

Barnes and the other officers step out of the car.

'A call was made by Zelda someone,' says one of the response officers.

'That's me,' Zelda calls. Archer looks round, relieved to see three of them are OK. They are no longer carrying weapons. Not that Zelda was carrying anything that could be described as a weapon.

'Are you OK?' Jimmy asks.

Archer catches her breath. 'Fine. Hicks was here.'

He stiffens. 'Did you see where he went?'

'Into Kennington Park,' says Maureen. 'I saw it.'

'Makes sense,' says Archer. 'It's dark and easy to get away unseen.'

Barnes nods his agreement. 'I'll head there now.'

'I'll come with you.'

'No! Too dangerous. He has a gun. Go back inside, we can take care of this.'

'I don't think he means to kill me.'

'What makes you think that?'

'A hunch.'

Barnes shrugs. 'I've got to know him over the past few months. He's unpredictable and clearly dangerous.'

'Sir, where do you want us?' one of the responders asks Barnes.

'One of you scout the perimeter of the block. The other come with me. I don't care which of you. We'll comb the park together.'

'Yes, sir,' replies the uniform. 'I'll come with you and Nick; you can do a reccy on the block.'

'You say you've come to know him,' Archer says. 'He's been off sick for most of the time you two were partners. Have you seen him at all during his time out?'

Barnes blinks. 'Sometimes we'd talk. We've known each other for a few years.'

'I see. Do you think he's changed much in the past six months?'

Barnes shrugs. 'He seemed normal.'

'And you didn't notice anything different about his behaviour, even since he returned to work?'

'No. Can't say that I did.'

Archer holds Barnes's gaze. His mouth twitches. 'I need to go, Grace,' he says.

'Go,' she replies.

'It'll be safer inside.'

Barnes turns to leave. Archer watches him and the responder hurry into the Kennington Park gloom and wonders if Jimmy Barnes is hiding something.

Chapter 31

THE NIGHT HAD PASSED WITHOUT incident. Archer wakes to the 7 a.m. alarm, having slept uneasily. She checks her phone. No messages or missed calls. Sliding out of bed, she pads barefoot across the cold vinyl tiles, making her way to the kitchen. She fills the kettle with water, boils it and searches for Quinn's fancy coffee and cafetière.

After coffee and a slice of dry toast, she showers and dresses. In the living room, she opens her laptop and logs into the Home Office Large Major Enquiry System, or HOLMES as it's commonly known. She searches for an update on the pursuit of Hicks but finds nothing. According to the report, Barnes had combed Kennington Park, but Hicks had disappeared and was still at large. Last night she had waited for Barnes to return. She had wanted a briefing, but he got into his car without checking in with her. That irked her. She had called him, but his phone went straight to voicemail.

She checks WhatsApp and sees Quinn has been online in the last five minutes. She calls him.

'Morning,' he croaks. He sounds tired.

'Are you OK to talk?' she asks.

'Of course.'

'How're you feeling?'

'My head's still pounding. I think they took a pneumatic drill to it in the few moments of sleep I managed to catch last night. Otherwise, I'm peachy. What's the news?' he asks.

Archer tells him about Hicks's visit, the intervention from Zelda's 'crime busters' and Hicks fleeing across Kennington Park with Jimmy Barnes in pursuit.

'Jesus, Zelda and her neighbourhood watch crew. They have no fear.'

'They have some balls.'

'Did you meet Maureen?'

'Of course.'

'Hicks was lucky to escape. She'd have had his balls dangling from her ears, had she caught up with him.'

'She is quite intimidating.'

'The obvious question is how did Hicks know you were staying at mine?'

'I don't know. Could he have overheard us talking about it?'

'I don't recall discussing it in the office or in earshot of anyone else.'

'Only Clare knows. When we were with you yesterday, she said she was going to ask Jimmy to check in. So only those two.'

'Hicks must have followed you.'

'I took Clare's car. He could have got lucky and spotted me, or maybe he's been staking the place. Maybe he assumed I'd be staying there. He'd seen us work late and leave the office together. He knew I wasn't at home. Perhaps he put two and two together.'

'Perhaps.'

'There's something else.'

'What?'

'I don't think he intended to kill me.'

188

'Grace, he shot me in the head. The bullet was meant for you.'

'I know. I'm sorry but hear me out. It's just that last night he was scared. I asked him to wait. I told him we could bring White down together. He hesitated. He was considering it, I know he was.'

'But he didn't.'

'The responders freaked him. He bolted.'

'We both know what Hicks is like, Grace. Don't forget that he has not made life easy for you since you started last year.'

'I know. But there's something more going on inside him. He's desperate and will do anything to save his family.'

'That includes shooting you.'

Archer hesitates before replying, 'He's a frightened man, Harry.'

'He's made his bed. Listen, I think you should get out of the flat. Find a hotel. Get Clare to sign off on somewhere decent. Somewhere expensive and secure. Might as well be comfortable.'

'I'm fine here.'

Quinn sighs. 'You do realise I'll have to re-engage with the Brandon Estate Crime Busting Association.'

'I feel safer already. Hey, there's one more thing.'

'What's that?'

'I spoke to Jimmy about Hicks and—'

'Grace, sorry, the doctor has just appeared. I have to go.'

'OK. Talk later.'

'Stay safe.'

Archer ends the call and sits on the Chesterfield. She had wanted to talk about Jimmy. She didn't know him as well as Quinn did and was hoping he could shed some light on the man. Last night, when she had asked him about Hicks and his behaviour, Jimmy seemed guarded and stated that there had been no change as far as he could tell. But how could the closest person working with Hicks not notice what everyone else saw? Perhaps it was her imagination. Besides, Jimmy and Hicks seem to get on well. Jimmy is a good, conscientious copper. He had even worked with her father back in the day. Archer rubs her neck. Something is niggling her. Something is out of place and she can't put her finger on it. She needs to think it over. For the moment, she needs to catch up on the Todd murder investigation.

She sets up a conference call with the team – Marian, Mel, Os and Klara – later that morning. They had missed half a day after the incident with Quinn, which they are all, understandably, still in shock about.

'I spoke to him this morning. He's doing much better,' says Archer.

'And I saw him yesterday. He's on good form, considering,' adds Klara.

'When will he be back?' asks Os.

'We don't know. It could be weeks, months possibly,' Archer replies. Saying it out loud instils a sense of selfish dread in her. What if during his recuperation he decides he doesn't want to come back? What if he thinks risking his life for this job is just not worth it? What would she do then? Who would be her partner? Jimmy? Phillips? She taps the arm of the Chesterfield, pushes these thoughts from her head and continues.

'I just updated HOLMES although I don't expect any of you had time to read it, so I'll brief you now. Harry and I met with Derek Fox. To start, he claimed he didn't really know Jason Todd. When we pressed him and mentioned his colourful emails and texts, he came clean. Jason is not Katie's first lover, it seems. Derek has a somewhat reluctant tolerance to his wife's occasional lovers. Not so for Jason Todd though, who he considers an abuser and a drunk.'

'So he's definitely a suspect?' asks Marian.

'Yes.'

When the meeting ends, Archer considers that there had been little in the way of progress from the team. Also, the call had been subdued with less of a buzz than normal. Archer knows the shooting of Harry by one of their own has impacted them more than they realise. This is not an easy time for any of them. They'll need time to process what has happened to the much-loved Quinn, as well figuring out what is going on with Hicks.

A knock on the flat door. Three slow raps. A code devised by Zelda, who has clearly been watching too many mystery movies. A text comes through at the same time.

It's me. Over. Z. LOL

Despite herself, Archer smiles. Through the peephole, Zelda is tiny. Archer unlocks the door and opens it.

'I'm bringing food,' she says, 'as I know Harry never has anything in his fridge or his cupboards. He needs a woman in his life. I've always said.' Zelda is wearing her coat and holding out a carrier bag in each hand. 'This is for you. Inside is some matzo ball soup. Just heat it for three minutes in the microwave.'

Archer takes the bag. 'Don't know what to say. Thank you, Zelda.'

'There's some potato latkes too, and a tub of kibbeh. You're not a vegetarian or one of those vegans, are you?'

'No.'

'Good. Don't understand veganism one bit.' She nods to the other bag. 'This is for Harry. He won't like that food at St Thomas's. It's inedible. I wouldn't feed it to my cat, if I had one. So, listen up, the ladies are patrolling today, so rest assured

191

you're safe. Betty, as you know, is our eyes, and ears too, I decided. Maureen is the muscle. You may have reached that conclusion. I have to go. I'm going to the hospital to see Harry.' She places her palm on her chest. 'I still can't believe he's been shot, but there we go. It's a hard, dangerous world out there . . . '

'Zelda, I really appreciate what you, Maureen and Betty are doing but you need to stop. It's dangerous, and besides, the police are keeping an eye on this place.'

'Detective Archer, with all due respect, Harry was almost murdered outside Charing Cross Police Station by another detective. Where were your fellow officers?' She shrugs her shoulders. 'You'll forgive me if my opinion of the Metropolitan Police Force is somewhat tarnished right now.'

'Fair enough.'

'I better get going. You take care of yourself. Goodbye for now – and lock the door behind you.'

'Thanks for the food.'

'You're welcome.'

Archer realises she's starving and hasn't eaten since yesterday morning. The food is warm and smells spicy and delicious. Her mouth waters. She heats the soup, as suggested, eats it all, dumplings too, and then finishes the meaty kibbeh snacks. She is full and has no room for the latkes, despite the fact they look so tasty.

A call comes through on her phone. It's a Charing Cross Police Station number.

'Archer speaking,' she says.

'Grace, this is Clare. I'm in a meeting room.' Her voice has an echo. She is on the conference speaker. 'Klara and Marian are here.'

Both Klara and Marian greet her.

'What's this about?'

'Give me one moment, Grace,' says Pierce. 'You know I'm not technical. I don't know how to use this bloody machine. Klara's figuring it out.'

'Hello,' comes a man's voice. Archer doesn't recognise it.

'Shaun, hello this is Clare Pierce. Can you hear me?'

'Yes, I can. Hello, Clare.'

'Hi. Everyone, this is DI Shaun Greene from Islington. Shaun, present we have SIO DI Grace Archer, DC Marian Phillips and analyst, Klara Clark.'

'Hello,' says Greene.

'Shaun, we've already had a brief discussion. For everyone else's benefit let's start at the beginning.'

'Will do. This morning we were called to the home of Robert Whitmore, a thirty-eight-year-old banker. He was murdered last night in unusual circumstances. He died from asphyxiation. His head and neck were covered in duct tape ...' Archer feels her muscles coiling. '... And here's the thing. The killer drew a sad smiley face on the tape. I had heard that you were investigating a similar murder and immediately got in touch with Clare.'

'So, there it is,' says Clare. 'I don't think this is a coincidence, do you, Grace?'

Archer's mind is racing. The Todd case had suddenly taken an unexpected change in direction.

Chapter 32

ARCHER'S PATIENCE IS WEARING THIN at the end
of the day, having been stuck indoors and waiting
hours for DI Greene's report to appear on the HOLMES
database. She finally gets the alert that the information has
arrived and reads it carefully. To her frustration, the details are
sketchy and there's a lack of clarity, as if the author had been
in a hurry. Greene had sent across two photos of the mask. It's
made from duct tape and has a daubed sad smiley face similar
to Jason Todd's.

With Hicks still at large, *The Pride of Elizabeth* bombing and
Frankie White, Charing Cross has its work stacked up.
Consequently, Archer's investigation has been impacted. No
one on her team has been able to go to the Whitmore house.
Only Greene and his DC have been. Archer feels like she's
getting nowhere. She needs to do something other than being
isolated in Quinn's flat.

She paces around the living room and glances at the clock
on the fireplace. It's 5.33. Then 5.36. Then 5.45. She stands at
the window, arms folded and looks over the luscious green
expanse of Kennington Park. It's raining but not as heavily
as it has been. There are several people coming and going.
A woman with two kids and a buggy. A man carrying his
shopping. A woman on a motability scooter. Archer sighs,

takes out her phone. No messages. No calls. She's had enough. She dials the mobile number DI Greene had sent her earlier.

A woman answers. 'Shaun, is that you?' she asks.

'This is Detective Inspector Archer from Charing Cross.'

The woman giggles. 'Oh, I'm sorry. I thought you was Shaun calling in.'

'Is this not his number?'

'It is. But he's gone home without his phone, the silly bugger.'

'How can I get hold of him?'

'You could call his home number but I don't think he'll be there. He's attending a function somewhere. Can I help?'

'Shaun and I met this morning with my team to discuss the Whitmore murder.'

'Oh yes.'

'I'd like to see the house.'

'But there's no one there at the moment.'

Archer bites her tongue. 'I need access. Can you give me the keys?'

'Oh yes. I can do that.'

Archer hears a rummaging sound and the jangle of keys.

'Here they are.'

'I'm going to go there now. Could you leave the keys somewhere for me to pick up.'

'Even better. I'll meet you there. It's on my way home. I can pop by before I go home and feed the kids.'

'That would be great. Thank you. I didn't catch your name.'

'Sara Clegg. DC.'

'Thanks, Sara. See you in say thirty minutes?'

'Perfect. See you then.'

'Bye.'

Archer looks outside again. She sees Maureen's bright blonde hair circling the front of the building. She smiles and feels more reassured and safer thanks to these three women than she does with an overworked police force crippled by government cuts.

She needs to go and decides she must wear something that doesn't scream Detective Inspector Grace Archer. In other words, she needs to ditch the peacoat. In Quinn's bedroom she opens the wardrobe and finds only shirts, folded T-shirts, and jeans. On the top shelf she spots a navy baseball cap. *Perfect.* Standing in front of the mirror, she pulls it on, tucking her hair inside. She recalls the hallway cupboard, where he hides the baseball bat, is also where his jackets hang. She finds a casual plain green military style jacket and pulls it on. It has Quinn's smell, a faint lemony scent, like the soap he uses. She puts it on and turns up the collar, grabs her phone and peeks through the peephole. There's no one there. She opens the door and hurries out of the flat.

What she considered her 'escape' from the Brandon Estate was relatively easy. There was no one watching as far as she could determine. That said, Archer had suspected Betty's binoculars had tracked her down and Betty had recorded her description, movements and time.

Archer parks near the Whitmore family home in Islington. The engine is still running, the wipers swipe like a metronome, clearing the soft rain from the windscreen's surface. She makes a call to Charing Cross. Marian picks up.

'Hi, Marian, it's Grace.'

'Hi, Grace, how's it going?'

She hears a male voice speaking to Marian. 'One moment, Grace. Sorry.'

Archer waits, tapping her finger on the wheel.

'I'm back. Sorry. That was Jimmy just being nosy. He asked where you were.'

'But he knows where I am. Anyway, just wanted to let you know I'm at the Whitmore house so don't worry about coming up here.'

'The Whitmore house in Islington. OK, great. That's good to know. I can crack on with some other stuff.'

'I'm going to look around and compile a report. We can talk tomorrow.'

'OK.'

'Talk tomorrow then. Good luck.'

Archer ends the call and looks across at the tall yellow-brick semi-detached Georgian villa in Englefield Road. A grand town-house with a private alley separating it and the property on the left. A possible unobserved exit point, she thinks. Police tape covers the glossy black panelled front door and the entrance from the side.

After a thirty-minute wait, she sees a woman with short brown hair, round glasses and a dark green puffer jacket hurrying towards the house. She stops outside and looks around.

Archer gets out of the car. 'Sara Clegg,' she calls.

'DI Archer,' the woman calls back, her hand waving enthusiastically.

'Sorry, I'm late.' She is out of breath as she reaches for Archer's hand and shakes it. Her grip is warm and soft. 'Pleased to meet you,' she says, taking off her steamed-up glasses and fanning her face.

'You too.'

She reaches into her pocket and takes out two sets of blue overshoe covers in plastic bags. 'Forensics are pretty much done but I think it's always best to be on the safe side, don't you?' After peeling the tape back from the entrance, she unlocks the door and pushes it open. It looks heavy and makes a creaking sound. It's dark inside. She turns on the light.

The floor of the entrance hall is herringbone parquet wood with a slightly worn path running through the centre. The walls are painted a crisp white eggshell with occasional chips on the edges and crayon marks on top of the high skirting board. Stark yet stylish art hangs on the walls at eye level. In contrast, a rustic block of wood with key hooks hangs to the left of the front door.

'Mrs Whitmore runs a gallery in central London,' says Clegg.

'Where was she last night?'

'She was away on business. She returned first thing and is staying with her sister-in-law.'

The house is as quiet as a crypt.

'Where to first?' asks Clegg.

'The bedrooms,' replies Archer.

'This way,' says Clegg, leading her to a wide stairwell. 'It's a beautiful house. South-facing garden.' She gestures to an immense sash window with a stained-glass border. 'During the day the light from this window is extraordinary . . . '

If Quinn was here, he'd say, 'Did you ever think of becoming an estate agent?' DC Clegg would probably giggle and blush.

They stop outside Uma Whitmore's bedroom. Archer pictures the killer concealed in the shadows, standing in the doorway watching the sleeping girl. The furniture is Scandinavian pastel colours, mostly pink. It reminds Archer of a scene from the children's section of an IKEA catalogue. Disney princesses line the skirting boards like miniature debutantes in a large Swedish ballroom waiting for a prince to ask them to dance. Around her bed is a ring of teddy bears.

'Apparently Uma keeps the teddies there to protect her from the bogeyman.'

They failed, Archer thinks.

'Have you spoken to Uma?'

'Very briefly. We weren't really supposed to at this stage, but Shaun was keen to move fast. Anyway, it didn't turn out so well.'

'Why was that?'

'She got quite upset.'

'I'm surprised that she was interviewed so soon after the murder. Did the mother consent?'

'She did. Shaun may have persuaded her.'

'I see.'

'There's a recording. I sent it to you after you called.'

'Thank you.'

Archer stands outside Robert Whitmore's bedroom. Inside is a depressing scene. The room is stuffy and smells of unwashed sheets and stale wine.

'There was a struggle here, we believe. A bottle of wine had been consumed. The victim was attacked and murdered in bed. The covers were pulled over him, neatly as if he had been tucked in for the night. Quite creepy, if you ask me.'

'In his report, Shaun wrote that this was not a break-in.'

'That's right. It's possible a door was left unlocked or open.'

'He didn't mention which door.'

'Oh really? He's normally so thorough with his reports.'

Archer had seen no evidence of thoroughness in his report. 'He's obviously got a lot on his mind.'

'He does. Shall we go down and have a look at the door?' says DC Clegg.

The kitchen is large, gleaming and modern with a polished concrete floor and windowed doors looking over an expansive lush garden.

Clegg turns to face her with a serious expression. 'It's my opinion that the killer exited through the back and into the side alley.'

200

Archer had also considered this. 'Why do you think that?' she asks.

'Well, you wouldn't go out the front door. Someone would see you. No?'

'True.'

'Also, it's quite dark out the back and easy to sneak up the alleyway and disappear unseen.'

'Was the rear door locked or unlocked when the killer arrived?'

She thinks this over for a minute. 'It was locked when we got here, and all the windows were secured too.'

'There's no sign of forced entry. There's also a key rack by the front door with no keys on it. Seems possible the killer might have acquired a set.'

DC Clegg tilts her head. 'Oh my. I think you might be right.'

Outside the rain begins to pour.

'In his report, Shaun mentioned a neighbour who found Uma standing on the pavement early this morning.'

'That'll be Oliver Stocker.'

They hear the front door creaking open.

'Who could that be?' says DC Clegg, frowning. 'Hello!' she calls, but no one responds.

'Did you just say Oliver Stocker?' asks Archer.

'Yes. Do excuse me, I must have left the front door open.' Clegg walks to the hallway. She stops and flinches, her hand jumping to her chest. 'Oh, you gave me a fright!'

Archer wonders if Greene has made an appearance.

'Who are you? You can't be here. Oh my . . . no, please.'

A muffled gunshot fills the air. In the blink of an eye DC Clegg is knocked off her feet and onto her back. Archer freezes. A shadow appears in the door frame. Pointing a pistol fixed with a silencer is DS Jimmy Barnes.

Chapter 33

RCHER RAISES HER HANDS IN an appeasing gesture. 'What are you doing, Jimmy?'

Her eyes dart between Barnes, the silencer fixed to his pistol and the body of DC Clegg lying on the floor of the Whitmore family home. One of her shoes has fallen off, a worn sensible flat shoe, lying askew on her right foot. Despite knowing the woman for no more than ten minutes, for some unfathomable reason, Archer feels a crippling sorrow and has the urge to fix the shoe back on as if it will somehow make things better. *She'd like it if I did that.* Archer swallows, overcome with discombobulation.

'This way!' says Barnes, his voice cold, emotionless.

He beckons her into the hallway. Archer's hands curl into fists. She appraises him and realises what she has missed all this time. 'You're also working for White. You and Hicks. Two of White's undercover clowns. Both of you, Jimmy. Both of you on White's payroll. Coppers by day, robbers and murderers by night.'

'Into the hallway. Now!' he demands, unmoved by Archer's goading.

'You're good, Jimmy. I'll give you that. You had us all fooled.' Archer claps her hands slowly. 'You must be so proud.'

Despite her words, she is terrified, yet rippling through every fibre in her body is a burning, consuming fire.

'Are you going to kill me here, Jimmy, with your little gun? Or are you going to lose your nerve like Hicks did?'

'Shut up.'

'What is it with blokes like you using your little weapons to kill women? Have you any idea how pathetic you are?'

Barnes rushes at her and slams his fist hard into her face. The pain is blinding. Light appears before her eyes, her knees wobble, she crumples to the floor. Barnes grabs her by the hair and hauls her up, the gun barrel lodged in her throat. Her heart is pounding, her eye throbbing.

He turns her around, pushes her against the wall and deftly wraps a plastic tie wrap around her wrists. Her hands are secured behind her back. She's powerless.

'We're going to walk out of here and go for a little drive. You and me. I'll be an arm's length behind you with the gun pointing at your back. You make a move or cry out then it's over. Bang, bang. You're dead. Understood?'

Trembling, Archer nods.

'Good. Now move.'

Barnes switches off the kitchen light as Archer, her head spinning, steps over DC Clegg's legs. She can't help but look at her in the hope that maybe she has just a superficial injury like Quinn's. But her stomach turns. There's a bullet-sized hole in the centre of the woman's forehead. Archer looks away and moves slowly down the hallway. Barnes urges her forward with the barrel of his gun. She steps out into the wet night. The cold rain soothes the throbbing flesh and bone around her left eye. The hallway light behind her goes out. She looks across the street to see if anyone is watching. Someone who might think this suspicious and report it to the police, but there is no one. The street is quiet and empty of people. The rain is keeping people indoors.

Barnes closes the door behind them. Archer walks down the short pathway and sees Barnes's car parked across the road. Someone is sitting in the driving seat looking their way. The rear windows are tinted black.

'Where are we going?' Archer asks, a dumb ploy to maybe get him to say it out loud in case someone hears and calls it in. Unlikely, but desperate times and all that.

'Keep moving,' he says, herding her forward. He slides the gun under her coat, digging the barrel into her ribs. He opens the rear passenger door. 'Get in.'

Archer climbs inside.

'Move across,' he says, climbing in beside her.

Archer slides across. Barnes closes the door behind him.

'Let's go,' he says to driver. 'And put the locks on.'

Archer looks across at the driver and shakes her head. 'Of course it's you.' Looking back at her through the rear-view mirror is Hicks.

They drive south.

Barnes leans across and begins searching through her pockets. He takes out her phone. They are somewhere in Haggerston. Opening the window, he tosses the phone on to the road. Through the rear window Archer watches regretfully as her only lifeline skims across the damp surface and finishes up in a puddle that is about to be obliterated by the tyre of a mammoth Routemaster bus.

'Nice throw,' she says, icily.

He ignores her.

'You have no remorse, do you? You just murdered DC Clegg in cold blood. A policewoman, a wife and a mother.'

Archer catches Hicks glancing at her in the rear-view mirror, his eyebrows knotted.

'Is that what you had planned for Tanya, Dylan and Daniel too? Put a bullet in their heads if Hicks didn't toe the line.'

Barnes says nothing.

They drive through Shoreditch and turn east at Spitalfields, Archer tensing by the minute, sweating beneath her jumper.

She turns to Hicks. 'You know White's not going to let you get away with any of what's happened. He knows you bottled it and accidentally shot Harry, who, by the way, is actually doing well, not that you care.'

Neither Barnes nor Hicks respond.

'I would bet my life ... ' Archer lets out a dry laugh. 'How ironic is that? My "soon to end" life ... funny that ... anyway, I digress ... I would bet my life that as soon as Rod puts a bullet in my head, assuming of course that is why he is here, then happy chops sitting next to me puts a bullet in the head of either Tanya, Daniel or Dylan. Or all three, if he feels like it. Just to teach you a lesson, Rod. Think on that. Just chew on that when you raise your gun. Loyalty is of supreme importance to that piece of shit you work for. And trust me, he does not forgive.'

'Rod's family has nothing to worry about,' says Barnes.

Archer meets his gaze and holds it as the car stops at a red light. Barnes blinks, his mouth twitches. She looks at Rod in the rear-view mirror. 'He's lying,' she says. 'He will make an example of your family just to send a message to anyone else who might defy him.'

'I told you to shut up!' says Barnes, poking the gun barrel hard into her ribs.

They drive past Canary Wharf and onwards to the Isle of Dogs and a remote location that she doesn't recognise. Hicks parks at the rear of a large building, a warehouse perhaps. There's a yellow glow coming from a small window on the ground floor. Someone's home. Archer's belly quivers.

She hears the click of the car doors unlocking. Barnes gets out, circles round to her side, opens the door and points the pistol at her. 'Out.'

She hesitates for a moment but what's the point? She heaves herself out. It's tricky with her hands bound, but she puts her weight forward and slides out. Looking towards the lighted window, she sees a profile pass across it. A door opens, light spills outside. Framed in the doorway, wearing a long black coat, is Frankie White.

Chapter 34

'MOVE,' SAYS BARNES, TAKING ARCHER by the elbow.

She pulls away from him. 'I can walk by myself!'

The terrain is rough. Loose stone, mud and patchy grass. Is their intention to bury her here or dump her corpse in the Thames nearby? Her skin crawls at the thought of either. She thinks about Grandad alone in hospital, frightened and uncertain of what the future has in store for him. She could cry at never seeing him again. Not even having the chance to say goodbye. She thinks of Quinn too. Her colleague, her friend, the man who literally took a bullet for her. What would he think now that she had put herself in this situation? He wouldn't be impressed. *Told you to stay indoors*, he'd say. *Zelda, Maureen and Betty had you covered.*

Frankie White is watching her approach through his thick-lensed tortoiseshell glasses. He's wearing leather gloves; his white hair is combed neatly in a side parting. 'Good timing,' he says. 'The camera's all set up and ready to go.'

Archer feels her nails digging into her palms. She thinks of her father who was murdered at White's command. She thinks of the weeks she endured as an abductee of her father's killer, Bernard Morrice, the child serial killer and employee of the man standing across from her. She stares at him, hate rippling through her body like an electrical charge. The years after her father's death and Archer's abduction had been hard on her grandparents. Archer too. All because of this one man. He has so much to answer for. She feels her body shaking in rage and lunges at him, screaming. His eyes widen in surprise, he stumbles backwards. She feels Barnes's strong hands grip her shoulders and haul her back.

White gathers himself and fixes his glasses. He smiles coldly at her. 'You almost got me.' He laughs. 'You so deserve what's coming to you, my girl.'

'I'm not your fucking girl!'

'Where do you want her?' Barnes asks.

'Over there, wall behind the table.'

Barnes takes her by the arm and shoves her against the wall. The room is filthy, once a kitchen, maybe it still is, rectangular in shape, around ten feet by twenty. It stinks of rotten meat. There is a door to the right of the room, presumably leading into the warehouse. Beside it stand two waist-high cupboards, 1960s style, with a dirty stand-alone stainless-steel sink. She notices a small paring knife resting on the worktop next to a kettle and a mug. The table in front of her is covered in dried blood; a thick grubby chain lies on the floor underneath. No guesses for what happens here. Behind White is a tripod with an iPad secured onto it.

'Making your own snuff movies. No end to your talents, is there?' Archer says.

'This is one movie I will enjoy watching over and over again.'

Archer trembles and spits in his direction.

White chuckles darkly.

Hicks appears at the door, wiping the smile from White's face. The gangland boss's lips curl into a sneer. Hicks steps

210

inside, eyes down. White frowns at him. 'What have you got to say for yourself?'

Hicks hesitates before responding. 'I'd like to just get this over with. Please,' he says quietly.

'"I'd like to just get this over with. Please!"' White repeats, mimicking his voice in an affected manner. 'You and I are not done,' he adds, pointing a gloved finger at him. 'Get on with it then.' White moves to the right of the room. Barnes follows and stands next to him. Their eyes focus on Hicks. 'When you're ready,' says White.

Hicks stands on the other side of the table from Archer. He reaches into his pocket and takes out the Glock, the same gun he used to shoot Quinn. Archer's muscles coil like snakes.

White lets out a snorting laugh and says, 'Hey, Jimmy. This reminds of that time twenty years ago. You was just a whipper-snapper. I sent you to Hendon for training. Remember that?'

'I remember it well.'

'Then you was set up in Charing Cross, all smiles and charm, eager to work with everyone, including a certain someone. Remember him?'

Hicks is frowning, nervous, unsure where White is going with this.

'That would be DI Sam Archer,' says Barnes.

Archer feels a chill in her heart. Had Jimmy Barnes been involved in her father's death? She turns to Barnes, who is looking at his boss like an obedient puppy. White is looking her way, smiling.

'Correct, Jimmy,' says White. 'You had become mates. He trusted you, didn't he?'

'He did.'

Archer looks down and closes her eyes.

'I think we've hit a nerve, Jimmy.'

Shut up, please just shut up.

'Remember we was sitting in the back of my car watching little Bernard at work?'

'I remember, sir.'

'He might have been a kiddie fiddler, but he was fucking efficient all right,' says White.

Archer feels her stomach turning.

'We watched him put a bullet in Daddy Archer's head, didn't we?'

'We did.'

'You got quite the thrill, if I remember, Jimmy.'

'I didn't much like him. He was . . . full of himself.'

'A do-gooding cunt, you might say.'

'That's pretty accurate.'

Archer breathes steadily through her nose, calming the fury rising inside her.

'Get on with it, Hicks,' says White. 'Wait – the camera isn't running.' He hurries to the iPad and presses the screen. 'Action!' he cries, laughing his guttural laugh.

Archer looks at Hicks, who meets her gaze with what seems a like a lost, frightened expression. She has never seen him like this. He raises the Glock but casts his eyes downwards. He can't bring himself to look at her.

'Try and look like you're enjoying yourself for fuck's sake,' White calls to Hicks.

Archer braces herself. She has faced death before, but it's different this time. Her hands are bound behind her back, in front of *him*, and he is enjoying every minute of it. Despite her burning fury, there is just no hope. She's alone and so far from anywhere and anyone who could intervene. Desolation begins to creep in, clawing at her soul. She can't die. Not like this. Not now. She has so much to live for. Her eyes water, a tear rolls down her cheek. She says quietly, 'You don't have to do this, Rod. He will kill you. He will destroy your family.'

Hicks's eyes snap up at her.

'What'd she say?' White asks.

'I'm not sure, sir,' says Barnes.

Hicks shakes his head. His arm trembles.

'For fuck's sake get on with it!' shouts White.

'You can end this, Rod,' Archer says, desperation peppered in her voice.

He steadies his arm.

'You have the gun. You have the advantage. Save your family. Kill him.'

It feels strange saying those words out loud. It goes against everything she believes in. Everything she signed up for as a police officer. But she feels no guilt and is oddly comforted by them.

'No!' Hicks replies quietly, his head shaking. 'No.'

'Think of your family. Your boys, Rod. What would they think if they ever found out you killed another officer?'

His eyes begin to brim, his bottom lip quivers. 'My boys,' he whispers.

Archer is trembling inside, her life flashes before her: her dad, her love for him, his murder, her abduction, the death of Bernard Morrice, her grandmother's demise and death, Grandad, who looked after her for all those years, her unhappy schooling, her years as an NCA detective and her time as a DI with Harry Quinn. Everything leading to this final moment.

'Your boys deserve a hero,' Archer says.

'For fuck's sake, I knew this was a waste of time. Take her out, Jimmy,' White says to Barnes. 'And finish him off too.'

'Yes, sir.'

Terror scorches through her soul like a fever burning her from the inside out. Her eyes remain fixed on Hicks. She can hold it in no longer. 'Kill him!' she cries.

A flicker on Hicks's face. A dawning realisation. He nods at Archer, and in the blink of an eye, spins and points the gun at White's confused face. He squeezes the trigger. An explosion fills the air. Archer gasps and crouches down. It all happens so quickly. At such short range, the bullet enters Frankie White's surprised open mouth; a mist of red sprays on the wall behind him, and on Barnes's face too. Barnes pulls out his pistol and takes aim. Hicks pumps two shots, one into his neck, the other into his chest, as Barnes squeezes the trigger. Barnes blinks, clutches his neck with his free hand and shoots. The bullet goes wide and lodges in the ceiling above Hicks. Barnes stumbles and falls to his knees, eyes wide in disbelief, blood spilling from his neck.

Archer's heart is pounding. Her head is spinning. She feels as if she might be sick.

Hicks is looking down at the bodies, his arm hanging loosely by his side, the gun still gripped in his hand.

'Rod, we need help. White's men could come here any moment.'

He seems not to have heard her.

'It should be safe for them now. My boys. Tanya, too.' Tears drop from his eyes and roll down his face. 'They're safe. I hid them away, I had no choice.'

'You did the right thing. But for now, we need to phone the police. We need backup, Rod. White's men could come by at any time.'

Hicks is not listening. Reaching into his coat pocket, he takes out a phone and chucks it on the table. 'It's a burner. You can contact Tanya on this.'

Archer is unsure what's going through Hicks's mind. 'Untie me and we can fix this mess,' she says.

'It's too late for me.' He's speaking in an almost dreamy fashion. 'I'm a lousy cop. I know it . . . everyone knows it . . . '

'Rod, listen to me—'

'I want them to know I died in the line of duty.'

Archer tenses. 'What are you talking about?'

'I'm a hero to my boys, you see. But the reality is, I'm not what they think I am.'

'Don't talk like that, Rod. Untie me and give me the gun.'

'I want them to remember me as somebody good. Not the person I am. Maybe they can grow up to be better than me.' He looks across at her, his face gaunt and haunted.

Dread seizes Archer. 'Rod—'

'I'm sorry . . . for everything,' he says, placing the gun barrel in his mouth.

'Rod, no!' she cries.

He squeezes the trigger.

She gasps, turns away and shuts her eyes as the gunshot explodes through the room.

Rooted to the spot and unable to move, Archer breathes rapidly through her nose, trying her best to compose herself.

Outside, she hears the rumble of a car approaching, the tyres cracking on loose stone.

Chapter 35

ARCHER PUSHES HERSELF UP AND hurries across the kitchen, carefully stepping over Hicks's legs. With her back to the worktop, she stands on her toes, leans back, fingers frantically scrabbling for the grubby knife.

The car stops, the handbrake creaks. She hears rap music and can see the beams of the headlights shining through the open door.

The headlamps switch off. Darkness outside.

The knife is a hair's breadth from the tip of her fingers.

The car door shuts.

Archer's heart pounds in her chest. She can feel the edge of the knife but there's not enough purchase. She leans back further; pain shoots up her arms and into her shoulders. Just a little more. Her middle finger touches the blade. She presses down on it and slides it to her.

'Boss?' a man's voice calls.

'Shit!'

She eases the knife into her fingers and deftly turns it so that she is holding it by the handle. Manoeuvring the blade against the plastic tie, she begins to saw.

'Boss. Are you there?'

Her fingers are cramping. She bites down on her lip, ignoring the pain.

Footsteps approaching.

Panic hits her like a slap, she loses her confidence, the knife slips. She holds her breath as her fingers squeeze together, catching the blade as it falls. It pierces her skin, opening a stinging cut. Panting, she slides it upwards and begins sawing once more, harder this time. She feels the tie loosening and tries to pull her wrists apart but the plastic slices into her skin, tearing open the flesh. She saws faster, her face is sweating, her eyes never leaving the door.

She sees a half-silhouette looking in at the bodies of White and Barnes. 'Jesus Christ!' he says.

He has still not seen her. She is on the other side of the room. Teeth gritted, Archer pulls at the tie with all her strength.

He enters cautiously and peeks inside, a pistol in his hand. Archer recognises him. The young mixed-race guy she saw with White at Ethan's funeral. Their eyes meet. Confusion in his. She pulls at the tie with all her strength. The plastic snaps. She snatches the Glock from Hicks's still warm hand. She is weapons trained. She knows how to use a gun and can tell from the Glock's weight there is still a round, perhaps two, inside. Archer points it at the man, her breathing coming to her in rapid bursts.

'Drop the gun!' she commands.

'What the hell happened in here?' he asks, peering across at Hicks's corpse. 'This is some bad shit.'

'I won't ask you again,' Archer says.

'It's OK,' he says. 'DI Archer. My name is Toby Cullen. I work for Charlie Bates.'

Archer blinks, unsure she heard correctly. 'What?'

'I work for the NCA, undercover.'

It takes her a moment to process what he has just said. 'You work for Charlie?'

'I do.'

'Prove it.'

'Please put the gun down. You're making me nervous.'

'Prove it!' she repeats.

'If I drop mine, you drop yours,' he says placing his pistol on the tabletop. 'OK. I'm going to slowly reach into my jacket pocket and take out my phone.'

Archer keeps her eyes firmly on him as he removes a phone from his inside pocket, dials a number and places it on speaker. After three rings the call is answered. 'Everything OK?' asks Charlie Bates.

Archer lets out a breath she didn't realise she was holding. She lowers the weapon.

'Charlie, we have a situation,' says Toby.

'I'm listening,' he replies.

'Frankie White is dead.'

'What the fuck?'

'Charlie, it's Grace,' says Archer. She can hear the exhaustion in her voice.

'Grace? What's going on?'

Archer places the Glock on the table, takes a breath and tells them what happened, but leaves out her desperate cry for Hicks to kill White.

When she finishes, Charlie speaks. 'Right, first things first. I'm on my way. I'll come in with backup. We'll be there in fifteen. Toby, hang around as long as you can with Grace in case any of White's crew return. Understood?'

'Yes, Charlie.'

'Wipe down Hicks's gun. Get Grace's prints off it and get it back into Hicks's hand. Grace, the story you told me is the one we will tell everyone else with the omission of Toby, who was never there. Toby, I need you back in the field. As soon as you hear our sirens, clear out.'

'Got it,' says Toby.

'This is terrific,' says Charlie with a triumphant tone in his voice. 'We have them now. We have his network, his weapons, his drugs. It's over.'

Archer looks down at Frankie White's bloody face. The bullet had entered his mouth and probably severed his spinal cord. Broken teeth lie scattered, some on his face and on the floor. She looks away and tries to figure out if she feels relief or not. In some respects, she supposes she does. However, despite Charlie's assertion that 'It's over', she is not sure that is entirely accurate. White's life, and his reign, are certainly over. But the impact he has had on her life, Hicks's life and now Quinn's too will be felt for a long time to come.

'Toby, put me onto Grace. I want a private word,' says Charlie.

'Will do.' Toby takes the call off speaker, hands across the phone with a nod and a reassuring expression.

As Toby gets to work on cleaning Hicks's Glock, Archer places the phone to her ear. She hesitates before speaking. 'It's me, Charlie,' she says, her voice a whisper.

'How're you bearing up?'

Archer has no answer to this. Only ten minutes before her life was in the balance. 'I'm still here.'

'Amen to that. Listen to me, Grace. I know you and I know what's going through your head right now. Rod Hicks's death is not your fault. He was on a downward spiral. You did what you had to do to survive. And survive you did.'

'Four people are dead, Charlie.'

She can hear Charlie breathing heavily as he hurries. 'Grace, the world is a better place without Frankie White. We both know that. I don't know this Barnes. He wasn't on our radar. He was clearly a skilled mole. Listen, I'm sorry about Hicks and DC Clegg too. That was Barnes's doing, with White pulling the strings. Grace, it seems to me Barnes got what was coming. I'll get in touch with Islington on my way. Let them know.'

Archer closes her eyes. 'Rod Hicks . . . his family,' she says, a tremor in her voice.

'Judging by what you told me, I'd guess he's been unstable for some time.'

'I . . . I didn't know he was going to kill himself, Charlie.'

She can hear traffic down the phone. 'I know that. My car's here, Grace. I have to go. I'll be there shortly.'

'OK.'

'Take it easy. I'll see you very soon.'

Archer rubs her aching wrists, gives Toby his phone back and steps into the cold night air. She feels spots of rain on her hot face and welcomes them. Leaning on the bonnet of the car Toby has just arrived in, Frankie White's treasured Mercedes, she tries to distance herself from the events of the evening. Just a few moments. That's all she needs. She can feel a headache coming and knows it will be a banger. Aside from the glow coming from the kitchen at the rear of the warehouse, there is no light pollution. She steadies her breathing and for just a few moments, she is content to be cocooned in the darkness.

Chapter 36

ARCHER HAS BARELY SLEPT. As much as she tries not to think about them, Hicks, Barnes and White cling to her like a bad hangover.

Kill him!

Archer's words to Hicks, her instructions bellowed as a frantic final command, reverberate inside her head like a banshee's wail. She tries to push them away as she stands under the steaming shower in Quinn's bathroom. She'd decided not to return to Roupell Street, for now. Quinn is still in hospital, and despite the current dismantling of White's empire, his people are still dotted around, hiding from arrest. It remains unsafe for her. Quinn's flat has become a quiet space to think and the place she feels safest for the time being. Add to that, both Charlie and Pierce had advised her not to go back home until the dust has truly settled.

Frankie White is cold and prostrate in the mortuary with a bullet hole in his mouth and skull. But Janine is still around, and who knows what she is capable of now that both her son, Ethan, and her father are dead. There's also a more personal reason too for not returning home. Grandad is still in hospital and the house would just be empty and cold without him.

Turning off the shower, Archer steps over the tub, dries herself down with a clean towel and uses a second to dry her sodden hair. Opening the window, she lets in the cold morning air, sits on the edge of the bath and brushes her hair. The cool feels good on her hot skin. The steam evaporates, the mirror above the sink clears. She stands and looks at her tender eye, pressing it gently with her fingers. Barnes had swung a hard punch, yet the bruising is not as bad as she had expected. He had worn gloves when he entered the Whitmore house to prevent leaving prints at the scene. The glove had cushioned the blow, a small silver lining in what otherwise had been a traumatic day.

She gets dressed and calls Grandad.

His phone rings four times before he answers. 'Hello,' he says. 'It's Jake Archer speaking.' He sounds tired.

'Grandad, it's me.'

'Oh hello, dear,' he replies, his voice lifting.

'How're you feeling?'

'Much better.'

'That's good.'

She feels her eye throbbing. They say nothing for a moment.

'Are you coming to visit?'

She can't bring herself to tell him it's still not safe for her to be out on the streets at the moment. 'I can't today, Grandad. Sorry. It's a long story. Listen, I need to tell you something. It's important you hear from me first.'

'Oh . . . ' A quiver in his voice.

'First thing to know is I'm fine.'

'OK . . . '

She hesitates before telling him. 'Grandad, Frankie White is dead.'

Silence. She hears his steady breathing. After a moment he asks, 'How?'

'I can't say for now. The investigation is underway. But please keep this to yourself for the time being.'

'I understand. Were you there when it happened?'

Her grip on the phone tightens. She closes her eyes. 'Yes,' she replies quietly.

'Are you hurt?'

'No.'

She hears him sniffing followed by the quiet sound of weeping.

'It's over, Grandad. It's over.'

She had spent the morning trying to catch up with admin. Quinn had called, having heard the news from Pierce. She told him what she'd said to Grandad, leaving out the sordid details.

Her phone rings. It's Charlie.

'I'm outside,' he tells her. 'Are you free?'

'Come up.'

Five minutes later, he's standing outside Quinn's flat, panting, his face red. 'Those bleedin' stairs will be the death of me.' Despite this, he smiles, opens his arms and embraces her. 'Thank Christ you're OK.'

She hugs him back, grateful for the affection, which she has not had a lot of recently. 'Come in,' she says, extracting herself. 'Can I get you a drink?'

'Coffee, ta.'

Charlie follows her into the kitchen, where she boils the kettle.

'How're you doing?' he asks.

Archer shrugs as she lifts the cafetière from the drainer and drops three scoops of Quinn's special blend into the jug. 'I don't know how to feel anything right now.'

Charlie nods his head. 'No one should have to see what you saw yesterday.'

Archer is still holding the cafetière and plastic scoop. The kettle boils but she barely notices. 'Four people died, Charlie.

225

I watched as their lives ended abruptly.' She frowns as she tries to wrap her head around it. 'DC Clegg ... Rod ... '

'None of it was your fault. You must remember that, Grace.'

She places the cafetière on the worktop, pours the hot water into it and puts the press on top. She opens a cupboard door and lifts out two mugs. She sighs. 'He was going to kill me. Hicks. That's why he was there. White had threatened his family.'

'But he didn't. You're still here, thank Christ.'

Archer is only half listening. 'I could see that he was troubled. That he was conflicted. He didn't want to shoot me but what choice did he have? What choice would anyone make in that situation?' She pushes down on the press. 'I told him he didn't have to do this. I told him to think of his boys. I ... I told him to kill Frankie White.' Archer pauses, her hands resting on the lid of the coffee jug. 'And he did. Just like that. He put a bullet in Frankie White's face and then two in Jimmy Barnes. He saved me.' She sighs heavily once more. 'And then he turned the gun on himself.' She dips her head and closes her eyes.

'I'm so sorry, Grace,' says Charlie.

She feels his arms wrap around her again. Leaning into his coat, she feels her shoulders shaking. Her eyes begin to sting as they well with tears.

'Just let it all out,' says Charlie, squeezing her. 'Let it out.'

Part 3

Chapter 37

TOMMY McKENNA IS A CUMBERSOME piece of shit. A wriggling, sobbing, good-for-nothing whale of a man. His thick lips and uncouth mouth are bound in duct tape. His meaty wrists and ankles too. Hauling him down the stairs by said ankles is testing his stamina. But that's a minor complication. He has strength in reserve and an unstoppable purpose.

At the bottom, he hooks his arms around McKenna's elephantine knees, hoists them up and spins him around the narrow hallway so that the soles of his feet face the kitchen and the rear of the house. Gripping his ankles once more, he drags McKenna across the rough carpet and down the step to the stone tiles of the kitchen floor. His quarry's head slams against the step. He roars angrily through the layers of tape, his face crimson in the kitchen's half-light.

The door to the garden is open, rain is falling in sheets outside. Four slugs escaping the cold have crawled into the kitchen, their shiny trails criss-crossing his path. He watches them with interest for a moment. Dropping McKenna's feet, he bends over, picks them up and places them in the palm of his gloved hand. He pokes and strokes them, enjoying their writhing confusion. Crouching beside McKenna, he looks down at him and affects a sad expression. McKenna stares back at him, his eyes brimming wide with terror.

Gently, he lifts one of the slugs with his thumb and index finger and hovers it over McKenna's face. The man's eyes dart from the slug to his. He shakes his head rapidly and lets out a muffled, 'Noooo!'

One by one, he places the slugs on McKenna's face, allowing them the freedom to crawl over his nose, eyes and ears. Cocking his head, he admires the writhing orgy upon the man's face.

McKenna stares at him in disbelief.

Shrugging, he pushes on. Switching off the kitchen light, he drags McKenna out into the garden and the rain, pleased that the man's bulk slides effortlessly across the sludgy, wet surface. The alder tree looms ahead, its craggy, muscular branches folding out like a giant's embrace.

He unhooks the rope from his belt and tosses the noose end over a branch almost ten feet above him. More muffled cries from McKenna, who has caught sight of the noose hanging from the branch. He shakes and kicks at him, writhing in the mud like a giant slug on speed.

Crouching down, he spins McKenna around so that his head is at the base of the tree. The man tries to slither from him, but his bonds are strong and tight, and he isn't going anywhere. He straddles McKenna, sitting on his thick comfy thighs. Three of the slugs have slid from his face to his chest but one remains clinging on to his stubby nose.

The rain stops. From the pocket of his coat, he takes out the roll of duct tape. McKenna's shoulders are heaving, he is crying.

He tapes the remainder of his head and face, takes out the marker and draws a sad smiley on the man's face. Looping the noose over McKenna's neck, he tightens it. The man begins to squirm and shake but he is fast and runs to the other side of the rope, gripping it with his strong, gloved hands. Using all his strength, he pulls and pulls, lifting the choking McKenna higher and higher until the tips of his toes wriggle for purchase on the muddy surface.

His eyes flash in wonderment and he leans back, pulling harder and further. There is a half-built fence with a wooden frame fixed into a concrete perimeter. He loops the rope around a tall stake and ties it firmly. Tommy McKenna's large body jerks violently. Piss runs down his leg and feet and drips to the ground. Seconds pass, his body is calm, he sways gently in the breeze like the pendulum of a grandfather clock.

Returning to the kitchen, he hears McKenna's phone ping. A message from *the missus*.

On my way home. Had a few too many. Pissed.

He types a return message:

See you laters. Ta ta. X

She is typing back.

Ta ta??? You're such a twat! LOL

Fifteen minutes later, he hears a taxi pull up outside. Peeking through the blinds of McKenna's bedroom, he sees Lowri McKenna stumble on all fours out of an Uber, heels off and in her hand, a glittery handbag in the other. She mutters something he can't hear and staggers away from the car towards the house. The driver gets out and shuts the door, shaking his head at her.

He hears the key punching at the keyhole downstairs. She can't quite get it in. She calls Tommy's name several times through the letter box before trying the key again. Eventually, she succeeds and falls into the hallway. Slamming the door behind her, he hears her throw down her shoes and bag. She stumbles up the stairs and into the bedroom. The light goes on.

'Oi, Tommy, are you sleeping?'

A cocktail of aromas fill the bedroom: sour wine, stale sweat, cheap perfume, cigarettes. He watches her clumsily pull off her dress, stripping down to her bra and pants. She waddles down to the toilet, where she pees and breaks wind. *Charming.* She is coming back, her arms reaching against the walls, helping her stay upright.

'Why's it so muddy in here?' she slurs. 'It's fucking filthy. What's going on, Tommy?'

She perches on the edge of the bed, belches and drops her head into her hands. After a moment, she says: 'Fucking hell!' And bolts down the hall to the toilet, where she throws up. He hears water running. She brushes her teeth, rinses and spits. He hears her returning. She tugs at the duvet cover. He is underneath and gripping it tight.

'Stop messin' around, Tommy. I'm knackered!'

She pulls and pulls but he holds on, waiting for his moment. 'Tommy!' she yells.

He eases his grip. She yanks the duvet off him.

Her mouth drops open. She blinks.

He beams at her.

Her eyes widen, her face frowns and twists into a terrified expression. She screams. He leaps from the bed and pushes the taser into her throat, releasing a powerful charge. Yelping, she falls to the floor, shaking. Taking the tape from his coat pocket, he wraps it tightly around her head and neck. In moments, she begins to shake and thrash. He holds her still.

She struggles for breath as the tape shrinks onto her mouth and nose. In moments she is still.

Lifting her from the floor, he places her in the bed. He tucks her under the covers and pats her head gently. From his coat pocket, he removes a black marker and draws a sad expression on the tape.

He returns to the garden and stands as still as a statue, enjoying the gentle sway of McKenna's bulk. The branch holding his weight creaks in protest. He feels nothing, other than pleased with his work.

He hears something smash like a glass breaking, and a gasp. In the rear window of the house on the adjoining garden, someone is looking his way. It's time to go. He turns and runs, leaping over the fence, disappearing into the night.

Chapter 38

THREE DAYS HAD PASSED SINCE Charlie had visited her at Quinn's flat. She had spent the time catching up on admin and getting her head together. It's early morning, and she is in Quinn's living room, sifting through reports.

She startles at the sound of keys rattling and the flat door being pushed open. Her eyes scan the space for something to use as a weapon.

'Hello,' comes Quinn's voice.

Relief washes over her. She exhales and steps into the hallway.

Quinn closes the door, jacket folded over his arm, a small white carrier bag in his hand. 'Honey, I'm home,' he says in a sing-song manner. His hair is untidy, he is unshaven, tired-looking.

'Yes, you are,' Archer replies, grinning and happy to see him.

'Couldn't stay at that place any longer. Too depressing.'

'Hospitals are never fun.'

'Ain't that the truth.' Quinn hangs his coat in the hallway cupboard.

'How are you feeling?' she asks.

'Better.' He holds up the plastic bag, 'Got some meds to see me along.'

He makes his way up the hall. Archer looks at the side of his head. The scar is neatly stitched but still raw. 'Does it hurt?'

'Only when I'm headbanging. Otherwise, it's manageable.'

'Best you take it easy with your choice in music then.'

'Good advice.' Narrowing in on her eye, he arches his brows. 'I've seen worse.'

Archer shrugs.

'I'm sorry about what happened. I wish I'd been there.'

'I'm glad you weren't. Barnes would have killed you. Besides, you took a bullet for me. I forgive you.'

'I still can't believe Rod did what he did . . . '

The memory of Hicks's haunted expression, the gun barrel in his mouth, flashes in her mind. *Kill him!* Archer thinks and shifts on her feet.

'Clare told me, by the way.'

'I know. Sorry I didn't tell you first. I had a lot to process.'

'Don't sweat it. I completely understand.'

'Despite my chequered relationship with Rod, I can't help but feel so sad for him, his family, especially,' says Archer.

'It sucks for Tanya and the kids. It really does. As for Rod himself, I have less sympathy. He knew what he was getting into.'

'Clare said she wanted to keep his involvement and his suicide under wraps. I agree with her. It's bad enough with two officers working for White. And one of them killing another. The press would crucify us. The public would lose confidence.'

'DC Clegg?'

'He didn't hesitate. Just put a bullet in her brain.' Archer shudders. 'Her kids have no mother now.'

'Jimmy Barnes . . . How did we not see that?'

'He was good at hiding it. Had years of practice. He stayed way under the radar in the Met, which is why no one suspected.'

'Jimmy was always the cop people wanted to be mates with. A gentleman to the ladies and one of the boys for the blokes.'

'White said that Jimmy had been working for him since he joined the Met twenty years ago.'

'I still can't get my head around that. Jimmy and I go way back.'

'He betrayed my dad. He watched him die.'

'I know.'

'It's over for him now.'

'How're you doing, in yourself?' Quinn asks.

'I'm still figuring it all out. It hasn't quite registered that White is actually gone . . . ' *Kill him!* Her cry to Hicks to finish White echoes once more through her mind. She feels a chill and rubs her arm.

'I know. Could any of us have predicted that he would come a cropper from a shot fired by a gun-wielding Hicks?'

'The last thing any of us could have predicted.'

Quinn's face scrunches.

'Are you all right?' Archer asks.

'Might be time for my pills. Also, I might grab a shower.'

'Good idea. Can I get you a coffee and something to eat?'

'Maybe just a coffee.'

'I'll sort it out.'

'Thanks, Grace.'

In the kitchen, Archer boils the kettle and prepares the coffee. She hears a knock on the flat door. Quinn ducks his damp head into the kitchen. 'If that's the "crime busters", I'm not here,' he says, zipping quickly into the bedroom.

'Understood.'

She makes her way to the front door and peers through the peephole. Zelda, Maureen and Betty are gathered outside. She opens the door. 'Hey, I was just leaving.'

'Where is he?' asks an expectant Zelda.

'Who're we talking about?'

'We're the eyes, ears and noses of the block, my dear,' says Zelda, pointing to her eyes and ears. 'We know he's in there.' She points into the flat.

'Zelda . . . '

'We'd better come in,' Zelda says and pushes her way past.

'Morning,' says Betty as she gives Archer an informal air-kiss.

Maureen is last. She takes stock of Archer, frowns at her bruised eye and leans across, embracing her with strong arms. 'God, you two has been through it all right.'

'Come in, Maureen.'

'Don't mind if I do.'

'Take a seat in the living room, everyone. I'll see if he's ready.'

Quinn appears dressed at the bedroom door.

'Sorry,' says Archer.

'No worries. I heard everything. On my way.'

'I'll bring your coffee.'

She hears the women fussing over him as she carries the mug down to the living room.

'The news is about to start,' says Maureen, brandishing the television remote control.

Quinn is sitting on the sofa flanked by Betty and Zelda, who is half watching the television, half staring at the scar on the side of his head.

'Will the hair grow back?' she asks.

'I don't think so, Zel,' he replies. 'Rest assured, there'll be enough hair to cover it.'

'It hasn't ruined your looks too much. You can still claim yourself a trophy wife, when the time comes.'

'That's the dream, Zel.'

Archer catches his eye and smiles.

Maureen points at the television. 'Here. It's coming on now.'

A picture of Frankie White appears on the screen. The sight of him makes Archer's skin crawl. The news anchor begins his summary: *'The National Crime Agency has confirmed the connection between the bombing of* The Pride of Elizabeth *on the Thames and the recently deceased Frankie "Snow" White, a businessman with links to organised crime, violence, money laundering, county lines drugs and weapon importation. More on that to follow. Also, in conjunction with the Metropolitan Police, they have seized a further consignment of Class A drugs to the value of £800,000. A shipment of Colombian cocaine was found in a warehouse in south London. This is in addition to the haul of heroin valued at £900,000 and the arsenal of illegal weapons discovered yesterday in a warehouse in the Isle of Dogs. Both properties belonged to Mr White. Eleven more arrests have been made today, including Janine White, the daughter of the deceased crime boss. That brings the total to thirty-one . . .'*

'Bravo!' Zelda says.

'Strange to think all this is going on around us and under our noses,' says Maureen.

Quinn reduces the television volume. 'I think we've heard enough of that. Listen, ladies, Grace and I need to shoot and start catching the bad guys again.'

'We just wanted to check in on you and make sure you're OK,' says Zelda.

'Thank you. I'm doing just fine.'

'What's a county line?' Betty asks.

Zelda pushes herself up. 'I'll explain later, Bets. We should get going and let these two get back to it. Although I do think you should take at least another two weeks off, Harry. You too,

Grace. With his stitched-up head and your black eye, you're like the walking wounded.'

A murmur of agreement from Maureen and Betty.

'That'd be nice. But we're now two men down and double the workload.'

'We can help,' says Betty. 'We have experience now.'

'Aye. I'll put a word in with the governor. See what she says.'

'Ooh, marvellous. That's exciting.'

Zelda rolls her eyes. 'If they recruit you into the police, we're all truly doomed.'

Maureen laughs. Betty purses her lips.

Archer sees them to the door. 'Thanks for popping in.'

'Look after him. And yourself.'

'I'll do my best. Bye, all.' She closes the door.

'Grace, quick, come and see this,' calls Quinn.

Archer enters the living room at the tail end of a breaking news report. A news helicopter is filming the scene of a police investigation in a cul-de-sac in Bermondsey.

'... *the man's body was found hanging from a tree in his back garden. A second body is also believed to have been discovered inside the house. That's as much as we know for now. We will release more information as it comes in.*'

Quinn is on his phone, searching the internet. His eyes widen. 'Shit,' he says, handing the device to Archer. 'A neighbour took this photo this morning and posted it online.'

Archer feels her stomach twisting. The photo depicts a large man dressed only in his underwear, hanging by the neck from a tree. Wrapped tightly around his face is a mask of duct tape with a smudged smiley face drawn upon it.

Archer looks at Quinn. 'Are you serious about returning to work?'

'One hundred per cent.'

240

'We need to go to Bermondsey. Are you good to go now?'

'I have meds, try and stop me.'

'I'll call Marian. We need to bring Oliver Stocker in. He's our number-one suspect.'

Chapter 39

'WAKE UP, BRYNN. IT'S TIME for school.'

Brynn blinks his eyes open and peers up from under the blankets keeping him warm on Mrs Toolan's sofa. She is smiling down at him, a brown towel draped over her arm. Wearing paisley slippers, a thick cotton nighty and a fleece dressing gown, the woman is five foot five tall and almost the same in width, according to Iris anyway. Brynn smells toast and hears the kettle boiling.

'Iris is making breakfast, God help us. Do you want to get ready and meet us in the kitchen?'

'Thank you, Mrs Toolan, I'm really grateful I am.'

She hands him the towel. 'The bathroom's empty if you want to go in and do your business.'

Since the incident with Dad two days ago, Brynn has stayed with Mrs Toolan and Iris, sleeping on the sofa and keeping out of his way. After a quick shower, he gets dressed and enters the kitchen, tucking his shirt into his school trousers. There is a burning smell in the air. Iris smiles at him. He smiles back and sits opposite her.

'How did you sleep?' Iris asks.

'OK,' he replies.

'Did you have any dreams?' she asks with a furtive wink.

'Erm . . . ' He feels his face going hot and slides his gaze to Mrs Toolan, who is looking at the plateful of blackened toast. That explained the smell.

'I don't know how you managed to burn all the toast, Iris,' says Mrs Toolan.

Iris holds up her slender hands. 'These babies were not made for hard labour.'

'I wouldn't say making toast is hard labour, dear,' says Mrs Toolan.

Iris stretches her arms across the table and turns her hands gracefully. 'Brynn said I could be a hand model one day.'

'Did he now?' says Mrs Toolan, with a smirk on her face.

'Did I?' says Brynn, with no recollection of saying any such thing.

'You have your mother's hands,' says Mrs Toolan. 'Not like mine.' She holds up hers and wriggles them. 'Mine are like sausages sticking out of two pork pies. Then again, I never was much to look at.'

'We can't all be beautiful, Aunty Jean,' says Iris.

Mrs Toolan chuckles. 'I learned that lesson a long time ago.' She pats her chest. 'But you know what I say, beauty on the inside is where it really counts.'

'Love you as much as I do, Aunty Jean, but I have to tell you that this notion of beauty on the inside where it matters is so overrated and outdated.'

Mrs Toolan snorts a laugh. 'Yes, dear, beauty on the outside is what really matters.'

'Thank you.' Iris grins at him.

'Do you know what they used to call me and your mum when we was kids?' says Mrs Toolan.

'Yes. But I still have no idea who *they* are,' says Iris, rolling her eyes.

244

Mrs Toolan turns to him. 'Brynn, you must. Have you heard of Laurel and Hardy?'

Brynn thinks the names sound familiar but can't picture their faces. 'I'm not sure.'

'Anyway, that's what they called us. It was cruel. Especially for me, being heavier and all.'

'People can be cruel, Mrs Toolan,' Brynn says. 'Other kids. Parents . . . fathers. Just, cruel.'

A silence falls over the table.

Mrs Toolan reaches across and squeezes his hand. 'I'm so sorry, Brynn.'

He squirms inside, unused to any sort of affection. Iris is watching him. He looks away.

'Is your mum living with another bloke?' Iris asks.

'Iris!' says Mrs Toolan in alarm. 'That's none of our business.'

'I'm only saying what you told me.'

Brynn does not look up. 'Yes. She is.'

He senses a change in the atmosphere at the table and imagines Mrs Toolan giving Iris daggers. He sighs. What does it matter?

Mrs Toolan changes the subject. 'I just wanted to say, Brynn, that I spoke to your dad this morning, while you were sleeping. I popped out to get some milk and bumped into him in the shop. He'd been out most of the night. He woke me in the early hours as it happens. I told him that too. Where does he go to at night? Does he have another job?'

'He does security work, checking in on buildings for a few hours each night. Something like that. He doesn't ever say much to me.'

'And he's a builder too. I don't know where he gets the strength to do two jobs.'

Brynn has never really given this much thought.

'Anyway, I told him you were with me. He said he knew that. He asked how you were. I told him you were fine. He said you were to go home. I told him you'd go home when you was ready. He didn't like that, but I wasn't having any of his nonsense.'

Brynn casts his gaze downwards. He had pushed any thoughts of returning home from his head despite knowing that he'd have to go back sometime soon. Mrs Toolan's hospitality was never going to be a long-term solution.

'That's OK. I'll go home today after school, I will.'

'Please don't feel you need to rush back to your dad's.'

'It's fine. Honestly, Mrs Toolan, I'll be fine.'

'Only if you're sure.'

Brynn nods. 'I'm sure.'

Brynn and Iris walk in silence to the train station, sharing a fag, a film of drizzle coating their faces, hair and anoraks.

'Sorry about your mum and all,' says Iris.

Brynn dips his head. 'S'OK.'

'Do you miss her?'

Brynn nods.

'Can't you go live with her?'

'She doesn't want me.'

'Oh . . . '

Brynn takes a long draw from the cigarette, inhaling the bitter smoke into his lungs and exhaling quickly.

'Do you—'

'I'd rather not talk about her.'

'Sorry.'

Brynn pushes any thoughts of his mum from his head and is overcome with a glumness and sense of dread at the thought of returning to live with his dad after school. He refocuses and allows his mind to drift into fantasy as he imagines running away and following his dream.

'You're smiling,' says Iris, breaking him out of his fugue.

'Am I?'

'Not anymore.'

The butterflies have returned to his tummy.

'What were you thinking about?' she asks.

He shrugs. 'Nothing much.'

They're approaching Abbey Wood Station and close to merging with the melee of school kids and commuters.

Iris loops her arm under his and pulls him to her. 'Tell me!' she says.

Despite not being used to affection it's different with Iris. It feels good to be close to her, to melt into her warmth, her flowery scent.

'It's one of those clichés, I suppose. For as long as I can remember, I've wanted to run away from home – get away from my fighting parents ... my dad ... '

'And join a circus?' Iris asks.

Brynn pauses and looks at her. 'Have I told you this already?'

'No, you haven't, Brynn Hughes. It just so happens you and I are cut from the same cloth. We're two souls brought together as one. That's what we are.' She exhales the last of the cigarette and drops the butt on the station steps.

'Do you want to join the circus?' he asks.

Iris looks to the distance with a dreamy expression. 'I'd want to be a trapeze artist. Dressed in a sexy red and black corset, I'd swing from trapeze to trapeze, flying over the heads of my admirers and haters, performing a beautiful sky ballet of gorgeousness. My admirers would desire me more and my haters would be even more jealous. But I wouldn't care because

I'd be up there, alone like a beautiful bird uncaged for the first time.'

Brynn smiles. 'I like that.'

'What about you?'

Brynn looks down at his feet. 'Don't laugh.'

'I won't.'

'I just want to become someone else. Someone who isn't me. Someone popular. Someone who is fun. The circus could do that for me. I could be that person in another costume. I could wear it and become someone else. Someone who could make people laugh. I'm ... I'm not that person though.'

'You make me laugh.'

'Do I?'

Iris shrugs. 'Sometimes. You could do more though. I can help you.'

Brynn considers this for a moment. 'Really? But how?'

'I don't know. I'm sure there's a book we can find in the library or something.'

'You'd really do that?'

She grins at him. 'I will be the making of you, Brynn Hughes.'

Their train arrives at the platform. They hurry through the crowds and the turnstile, melding with the commuters as they pour into the carriages. Brynn and Iris stand together in a busy corridor, leaning against the wall and each other for support.

'Maybe we can look for a trapeze book too?' says Brynn.

Her face darkens. 'I don't think so.'

'If I can, you can too.'

'It's only a dream for me.'

'But why?'

'You know why.'

Brynn is confused. 'But ... '

'It's because I'm Epi-Iris!'

'Don't say that name. I don't like it.'

'Do you think I do?'

'No . . . but what difference would that make?'

Iris sighs. 'Because I could just flip at any moment. Like now, for instance, I could go into one. My eyes could roll back in my head, my body would start shaking and I'd fall to the ground. Picture the scene: me flying over the heads of my admirers and haters. Suddenly, the epi-switch flicks and they watch on, some in fear, others in pleasure, as the beautiful, uncaged bird falls to her death through the air like a trembling brick.'

'Oh.'

They stand in silence for a moment.

'I'm sorry,' he says.

Iris shrugs. 'It's OK. It's my life, I'm used to it. It wasn't always like this. Did I tell you how I became this way?' Brynn is about to say no but she doesn't wait for an answer. 'It's my parents' fault. They was fighting for a change. Arguing and screaming at each other. Trouble is, we was in the car driving. Dad was driving and we had an accident. I wasn't wearing a seat belt and flew from the back of the car and hit the windscreen. I was only nine. I had terrible head injuries. Nineteen stitches and hundreds of seizures ever since.'

Iris's eyes begin to water.

'They never cared much for me. Still don't,' she says. 'All they think about is themselves and who wins the argument.'

Brynn reaches across and takes her hand. She squeezes it and looks deeply into his eyes. 'Tomorrow, we're going to the library,' she says. 'I may not be able to live my dream, but you can live yours.'

Chapter 40

T HE SIO IS AT THE scene, a seasoned Bermondsey DI called Angela Carver, blocks their approach to the house, a shabby modern terrace with a large, rusted satellite dish situated above a bedroom window. A white CSI tent covers the entrance. Dressed in a forensic suit, Carver is a stern-looking woman of colour with a strong jawline and a sharp buzz cut. Archer introduces herself and Quinn.

'I heard you were coming,' she says, her brows knitted in a frown.

'It's not our intention to step on toes,' says Archer.

'It seems I may not have a choice.'

'It's our belief these murders may be connected to our current investigation.'

'Krish mentioned that.'

'He's here?'

'Just finishing up.'

'The other victims were found with their heads wrapped in duct tape and a smiley face drawn on them.'

'You'd better suit up,' she says.

As Archer and Quinn pull on their PPE, DI Carver gives them a run-down. 'We believe the victims are Thomas and Lowri McKenna. Mr McKenna was home alone last night, it seems. Neighbours reported Mrs Kenna returning home drunk in an Uber at around two o'clock this morning. She had difficulty getting access to the house. She shouted through the letter box, banged the door, but eventually managed to get her key in and open it herself. One neighbour said this is not unusual. And as you mentioned, both victims have taped-up heads with a smiley face drawn on them.'

Archer zips up her suit and pulls over the hood. 'Who found the bodies?'

'A neighbour called the police. He saw someone watching the swaying body of Mr McKenna.'

'Did he recognise this person?' Quinn asks.

'No. He ran away as soon as he knew he was being watched. Let's go in,' says Carver.

The house is cold inside, the damp morning air flows through the gap in the tent and out to the kitchen and rear garden, where another tent has been erected. Stepping across the forensic floor tiles, Archer notices a discarded pair of heels and a glittery handbag lying on the hall floor with numbered labels next to them.

'We'll go upstairs first,' says Carver. 'You can see muddy prints on the carpet where the perpetrator came in from the garden. Krish will make an imprint of those for shoe size and type.'

Archer climbs the stair plates. Carver leads them down a small hallway to a bedroom where the body of a woman is being placed and zipped into a black body bag.

'We cut the tape from her head.'

'Can we see it?'

'It's in a sealed evidence bag. Krish has videoed the removal. So, this room is where I believe it started for Mr McKenna and ended for Mrs McKenna. I think the killer got access to the house . . . '

'Are there signs of a break-in?' Quinn asks.

'None. Either the back door was left open, or the perpetrator had keys. That's yet to be determined. Anyway, the killer makes his way upstairs while McKenna is sleeping, tasers him, tapes his arms and legs while he's out of action, and drags him downstairs and out to the garden. McKenna is a big man so whoever did it is strong.'

'Is it just the two of them that live here?'

'No. They're fostering a teenager called Kirsty May. She was at a sleepover with a friend last night.'

'Has anyone spoken to her?'

'My officers are with her now.'

'Do you think the killer knew McKenna was alone?' Archer asks.

'Because of the way they died I'm inclined to say yes. But who knows? If both Mr and Mrs McKenna had been home together maybe they would still be alive.'

Archer doubts that. This killer has his modus operandi in place. He knows how he wants them to die and how their bodies will be discovered.

'There is no sign of the killer being in any other room upstairs,' says Carver. She leads them back downstairs. 'So he dragged McKenna down here, through the kitchen.' They are out in the garden, where a handful of CSI and police officers are assessing the scene. Carver points to a muddy trail leading to the alder tree at the end of the garden. 'There are footprints and a long drag mark in the ground suggesting McKenna was hauled across to the tree. His back is covered in mud and grass, which backs up that theory.'

Krish Anand emerges from the tent, carrying an iPad, and looks towards them. 'Be with you in a moment,' he says. He speaks quickly to one of his team before joining them.

'How're you both doing?'

'We're still alive,' says Archer.

'You dodged a bullet, Harry.'

'Kinda took it but not all the way, if you know what I mean.'

'I do. I'm relieved you're both OK.'

'What's your conclusions?' Archer asks.

'It'll come as no surprise that this has all the hallmarks of the Whitmore and Todd murders. The killer enters the home, tasers his victims, tapes them up and suffocates them with those charming smiley faces. The only difference between the four victims is Thomas McKenna, who died from hanging.'

Archer considers this.

'Maybe your killer is just getting into his groove,' says Carver.

'Possibly. Or maybe he really had it in for McKenna,' says Archer.

'So they knew each other,' says Quinn.

'Or had some sort of contact,' Archer replies.

'Are you certain it's only one person?' Carver asks.

'There's no indication of anyone other than the McKennas and the killer being here last night,' says Krish.

Archer turns to Carver. 'DI Carver, we will need to take control of this investigation.'

Carver nods.

'We really appreciate everything you've done.'

'No worries. I'll have my people write up our reports and get everything processed as soon as possible. If you need anything from me, you can contact me at Bermondsey.'

'I appreciate that. Thank you, Angela.'

Chapter 41

A DESOLATE MOOD HANGS OVER CHARING Cross Police Station. Archer has the sense it's like a final curtain call in a tragic play without the applause. Her colleagues are still in shock at the loss of two of their own. The details around Barnes and his connection with Frankie White have remained under wraps for now. There are whispers in corridors, different theories float around about Hicks and his partner. Some say they were shot by the police. Others say they were shot by White's men. Speculation is rife. Archer says nothing. DCI Pierce plans to make a statement in due course, once the NCA compile their findings.

Archer's team is severely diminished. DC Mel Anderson has been assigned to help with Barnes and Hicks's workload. The remainder are gathered in the incident room. Quinn, DC Marian Phillips and Klara Clark are all she has left. DCI Clare Pierce is present for the update.

Archer briefs them, bringing them up to speed with the McKenna house and what they discovered. She lays photographs of the victims on the table. Two sets: one with the duct tape on their heads, one without. A sombre ambience quietens the room as the team take in the pictures. A moment passes and Archer breaks the silence. 'There's a connection between Jason Todd and Robert Whitmore. That connection is Oliver

Stocker. What, if any, his connection to the McKennas is we have yet to determine. Harry and I will make that our priority. Following this meeting we're interviewing Stocker. We'll update you if there's anything to follow up on. Klara, what do you have?'

'Still nothing on similar murders. I read over Krish's report that just came in. The footprints in Jason Todd's flat from the night of the murder. They're a size nine Dr Martens boot or shoe. Jason Todd didn't own a pair. There are none in his flat.'

'The killer left footprints at the McKenna house too,' says Quinn.

'Schoolboy error,' says Phillips.

'Or he doesn't care,' says Archer.

'I looked into the McKennas while you were on your way back,' says Klara. 'Tommy McKenna, forty-two, was a builder. Lowri McKenna was a teaching assistant. Neither had children, but they did foster them. They were looking after a teenager named Kirsty May. She was staying at a friend's last night.'

'Where is she now?'

'She's gone into care with another family.'

'Do you know where?'

'I'm looking into it.'

'Thanks, Klara.' Archer turns to DC Phillips. 'What else do we have, Marian?'

'Apologies. I'm still catching up since Mel shifted across. Getting there though. In terms of our original cast of neighbours and lovers as suspects, they all have alibis for Jason Todd's and Robert Whitmore's murder. Except for Oliver Stocker, who was home alone, so he says, the night Todd was murdered. He has no one to back up that story. Also, Mel and I combed through the social media accounts, and I'm afraid at this stage, there's still nothing. Regarding the Whitmores, Christine

Whitmore has returned from her business trip and is looking after her daughter.'

'Did you meet with Mrs Whitmore?'

'Very briefly. As you can imagine, she's in shock. She isn't aware of anyone who would do this to her husband. He was ordinary. Not involved in anything illegal, as far as she knows.'

'OK, keep digging. There might be something. Also, I'd like you to lead a door-to-door in and around the cul-de-sac where the McKennas lived. Take two uniforms with you and find out what you can. We have a statement from a witness who saw the killer. He's a tourist named Mr Miguel Lopez, who's staying with a friend in a flat overlooking the garden. Make it a priority to talk to him again, see if anything was missed. I'll text you the address he's staying at.'

'Sounds like a plan.'

'Harry and I will check in with the McKennas' work colleagues. See what we can find out. Any questions?'

There are none.

'OK, everyone,' says Archer. 'That's all for now. Good luck and if anything comes up, send it to our WhatsApp group.'

The team stand and begin to shuffle their way to the door.

'One last thing,' Archer calls. 'Some homework for our next meeting. I want you to think about why the killer would suffocate his victims by wrapping their heads and faces in duct tape. And why draw a smiley face. Come back with your ideas.'

Oliver Stocker is sitting in the interview room, fingers knotted together, hands resting on the table in front of him. Seated next to him is his brief, an owl-like man called Hodson.

'What exactly is my client here for?' asks Hodson.

'Just to answer a few questions. Nothing more,' Quinn replies.

Stocker shifts in his chair, as he takes in Archer's bruised eye and Quinn's head wound.

'Don't mind us,' says Quinn. 'We had a run-in with the last person we interviewed.'

Stocker swallows.

'How well did you know Jason Todd?' Archer asks.

Stocker considers the question before answering. 'We weren't friends, if that's what you're asking.'

'So you didn't like him?' says Quinn.

'I didn't say that.'

'It's fair to say you and Jason didn't see eye to eye.'

Stocker looks at his brief, who nods his head.

'We weren't friends,' he repeats.

'Did you ever have an argument, or a fight?' Quinn asks.

'Certainly not.'

From a folder on the table, Quinn removes a sheet of paper with the printed text of Jason Todd's text to Stocker. 'We have a text from Jason Todd to you. Let me read it for you: "Fuck you, fucknuts! Who do you think you are telling me how and when to speak to my wife? Fuck right off! We may be separated but that could change tomorrow. She still loves me – don't you get it? She doesn't care about you. You're just a convenience—"'

'OK, OK!' says Stocker. 'What does that prove?'

'That you didn't like him? Even perhaps hated him for what he said to you.'

'Jason was hot-headed. Everyone knew. He had a drink problem. Penny had told me all about that.'

'She still had a thing for him, didn't she?' says Quinn. 'That must have hurt.'

'You're barking up the wrong tree, Detective Sergeant Quinn. I did not kill Jason Todd.'

'Mr Stocker, tell me about Robert Whitmore,' says Archer.

Stocker shrugs. 'What about him?'

'He's your neighbour, yes?'

'That's correct.'

'How well did you know him?'

'As well as I know my other neighbours. We weren't friends. We weren't enemies. We never had a run-in. And I didn't kill him either.'

'It's just odd that the only connection between the murders of Jason Todd and Robert Whitmore is you,' says Quinn.

'Can you explain why that might be?' adds Archer.

'It's a coincidence. Nothing more. I have nothing to do with either of those men's murders. Nothing!'

From the file, Archer removes a photo she had printed from Facebook. She slides it across the table. 'Do you know these people?'

Stocker leans over for a closer look. He frowns. 'No.'

'Their names are Thomas McKenna and Lowri McKenna. Do you recognise those names?'

'No, I do not!'

The brief named Hodson weighs in. 'You have nothing on my client, Detective Inspector Archer. He was home alone on the night Mr Todd was murdered. The GPS on his phone and his Fitbit prove that.'

'That's hardly a solid alibi,' says Quinn.

'It's true!' says Stocker with more than a hint of exasperation in his voice.

Hodson continues, 'The night that Mr Whitmore was killed, my client was with Mrs Todd. She has already backed this up. Now, we don't need to waste any more of Mr Stocker's time. I think we can wrap this up, don't you?'

'Sure,' says Archer. 'At some stage we'll need to talk to you again, Mr Stocker.'

On their way to the third floor, Quinn says, 'I'm not convinced he did it, to be honest.'

'I'm reserving judgement. For now.'

Chapter 42

THE DAY IN SCHOOL HAD passed with increasing anxiety for Brynn, who really did not want to return home. He had long ago worked out that each morning he woke, or each time he walked through the front door, there was an 85 per cent probability that his dad's head would be in a dark place. This was never, ever good for Brynn, who was his dad's physical and emotional punching bag. The other 15 per cent was a combination of Dad sleeping (6.5 per cent), Dad uninterested (6.5 per cent), Dad happy (2 per cent decreasing to extinction). He had overheard Mam once calling him 'all sorts of crazy'. At the time, Brynn had no idea what that meant. Since Mam had left, Brynn had learned the hard way.

Despite the drizzle, Brynn is hanging out at Abbey Wood playground, working up the courage to go home. Iris is with him, doing her best to keep his spirits up.

'The dust has settled. I'm sure your dad has calmed down,' she says, albeit with an unconvincing tone.

'You don't know my dad. He's . . . he's . . . all kinds of crazy, he is.'

'Oh . . . '

'Do you think I'm like him?'

Iris frowns. ''Course not! You're nothing like him. And I'm nothing like my parents. We're . . . we're . . . '

'No kinds of crazy?'

She leans into him. 'We're no kinds of crazy.'

''Ave you got a spare fag I can bum?'

'Sorry, I'm all out. Anyway, you shouldn't smoke. Stunts your growth apparently.'

Brynn arches an eyebrow at her. 'They haven't stopped you from sprouting. You're taller than me, you are!'

'Only just,' Iris giggles, kissing his cheek. She detaches herself from him suddenly. 'Look over there,' she says, grinning. 'The swings!' She grabs his hand and pulls him across the playground.

Iris practically launches herself at the swing and begins swinging like there's no tomorrow.

'I'm flying, Brynn,' she laughs.

Brynn swings next to her, smiling at the joy on her face.

She squeals in delight. 'It's a trapeze, Brynn. Remember my dream to run away to the circus? It's a trapeze and I'm living my best life.' On she pushes herself, throwing her head back and kicking her long legs into the air.

Brynn laughs too and howls like a wolf. In that brief moment he has never felt so free, so happy, so connected with someone else. Not even his mam, who he rarely thinks of now. He looks across at Iris. She meets his gaze and grins. He smiles back at her. But something in her expression changes. Her gaze becomes vacant, her eyes begin to flicker.

'Iris?'

Iris's head is shaking, her body is rigid yet at the same time trembling. She is still gripping the chains yet the more she jerks, the looser her grasp becomes. Brynn leaps off the swing, hurries behind her and takes the weight of her shoulders just as her hands slip from the chains. She falls into his arms. He eases her to the damp ground.

'Iris, can you hear me?' he calls.

Brynn has no idea what to do. He had never thought to ask Iris or Mrs Toolan what to do if she had a fit. He looks around, hoping for an adult who might be able to help. He hears laughter nearby and looks up to see Garret and Stevo Brown with two girls from school, across the park. They are shaking and mimicking Iris's seizure.

Brynn's jaw clenches. Red-hot anger burns inside him.

'Go, Epi-Iris! Go!' Garret shouts.

Brynn feels cold fingers on his face. His heart leaps and he looks down at Iris. She has a dreamy expression as if she has just woken up.

'Am I dead?' she asks in a timid voice.

'Iris, it's me. Brynn. Are you OK?'

Her fingers stroke his cheek. 'Are you an angel?'

'No, Iris. It's only me. Brynn.'

She blinks her eyes and after a moment says, 'Brynn. Is that you?'

'Yeah. It's me, it is.'

'Everything was white. Your hair. Your face. I thought you were an angel. I thought I was dead.' Her face contorts, tears fill her eyes. 'I thought I was dead, Brynn.'

'You're not, you're fine. I'm here.'

She cries quietly. 'I'm frightened, Brynn. Can you take me home?'

The Brown brothers and their girlfriends are hollering across the park. Brynn ignores them and is relieved Iris appears not to have noticed. Carrying both their school bags, he puts his arm around her waist. She leans into him, and they leave the playground.

As they walk up Holstein Way, Brynn sees Mrs Toolan and some of the neighbours clustered outside his house. Mrs Toolan catches sight of them. Her face drops when she sees Iris, who is pale and sick-looking. Mrs Toolan hurries towards them, her eyes wide with concern.

'Did she have a fit?' she mouths at Brynn.

He nods.

She takes Iris from Brynn and examines her head. 'Did you hit your head, dear?'

'No. I was there and caught her.'

'Good lad. Did something happen to bring it on?'

'No, we were just in the park . . . '

'She should be wearing her helmet. This is the third one this week, Iris. You should be wearing your helmet.'

Iris rolls her eyes. 'I just need to sleep.'

'Of course you do. Come on, I'll take you inside.' Mrs Toolan turns to Brynn. 'You should have a word with your dad. I've no idea what he's been up to in there.'

'What do you mean?'

'He's been banging all day. Driving us all mad. Is he knocking walls down or something?'

Brynn swallows. 'I don't know.'

'Please tell him to be mindful of the other neighbours.'

Brynn nods.

'I know this is your first day back. Good luck, Brynn. Any problems, you know where we are.'

'Thank you, Mrs Toolan. I appreciate it.'

Mrs Toolan helps her niece inside. 'Your mum and dad are coming to take you home tomorrow, dear.'

Brynn's heart sinks. He feels his world collapsing around him.

'But I don't want to go home,' says Iris.

'It was only ever temporary here, Iris. You know that. Your parents love you and want you home.'

'No, they don't.'

Mrs Toolan chuckles. 'Don't be silly. Of course they do.'

Iris turns to look at him. She has the same dreamy expression and seems achingly sad. 'Bye, Brynn.'

'I'll come and see you later, I will,' says Brynn.

But Iris seems not to hear.

Despite what Mrs Toolan had told him, Brynn does not hear any banging coming from inside his house. His stomach is in knots as he inserts the key into the front lock. He turns it and pushes open the door. There's a bitter smell when he enters. Concrete dust. The ground floor and wooden stairs are coated in it.

'Dad,' he says, his voice mouselike.

There's no response. The house is silent.

Post on the floor, beneath the letter box. Mostly junk mail. He picks it up and rolls it up in his hands, listening for any sign of his dad but there's none. He climbs the stairs to the first floor, enters the living room and switches on the light. Despite the coating of concrete, the space has been cleaned since he was here. The kitchen too. Brynn swallows. He knows his father. This is a game. A lesson for Brynn that everything is better when he is not here.

Brynn cautiously climbs the stairs to the second floor. Dad's bedroom door is half open. He peeks inside. The bed is made, pristine, like a hotel bed. Brynn looks down the hallway to his bedroom door. It's closed. Something just doesn't feel right. He has never felt so unnerved. He presses the light switch, but it does not come on. Maybe it's blown. He makes his way to his bedroom eager to get to his safe place. He stands at his door and pauses. Did he hear something? He waits, his hand gripping the handle. After a moment he relaxes, believing it was his imagination. Turning the handle, he pushes the door, but it doesn't budge. He pushes again, but it won't open.

He looks up and through the gloom notices the door has been fitted with a bolt lock.

A sigh behind him.

Brynn freezes.

'The prodigal son returns,' says Dad, from the bathroom.

Fight or flight. Fight or flight.

'I . . . I was just going to my room.'

'Hush . . . don't raise your voice.'

'I didn't. I . . . '

'Shh. Too loud.'

His father is inches behind him. He can smell his meaty stale sweat mixed with concrete dust.

'I'll go put the kettle on. Make us a nice cup of tea,' says Brynn.

Brynn makes to walk away but is yanked back by the collar. Dad covers his mouth with a thick calloused paw. Brynn can taste the bitter dust.

'Quiet now,' his father growls.

Brynn trembles and tries to wriggle free, but his dad is too strong and his grip tightens.

'Dad, stop it, please.'

'Shhh.'

Terror overcomes him, and fearing for his life, he begins to kick and punch at his dad. He bites down on his palm.

'Fucker!' Dad cries. Spinning Brynn around, he swings a punch at his stomach.

'Ooof!' Brynn crumples to the floor clutching his belly, winded, unable to breathe.

'I'll fucking teach you.'

Dad hauls Brynn up the hallway by the ankles and drags him down the stairs, his body thudding hard on each step. Brynn struggles to breathe. The pain is immense, he feels like he might be sick.

Dad takes him through the front hallway and into the garage. It's freezing cold. There's a rectangular hole in the middle of the concrete floor. Slabs of concrete lie in a mound beside it. Brynn's head is spinning. The hole is like a grave.

'Dad, please. Don't do this!'

But he ignores him as he searches through a cupboard. Dad takes out a roll of black duct tape.

'Please don't do this, Dad.'

'You see this house. You see how much better I am without you? Everything is better without you.'

'But you told Mrs Toolan I was to come home.'

Dad slaps his face hard. 'Stop shouting!'

'I didn't . . . '

Dad opens the tape and begins to wrap it around Brynn's ankles.

Brynn feels his heart pounding. He has never gone this far. 'Dad, stop!' he cries.

Dad backs away and covers his ear. 'You're too loud! Stop talking.'

'I will. I will . . . I'm sorry, Dad, honest, I'm sorry!'

'You need to learn your lesson.'

'Dad, no . . . '

Crouching down, he pulls Brynn's arms behind his back and tapes his wrists.

Brynn drops his head and begins to sob. He can't help himself.

Dad lifts his head and tapes his mouth, wrapping it several times.

'That'll keep you quiet.'

Tears stream down Brynn's cheeks. Dad tosses the tape aside, stands and looks down at Brynn. His face is covered in white concrete dust, his eyes are red, wide and wild. He looks inhuman. He slides Brynn along the floor and rolls him into the hole. He thuds to the bottom, landing on soft soil. It must be four feet deep. Horror ripples through every fibre of Brynn's body. He tries to break free from his bonds, but they are too tight. He sees Dad's silhouette looking down at him.

'Prreeaaase!' Brynn urges.

But Dad steps away. The light goes off.

Brynn shakes and tries to scream, but his voice is muffled, inaudible to anyone other than himself.

Chapter 43

SIFTING THROUGH HER INBOX, ARCHER finds an unopened email sent by DC Clegg the day of her murder. An image of the DC with a bullet in her head flashes in her mind. Archer's stomach clenches.

'You OK?' Quinn asks from the desk opposite.

'Fine . . . ' She takes a breath. 'I just saw this email from Sara Clegg. It contains a sound file. It's the interview with Uma Whitmore.'

Quinn joins her at her desk. Archer plays the sound file and turns up the volume.

They hear whispering, followed by DI Greene's voice. 'Interview with Uma Whitmore. Present are DI Shaun Greene, DC Sara Clegg, Uma Whitmore. The appropriate adult is Uma's mother, Christine Whitmore.'

'Uma,' says a woman's voice.

Archer can hear a child whispering to herself. She also hears a rustling sound like paper.

The child does not reply.

'Uma, sweetheart?' The woman's tone is soft yet formal. Archer assumes the voice belongs to her mother, Christine Whitmore. 'This nice lady and gentleman are from the police. Do you think we could take a break from that and talk for five minutes?'

More rustling, faster this time. She can also hear a child's voice, whispering rapidly.

'Uma, please . . . '

Uma does not respond to her mother.

'Uma, stop talking for one moment!'

The whispering stops.

A second woman's voice says, 'Hi, Uma. My name is Sara. That's a nice doll you're holding. Does she have a name?'

Silence.

DC Clegg continues, 'I'd love to see what it is you're drawing.'

The rustling slows to a stop.

'I bet you don't,' comes a child's quiet whisper.

'I really would.'

There's a pause followed by Uma's voice, which is too quiet to make out.

'Uma, dear, we can't hear you,' urges Christine Whitmore.

The little girl's voice rises slightly. 'It's Daddy.'

'Oh,' says DC Clegg. 'That's—'

'Horrible, Uma. How could you?!' her mother cries.

Archer hears a nervous cough from DC Clegg. 'Perhaps we can come back . . . another time.'

'He's in heaven,' says Uma.

'Oh God!' says Christine.

Shaun Greene's voice enters the conversation. 'Uma, my name is DI . . . well, why not call me Shaun . . . if you like. I have a little girl your age. Her name is Laura.'

Silence broken by whispers interrupted by Greene's bullish tone. 'Do you remember seeing anyone the night the man came into your house?'

Archer cringes and looks at Quinn, who is shaking his head. She hears a scratching sound like nails on paper.

'Uma! Uma!' says a distressed Christine.

The little girl starts to sob. Archer feels an overwhelming sorrow for her.

'You should go,' Christine says. 'Go now, please!'

'Of course,' replies DI Greene. 'We'll come back another time.'

The recording finishes.

'That went well,' says Quinn, drily.

'Each of the victims has one thing in common,' says Archer.

'Kids,' replies Quinn.

'Biological. With the exception of the McKennas, who fostered.'

'Plus, Lucas Todd and Uma Whitmore were at home the night their fathers were murdered. The McKennas' foster child, Kirsty May, was staying with a friend.'

'They are the wildcard in this mystery.'

'We should talk to Kirsty. And Uma too. They might know more than we think.'

'It's worth a shot.'

'Grace, Harry,' comes Klara's voice. 'I have two contacts for you. Paul Finch is Tommy McKenna's boss and Lily Smith is the teacher Lowri worked with.' She hands across a sheet of paper with work addresses scribbled onto them.

'Not like you to go old school with pen and paper, Klara,' says Quinn.

'Sometimes I just need a shot of nostalgia,' she replies, smiling.

Archer is driving. Quinn switches on the radio. The news anchor is talking.

'And finally, the two people murdered in their home in Bermondsey last night have been identified as Thomas and Lowri McKenna. We are still waiting on the details from the police, but our reporter managed to catch up with a witness. We go to John now in Bermondsey.'

271

'What bloody witness?' says Archer.

'Yes, from what we know, police are searching for a killer in connection with the murders of Thomas and Lowri McKenna, who live here in this quiet Bermondsey cul-de-sac. I managed to track down a witness, a Señor Miguel Lopez who saw the killer. He speaks little English, but fortunately his friend can translate his words.'

'Miguel, por favor dime?'

'Si. Estaba asomado a la ventana fumando ...'

'I was leaning out the window having a smoke ...'

'Yo le vi ...'

'I saw him ... '

'Vestido de negro, cara oculta ...'

'Dressed in black, face hidden ...'

'Mató a ese pobre hombre. ..'

'He killed that poor man ...'

'Fue terrible ...'

'It was terrible.'

'Estaba colgado del árbol. Le vi sólo mirándole ...'

'He was hanging from the tree. I saw him just looking at him ...'

'Estaba come el Ángel de la Muerte.'

'He was like the Angel of Death.'

'Fue terrible.'

'It was terrible.'

'Gracias, *Miguel.'*

'De nada.'

'And there we have it. A first-hand witness description of the killer, who is still at large.'

Archer switches off the radio.

'Why the hell is that witness talking to the media?'

'All the neighbours had been instructed not to talk to the press, Lopez included. Maybe this got lost in translation.'

'The press and public are going to have a field day now that the Angel of Death seed has been planted.'

Quinn is looking at his smartphone. 'Seems "*el Ángel de la Muerte*" is propagating across news channels and social media faster than an Australian bushfire.'

'That's just great,' says Archer.

Chapter 44

LILY SMITH, A TEACHER AT Southwark Road Primary School, is a slim young woman with a kind face and a nervous disposition. According to the clock above her desk, it's 3.40. Her students have gone home for the day. The walls are plastered with enough sheets of multicoloured stick people, houses and handprint paintings to make Archer's head spin.

'I couldn't believe it when I heard the news,' she says, scratching her forearms. 'I was just so shocked.'

'The headmaster told us you knew Lowri quite well,' says Quinn.

'Oh, I don't know about that. I suppose compared to the other teachers I knew her best because she worked with me. That's probably what he means.'

'Can you tell us a little bit about her?' Archer asks.

'She was terrific. Funny too. Made the kids laugh. I can't tell you how devastated they are. We had a little chat about it this morning. About heaven and that. You read about this stuff all the time and see it on the telly, but you never expect it to happen to someone you know.'

'Describe what she was like,' Archer tries again.

'Oh, yes . . . sorry. She was very nice. The kids liked her. She worked three days a week. She was a grafter, good with the children. Um . . . the staff liked her . . . I suppose.'

'What does that mean?'

Smith's face draws a blank. 'What does what mean?'

'You said, "the staff liked her ... I suppose".'

'Oh.' She presses her palms together. 'Well, we all did, sorry, I didn't mean to suggest ... ' Smith shifts uneasily on her feet. 'I didn't mean to say anything bad. She's dead after all.'

'Please be honest with us, Miss Smith.'

She considers her response for a moment.

'Well, I suppose there were times. Just the odd day here and there. That's all. When she'd come to work smelling of alcohol.'

'How often?'

Smith is practically squirming. 'Not very often.'

'Did you think she had a drink problem?'

'I assumed so, but I didn't like to make that conclusion.'

'Did you speak to anyone about it?'

'Not really. Although we all knew.'

'If you didn't talk to each other about it, how could you all know?'

'We'd exchange looks, that sort of thing.'

'Surely, it would be in the interest of the students to bring this up at least with the headmaster?'

Smith blanches. 'Oh God. Am I going to get into trouble?'

'Right now, we just need to know a little more about Lowri.'

'It wasn't worth gossiping about, especially as it's so hard to keep a secret here and Lowri was so ... unpredictable. I did talk to her one night. I didn't want her to get fired so I tried to help her. I asked her about it in the pub, ironically, when we were having a staff night out. A Friday evening, of course. She started crying and said that she felt really bad. She said she wouldn't do it again. I said that's fine and that was that. Then Monday came and she pulled me aside and had a right go at me.'

276

'Was she angry?'

'Very. Told me to mind my own business. Then she apologised later. That's how unpredictable she could be.'

'When was this?'

'Almost four weeks back. I can't remember the exact date but could figure it out.'

'Were you aware of anyone who had problems with her or her husband?'

'Sorry, no.'

'Did you know if she was having any problems at home?'

Smith shakes her head. 'She always said how wonderful her marriage to Tommy was. They were soulmates, she'd say.'

'Did they have children?'

'No. Lowri couldn't have them. They fostered over the years though.'

'They were fostering recently, we understand.'

'Yes. That's right.'

'Do you know who they were fostering?'

Smith frowns as she considers this. 'Oh, what's her name . . .'

'Kirsty May?'

Smith beams. 'That's her. A teenager. Fifteen, I think.'

'How did Kirsty get along with the McKennas?'

'OK, I believe. She's a good kid, from what Lowri told me. A bit highly strung though.'

'Did you ever meet her?'

'Just once. She was waiting outside for Lowri.'

'How did she seem?'

'She seemed happy enough considering what she'd been through.'

'And what was that?'

'I don't know the details, but she had a pretty rough time in the care system.'

Archer hands across her contact details. 'If you think of anything else, please let me know.'

'Absolutely.'

Thomas McKenna had worked at an office construction site in Clerkenwell. His manager, Paul Finch, a stocky, stony-faced man, meets them at the site entrance. He removes his helmet and gloves and keeps his attention focused on the activity at the site.

'We're running behind, so I ain't got a lot of time.' His tone is indifferent, his accent, south London.

'We know how that feels,' says Quinn, drily.

Finch shoots a frown at Quinn but then turns his attention back to the site.

'Thomas McKenna, and his wife, were murdered last night, Mr Finch,' says Archer. 'You've no doubt seen the news.'

'Yes.'

'Therefore, it's probably no surprise why he hasn't shown up for work this morning,' adds Quinn.

Finch barks something indiscernible at a builder and turns back to Quinn. 'That's right. It's no surprise.'

'You don't seem any way upset or bothered that one of your team has been murdered.'

'I 'aven't got any tears, if that's what you're expecting.'

'We'd just appreciate some cooperation. That's all,' Archer says.

Finch exhales through his nose. 'OK. Ask away.'

'Is it fair to assume you and Thomas didn't get along?'

Finch shrugs. 'We had a few run-ins.'

'What kind of run-ins?'

'He was often late, and some days wouldn't show up for work. He let me and the rest of the boys down.'

'Why didn't he come to work on those days?'

'There was always some excuse. He was ill. His wife was ill. Drunk, more like.'

'Did you know his wife?'

'No, but I heard she liked a bevy.'

'Did Tommy have a drinking problem?'

'That's an understatement. He kept telling us he was clean. I believed him at first. He was good at telling lies. Most alcoholics are. But there were the odd days when he would show up and the stench of whisky oozed from his pores. It was minging. I was his governor. I prefer to keep my distance, so we weren't chummy or anything and I don't know much about his personal life. You should talk to Marcel.'

'Marcel?'

'He works here. He knew Tommy better than most.'

'Is he here?'

'Should be.' Finch turns and looks into the site. 'There he is.' Raising his voice, he shouts, 'Oi, Marcel!'

A man wearing a high-vis jacket and a yellow helmet pushing a wheelbarrow looks their way. Finch beckons him over.

'Yes, boss,' says Marcel.

'These people are from the police. They have some questions about Tommy. Help them out but don't be all day about it.'

'Asshole,' mutters Quinn.

Marcel smiles and tilts the front of his helmet. 'Yes, sir.'

'I'll leave you to it,' says Finch, returning to the site.

'I'm Detective Inspector Archer and this is Detective Sergeant Quinn.'

'How can I help you?'

'You've heard about the murder of Tommy and his wife?'

'Yes, it's all we've talked about this morning.'

'Did you know Tommy well?'

279

'We weren't best mates. We got on all right but didn't hang out or anything like that. We just got on better than most.'

'How would you describe him?' Archer asks.

'Oh ... I dunno ... let me see ... big buffoon of a fella you might say. Likeable, though.'

'Did he have many friends?'

'I couldn't say for sure. Outside of work he had a few mates, but I didn't know them. It's quite an itinerant workforce here. There's a lot of foreigners who don't speak much English. They come for a few weeks or months and then disappear. There's not much time to get to know people. That said, most people that worked with him seemed to like him.'

'Except for Paul Finch.'

'Oh, Paul doesn't get on with many people. You might have figured that out already. Tommy and Finchy were OK. Just Tommy pulled more sickies than other people and Finchy had no time for that.'

'Did Tommy ever mention anything about being in trouble?' asks Quinn.

'No, can't say that he did.'

'Has he ever had beef with anyone here or elsewhere?'

'Not here as far I as know. Outside of work I couldn't say.'

'You are aware he had a drink problem?'

'I'd heard something about that. I don't think that he had a drink problem any more than anyone else.'

'Paul Finch might disagree.'

Marcel shrugs. 'That's Finchy for you.'

'OK, Marcel. Thanks for your help.' Archer hands across her contact details. 'If you think of anything else, please call me.'

'I absolutely will. Good luck finding whoever did this.'

'Thanks,' says Archer.

'Aside from liking a drink we're no closer to understanding why the McKennas were murdered.'

'We should talk to Kirsty May,' says Quinn.

'Agreed. Are you OK to work a little later?'

'Fine by me.'

'How's your head?'

'I'm doing OK. Don't worry about me. What about you? You've had a harsh few days.'

'Working this case is helping me focus. I'm good.'

Chapter 45

LYING IN THE COLD, DARK concrete hole, Brynn dreams of Iris dressed in her red and black corset flying through the air like the beautiful bird that she is. He is flying beside her, his face painted white, his lips daubed in a thick black smile. He is performing air acrobatics and making her laugh. But the laughter stops when she begins to tremble. 'Iris!' he cries. And suddenly they are falling, hurtling towards the ground and the two rectangular holes below.

Brynn jolts from his dream and hears the front door opening on the other side of the internal garage wall. His heart quickens. He hears it closing gently, the lock turning and his father's boots treading on the wooden floor.

Please, Dad, please don't leave me here any longer.

His feet and arms bound in tape, Brynn pushes himself up, leaning against the rough concrete to stop himself from falling over. He hops closer to the bottom end of the hole and peers across at the light coming through the gap at the bottom of the door. The floor is level with his neck. He can see the soles of Dad's boots. Brynn knows he is behind the door, listening. He tries to call but the tape around his mouth is multi-layered and fixed so tightly it's just impossible. He sees Dad's feet step away and hears his boots ascend the stairs. Brynn's heart sinks. He feels like crying again. But what good would that do? He wonders what time it is. It's quiet outside. Looking towards the garage door, he can see there is no light coming from the gaps which would suggest it's late, perhaps even in the early hours. He sits down and tries to make himself as comfortable as he can. With his arms behind his back, it's not as easy as he'd like. He's worn out, exhausted physically and mentally. Yet his heart is pounding, undeterred by his predicament. He thinks about Iris, the only good thing in his life right now. Mrs Toolan said her parents were coming for her tomorrow. He feels his stomach clenching. Could Dad come to his senses and let him out of here in time to say goodbye? He shudders. Would he ever get out of here? He doesn't want to think about that. He just can't. Lying down on his side, he pulls his knees to his chest and trembles.

He wakes to the sound of the doorbell ringing. There are voices outside. Mrs Toolan, a woman and a man's voice she doesn't recognise. And Iris. His Iris. His heart skips. He hauls himself up. The doorbell rings once more.

'Brynn. It's me, Iris. Open up.' She knocks heavily on the door.

'IRISSS!' he cries through the tape.

'I don't think anyone's home, dear,' says the woman.

'He must be. It's too early to go to school, Mum,' Iris replies, knocking on the door once more, harder this time.

Brynn hears his father's boots on the stairs.

'Someone's coming,' says Iris.

The front door unlocks and opens. 'What is it?' his father asks.

'I'd like to talk to Brynn, please.'

'He's not here.'

'What do you mean, he's not here?'

'Iris, mind your manners,' says her mum. 'Sorry, my daughter would like to speak to your son. They're friends.'

'Like I said, he's not here.'

'Are you sure?' Iris asks.

'This is my 'ouse. I would know who's 'ere and who isn't. He left for school this morning. He said you might come by. He told me to tell you if you did that, he doesn't want to see you anymore. It's over. Didn't have the balls to tell you himself.'

A surge of anger shoots through Brynn like lightning. 'IRISSS!'

'Charming,' says Iris's mum.

'I don't believe you,' says Iris.

'I don't care.'

'Come on, Iris. Let's go.'

'Can you please tell him I said goodbye.'

'I'll mention it, but I don't think he'll be bothered.'

'Can you give him this too?'

'I'd rather not.'

'Please.'

'If you go away, I'll think about it.'

After a moment, Dad slams the door shut. Brynn hears him climb the stairs.

Outside, Iris is talking and weeping. 'He's so horrible.'

'You're better off away from here,' her mum says.

'Can we go now?' says Iris.

'NO!' he cries.

'Yes. Let's do that.'

Brynn listens as their voices disappear. He sinks to the ground with a growing desolation spreading over his heart like a rash.

The day passes.

The second night passes.

Brynn lies awake stirring into darkness.

It seems like forever.

Outside, he hears people talking and laughing. Someone is whistling. He hears the clink of bottles. The milkman. It must be morning. He hears Dad's feet pounding on the stairs. 'Brynn! Son! What have I done?'

The door swings open and the light flickers on, almost blinding him. He closes his eyes, unwilling to move, unwilling to engage. Dad drops down into the hole and begins cutting at the tape on his wrists and ankles. He is sobbing. 'My son! Oh God! My son!' Dad cuts into the tape on his face and rips it off, pulling the hairs from the back of Brynn's head. It hurts but he doesn't care. It's as if he can't feel anything – emotion or physical pain. Brynn is weak, he feels lifeless and limp. Dad lifts him up and with all his strength, rolls him onto the garage floor.

'Let's get you cleaned up, son. I'll make us some breakfast, so I will. Fried eggs and bacon. You like that, you do.'

There's an expression. The lights are on but no one's home. In a literal sense that's exactly how Brynn feels. Dad is speaking but Brynn is not really taking the words in. He feels himself being lifted. Dad throws him over his shoulder and carries him up the stairs.

'Let's get you into the shower. You don't smell too good,' he says with a chuckle.

Brynn had lain in his own mess for . . . how long? Three days at least.

In the bathroom, Dad drops Brynn into the bath, still wearing his school uniform, and turns on the shower. The water is freezing. That's OK. Brynn's body and soul already feel like ice.

'That girl left you a present, she did. I'll get it for you, shall I? Stay there.'

Dad leaves and runs down the stairs. He hears him rattling around in the kitchen. And then he's running back up the stairs and down to the bathroom.

'Here it is. It was in the bin. Don't know how it got there. It's a book, I reckon. I've given it a wipe now.'

The water is warming up. Brynn stares blankly at the brown tiles above the bath taps.

'I'll set it here on the toilet. If you want to read it. She seems nice. That girl.'

Iris.

'I'll put the bacon and eggs on. You get cleaned up and perhaps we can do something together today. What do you think? Maybe we can fill that hole in the garage. What a mess that is.'

Dad hurries out of the bathroom and down to the kitchen. Brynn closes his eyes. Here he is once more pulled to the flip side of his father's personality. Brynn takes a breath. Tired and confused, he's unsure of himself and what to do next. The only thing he knows is that something inside him has died. Forever.

Chapter 46

THE McKENNAS' FOSTER CHILD, FIFTEEN-YEAR-old Kirsty May, is seated at the rustic pine kitchen table of her replacement foster parents, a middle-aged couple called Michael and Barbara Geary. The space is cluttered, painted rustic reds and greens, a shabby chic hippyish environment. An ancient golden retriever sleeps near a warm range cooker and a tabby cat patrols the space under the table, curious about the new visitors.

Archer and Quinn are seated opposite the teenager. Kirsty is a pale-skinned girl with thin lips and spots on her chin. She has large eyes, which are red from crying.

'We're so sorry, Kirsty,' says Archer.

She nods her head and dabs her nose with a crumpled paper hanky.

'We really appreciate you agreeing to talk with us so soon.'

'I just hope you can catch whoever did it.'

Barbara places a tray containing four large mugs of tea on the table. They're almost the size of toby jugs in the shape of laughing circus clowns. She hands them around and sits next to Kirsty.

'Is it true what that man said on the news about the Angel of Death?' asks Kirsty.

'That man has a vivid imagination. Please don't take his account seriously.'

'I ... I ... heard the news about Tommy hanging from the tree.' A quiver in her voice. A frightened expression on her young face.

Barbara reaches across and gently squeezes Kirsty's hand.

'I'm sorry you had to find out that way,' says Archer.

'It's just awful,' interrupts Barbara.

'Kirsty, can you tell us about Tommy and Lowri?'

'What'd you want to know?'

'Were they good foster parents?'

'Yes. They were nice people. Kind.'

'Were you aware of any trouble either of them might have been in?'

Kirsty looks across the kitchen, brow creasing as she considers this. 'Not really. They never had much money. They were always living hand to mouth. Shopping in the cut-price food aisles and all that.'

'Did they seem happy to you?'

Her eyes water. 'I never much thought about them in that way but I suppose they were, yeah. They had nothing but that never stopped them living. I'm sure they were in debt. They were always waiting on a lottery win. They spent a lot of money on the lottery. And scratch cards. Cigarettes and booze too.'

'Did they drink alcohol much?'

'They'd have a couple cans of lager every night. Sometimes more. I didn't mind. They always looked after me. Ensured I was fed and clothed, even if the clothes were a bit cheap.'

'Did you ever see anyone hanging around the house, watching it, or watching Tommy and Lowri perhaps?'

She takes a moment to consider her answer but shakes her head. 'Honestly, I don't think so. And they never mentioned anything.'

'On the night of your foster parents' death, you were staying at a friend's.'

290

The teenager nods her head. 'My friend Sally. I was there for a sleepover.'

'Did anyone other than Tommy, Lowri, Sally and her parents know you were staying out that night?'

'Lots of people, I suppose. My friends mainly. I couldn't say who else though.'

'And when you left, you did not notice anyone watching the house?'

'No, I went straight from school.'

'I'm sorry for pressing on some points, Kirsty, I just want to get a clear picture. Lowri was out with her friends that night and Tommy was staying home.'

'Oh, that's the odd thing,' says Kirsty.

'How so?' asks Archer.

'Because I was having a sleepover, both Tommy and Lowri had arranged to go out. But Tommy didn't.'

'Do you know why?'

'I don't.'

'Do you know where he was going or who he was going out with?'

'He was going to the pub, and he was going to meet someone. Oh God,' she says, shuddering.

'What is it?'

'The pub is called the Angel. Do you think that's a coincidence with the Angel of Death and all that?'

Archer offers a reassuring smile. 'We'll look into it. Is there anything else you can think of that might help us?'

She shrugs and shakes her head. 'I don't think so.'

Archer gives her contact card. 'If you think of anything, please call me at any time.'

On the walk back to the car, Archer calls DC Phillips. 'Marian, hi, it's Grace, did you talk to Mr Lopez?'

'Yes, we did. Eventually found him at home. He'd been drinking with his mate and was a little worse for wear. Oh, and the place he is staying at stinks of weed. As does he. And I do too, now.'

'Great! I suppose he was high last night when he saw the killer?'

'I'm afraid so. We managed to sober him up a bit with coffee and by opening the windows. He speaks a little English. Not much. His friend translated. Anyway, he apologised for speaking to the press and realises that was a mistake, yada yada yada.'

'It's a bit late now.'

'I'm sure they slipped him a bung. When we got to questioning him, he more or less told the same story he told the press but with less theatre. He remembers a tall man with a pale face concealed beneath a hoodie. Dressed in black or dark clothes. He isn't sure. He said the man wasn't like a "muscle Mary" – the expression he used – but he looked imposing. That was pretty much all from him. He's coming to the station tomorrow to make a statement. He's been warned to come in sober.' Phillips chuckles.

They are approaching the car.

'What about the other neighbours?'

'Zilch. Seems the McKennas were liked well enough. No one other than Lopez saw anything. A few heard Mrs McKenna return home that night. She made a lot of noise apparently, falling out of a taxi. One of our PCs spoke with the driver. He just recalls another drunk passenger.'

'OK. Thanks for the update, Marian.'

'No worries.'

'What're you guys doing now?'

'We're going to talk to Melissa Whitmore and then head to Tommy McKenna's local. After that, unless something comes up, we'll be back to the station.'

'See you there.'

'Will do.'

Archer ends the call.

Chapter 47

ELISSA WHITMORE'S HOME IN GREENWICH is
a mid-terraced Georgian house, a smaller, quainter
version of her brother's. She answers the door in
her dressing gown. She is pale, with lank brown hair, her eyes
are red with dark rings underneath them.

'Miss Whitmore, thank you for seeing us at such short notice.
This is Detective Sergeant Harry Quinn.'

She nods curtly. 'Come in.'

The house smells of warm toast and cigarette smoke.

'We're so sorry for your loss.'

'Everybody is,' she replies, thrusting her hands into
the pockets of her dressing gown. Her breath is sour with
morning-after wine.

'A silly question I know but how are you bearing up?' Archer
asks.

'Do I look like I'm bearing up?' Whitmore closes her eyes
and shakes her head. 'Sorry . . . it's just been so hard.'

'Of course it has.'

'Come through.' She leads them into a dishevelled living
room, littered with toys, crayons and children's books.

'Christine and Uma left this morning. They've gone to
stay with her mother. I haven't had a chance to tidy up yet.
We can talk in the kitchen.'

Whitmore leads them through to the kitchen. A six-seater oak table with matching chairs dominates the space. There's an open packet of Marlboro and a lighter on the surface. Bifold doors overlook a smart west-facing patio and garden. Cigarette butts litter the ground outside.

'You enjoy gardening?' Quinn asks.

'When I can. Which is not now for obvious reasons . . . never mind, the rain won't fucking let up.' She sighs heavily and shakes her head. 'I didn't mean to swear. Can I get either of you a drink?'

'Not for me,' Archer replies.

'No, thanks,' says Quinn.

Whitmore gestures at the table. 'Take a seat, please.' She sits at the head, Archer and Quinn on either side.

'Miss Whitmore, could you tell us a little bit about your brother?' Archer asks.

'He was a banker. Worked hard. Ambitious, and all he really wanted was a good life for his family.' From the pocket of her gown, she takes out a rolled-up paper tissue and dabs her eyes. 'Everything for him centred around Christine and Uma. They were his life.'

'When was the last time you saw him?'

'Two weeks ago. At Uma's birthday. There was a party at the house.'

'How did he seem?'

'Fine. Just himself really.'

'Did he seem out of sorts?'

'No. He was just Rob.' She takes a moment to think more on this. 'The party was going well. Everyone was having fun. But he was fussing. Trying to make everything perfect.'

'In what way?'

'My brother was a stickler for detail. I would often tease him that he was on the spectrum. But it was just a kids' party. There was no need for him to lose his shit.'

'How exactly did he "lose his shit"?'

'I don't recall the entire details. But Uma had been a nuisance. Something got broken. A glass jug . . . or a vase or something. Rob just lost it.'

'In what way?'

'He shouted at her. He had a short fuse, you see. Always did have. Drinking didn't help.'

'He was drinking at the party?'

Whitmore frowns. 'No. Why are you asking about Rob anyway?'

'We just want to get a sense of him. That's all.'

'Who else was at the party?' asks Quinn

'Kids mostly. Some parents. Not all of them. Many had the sense to stay away.'

'I get the sense they're not your thing.'

She snorts. 'Kids are not my thing. It's not that I don't like them. I mean, I love my niece. But being stuck in a room with a dozen of them is a horror movie.' She picks up the packet of Marlboro and the lighter and stands. 'I need a cigarette.' She makes her way to the bifold doors, opens them and stands half in, half out. Lighting the cigarette, she inhales deeply and exhales a torrent of smoke. 'I don't know the names of anyone at Uma's party, if that's what you're going to ask me next. I doubt Rob and Christine knew them that well either. They were Uma's friends and schoolmates.'

'Were any of the neighbours there?'

She arches her brows at this. 'Yes, of course. Oliver someone . . .'

'Stocker?'

'That's him. And someone else.' She bites her thumb as she tries to remember.

'Has Uma mentioned anything more about that night?' Quinn asks.

'She didn't see anyone and doesn't remember anything. She might still be in shock.'

'Indeed,' agrees Archer.

Archer stands. 'Thank you for your time, Miss Whitmore.'

'Can't imagine I was any help.'

'You mentioned there was another neighbour.'

'Oh yes. Actually, it wasn't a neighbour. It was Oliver's ex-girlfriend, Jenny Sinclair. She and Rob go way back apparently. Used to date. Now that I think of it, Oliver wasn't too happy when he found out.'

'Did he find out at Uma's party?'

'Yes. It was all very awkward.'

Chapter 48

FOR THE EIGHTH TIME THAT morning Linda Parker slams on the brakes.

'Every buggering light has turned red,' she hisses through gritted teeth.

'What did you say, Mummy?' asks Charlotte, her nine-year-old.

'Nothing, dear. Nothing, Mummy said nothing.'

'But I heard you speak. What did you say?'

The light turns green suddenly. Linda eases off the clutch and presses the accelerator, jolting forward too harshly for first gear. The engine cuts out. She is stuck in the intersection.

'Shit!'

She feels her heart racing.

'Mummy, why have we stopped again?'

Behind her is a long queue of cars. A horn blasts at her, followed by a second. Linda feels her face flushing. London drivers can be so fucking antsy.

She presses the ignition button and turns the engine. It chokes into life for a moment before dying once more. She tries a second time, but it seems unwilling to do her bidding. She's blocking the traffic from the left side and waves an apology at the furious-looking driver, a man in a white van. Of course, it would be a man in a white fucking van. He presses down hard on his horn. Her mouth dries. She tries again to start the car. Nothing. Soon there is a chorus of horns coming from all directions. 'Oh, fuck off!' she screams as she pushes the button once more.

The car starts. Thank God!

The traffic light goes red, but she doesn't care. Nothing is going to stop her. She eases forward gently this time and joins the traffic ahead. She is relieved but her heart is pounding. She wants to cry.

'Mummy?'

Linda takes a few calming breaths. 'What is it?'

'You said a bad word.'

'I know. It's a grown-up word and you are never to repeat it, ever. Remember what I said last time?'

Through the rear-view mirror, she sees Charlotte scrunching her face as she ponders the question. 'If you can't say anything nice . . . '

'Don't say anything,' says Charlotte.

'That's correct.'

'But you said it, Mummy. That word that Daddy hates.'

'And I shouldn't have. And he doesn't need to know. Our secret.'

Linda switches on the radio in the hope of diverting Charlotte's attention. 'Let's have some music, shall we?' They drive for ten minutes, listening to inane pop songs. Thankfully, Charlotte sings along and doesn't badger her.

The phone rings. It's Julian. She swipes to answer, putting him on speaker.

'Hi.'

'Hi. Where are you?'

'Traffic was horrendous. Be there in five.'

'Hi, Daddy!'

'Hello, sweet pea.'

'It's my birthday today.'

'We know, sweet pea. You've been reminding us all morning.'

'Did you get the cake?' asks Linda.

'I did. It looks great. Listen, I think we might need the gazebo.'

'Why?'

'It's going to rain.'

Linda glances up at the sky. Grey clouds are gathering. 'But my app said it would be dry today.'

'According to the BBC, we're about to get a downpour.'

Linda feels her anxiety kicking in. 'But the app on my phone ... '

'The weather apps are never accurate, Linda. I've told you that before.'

She squeezes the steering wheel and bites her tongue.

'I think it's worth putting the gazebo up just in case.'

'We don't have it. Jill borrowed it.'

'That's helpful.'

She indicates right and turns.

'We don't have time to drive across London to get it. We'll just have to improvise. I'm pulling up outside.'

This day just gets better and better.

'Shall I—'

She ends the call before he finishes.

Linda parks and helps her daughter out of the car. 'Go inside, Charlotte.' From the boot she hauls out the four heavy Marks & Spencer bags stuffed with kids' party food and drinks.

Julian opens the front door.

'Daddy!' cries Charlotte, running towards him. Always the daddy's girl.

He sweeps her into his arms. 'Is it someone's special day today?'

'Yes, it's mine!' she squeals.

As Linda walks up the garden path, a spot of rain splashes on her face. She rolls her eyes and really cannot wait for this day to be over. In the kitchen, she drops the bags on the marble worktop. Through the French windows she sees the rain coming down harder. Her lovely garden that she had spent the morning decorating with bunting, balloons and ribbons is slowly being destroyed.

'Daddy, Mummy said "fuck" in the car.'

Why do I even bother, she thinks.

'Charlotte, do not ever say that word again!' says Julian, harshly.

'I won't, Daddy, I promise.'

'Good girl.'

Linda can feel Julian's judgemental eyes boring into her. She turns and glares back at him. 'It's raining, Julian, just as the BBC predicted. Bully for them. Maybe you can help me rescue the decorations. We'll have the party in the dining room instead.'

Julian gives her an insincere half-smile. He sets Charlotte down. 'I'll get my coat.'

The rain begins coming down in sheets. Linda hurries out the door and runs to untie the balloons. The string is slippery and tricky to undo. Julian joins her. It takes them the best part of twenty minutes to dismantle the decorations and get them inside.

Charlotte is sitting at the kitchen table watching something on her iPad.

Linda's hair, face and clothes are sodden and cold. The strings of coloured bunting in her hands are dripping too. 'I'll put these in the dryer.'

'I'll dry the balloons with a towel,' says Julian.

Linda hears the toilet upstairs flushing. She frowns and looks at her husband.

'Oh, forgot to mention. The entertainer is here.'

'He's a bit early.'

'He got the times wrong. I couldn't tell him to go away. He'd travelled all the way across London.'

'That's not our problem.'

'He said he needs to get ready. He's in the spare bedroom. It's only an hour. What does it matter?'

'You could have told me.'

'I'm telling you now.'

'I have to go upstairs and get cleaned up and undressed with a stranger in the house.'

'Try locking the bedroom door.'

Linda feels her blood boiling. 'Fuck you, Julian!' she hisses and throws the bunting at him. She leaves the kitchen, pulls off her coat, flings it over the banister and marches up the stairs with Julian following her.

'Linda, just calm down.'

'Don't tell me to calm down!'

'Linda . . . '

'Just leave it, Julian. I need to get ready.' She enters their bedroom and slams the door. He pushes it open.

'What the hell is wrong with you?'

'What's wrong with me? What the hell is wrong with *you*?'

'There's nothing wrong with me! I'm not the one swearing in front of our child on her birthday.'

Linda pulls off her jumper and throws it forcefully into the laundry basket. 'Oh, I'm just fine. I've had the best day . . . '

'Keep your voice down. He's in the next room,' says Julian.

'I don't give a flying fig who's next door, Julian. I was up at the crack, doing everything in my power to make this day as perfect as it can be. I've cleared the garden, blown up balloons, put up the bunting, gone shopping for party food, stopped at every fucking traffic light, got blasted by every fucking driver in north London only to come home, get grassed up by my daughter and told off by my husband. Maybe put yourself in my shoes for a moment.'

'OK, OK, I get it. I'm sorry.'

Through the crack in the door, Linda notices a tall shadow flit past.

'Can you close the door, please,' she says quietly.

'Sorry,' he replies, shutting the door.

'Why is he wandering around the house?'

'I'll have a word with him.'

'I need to shower.'

Julian steps towards her and hugs her. 'I'm sorry. I know you've been working hard. I'll decorate the dining room. Might not be to your standards but who cares? The kids certainly won't.'

'True.'

She's too frazzled to fight and sinks into him, letting him kiss her full on the mouth.

'I'm sorry for swearing,' she says.

'Sounds to me like you had no choice.'

'I've had better mornings.'

'Take whatever time you need, and I'll get everything ready.'

'And tell that clown to stop walking around the house.'

'I will,' he replies and blows her a kiss.

Chapter 49

I T IS THE SAME STORY at the Angel pub in Bermondsey. Tommy and Lowri McKenna were salt-of-the-earth people. Regulars at the Angel, they were loyal and popular customers and friends. No one has a bad word to say about them. As far as they knew, neither Tommy nor Lowri were in any sort of trouble. There was nothing or no one who could shed light on why the couple had been murdered.

The manager is a broad, surly bloke in his mid-forties. His name is Maxwell.

'Did you ever notice anyone watching them, either if they were together or alone?'

'No, can't say that I did.'

'Did they ever bring anyone here that you didn't recognise?'

Maxwell considers this for a moment. He shakes his head but stops. 'Wait. There was that one guy from his work.'

'Do you recall his name?' asks Quinn.

'The guy told me, but I don't remember ... oh wait ... something to do with a bird.'

'Finch?' says Archer.

'That's him.'

'Strange bloke.'

'In what way?'

'Just odd. Didn't really say a lot. Tommy did all the talking as he normally did. Finch just sat there, brooding. They drank for a few hours and then left.'

'When was this?'

'Weeks ago.'

'Do you remember the date and time?'

'I could probably figure it out.' From under the bar, he takes out a well-thumbed diary. He licks his index finger and skips through the pages. 'Tommy usually came here on Tuesday and Friday evenings. Also, Saturday and Sunday afternoons. It was definitely an evening so that rules out the weekend. I'm sure it was three weeks ago. Tuesday is quiz night, so it wasn't a Tuesday. Therefore, it was a Friday. And I'm pretty certain it was this date,' he says, pointing to a day in the calendar.

'And you're certain?'

'Eighteenth of March, yes. It was because we had no barrels of the Dark Mild for a week and they'd arrived that morning. I remember telling him this. It was his drink, you see.'

'Was that the last time you saw Mr Finch?'

'Yes, it was. Tommy was supposed to meet him here the night he was killed, but he didn't show up.'

'Did Tommy tell you that?'

'He did. I asked who he was meeting, and he said that bloke from work he'd been drinking with a few weeks back.'

'That's really helpful. Thank you, Mr Maxwell.'

'Do you think it was this Finch fella what did it?'

'We don't know anything yet. Please don't mention any names to anyone.'

'Of course. Understood. I just hope you find whoever did it.'

Outside the rain is pouring down. They hurry to the car across the street and jump inside. Quinn starts up the engine and begins the drive back to Charing Cross.

'So, the question on both our lips is why was Paul Finch drinking with Tommy, whom he didn't much like?' says Quinn.

'He can answer that later.'

It's mid-afternoon in Charing Cross – Archer is pleased to see Pierce has followed through on her promise to expand the team. She counts five plain clothes detectives and six uniforms. Klara, Os, DC Phillips and DCI Pierce are all present as Quinn provides a full overview.

'And that's where we are to date. So, to summarise, we have a killer who tasers his victims and then asphyxiates them by mummifying the necks, heads and faces with duct tape and draws a sad emoji on their taped faces. Any thoughts since our last meeting?'

A murmuring in the room and shaking of heads. One detective, a stout man with receding hair, raises his hand. 'Is he mental?'

'Understatement,' someone says.

Laughter fills the room.

'Maybe he doesn't want to see their faces when they die,' says Klara. 'Maybe a smiley is a way of easing his guilt.'

'I like that,' says Archer.

'Perhaps he thinks it's funny,' says Phillips.

'Maybe.'

'It's his brand. Like his calling card,' says Pierce.

Quinn writes the suggestions on the whiteboard.

'The truth is we don't yet know,' says Archer. 'It might be all of those or a combination. What we do know is, he's clever and dangerous. He's also strong and, according to one witness, he's a broad man with a pale face. So, we know he's white. He wears a size nine Dr Martens boot. He kills in the night-time and then goes home unseen. He knows what he's doing. Why he is killing these people we don't yet know and with your help, I hope we can find out. The victims all come from different backgrounds. What they do have in common is that they are in their mid-thirties and above, white, and all have children. Or in the case of the McKennas, a foster child. He's been able to enter people's homes without breaking in.' Archer pauses to allow her words to sink in. She nods at Quinn to take over.

'So, either the killer has keys, or he got lucky because the victims left their doors unlocked. Which seems improbable. If he did have keys, how did he get them? Did he steal from either victim, or their foster child, at some stage prior to the murder? Perhaps he visited their home in some capacity to provide a service: gas, electric, building. Marian, could you allocate a resource to follow up on who has been to the McKennas' house?'

Phillips nods and says, 'I'll also talk to the foster child regarding the keys too.'

'Thanks.'

'Have we had any news from the CSI team?' she adds.

'Nothing yet, unfortunately. I was hoping Krish would be here, but he's caught up elsewhere. He said he has something interesting he's looking into. We have a call later. As soon as I know, I'll let you all know. Any more questions?'

There are none.

'OK, thanks, everyone. Marian will work with each of you on your tasks. Please make sure you're in the WhatsApp group. If you're not, then text me and I'll add you. My number is on the board.'

'Good work,' says DCI Pierce. 'How close do you think we are?'

'Hard to say. We're doing our best.'

'Of course.'

'I appreciate the extra heads. Thank you.'

'The reason I ask is we may have them for a limited time.'

'How limited?'

'A week or so. Possibly less. I've had to beg, borrow and steal.'

'That could finish us, Clare. We need a bigger team for as long as it takes.'

'I know that, but we're at breaking point. The most I could do is gather a few inexperienced detectives and uniforms. I'll fight to keep them longer. Just bear with me. I'll do what I can.'

'Thanks.'

Chapter 50

THE FOLLOWING MORNING, ARCHER AND Quinn are leaving the office to drive to the construction site in Clerkenwell for a second interview with Paul Finch. It's a grey morning but at least the rain has stopped.

They walk up Chandos Place and Archer gets a chill. She glances at Quinn, who slows his pace, stopping at the same point where Hicks had shot him last week.

'Sorry, we shouldn't have come this way,' says Archer.

'The déjà vu feels really weird.'

Quinn seems rooted to the spot, as if he is unable to move forward. 'It's been five days now. Rod almost killed me. And you. But now he's dead. Fuck me, that's a *trip*.'

Archer knows only too well.

'I'll drive,' she says.

'I'm fine.'

'That wasn't a request.'

'Yeah. Maybe you're right.' Quinn hands her the keys.

They drive in silence for ten minutes as the shock of the shared déjà vu moment subsides.

'How was your first night back home?' Quinn asks.

'The evening flew by. I spent the entire time vacuuming, dusting, cleaning clothes and bedlinen. It was almost midnight by the time I was done. I literally passed out in bed.'

'How'd you sleep?'

The bloodied corpses of Frankie White, Jimmy Barnes and Rod Hicks had all jostled for attention in her dreams. It had not been the easiest of nights.

'I slept OK.'

'Good.'

'How about you?'

'Once I ejected the Kennington Park Thursday Murder Club from the flat, I was able to get some shut-eye dosed up on painkillers.'

'Are you in pain now?'

'It's constant, but manageable.'

'I know you said you'd prefer to be at work, but should you change your mind and need some time off, just take it. You've earned it. To be honest, I'm surprised Clare allowed you back.'

'Thanks, but I'm good. If I can walk and talk then I'm fit for purpose.'

'That's very much Clare Pierce's approach.'

Quinn chuckles. 'If I had a bullet in my head and could still think and walk, Clare would have me on the streets. It's not all down to her though. I did insist on coming back. Anyway, you need me. Or else you won't catch this killer.'

Archer smiles. 'Is that right?'

'Oh yes.'

The Clerkenwell construction site is a hive of activity with high-vis-wearing builders streaming around the place like orange and yellow worker ants. Archer scans for Finch but can't see him.

She hears Quinn talk to one of the builders.

'Where can we find Paul Finch?' he asks.

310

The man points to an off-site shabby portable cabin down the road near to where she had parked the car. 'The last I saw, he was in his office,' says the man. 'And was in a right mood.'

'That's nice to know. Thanks,' says Quinn.

'Between you and me, we're getting a bit fed up with him and this place.'

'Why's that?'

'We haven't been paid today. We ain't putting up with this any longer. I'll tell you that much. He better sort that out.'

Quinn meets Archer's gaze. 'He's in a mood, apparently.'

'Seems to be his default disposition.'

'And he hasn't paid anyone.'

At the cabin, they knock on the door. 'Come in,' says a woman's voice.

Pushing open the door, they enter the office. There are two desks facing the entrance and positioned diagonally on either side of the small office. A window divides them with a view of Clerkenwell Road. A second window provides a view of the site entrance. Finch is not here. Seated on the desk to the left is a broad woman with an anxious expression. 'How can I help you?' she asks.

'We'd like to speak to Paul Finch.'

'He's not here.'

'What's your name?' Archer asks politely.

'I'm Jenny Barclay. His assistant.'

Archer shows her ID. The woman's face flushes. 'The police. Oh my.' She begins to fidget and arrange the paperwork on her desk. 'I . . . I don't know where he's gone. He was just here a moment ago and then he left. Quickly.'

'Why would he do that?' Archer asks, but looking out the window at the entrance to the site she can guess he has just clocked their arrival.

'There!' says Quinn, pointing at the rear window.

Paul Finch is running down Clerkenwell Road, occasionally glancing back at the cabin. 'Great!' he says drily and bolts out the door. Archer is behind him. 'Harry, wait!' Quinn turns and gives her a quizzical look. She tosses the car key. 'You're in no state to go running after him. Not with your injury. I'll go. Follow me in the car.' She can see Quinn is about to protest. 'I'll be on my phone,' she says and hurries down Clerkenwell Road, dodging traffic and waving apologies at horn-blasting irritated drivers. She sees Finch's bald head in the distance, pushing his way through the pedestrians. Archer glances to her right, checking the oncoming traffic and jumps on to the edge of the road, sprinting over the double yellow lines. Behind her, she hears Quinn's siren. Her phone is ringing, she swipes and turns on the speaker, almost tripping in the process.

'Where are you?' says Quinn.

'Approaching Farringdon Road. There's a Pret A Manger on the corner.'

'I know it.'

'I can see him. He's running across Farringdon Road ... he's going up another street, a bridge over the railway. It's a dead end.'

'That'll be Vine Street Bridge,' says Quinn. 'I'm almost there.'

Panting and almost out of breath, Archer dodges oncoming cars, waving more apologies at the traffic on Farringdon Road. She wants to bolt across the final lane, but a large green Land Rover is hurtling her way. She waves for it to slow but the driver, a blonde woman with a tan, is having none of it. She glares angrily at Archer and blares her horn for all to hear. The sound dissolves in the distance as Archer reaches the Vine Street Bridge. 'I've lost him,' she says, hurrying up the bridge. Ahead is Clerkenwell Green, to her left and right is Farringdon

Lane. There is no sign of Finch. She catches her breath and sees Quinn turn off Farringdon Road. He pulls up beside her. She gets inside. They drive around for almost twenty minutes looking for him, but he is nowhere to be seen.

'Let's head back to his office,' says Archer. 'I'd like to speak to his assistant.'

'I really don't know what all that was about,' says Jenny Barclay.

'He saw us and ran. Is that a fair assumption?' Quinn asks.

'But I don't know why he would do that. Yes, he was looking out the window and something spooked him.'

'We spooked him,' says Quinn. 'The question is why.'

'Why has he not paid anyone today?' Archer asks.

'Some sort of computer error. It'll be sorted this afternoon, he said.'

'Where does he live?'

'In Bermondsey. I'm not sure of the exact address.'

'You must have everything on file here. The names and addresses of everyone who works here?'

'Yes. Sorry. I'm not thinking straight. This is all such a shock.' She starts typing on her laptop. 'Here it is.' She writes on a Post-it note and hands it across. 'This is his home address and his mobile number.'

'Thank you,' says Archer.

'What should I do if he returns?'

'I'd be surprised if you see his face any time soon,' says Quinn. 'But if you hear from him, tell him we want to talk to him.'

They're driving to Paul Finch's house. Two response vehicles with wailing sirens are ahead of them. Four uniforms in total.

Archer's phone rings. It's Krish. She swipes it open on speaker.

'Hi, Krish,' says Archer.

'Hey, stranger,' says Quinn. 'Long time.'

'Yeah, sorry. We've been stacked up. Sounds like I've caught you guys in the middle of something important.'

'You know us. Just chasing the bad guys, as always.'

'I'd call you back, but I think this is important. It's been bugging me for a while.'

'We're all ears,' says Quinn.

'At the McKennas' house I came across a white, waxy residue on the duvet where we found Mrs McKenna. I wasn't sure what to make of it. Looking through my team's reports, I found records of a similar substance. There was a trace of it in Jason Todd's hair and some on the fingernails of Robert Whitmore. I had it analysed and got the results back this morning. It contains petrolatum, talcum powder, lanolin and beeswax, among other things.'

'That sounds like some sort of moisturiser,' says Archer.

'Not quite but close. I'd hazard a guess and say it's makeup of some sort.'

'Makeup?' says Quinn.

'Yeah. It's feasible.'

Archer's mind is racing as she navigates the road ahead.

'That's all I had for now. I'll get it written up and sent across,' says Krish.

'Thanks, Krish,' says Archer.

'No worries.'

They say their goodbyes and Archer ends the call.

'A killer wearing makeup . . . ' says Quinn. 'Are we looking at a very strong woman, or . . . don't cancel me . . . a man dressed as a woman?'

In her mind, the pieces of the puzzle begin to inch slowly together. 'No. Think about it. Krish mentioned the substance is white. Where do you find white makeup?'

After a moment Quinn says, 'Fuck . . . the theatre.'

Archer is focusing on the response cars ahead, watching her speed, checking her mirrors, but her mind is racing. 'Lucas Todd,' she says. 'The birthday party. There was an entertainer in the picture, remember?'

'I remember a clown of some sort. Christ, Paul Finch is the murderer and he's also a clown.'

'It gets him access to people's homes.'

They're approaching the street where Paul Finch lives. The response cars are already outside his small terrace house. The officers are running to the house with a battering ram.

'Christ . . . I hate clowns,' says Quinn.

Archer parks behind the response vehicles and joins the uniforms. One of them, a sturdy officer called Lee Carling, takes the lead and bangs the front door. There is no response. Carling bangs the door and shouts, 'Officers coming through.'

Archer steps back and sees a silhouette in the bedroom peering down. 'Someone's inside,' she says.

Carling nods an acknowledgement at her.

'Let's go in,' she says.

One of the officers slams the ram against the PVC door. It caves in after two blows. The officers swarm the house. Two downstairs. Two upstairs.

'He's up here,' comes a voice. 'We have him.'

Lee Carling and his colleague wrestle a cuffed, angry-looking Finch down the stairs.

Archer approaches him. 'Paul Finch, I'm arresting you for the murders of Jason Todd, Robert Whitmore, Thomas McKenna and Lowri McKenna. You do not have to say anything but it may harm your defence if you do not mention when questioned something that you later rely on in court. Anything you do say may be given in evidence.'

His face is flushed with anger. 'Fucking get off me, you cunts!'

'He was shredding papers upstairs, ma'am,' says Carling. 'Whatever it was, he didn't want us to see it.'

Chapter 51

IT'S LUNCHTIME AND ARCHER IS in the incident room with Quinn and Klara waiting on DC Phillips and two of the available detectives that DCI Pierce pulled from other teams. Archer wants everything in place before they interview the suspect. Klara has compiled a presentation using an iPad. It contains photographs of the victims, before and after their murder, and shots from the crime scenes including the masks. Finch is being processed downstairs and awaiting his brief. They had found him shredding and burning paperwork. He had also smashed up a laptop.

Archer looks at the picture of Lucas Todd's birthday party in the garden of Penny Todd's Battersea home. Using her fingers, she zooms in on the children's entertainer. He is an eccentric figure. Wearing a long, dark double-breasted coat, he brandishes a magician's wand in one hand and flowers in the other. His face is painted white, his eyes are black and hollow like a skull's. A piece of thick black electrical tape covers his mouth. Daubed on it, in white paint, is what looks like an emoji-type smile. On his head is a weathered bowler hat. Pinned on it is a badge depicting the comedy and tragedy theatre masks.

'It's definitely him, isn't it?' says Quinn. 'He's even wearing DMs.'

Archer looks at the thick black boots with yellow laces. 'No question.'

'Everyone that's available is here,' says Klara.

'Let's begin then,' says Archer, nodding at the analyst.

Klara kicks off. 'Paul Finch. Age forty-five. Divorced. No kids. Site manager and business partner at Clerkenwell Construction. Has a record. Bit of GBH from drunken fights. Stole a few cars when he was young.'

Archer says, 'We have a team at Finch's house right now. We need volunteers at Clerkenwell Construction to talk to the people who work for him.'

'Dawn and I can go,' says a bearded DC named Collins.

'Thank you,' says Archer. 'Gather whatever info you have. Find out who knew him best. His assistant, Jenny Barclay, would be a good start. What is he like? What are his habits, et cetera?'

'Understood, ma'am,' says Collins.

Archer turns to DC Phillips. 'Marian, what have you got?'

'I spoke to Penny Todd,' says Phillips. 'She hired Paul Finch to entertain the kids at her son Lucas's birthday party. She said he calls himself The Silent Man. Penny recalls giving the contact details to her partner, Oliver Stockwell, who passed them on to his neighbours, the Whitmores.'

'So, children's parties are the connection,' says Archer, her mind processing all possibilities.

'I had a word with Kirsty May just before this meeting,' says Quinn. 'She's never had a party at the McKennas with any children's entertainer. But she did know that one of Tommy's friends – she doesn't recall his name – did this line of work on the side.'

Klara speaks. 'Looking at the big picture, the McKennas remain the outsiders in this puzzle. No party for Kirsty. Kirsty is a foster child. The other kids are not. Plus, it seems Finch has a personal connection with Tommy McKenna. What we know so far, the relationship with the Todds and the Whitmores was professional. He provided a service.'

'A clown service. With extras,' says Quinn.

'The parents are the victims always. Why?' asks Archer.

'We know Finch had beef with Tommy despite others telling us they were drinking buddies,' says Quinn.

'Tommy's other mate, Marcel, confirmed that. He said that Finch and Tommy were "OK". Obviously, there was other stuff going on that Marcel was not privy to.'

There's a knock on the door. PC Carling is standing outside, holding a brown evidence envelope. Quinn opens the door. 'Come in, Lee,' he says.

Archer introduces him to the team.

'We just finished the search, ma'am. Unfortunately, we didn't find any duct tape, or white makeup. No Dr Martens boots either. We looked pretty much everywhere and left no stone unturned. I can only imagine he keeps that stuff elsewhere, at a lock-up or another place.'

'One for you and Dawn, DC Collins. Look around the site and see if you can find any of those items.'

'Yes, ma'am,' says Collins.

Archer turns back to PC Carling. 'Did you talk to the neighbours?'

'Yes, ma'am. That's still ongoing. He lives alone. Keeps pretty much to himself. It was a surprise to them when I asked if they'd ever seen him dressed as a clown. Some laughed. One even said, "What? That miserable git."'

'The more we hear about Finch, the more we warm to him,' says Quinn.

Carling continues, 'He'd pretty much shredded and torched most of the paperwork. It was obvious he did not want us to find it, whatever *it* was. That said, we managed to salvage some of it. Not much, but some. It's bank statements from different accounts. One of the accounts has the Clerkenwell Construction name on it.' He hands across the evidence envelope. 'It's all in here.'

'Thank you, Lee. This is really good work,' says Archer.

Carling smiles. 'Anytime,' he replies and leaves.

'Could be embezzling,' says Klara. 'He's a business partner and presumably has access to the company account. I'll get to work on his laptop and phone. See what I can dig up. Do you need anything else from me?'

'Nothing, thanks, Klara. If you find anything important, let us know straightaway. Even if we're interviewing him.'

'Will do.'

'Can someone find out who his business partner is and talk to him?' Archer asks.

'I can do that,' says Phillips.

'Thanks, Marian.' Archer addresses the room, 'Any questions?'

A collective murmur of no.

'Good luck today and let's find out as much as we can to nail this guy,' says Archer.

Why is he killing the parents? she wonders. Her mind reaches for something across what seems an empty void. And then it comes to her. She looks back at the iPad and the photo of Lucas Todd's party. She focuses in on the boy. His arm. 'Lucas Todd broke his arm at his birthday party,' she says.

Quinn says, 'Something happened between him and his dad.'

'Penny Todd said it was an accident but no one else quite saw it that way.'

'Derek Fox blamed Jason Todd for breaking Lucas's arm.'

Archer turns back to the iPad, opens Instagram and searches through Christine Whitmore's photos. She finds Uma's birthday party. There are several photos. She swipes through a mostly happy scene. Four photos in, she sees the white-faced children's entertainer in the background, performing and wearing his joyless black tape smile. In the next shot, Uma is crying. Robert Whitmore is frowning at her. Below the photo is the caption 'Father and daughter clash at party LOL'. In the background, the clown is watching, a malevolent figure taking in the scene. Archer feels the hairs on her neck stand. His hands are curled into fists, and he has turned his taped smile upside down into a frown.

'He's triggered by something to do with the parents. They get angry at their kids or in extreme cases accidentally break an arm.'

Paul Finch is seated in an interview room talking to his brief, a thin grey man named Jacob Goldman. Archer and Quinn sit at the table opposite them.

'OK, let's begin,' says Archer. 'For the purposes of the recording, Paul, could you please state your name and date of birth.'

'Paul Joseph Finch. Born 10 May 1980.'

Before Archer can ask the first question, Jacob Goldman leans across and says, 'What you're accusing my client of is absurd, DI Archer. He refutes all the accusations laid at him.'

Archer's eyes slide to Finch's. 'Then why did you run from us, Paul?'

'No comment,' he replies, without meeting her gaze.

Archer turns to Goldman, who arches an eyebrow at her.

'What were you burning at your house, Paul?' asks Quinn.

'No comment.'

'What were you shredding at your house?'

'No comment.'

'Why did you smash up your laptop?'

'No comment.'

'You resisted arrest, didn't you?'

'No comment.'

'Is that going to be your answer for every question, Paul?' Archer asks.

'No comment.'

Archer slides open the iPad and brings up a photograph of Jason Todd.

'Do you know who this man is?'

Finch looks at the picture with a puzzled expression and frowns at Archer. 'No comment.'

'His name was Jason Todd. He was thirty-five years old, a father, he lived in Albany Mansions in Battersea. Look again. Do you recognise him?'

'No comment.'

'Have you ever spoken to him?'

'No comment.'

'Have you ever been in the same room as him?'

'No comment.'

Archer opens the second photograph. 'This is Robert Whitmore, a thirty-eight-year-old banker, who was also a husband and father. Do you recognise him?'

Finch shifts on his seat. 'No . . . no comment.'

'Have you ever spoken to him?'

'No comment.'

'Have you ever been in the same room as him?'

Goldman intervenes. 'I don't know where you're going with this, DI Archer. My client does not know nor has he ever met any of these people.'

Archer shows him a photograph of the McKennas. 'Do you recognise the couple in this picture, Paul? I'm not sure a "no comment" will hold, considering he did work for you.'

Finch shoots a nervous glance at his brief. Goldman nods. 'Yes,' replies Finch.

'Tell us their names,' says Quinn.

'Tommy and Lowri.'

'You and Tommy were mates,' says Quinn.

Finch frowns again. 'No, we weren't.'

'You'd been drinking with him. At the Angel in Bermondsey. We have a witness.'

'Your witness is lying. I haven't been to the Angel in years!'

'Our witness says you were supposed to meet Tommy McKenna at the Angel the night he was murdered.'

'Your witness is wrong.'

Archer brings up a shot of Tommy McKenna's corpse. 'Where were you on the twenty-third of March, the night Tommy and Lowri were murdered?'

A sly smile creeps over Finch's face. 'I wasn't anywhere near Tommy or his wife.'

'You didn't like Tommy, did you?' asks Quinn. 'Did you want him out of the way? Why?'

'I didn't kill him or his wife.'

'Do you have another job, Paul?' Archer asks.

He rolls his eyes as if bored. 'No. I don't.'

'Do you like clowning around?' Quinn asks.

Archer slides the laptop across displaying the picture of Lucas Todd's birthday party with the white-faced trickster. 'Jason Todd's ex-wife Penny Todd claims that she booked Paul Finch otherwise known as The Silent Man to entertain the kids at her son's birthday party. This is you, isn't it?' Archer points at the sinister figure in the photo.

Finch stares at it in what seems like disbelief. 'That fucker. He's set me up.'

Archer exchanges a concerned glance with Quinn.

Finch looks up at them and grins a smug smile. 'You two are barking up the wrong tree. It's not me that you want.'

Archer's patience is thinning. 'Who is it we want, Paul?'

'If you want him, you might want to hurry across to Covent Garden Market or Leicester Square. He might just be performing at one of those spots. Better be quick or you'll miss the show.'

Archer feels her grip on this investigation loosening, 'Who's performing?'

Finch leans back in his chair, enjoying the twist in this interrogation. 'No comment,' he laughs.

Chapter 52

'**D**O YOU THINK HE'S BULLSHITTING us?' asks Quinn.

They are standing in the processing block, watching Finch being escorted back to his cell.

'I don't know.'

'It's a shame those days are gone.'

'What days?'

'The days when we could tie a suspect to a chair and beat the truth from him.'

Archer folds her arms. 'I think we should go take a look. What do we have to lose?'

'You know I'm kidding, right?'

'About what?'

'Beating the truth from suspects.'

'Sometimes I prefer to let your jocularity sail over my head.'

'That's nice.'

'You're welcome.'

He smiles. 'Anyway, I'm inclined to agree. We could take one location each. Any preference for Leicester Square or Covent Garden?'

'I'll take Covent Garden,' says Archer.

'OK. Do you want a couple of chummy bobbies to accompany us?'

'I think we'll be fine. To be honest, I'm not sure this will come to much. That said, if you catch sight of him, call it in and call me, obviously.'

'Obviously,' Archer replies with a wry smile.

She crosses Chandos Place and turns left up Bedford Street. It's late afternoon, the bars and restaurants are beginning to fill with the after-work and pre-theatre clientele. A gap clears in the traffic, and she hurries across the road, turning right up Henrietta Street. Her phone rings. It's Grandad.

'Hey. How're you doing?' she says.

'Hello, dear. I'm doing very well. How're you?'

'Good.'

'We have cause to celebrate.'

'We do?'

'I'm getting out tomorrow.'

'Oh, Grandad, that's wonderful. What did the doctor say?'

'Just that I had a small stroke but I'm doing fine now. So, they want to send me home and give the bed to a more needy patient.'

'I'm so happy to hear that. I'll pick you up.'

'If you're able.'

'Did they give you a time?'

Above the heads of the hordes, she sees the spiral arched window of the London Transport Museum ahead. To its left, the sound of old-style scratchy gramophone music drifts from the piazza. She hears cheering and laughter too.

'They didn't specify a time. You know what they're like. It'll happen when it happens.'

'OK. Will you call me when you know?'

'Yes, I will.'

'That's such great news.'

'I thought I'd call you now. I didn't want you to come by later and find me sleeping.'

'Are you tired?'

He yawns. 'I just sent Cosmo home. He wore me out. Not his fault, I just need some sleep.'

'I'm sorry I won't see you later.'

'We can make up for it tomorrow when I get home.'

'Yes, we will.'

'Bye, Grace.'

'Sleep tight. See you tomorrow.'

Threading through the clusters of people, her eyes slide to a small restaurant on the ground floor of an old townhouse. Named after a local English courtesan, Cora Pearl, the interior's dimly lit comforting Parisian-style decor glows warmly inside. Quinn had been going through a tough time recently after the death of a girlfriend. Archer and Klara had taken him there for a blowout. She smiles at the memory. It had been worth every penny.

Turning left, onto the West Piazza, she stops at the edge of a twenty-deep circle of people standing on the damp cobbles, opposite the NatWest Bank. They're cheering and laughing at whoever is entertaining them in the centre. She sees three large daggers spinning in the air and slips sideways into the throng, apologising as she inches her way through the close-knit audience. Her phone rings once more. It's Quinn. She answers, 'Any luck?'

'Nah. No sign of him. How about you?'

'It's crammed here. I'm just making my way through to take a look at a street performer.'

Archer is near the centre. She stands on her toes and peers over the shoulders of the people in front. She sees a shirtless, smiling man of colour with dreadlocks sitting on the shoulders of an identical man. Both are juggling knives.

'Is it him?'

327

'No. I'll keep looking.'

'I'm heading your way. Just walking down Cecil Court. I'll be with you in five.'

'See you shortly.'

Archer leaves the gathering and sees a second crowd gathered outside the four columns of the immense portico entrance to The Actors' Church, St Paul's. A rope has been tied between two of the pillars. Walking gracefully across it is a muscular, bearded lady wearing a tight basque and a wide Victorian skirt. She is cheered and clapped by a captive audience.

Archer leaves the West Piazza and crosses to Covent Garden, where a man dressed in Union Jack underpants lies on a bed of nails. A Japanese tourist balances precariously on his chest, much to the amusement of his friends.

Archer hears a woman scream followed by laughter. A group of people have gathered at the corner of James Street and Covent Garden. Music is playing. A haunting gothic punk song with a jagged guitar, echoing bass, and a fast-tapping drumbeat. She makes her way towards them. The singer chants about Bela Lugosi being dead.

Above the onlookers' heads a dark coat flaps in the air like a giant bat and floats down inside the circle.

Archer slides inside the crowd. They're watching a man lying on the ground, the coat lies on top of him like a shroud. His body begins to jerk to the rhythm of the music. And then he slowly sits up, like one of the undead rising from his coffin.

'He's freaking me out!' someone says, giggling.

'Wait till you see his face,' someone else says.

The performer rises jerkily to his feet. He's wearing a threadbare double-breasted baggy pinstripe suit and white Converse trainers. *No Dr Martens*. His arms flail in a strange, crooked dance. He throws himself into the air like a broken marionette and then stands with his arms folded across his chest like a corpse in a coffin. Cheers and claps from the crowd.

As the song reaches a crescendo, he spins, turning his back to Archer. He tears the coat from his shoulders and throws it into the air. It floats above them and falls to the ground by his feet. She sees the back of his head. Large protruding ears. Black hair, short and spiky.

The audience opposite cower and shriek in delight.

Her phone rings. It's Quinn again. She swipes it.

'Any luck?' he asks.

'I'm not sure.' Archer edges around the rim of the crowd, leaning forward to get a better view of the performer's face. But he turns in the opposite direction almost as if he is gliding, revealing himself to his captive audience.

'Where are you?' she asks.

'Bottom of James Street.'

'I'm fighting my way through the hordes. Be there in a few minutes.'

He turns and she sees his face for the first time. Her heartbeat quickens. His face is painted white, his eyes are closed and black as coal. Dark tape with a daubed smile covers his mouth.

'It's him!' says Archer.

'Oh my God!' someone says.

The Silent Man opens his eyes wide. They are bulbous and yellow with coloured contacts.

'I'm running,' says Quinn. 'Don't try anything until I get there!'

'I'll call for backup.' She ends the call and phones Charing Cross.

The Silent Man's eyes clock Archer's. His brow knots.

Her call is picked up. 'This is Detective Inspector Grace Archer. I need backup at the corner of James Street and Covent Garden immediately. Now!'

Archer raises her free arm. 'Police. Stay right where you are!'

Peeling off the tape, the Silent Man turns it over, sticks it back on, reversing the smile into a frown.

'I'm Detective Inspector Archer. I'm arresting you—'

But before she can finish, he charges her, his eyes wild with anger and shoves her hard.

'Oof!' The wind is knocked from her as she tumbles backwards, thudding on the damp cobbles, her phone slipping from her hand. He stands over her, hands curled into fists, shaking them at her in an odd theatrical manner. And then he turns, snatches up his coat and bolts up James Street.

'What the hell was that about?' someone says.

Archer grabs her phone and pushes herself up.

'Grace!' comes Quinn's voice.

She turns to see him hurrying towards her.

'What happened?'

'He got away. He's gone up James Street.' Archer calls Charing Cross again, as they hurry up James Street. 'He's wearing a pinstripe suit, Converse trainers, short spiky dark hair. Really, he won't be hard to miss.'

There's no sign of him.

'I'll take Floral Street,' says Archer.

'I'll take Long Acre and anywhere else I can.'

Archer searches everywhere in and around Floral Street. She exits the narrow walkway of Rose Street, sees Quinn running down Long Acre, his eyes scanning every person and every store. He spots her and shrugs. 'He could have turned right up Long Acre or gone down Neal Street.'

'He recognised me. I'm sure of it.'

'We should go back to the station and put the thumbscrews on Finch. That fucker has to speak.'

'Agreed.'

On their way back, Archer calls Klara. 'Hey. Did you get anything from Finch's laptop?'

'Aside from watching a lot of porn he also likes to gamble. He visits various gambling sites three or four times a day, every day. Seems he has a problem. He's in debt and has been taking money from the company account.'

'You were right about the embezzling.'

'An informed guess.'

'We'll be back at the station shortly. I want to talk to Finch once more. Listen, I need you to drop everything and find out what you can about a Covent Garden street performer called the Silent Man.'

'Is this a new case?'

'Same case. I'll explain everything when I see you.

Quinn practically kicks open Finch's cell door. He frowns when they enter and shrinks back against the wall. Quinn pulls him off the bed and squares up to him. 'Who the fuck is he?'

'You can't just come in here and rough me up. I want my brief. I have rights.'

'Four people are dead. Possibly more for all we know. So, screw your rights.'

'Mr Finch, we know you've been embezzling,' says Archer. 'We have the evidence from your hard drive. We're going to keep you here for the next twenty-four hours, and once I leave here, I will apply for a further twenty-four hours, if not more, to keep you here until you tell us who the Silent Man is. As I see it now, you're complicit in these murders if you do not cooperate. We'll leave you to make that choice.'

Quinn shoves him back on the bed.

They turn to leave.

'Wait!'

Archer and Quinn turn to look at him.

'You've met him. He works for me. Marcel.'

'Marcel?' says Archer.

Finch nods. 'That's not his real name. It's a nickname we give him.'

Archer frowns.

'You know ... ' Finch starts pressing his palms in the air like he's pushing against a sheet of glass ' ... the mime bloke. Marcel Marceau.'

'Hilarious,' says Quinn.

'His real name's Hughes. He's Welsh, I think.'

Part 4

Chapter 53

OVERNIGHT, BRYNN HAD SLEPT UNDER the bushes in Abbey Wood Park. It had been damp and cold, but he'd had the presence of mind to grab a sleeping bag when his father returned home like an angry bear, stinking of whisky and vomit. In his drunken state, he had swung clumsily for Brynn and missed. As a result, he'd fallen over, allowing time for Brynn's hasty exit.

Rolling up the sleeping bag, he inserts it into the nylon carrier, makes his way across the park and onwards to Holstein Way, where he watches his house from behind a wall at the corner of the street. The light is on in the living room. Silhouetted in the net curtains is Dad, rubbing his hands backwards and forwards over his head. After a moment he disappears and returns, pulling on his high-vis jacket. Further down the street, Brynn notices the postman pushing his trolley. He hears a hacking dry cough and sees his father closing the front door. Dad makes a loud choking sound to clear his throat and spits a disgusting globule of green phlegm on to the ground. He pauses to look at it before turning down the street away from where Brynn is hiding. When his father is out of sight, Brynn makes his way down to the front of the house. He inserts the key.

'Mornin'. Got mail for ya,' comes a voice.

Brynn turns to see the postman, hand extended. Mail in his hand. Two brown letters and one lavender envelope with green writing. He recognises the handwriting. His heart skips. *Iris?*

'Thanks,' he says, taking the letters.

Closing the door behind him, he then hurries up the stairs, drops the brown letters on the kitchen table and makes his way to his bedroom on the second floor. He sits on the edge of the bed and opens the lavender envelope. Inside is a greeting card with a drawing of the Victorian clown, Joseph Grimaldi. Brynn has seen the picture before. Grimaldi is wearing a Russian-style, long green overcoat with furred collar and cuffs. His wide, round head is painted white, his large eyes daubed blue, and his thick smiling lips are coloured a deep red. There is something deranged in Grimaldi's expression that resonates with Brynn. An image flashes in his mind, triggering a bout of nausea. He sees his father looking down at him in the hole in the garage floor, his face with its unhinged expression, coated in concrete dust. He pushes the image from his mind and opens the card.

Dear Brynn,

I was passing a shop in Bristol, saw this card in the window and thought of you. Remember that book I found among Aunty Jean's collection. The one I left with your dad? Memoirs of Joseph Grimaldi, *I think it was.*

Brynn looks across at the weathered hardback on his bedside table. He had read it many times.

Anyway, I still think of that day when we walked to school and talked about our dreams of joining a circus. I was going to dress in a sexy corset and fly from trapeze to trapeze, whirling through the air like a beautiful bird. And you would be dressed up in your funny outfit, making us all laugh. It seems like an age ago but it's only three years. Can you believe it?

I often wonder about you. Shortly after Aunty Jean died, we moved to Bristol. It's nice here but I miss London. I still miss you. I sent you letter after letter and two gift boxes. One for Christmas and one for your birthday. I never heard back from you. I want you to know I'm not cross. I know people move on. I assumed you'd found a new girlfriend. Is she as kooky as me? I bet she's not. But I hope you're happy anyway.

Confusion swirls through him. What letters? He thinks about his father. Did he throw them away or hide them? He wouldn't put it past him! He continues reading.

My parents separated, but you probably know that already from my previous letters. I live with my mum, who's not as mental as she was when my dad was around. She's helping me out a lot. Oh, my other news. I'm pregnant! Can you believe it? I'm going to have a baby girl. Mum's going to help me look after her as the bloke I was seeing was (is) an asshole. Anyway, she's going to be born either at the end of this year or in the first few days of the new millennium. I'm so hoping that she will be one of the first babies born in the year 2000. That would be so cool, don't you think?

The downside is that there's no hope of me living my dreams now. Haha! Not that there ever was with my turns and all. Although they have calmed down, thank God.

That's all my news. I think about you as the new Grimaldi. London's finest entertainer with his wacky suit and painted

337

face. I love that idea. I hope everything is good for you,
Brynn, I really do, and I hope you become the person you
were always meant to be.

> *Love,*
> *Iris*
> *XXX*

He trembles, his jaw clenching. Rage sweeps through him like a blizzard freezing what remains of his broken soul. He drops his head, rubs his eyes and forehead over and over with his hands. He rocks back and forth on the bed, groaning. His hands clutch at his hair and tug it, pulling it until it hurts, and tufts lie between his scrunched fingers. He opens his mouth and screams until his throat goes dry. Tears sting his eyes, and he screams once more. He shakes his head and pounds it with his fists.

Three years have passed since Iris left with her parents. He had written to her every week in the beginning. Desperate letters of teenage love that was not meant to be. Had her parents kept his letters from her? He never saw hers and always lived in hope that she might write back. But then he had come to believe that she had given up on him and found someone else. Despite being in his life for just a short period there had not been a day when he did not think of her. His thoughts turn to his father. *That bastard! He's killed me.* He screams once more and stands, every muscle in his body taut like fists. Trembling, he lashes out with his foot at his bedside table, kicking it hard, stomping on it, shattering it to pieces. He rips his mattress from the bed and tosses it across the room.

He thinks about Iris's letters. Could they be hidden somewhere? Was it Dad's intention to show them to him one day? To mock him or to ease his conscience with one of his rare guilt trips? Brynn needs to know if they're hidden. He must find the truth.

He hurries down to his father's bedroom and searches through every drawer in the dresser, the wardrobe, under the bed. His rage burns cold as he rips the room apart. But he finds no letters. Without a thought for the consequences, Brynn tears up the living room, the kitchen, every corner, every space in the house but still he finds nothing. Hot, sweaty and out of breath, he sits on the stairs looking down at the front hallway. He notices the doorway to the garage is slightly ajar. Brynn shudders. He has not set foot in there in three years. Not since the day Dad put him there and left him alone in that grave. Since then, Dad had wanted Brynn to fill in the hole. It was his penance. His 'manning up'. But there was no way he was ever going back in that room. He recalls something Dad had said to him: 'Face your fears. Go back into the garage. You may be surprised at what you find.' What had he meant by that?

Brynn stands and slowly makes his way downstairs, his eyes never leaving the darkness oozing out from the gap in the entrance to the garage.

His heart is pounding.

That room has filled him with terror, which deep down he knows is illogical. *You may be surprised at what you find.* Had Dad put the letters there knowing that Brynn was too frightened to go poking around? He closes his eyes. Shoving all thoughts of the trauma from his mind, he pushes open the door, reaches for the light switch and turns it on. He hears the tube light flicker and fizz into life. Brynn takes a breath and opens his eyes. He cannot bring himself to look down at the hole. His eye slide across the worktop on the left side of the garage. There's a barstool on top, a toolbox, a drill, a large mallet, and a roll of black electrical tape. The space underneath is clear. No sign of any letters. On the right side of the garage there are two pairs of Dad's boots, a spare builder's helmet and a high-vis jacket hanging on the wall. There are also three large bags of cement that Dad expected Brynn to mix up and use to fill in the hole. But there are no letters. Only one place remains where the letters could be if they still exist.

Slowly, he drops his gaze to the floor. He hadn't realised the hole is now covered with a sheet of MDF peppered with his father's boot prints. He crouches down, slides the MDF across, revealing the grave beneath. He swallows, peers down and gasps. Lying at the bottom of the pit are dozens of scattered letters and unopened packages. Iris's correspondence to him. His eyes begin to well, his fists clench. He is broken. Pushing his fists into his eyes, he opens his mouth wide and screams a silent scream.

Chapter 54

ARCHER HAS FAST-TRACKED A TEAM of MO19 Specialist Firearms Command. Hughes is using an illegal taser. Who knows what other illegal weapons he has. She's not prepared to put an officer's life at risk. Wipers on full, she steers the Volvo, keeping pace behind the police van as it speeds through Greenwich and the pouring rain and onwards to Holstein Way in Erith, south-east London.

Klara is on the phone speaker.

'I found him on the Police National Computer database. He has previous for stalking.'

'We have his fingerprints and DNA then,' says Archer.

'We sure do. He was arrested for stalking a woman in 2005. He was prosecuted but not sentenced because he was the sole carer for his sick father. Hughes also claimed he suffered from a learning disability, which had held him back all his life. For those reasons he was cautioned. In 2012, he was arrested a second time for stalking a man. He got off lightly again. Apparently, his father had recently passed. Hughes said he was "broken-hearted". He also claimed he was full of remorse for what he had done. He ended up with community service and a fine.'

'Did Hughes explain why he stalked these people?' Quinn asks.

Archer eases on the brakes as they reach a busy junction with traffic pouring from all directions. The MO19 van pushes through, lights flashing, siren howling. Archer stays close behind, following in its wake.

'Yes, I scanned the transcripts, and this won't come as any surprise. He said they were "awful people". What he meant by that was they were, in his opinion, terrible parents. "Abusers" was the term he used. He said he had witnessed them "harming" their kids in public. When asked to elaborate, he said both parents had lost their tempers. One had slapped their kid's wrist; the other had caused a scene and shouted at his child. Both kids had screamed and sobbed, apparently, so he said. There was no evidence to back up these claims, by the way.'

'What parent hasn't lost it with their kid?' says Quinn.

'He has a warped view of the world around him. He's triggered by what he perceives as child abuse,' says Archer, breaking through the gridlocked junction. 'As far as we can tell, all of his victims have been regular people. Parents with short fuses or in some cases, drink problems. Jason Todd was drunk when he accidentally broke Lucas's arm at his birthday party. Hughes was present with the other adults. He witnessed the whole thing.'

'Right. There's also that Instagram picture from Uma Whitmore's party,' says Quinn. 'The sinister one with an angry-looking Silent Man watching a distressed Uma.'

'Exactly,' replies Archer. 'The McKennas – Hughes knew them. They were good people, but they drank almost every night. Did he think them unfit to be foster parents?'

'Considering his previous arrests and conviction, why is he killing now? Why wait this long if you're that fucked up?' says Quinn.

'We don't know that he hasn't killed before,' says Archer.

'We know no one has been murdered in what is Hughes's signature method: the duct tape, the sad smiley,' says Klara.

Archer says, 'That's right. But maybe Jason Todd is not his first. That we need to find out. Also, the thing about these murders is they are all quite close together. Regardless of whether he's killed before or not, he has been thinking about it, probably for years. These thoughts have been cooking in his head and it was only a matter of time before he acted on his urges. Killing, to him, is like heroin to an addict.'

Quinn says, 'Is it possible his alter ego, the Silent Man, is the real killer here?'

'A split personality?'

'I'm no expert but perhaps by putting on his makeup, transitioning from Brynn Hughes to the Silent Man, it changes who he is. It gives him the confidence to act on his urges. Like Norman Bates dressing up as his mother.'

Archer considers this and shoots a smiling glance at Quinn. 'I think that's a sound theory, Harry. I like it.'

'You can quote me later on the report.'

'Do you guys need anything else?' asks Klara.

'I'm good for now, Klara. Harry?'

'Nothing from me.'

'Good luck both of you and stay safe.'

Ten minutes later, the van drives on to a grass verge at the edge of Alsike Road. A group of youths walking past stop and watch with interest. Archer parks near the entrance to Holstein Way. She and Quinn exit the car and pull on their bulletproof vests.

'Woah! What's going on here?' calls one of the youths.

'Piss off, pigs!' says another.

The firearms team leader, a stocky Newcastle man, Sergeant Bill Armstrong, hops out from the van and circles back to the Volvo.

'He lives in a townhouse. We'll go on foot from here and cover the front and rear,' he says.

'Understood, Sergeant.'

The team of six, carrying assault rifles and armed with pistols, split into two teams of three. Squinting through the rain, Archer and Quinn hurry after Armstrong and his two officers.

'What you doing here with those little peashooters!' calls one of the youths.

Archer ignores them and hurries through the evening gloom, the officers' heavy boots echoing on the wet street. Holstein Way is a charmless row of ugly three-storey concrete townhouses with front gardens. They could have been designed and made in the seventies or eighties. Who knows? She doesn't much care. Hughes' garden is unkempt and overgrown with grass and weeds and a rusted garden table. A single plastic chair lies on its side.

From what she can see, there are no lights on in his house. Armstrong is making his way cautiously up the garden. He looks back quickly and signals for his men to come closer. One of them is carrying a battering ram. Archer and Quinn hang back as the sergeant knocks three times on the door.

'Mr Hughes. Police. Please open the door,' he calls.

They wait for two minutes. No response.

Armstrong knocks harder this time. 'Mr Hughes. Police. Open up.'

Still no response. The sergeant nods to the officer with the battering ram. They switch places. On the second attempt, Hughes's door caves in like cardboard. The officers charge inside. She hears them shouting and Armstrong barking orders. Minutes pass and the sergeant emerges. He shakes his head. 'No one here, I'm afraid.'

'Shit!' hisses Archer.

'Did you want to take a look inside?'

'We do. Thanks, Sergeant Armstrong.'

'Thanks, Bill,' says Quinn.

'No problem. We'll be outside. Let me know if you need anything.'

The entrance to the house is through a weathered sunroom containing several gardening tools that have evidently not been used in a long time. There's a fusty, unaired smell as they enter the narrow hallway. There are two doors. One room leads to a storeroom stuffed with bin bags full of what looks like old clothes and a washing machine. The second door leads to an empty garage. Upstairs, they turn right into the living room. The walls are painted magnolia, the carpet is a threadbare navy colour with a grubby zebra-patterned rug laid on top. A fake baroque fireplace with an electric fire is the focal point of the room. The decor has not been changed in thirty years or more, she reckons.

'I wonder if we have the same decorator,' says Quinn.

'That had crossed my mind.'

'I'm not sure his has the wow factor that mine does.'

'There's no competition.'

With little to see, they leave the living room. In the kitchen, Archer notices a Post-it note stuck to the battered door of an old fridge freezer. It contains a mobile phone number. She peels it off and reads it.

The Parkers 12 p.m. 24/03

'That was yesterday,' says Quinn.

She takes out her phone and calls the number. It rings but goes straight to voicemail.

'Hi. This is Linda. Can't take your call right now. Leave me a message and I'll get right back.'

345

'Hello, Linda. My name is Detective Inspector Grace Archer. Please could you give me a call back on this number urgently. Thank you.'

She ends the call and phones Klara.

'Hey, Grace. Was he there?'

'No. He may show up yet. We're inside his house and we'll hang around for a bit. Listen, could you get me the details of a mobile number?'

'Sure. What do you need?'

Quinn is making his way to the next floor.

'It belongs to a Linda Parker. I need her address, if possible.'

'I'll get on that now and call you back as soon as I can.'

'Thanks.'

Archer ends the call, pockets the phone, and makes her way upstairs. The ceiling has nebulous grey damp stains that are spreading to the walls. There is a ripe and unpleasant smell.

Quinn is emerging from one of the bedrooms. 'This room and the rear bedroom are empty.'

Brynn Hughes's bedroom is above the living room over-looking the garden. It has an underlying smell of stale sweat and sweet chemicals of Lynx deodorant that clings to the walls and surfaces. Her eyes are drawn to a dressing table with an old bar stool in front of it. On top of the dresser is a triple mirror and a Tiffany lamp. Scattered on the surface are several jars of face paint. Four white and two black.

There's an unmade double bed and a wobbly fake pine wardrobe that looks set to return any minute to its original flat-packed status. Hanging inside are rows of horizontal striped shirts. There is also a baggy suit similar to the one he was wearing today, and a long double-breasted coat. On the top shelf is a bowler hat. Pinned to it is the comedy and tragedy theatre masks badge.

'I found his boots,' says Quinn from the other side of the room.

She looks around and sees him crouched by the bed. There are a pair of old Dr Martens with yellow laces lying underneath. She gestures at the wardrobe. 'The rest of his "murder drag" is in here.'

They return downstairs. Sergeant Armstrong is waiting. 'I've put some of the team in with some of the more agreeable neighbours to keep eyes front and back.'

'Thank you, Sergeant Armstrong. We'll be in the car if you need us.'

They wait in the Volvo, listening idly to the police radio.

'Can't see him coming back here tonight. He'll know we're waiting,' says Quinn.

'It's worth a shot.'

Archer's phone rings. It's Klara.

'I have the address. It's forty-two Osbald Road in Stoke Newington. I looked her up. She lives there with her husband, Julian Parker, and daughter, Charlotte.'

'A family unit that fits the profile for the Silent Man.'

'That's what I thought. I'm scanning through the photos on Linda Parker's social media. So far I'm not seeing any parties with the suspect in attendance. I'll keep searching. If I find anything, I'll call you.'

'Thanks, Klara. I'll see if I can get someone to call in on the Parkers.'

'Talk later.'

'Bye.'

Chapter 55

STRIPPED TO HIS WAIST AND seated on the barstool perched at the worktop in the garage, Brynn takes a swig from a bottle of whisky he had found in a cupboard in the kitchen. Despite his father's ban on all music in the house, Brynn is playing a mix tape on the portable cassette player he keeps hidden in his bedroom. He likes dark music, melodic guitars, haunting bass, gloomy songs of regret and anger. Radiohead's 'Creep' is playing: it has a special place in his busted heart.

He has read through all of Iris's love letters in order. They began with a tearful Iris missing him, wanting to run away with him to flee her 'terrible' parents. This thread carried through to later letters when she questions why he was not writing back to her. Eventually, she sent what she claimed was her final letter, almost eighteen months ago. That was the hardest one to read. Her heart was broken. His is crushed.

There were packages too. Chocolates, long out of date, which he eats anyway, washing them down with the harsh whisky that tears at his throat. He feels light-headed.

One package had captured his interest. A birthday gift containing two tubs of face paint. One white. One black. There is a card depicting a gothic-looking mime artist with black stitches painted as a smile. Inside, Iris has written:

Always follow your dreams.
Happy birthday.
Love, Iris.
XXX

Brynn has taken the mirror from the bathroom and set it on the worktop. He smiles dreamily at his reflection. He barely recognises himself. He has smeared his face and neck in white face paint. It's amateur-looking but has the desired effect of making him feel like a different person. His eyes are daubed roughly with black paint, almost like a mask. He grins. His teeth seem more yellow than usual. He frowns in an exaggerated fashion and grins again. Something is not right. He looks at the picture of the gothic mime with his sinister smile. Brynn's eyes catch the roll of black tape across the worktop. A memory flashes in his mind. His mouth bound and layered with tape. For the first time, he feels no fear. He picks up the roll, bites off a strip and sticks it over his mouth. He looks at his reflection, his eyes widening. Joy Division's 'Transmission' begins playing on the cassette player. He has found himself. He dips his finger in the white paint and draws a smile on the tape. His eyes well. Ian Curtis's dark baritone vocals resonate around the garage. Brynn cocks his head, admiring himself. He cranks up the volume and begins to dance in a jerking fashion like he'd seen Ian Curtis do on the television. He catches his reflection in the mirror and feels like he's in another world.

'What the hell is going on here?'

Brynn freezes. Dad's large silhouette is framed in the doorway, his hands covering his ears. He can see Dad's body go rigid as he takes in Brynn, his painted face and the half-drunk bottle of whisky.

'That's my whisky, you fucking little shit!'

He charges into the garage, fists clenched, ready to do damage. Brynn reaches for the mallet, which he has kept close by all day. As his father rounds on him, Brynn swings it with all his might, slamming it hard into Dad's temple. His eyes blink in confusion, he stumbles and tries to retain his balance. Brynn raises the mallet once more and hits him a second time. Dad falls face down to the ground. Brynn grabs the duct tape and binds his wrists and ankles. He then binds his mouth but that doesn't satisfy him. Dad's eyes are twitching. Brynn wraps the tape over them and continues until his head and neck are completely covered. Dad begins to shake and tug at his bonds. Brynn feels nothing. He rolls him over to the hole and pushes him inside. Dad falls to the bottom. It takes only moments for him run out of air and stop shaking. Still Brynn feels nothing. All he knows is that Dad is gone forever and he, Brynn, is free.

He rewinds the track and starts dancing again, feeling the happiest he has felt in a long time. He stops and looks at his reflection. Tearing off the tape, he turns it upside down, reversing the smile into a frown and sticks it back on. He rubs his eyes, pretending to cry, and then looks across at the bags of cement. Time to fix that hole.

Chapter 56

UNDER THE DIM, CALMING LIGHTS of her gleaming kitchen, Linda Parker removes the last of her French crockery from the dishwasher and neatly stacks them in their allotted spaces inside the cupboards. It's dark outside and the rain is relentless. She glances across at the bifold doors and the water streaming down the glass. She shakes her head, disapprovingly. When will it ever stop?

With the dishwasher empty, she turns to the sink and runs the hot water. From the cupboard below, she grabs the non-toxic clementine kitchen spray and a brand-new dishcloth. She rinses the cloth in the water and squeezes out the excess. Spraying the white granite worktops with several layers of orange-scented mist, she begins to vigorously wipe and clean.

'Julian?' she calls.

He does not respond. She glances back towards the rear of the kitchen and the hallway but doesn't see any sign of him. She listens but hears nothing, not even the television. 'Julian, do you want a drink before bedtime? I think I'll have a peppermint tea. What do you think?'

Still, he does not respond. She shrugs. Perhaps he's upstairs, brushing his teeth.

She sprays one extra layer and rinses the cloth again. Through her peripheral vision she sees something move.

She looks across at the glass doors and in the reflection sees a pale face looking down at her. Linda's heart leaps into her mouth and she jumps.

She feels hands on her arms. 'Darling, it's only me,' laughs Julian.

'Oh God. Don't do that, you frightened the life out of me.'

'Why so jumpy?' he says, locking his arms around her waist and pulling her to him.

'I'm not. I was just elsewhere.'

'Focusing on your worktops.'

She clicks her tongue and slips from his embrace. 'Someone has to clean them.'

'Linda, they're spotless. You cleaned them twice after dinner.'

She rolls her eyes and wipes. 'Why did we have to get white? Of all colours. White! We should have gone darker.'

He places his hands gently on her hips and kisses her ear. '*We* didn't, darling. I recall that might have been my dear wife's decision.'

He lifts the back of her hair and kisses her neck. She feels a shiver down her spine.

'Give me your hand,' he says.

She frowns. 'Why?'

'It's a surprise.'

'What kind of surprise?'

'Just give me your hand.'

He reaches for her wrist and takes it gently in his hand. 'Relax,' he says.

She smiles. 'I know what you're doing.'

'I'm not sure that you do, madam.'

He places her palm onto his crotch. Under his tracksuit bottoms, he's hard, as she suspected.

'There's something about a gal who cleans so meticulously that just fires up my loins.'

He lets go of her wrist. She lifts her hand away and turns to face him. 'I'm a gal who could do worse than cleaning her husband's dirty mind.'

He presses himself into her and hugs her gently. 'Love you, my little sparrow.'

She kisses him and he begins to grind against her. 'Let's do it here,' he says.

Placing her hands on his chest, she looks directly into his eyes and smiles. 'Let's do it in bed.'

He arches his eyebrow at her. 'Are we on a promise?'

'Maybe.'

Julian slaps his palms together and rubs them. 'OK. Wasn't expecting that, but I'm delighted. I'll go shower,' he says with a boyish nervousness.

'You do that.'

'Want me to take the rubbish out?'

She shakes her head. 'I'll finish up. See you in a moment.'

As Julian hurries upstairs, Linda puts away the spray bottle and hangs the dishcloth to dry over the edge of the sink. From the stainless-steel kitchen bin, she hauls out the black rubbish bag and ties the top corners together. Switching off the kitchen lights, she carries the bag down the hallway to the steps leading to the lower ground door at the front of the house. She opens the door and hurries across to the bins. Aside from the falling rain, the street is pleasantly quiet and dark, the street lights obscured by the shade of the trees lining the pavement on either side. She lifts the bin lid, deposits the bag and drops the lid. She notices someone across the street, standing by a tree, watching her. Linda blinks the rain from her eyes, but whoever it is, if indeed there was someone there, is gone. She feels a chill in her stomach and hurries back inside, out of the rain.

Glancing back, she sees no one. 'Pull yourself together,' she says. There's a small utility room with a sink in the basement. She rarely comes in here and clicks her disapproval at the mess left by Julian. Household tools, rolls of masking tape, half-empty buckets of paint are stacked untidily on the floor. She cleans her hands at the sink, rubbing thoroughly with antibacterial soap, and thinks nothing more of whoever she may or may not have just seen outside.

After hurrying upstairs to the first floor, she stops outside Charlotte's room and peers inside. Her heart warms at the sight of her nine-year-old daughter sleeping soundly on her bed. She pulls the door closed. Best not to wake her just in case she and Julian make too much noise.

Julian is on his front, lying naked on the bed reading the news on his phone. His bottom is large, round and smooth like an adult baby's. She leans across and slaps it. His cheeks wobble like jelly. Julian tosses his phone aside, turns over onto his back and grins. 'Hey, Mama, I like me some of that.'

She notices his penis is still erect. 'What were you reading to keep that up?'

He takes it in his hand. 'Honey, this baby is powered by love alone.'

She pulls off her blouse and jeans and puts them into the wash basket.

'Come to Daddy.'

She laughs. 'What on earth has got into you tonight?'

'I'm of the mind that we fuck like it's the last fuck we'll ever have.'

'I need to shower first.'

'No, don't do that. I like you a bit . . . grubby.'

'Eww,' she says, slipping out of her bra and pants. She drops them in the basket, enters the en-suite bathroom and runs the shower as she brushes her teeth.

Above the din of the water, she hears Julian's voice.

'What?' She calls with a mouthful of toothpaste.

'Your phone's ringing. It's downstairs. Do you want me to get it?'

Who could be phoning at this time? 'No, leave it. I'll call them back tomorrow.'

With a shower cap on her head, she enters the hot shower and lathers herself in soap. She hears Julian's voice again. Shouting this time. 'I can't hear you,' she calls.

She finishes and dries herself down.

'OK. I'm ready,' she says, walking into the bedroom.

She stops, her heart jumps to her mouth. 'What the fuck?' Julian is sitting on the floor, his wrists bound to his ankles with black duct tape. His neck, face and head are completely covered in tape also. 'Julian?' The room has a strange smell, like cold damp clothes. For the second time that evening she sees the reflection in the window of a pale face standing over her. He is raising his arm. She looks up and sees the glow of small blue lights rushing towards her. A blinding bolt of electrical pain surges through her neck and body and then everything goes dark.

Chapter 57

IT HAD NIGGLED ARCHER THAT Linda Parker had not returned her call. Plus, it didn't help that no one was available to look in on the family. The fact that her phone kept ringing to voicemail bothered Archer too. Quinn had suggested the Parkers might be out for the evening or had gone away for a break, although he had said this with a degree of hesitancy. She knew he shared the same discomfort that she did. So, Archer decided to drive up to Stoke Newington and check out for herself. Quinn would remain as the senior officer and supervise the stake out at Brynn Hughes's house with Sergeant Armstrong and his team. She promised she'd be back as soon as she could.

It's almost ten thirty in the evening. The traffic has thinned and her journey to Osbald Road was thankfully the best part of forty-five minutes and no more, despite the driving rain. Indicating left, she brakes and reverse parks into an available space outside number thirty. Locking the car, she walks up the leafy affluent street of Edwardian houses, under the shelter of the trees. The Parker house has two front doors, both painted a glossy blue. One is at the top of five steps, the main door; the other is adjacent to the steps on the lower ground floor. A kind of tradesman's entrance. Her heart sinks when she sees there is no light or sign of life from any window. Perhaps, as Quinn had suggested, the family has gone away or is out for the evening. Other people have lives after all. Grabbing the rail, she climbs the steps up to the door and presses the doorbell. An electronic chime tolls inside. She waits but no one answers. She pushes the button once more. Moments pass, no lights switch on, no one answers. Glancing around the neighbourhood, she sees warm lighted rooms in all the homes. Focusing back on the Parker house, her eyes catch the letter box. Crouching down, she peers through it. Inside, the hallway is gloomy and full of shadows. Taking out her iPhone, she presses the torch button and points the beam through the narrow slot. She sees a console table. Something on top grabs her attention. Narrowing her gaze, she sees a mobile phone. Archer redials Linda Parker's number. The phone on the console table glows and rings. Pulling back, she stands and catches her breath. Part of her thinks this could mean nothing. It's really not unfeasible that Linda has left it behind if she has gone out for the evening. She mulls this over and can't shake the feeling that something just isn't right.

She peers over the rail at the tradesman's entrance below. It's dark and difficult to make anything out. She points the phone's torch beam at the door. Her stomach clenches like a fist. The door is slightly ajar. She hurries down the steps and hesitates at a thudding sound coming from above. Looking up, she sees a child looking down at her from the second floor, her hands pressed against the pane. Her small pale face is twisted in terror. Archer's pulse begins to quicken.

Her grip tightens on the phone. She dials Quinn.

'I'm beginning to think this could be a long night,' he answers.

'He's here, Harry. He's here at the Parkers.'

'What?! Have you seen him?'

'No . . . no. He may even have gone. I've seen Charlotte. She's terrified. I'm going in.'

'Grace, wait—'

'I have to.'

'Grace, if he's in there—'

'Call in local backup and get over here as quick as you can.'

'Don't do it. What're you going to do if he's there?'

'I'll think of something. I'm not waiting, just get me backup.'

'Fuck! I'm on it.'

She ends the call and takes three calming breaths. The trades-man's entrance has been forced open. The wood is chipped, the lock is old. It looks like it's been forced with a flat blade screwdriver to get access.

Archer is inside. There are steps leading up to the ground floor. To her right is a half-open door. She points the beam inside. It's a utility room with tools piled on the floor. She spots a Stanley knife on a table and reaches for it.

Archer climbs the stairs, quietly, listening, eyes scanning, heart pounding. Her priority has to be Charlotte. If her parents are dead, she must get the girl out of here before she sees something that will scar and haunt her for the rest of her life. Considering the terrified face Archer has just seen at the window, it may already be too late. If the Silent Man is still here, then this story may not end as she would like it to.

Archer passes the console table and ascends the stairs, quiet as a mouse. She reaches the landing and looks down the hallway to the bedroom at the end. The door is half open. She makes her way down, her senses alert.

Her heart leaps. The door begins to open slowly inwards.

Through the gloom, she can see two shapes on the floor. Her throat dries. She points the torch at them. Two naked people: a man and a woman, sit back to back with their knees up and their wrists taped to their ankles. Their heads and necks are taped together, mummified as one. Archer feels sick.

'Linda Parker. Julian Parker. This is the police. Are you OK?'

No movement from the man. The woman twitches.

Relief surges through Archer.

'Is he still here, Linda?'

She can't move her head, but Archer can see her hands. They are trembling but with one she manages to give a thumbs-up.

'Brynn Hughes, officers will be here any minute. There is nowhere for you to go.'

There is no response. She knows he's in the bedroom, waiting for her. She is a fly to his spider. Archer listens for the sound of sirens, praying they are close. But there is nothing. Dismay hits her when Linda's body begins to shake and spasm: she's running out of air.

'Shit!'

She has to do something now or the woman will die. Archer cannot let that happen. Pocketing her phone, she presses the button on the Stanley knife and slides out the blade.

She runs, charging through the door, swinging the blade. She frowns. There's no sign of him. She switches on the light, but it doesn't come on. Has he turned the mains off? She sees a door. An en suite perhaps. Is he in there? Her heart's racing. No time. Hurry. She crouches down, eyes everywhere. She feels Linda's face with one hand and finds the imprint of her lips. With the other, she cuts a hole in the tape and quickly does the same with Julian, who is still not moving. She hears Linda gasp. Archer begins to cut her wrists. She jumps at the sound of pounding feet. Looking up, she sees his silhouette rush from the bathroom.

The Silent Man leaps at her, and hooking his arm around her neck, yanks her off Linda. The Stanley knife slips from her grasp as he hauls her off her feet and drags her across the room, choking her. Lifting her arm, Archer drives her elbow into his side as hard as she can, once then twice. Black spots appear in front of her eyes. Desperate, she kicks back at his shins and reaches for his face, scratching, tearing, but all she gets is the tape covering his mouth. She hears him groaning angrily at this. Through the corner of her eye, she can see the small blue flashing lights of the taser in his other hand getting closer. He pushes her towards the wall, but she lifts her legs and pushes back with all her strength. They fall back onto the floor, his grip loosening.

Archer turns quickly, facing him, and punches him twice in the face. The black and white paint is smeared. He looks even more deranged. She grabs his hand holding the taser and slams it three times against the leg of the bed. His face contorts and he drops the weapon. She reaches for it, but he is strong, grabs her arms and twists her over onto her back. With one arm pressing her neck, he uses the other to try and grab the taser. Archer's heart sinks. Gritting her teeth, she tries to push his arm off her neck but she is weakening. His eyes are wild, his lips remain tightly closed. She turns her head, searching for the taser. She sees it. It's about an inch from her hand. She pushes against him and tries to get to it before he does. Her head is spinning. Her eyes blinking. She sees a third arm reaching down. A bare slender arm, with manicured nails, picks up the taser.

Archer looks up to see Linda Parker, her face half concealed in black tape that hangs off her like charred skin. One eye is visible and it's wide with fury. She screams and slams the taser into the Silent Man's neck. She cries a visceral, primal scream as he tumbles off Archer and falls unconscious to the floor. Outside, she hears sirens approaching. Archer breathes a sigh of relief. She looks across to see Julian Parker slumped on the floor. Archer wastes no time, jumps to her feet, and runs to him. She checks his pulse. Nothing.

'Oh, Julian,' cries Linda.

Archer inserts her finger into the hole she had made in the tape covering his mouth. She pulls at the tape covering his nose and mouth, tearing it from his face. As the police boots pound up the stairs, Archer pushes down on Julian Parker's chest and tries to resuscitate him.

Chapter 58

I T HAD BEEN ALMOST 2 a.m. by the time Archer returned to Roupell Street via the hospital, where she had been checked for her injuries. There was nothing serious, just some bruising on her neck to match the bruise on her eye. Terrific.

Quinn had insisted that she not be alone.

'I'll be downstairs while you get some shut-eye. If you need me, just shout,' he had said.

Archer's adrenaline had subsided. Her mind was racing but she was also too drained to argue. Besides, with Grandad absent, the house felt like the heart and soul had been yanked from it, and for that reason she just couldn't bear to be alone in it. She thanked Quinn and climbed the stairs in what she would think later was an almost zombie-like trance.

She had stripped, put all her clothes into the wash basket and taken two Nytol to get her on the path to a half-decent night's sleep. She showered and shampooed, scrubbing off any trace of the killer that might have lingered on her body. Pulling on clean pyjamas, she slipped under the covers and closed her eyes. The search for the Silent Man was over. They had found him, arrested him and put him into a cell in Charing Cross. It was a relief to think that no one else would suffer at his hands. That's what made this godforsaken job worthwhile.

Archer stirs and wakes to the sound of the kettle boiling and the chatter of a television news anchor coming from the living room downstairs and remembers Quinn stayed last night. She slides out of bed, yawns, stretches and caresses her sore neck.

After a shower and a light breakfast, they make their way to the car which Quinn had parked in the only available space at the opposite end of Roupell Street. It's a crisp cool morning. The first without rain in what seems like weeks.

'Thanks for staying last night,' says Archer.

'No worries. Happy to. You've had a tough two weeks.'

'We both have,' she replies, looking at the scar on his temple. 'How's your head?'

'With these painkillers it feels like it's just a scratch.' He takes out a small brown plastic bottle. 'These are some top-quality gear, Grace. Recommended for all occasions. I'll do you a mates rates deal if you're interested?' He winks at her.

Archer smiles. 'Considerate of you but I'll pass.'

They have an 8 a.m. meeting with DCI Pierce, who is waiting for them in her office. 'Come in. Sit down.'

They sit opposite her.

'First up, how are you doing, Grace?'

'A bit bruised but fine.'

Pierce holds Archer's gaze for a moment. 'Are you sure about that?'

'As sure as sure can be.'

'OK then.' She turns to Quinn, 'Harry?'

'All good here.'

'Splendid. I'm really grateful to both of you for all that you've done on this case. Top work. Grace, I can't say that I like the idea of you putting your life at risk, but you followed your

366

instincts last night. You caught the killer and saved both Linda Parker and Julian Parker. I couldn't be prouder. This is a major feather in our cap.'

'We're all about the feathers,' says Quinn.

Pierce purses her lips. 'They can do us no harm, Harry.'

'I suppose,' he replies.

'So, you're interviewing Hughes this morning?'

'At nine,' says Archer.

'Grace, are you sure you want to do this . . . he tried to kill you after all.'

'I want to see this investigation through to the end, Clare. Besides, it's not as if he's my first. I have fewer exes than I have men who have tried to kill me.'

'Good Lord . . . OK. Please go ahead and do your best. By the way, apparently, they had problems processing him last night.'

'What happened?'

'He wouldn't talk. Remained quiet the whole time. Refused to answer any questions. You may get the same response this morning.'

'Understood. We'll work on him.'

'Good luck.'

At her desk, Archer picks up the case folder containing the notes and photos of each victim. She searches through her drawers and finds what she's looking for. She takes out a packet of wet wipes.

'Grace, Harry,' calls Klara.

Archer looks up to see her walking towards them from her office.

'How're you doing, Grace?' Klara asks.

'Still here.'

'I won't keep you. I know you're heading down to interview Hughes. He applied for his street performers licence ten years back under a different act called The Ghost, in which he stood still for ages but would occasionally come to life and jump at people. That licence expired in 2018 and was not renewed. I searched for the Silent Man and found it registered under Paul Finch's name and a Royal Mail Post Office Box.'

'Cunning,' says Quinn. 'And why Paul Finch?'

'He can tell us,' says Archer.

'OK. Thanks, Klara. Great work as always.'

Brynn Hughes is waiting for them in one of the interview rooms in the basement. His face remains partially coated in streaks of black and white grease paint. Archer and Quinn sit at the table opposite him. He's sitting upright, hands splayed on the table. Eyes wide, he wears an innocuous, surprised expression as if he's not quite sure why he's here.

'Hello, Brynn. Remember me?' asks Archer.

He cocks his head and arches his dark eyebrows, affecting a questioning expression. He doesn't respond. He doesn't even blink.

Quinn speaks. 'Are you going to keep up this silent treatment, Brynn? We don't really have the time, the inclination or the stomach to put up with it for more than we must. Happy for you to go back to your cell because, buddy, you were caught in the act and you ain't going anywhere.'

Hughes gives Quinn a benign and helpless look.

Archer slides across the packet of cleaning wipes. 'It's time for the Silent Man to leave, Brynn. Wipe him away. Take off that mask, come out of there and talk to us.'

A murderous look flashes on his face.

Archer tenses but holds his gaze as she slowly retrieves her hand. 'It's over, Brynn.'

A moment passes. Hughes closes his eyes and breathes slowly through his nose. He reaches for the wipes, removes two and begins to clean his face and eyes. He removes two more and rubs them over his forehead. Archer takes out her iPhone and switches the camera to selfie mode. She turns it towards Hughes. He looks at his image on the screen and uses it as a mirror to finish his ablutions. It takes him almost five minutes and the entire pack before he is done. He sits back and looks at Archer.

'Thank you,' he says.

'Are you ready to talk?' Archer asks.

Hughes clasps his hands and rests them on the table. He stares down at them blankly. After a moment, he replies, 'Yes.'

Chapter 59

'I'M NOT A BAD PERSON,' says Hughes.

Archer pauses at this statement, exchanging a glance with Quinn.

'You don't have a brief,' she says, after a moment.

'I don't need one.'

'Very well.'

Quinn starts the recording.

Archer begins. 'This interview is being recorded and may be given in evidence if your case is brought to trial. We are in an interview room at Charing Cross Police Station. I am Detective Inspector Grace Archer. The other police officer present is Detective Sergeant Harry Quinn. Please state your full name and date of birth.'

Hughes pauses before answering. 'Brynn Hughes. Twenty-first April, 1983.

'Brynn, on the evening of the twenty-fifth of March, you were arrested for the attempted murder of Linda Parker and Julian Parker of forty-two Osbald Road.'

'Yes, that's correct.'

'Can you tell us why you tried to murder them?'

'I'm not a bad person,' he repeats. His hands, bunched into fists, gently massage his eyes, leaving the skin pink and sore-looking.

'Brynn, please answer the question.'

'They're bad people.'

'What do you mean by that?'

'They're terrible parents. Abusers. Vile abusers.'

'What makes you say that?'

'I was there.'

'What did you see?'

'I saw a desperate child damaged by the behaviour and actions of her parents.'

'Can you give us examples of this behaviour and actions?'

'I saw them argue before and during Charlotte's party.'

'What type of argument?'

'Snapping at each other. Swearing, they were. Snide comments and the like. Charlotte was taking it all in.'

'Did she tell you that?'

He pauses before answering. 'She didn't have to.'

'But how do you know she was so affected by this argument?'

'I could feel it.'

'You could feel her pain?'

'Every bit of it.'

'Describe it.'

Hughes looks down at the table. 'She was upset. Angry. Terrified. She wanted to leave . . . to run away.'

'Did you talk to Charlotte at any stage?'

'Of course not. It would ruin the experience.'

'What experience would that be?'

'The magic of the Silent Man. He can never speak.'

'How could you feel Charlotte's pain?' asks Archer.

Hughes places his hand on his chest. 'She reached out to me. In here.'

'OK,' says Archer as she removes photos from the folder and places them in front of Hughes. 'Do you recognise the people in these photos?'

372

He scans the pictures. 'Yes.'

'Did you murder Jason Todd, Robert Whitmore and Thomas and Lowri McKenna?' Archer asks.

'What do you think?' replies Hughes.

'Please answer the question, Brynn.'

'Yes.'

'You covered their heads and necks with duct tape, strangling and suffocating them. Why kill them in that way?'

'They had to be silenced.'

'But why cover their heads in tape?'

'Taping just the mouth and nose is not enough. Restricting their sight and hearing is justice for their crimes.'

Archer feels her skin crawling. 'Do you feel nothing for the terror your victims suffered?'

'I was doing it for the children. They are safer now.'

'Do you really believe that?'

'I do.'

Archer looks down at the photo of Jason Todd. 'OK, let's start with Jason Todd. Why did you kill him?'

'I told you: he was a bad person. They all were. Abusers and bullies. I saw the way they treated their children and other children too. I felt it.'

'What did you see?'

'Violence. Physical. Mental. They deserved what was coming to them.'

'Did you witness Jason Todd abusing his son either physically or mentally?'

'Yes.'

'Can you elaborate on that?'

'At Lucas's birthday party, I saw Jason Todd was drunk. He was angry. Lucas was terrified. As a consequence, Jason Todd broke the boy's arm.'

'The other witnesses will tell you that was an accident.'

Hughes levels his gaze with Archer's. 'He was not fit to be a parent.'

'How do you think Lucas feels about you murdering his father?'

'He will thank me one day.'

'You said Lucas was terrified. Did he communicate this to you?'

'He didn't need to.'

'Then how did you know?'

'I could feel it.'

'You keep saying that you feel the emotions of the children. That is just bullshit,' says Quinn.

'I have strong empathy.'

'Do you now?'

'How did you get into Jason Todd's home?' asks Archer.

'I was watching him from outside. He left the door open.'

'Simple as that,' says Quinn.

'Simple as that,' Hughes repeats.

'Why did you kill Robert Whitmore?' Archer asks.

'He was cruel ... to his daughter ... to the other kids.'

'In what way was he cruel?'

'He made Uma cry. I didn't like that. It was her birthday. It upset me.'

'Could you feel her pain too?'

'Naturally.'

'All parents at some stage make their kids cry. It's part of being a parent,' says Archer.

Hughes snorts. 'Whitmore was the same as the others.'

'What do you mean by that?'

'He was no different to Todd. To the Parkers. The McKennas. He also liked to drink. You should never drink when looking after children.'

'Sounds to me like you're triggered when you witness something you don't like,' says Quinn.

Archer notices a brief twitch in Hughes's eye.

'They were bad people.'

'So you keep telling us.'

'How did you get into the Whitmore house?' Archer asks.

'I was in the kitchen after Uma's party. I saw the keys and took them when no one was looking.'

'Why did you kill Thomas and Lowri McKenna?'

'They were vulgar drunks. Every night they were pissed. No parent, no matter who they are, should be off their heads when looking after a child. They got what they deserved.'

'How did you know they were off their heads every night?' Archer asks.

'I knew McKenna. I worked with him. He would come to work boasting about him and his wife and how they were amazing foster parents but all the while he was stinking of alcohol. It infuriated me. I followed them and watched them. Sometimes when they left the pub. Sometimes when they were at home.'

'Kirsty May was their foster child. If she was here, she would tell you a different story.'

'Children do not see what I see.'

'Kirsty May is not a child.'

'That's your opinion.'

'Did you feel Kirsty May's pain too?' Archer asks.

'I freed her from them.'

'Is Jason Todd the first parent you've killed?'

He shifts in his chair. 'Yes.'

Archer holds his gaze, but Hughes looks away.

'Have you been to any other parties as the Silent Man and witnessed this so-called abuse?'

'No.'

'So, Lucas Todd's party was the first?'

'Yes.'

Archer tries a different approach. 'As the Silent Man, have you murdered anyone prior to Jason Todd?'

'No.'

'As Brynn Hughes, have you murdered anyone?'

A knock on the door interrupts the interview.

Tianna Rowland, the custody officer, a sturdy woman with a friendly demeanour, says, 'Excuse me, DI Archer, Klara would like a quick word.'

'Pausing the interview for a quick break,' says Archer. 'I'll be out in one moment.' Archer turns back to Hughes. 'Brynn, can I get you a drink?'

He shakes his head.

Archer and Quinn leave Hughes. Klara is waiting in the custody suite corridor with her iPad.

'Sorry for the interruption but I thought this important. Marian and Mel are leading the house-to-house interviews in the street and area where Hughes lives. They were able to get a contact in Bristol. An ex-girlfriend of his. Iris Wilson. Before she married, her name was Pond. She was very helpful. Apparently, Hughes has lived in Holstein Way since he was fourteen. His parents moved from Swansea to London in early 1997, looking for better job opportunities. Hughes's mother had an affair with a man she worked with and left the family home, abandoning her son and leaving him with his abusive father. She said Brynn was a sweet, shy and introverted kid who had a tough time from other kids at school too.'

'Are his parents still alive?' Quinn asks.

'His mother certainly is, but they have nothing to do with each other. His dad, we're not sure about. On paper it would seem his father, Ifan Hughes, is still alive, but no one has seen him, by my current calculation, in almost twenty-two years.'

'Has he been reported missing?' asks Archer.

'No. There are no records. But look at these.' Klara swipes open her iPad screen. 'Marian sent these photos through. They were taken this morning inside Hughes's garage.'

Archer flicks through a series of photos depicting a concrete floor with a rectangular indent in the centre.

'Remind you of anything?' Klara asks.

'A grave.'

'His father's final resting place,' says Quinn.

Archer's mind is racing. 'Bullied at school. Abandoned by his mother. Abused by his father.'

'Perhaps that sweet, shy, introverted teenager had had enough and flipped and killed his father,' says Quinn.

'The father was the spark that lit the fuse,' says Archer.

'I've started the ball rolling for the Ground Penetrating Radar. Should take a day or two,' says Klara.

'Excellent work. Thanks, Klara.' Archer turns to Quinn. 'Could you lead with stealing Paul Finch's identity? I want to get my head around Klara's update.'

'No worries.'

In the interview room, Quinn restarts the recording.

'Brynn, why did you use Paul Finch's name when you arranged to meet Tommy McKenna at the Angel in Bermondsey?'

'Obviously I couldn't use my own name, could I? Best the bar staff have Finch's name. He's an asshole, anyway.'

'You used his name again when people booked the Silent Man for their parties. You told them your real name was Paul Finch. You even applied for your Covent Garden street licence using his name.'

'Less attention focused on me the better.'

'What is it about Paul Finch that you don't like?'

Hughes considers his response. 'I never liked him. He's a bully and a crook, he is. Treats the people that work for him like garbage.'

'Was using his name some sort of payback?'

'As I saw it, if things turned to shit, then the scent would be on him and not me.'

'That didn't quite go to plan, did it?' says Quinn.

Hughes does not respond.

'Who's Iris?' asks Archer.

Hughes blinks and hesitates. 'Could I 'ave a glass of water, please?'

Quinn is up and returns moments later with a plastic cup of water.

Hughes drinks it. 'Thank you.'

'So, Iris Pond, as she was back then. Tell us about her.'

'She was my girlfriend, I suppose. For a time. And then she wasn't.'

'What happened?'

'She left. With her parents. Moved to Streatham and then to Bristol.'

'Was she important to you?'

'Back then, yes.'

'Did you love her?'

Hughes's eyes begin to well. 'With all my heart.'

'Did you not keep in touch?'

Hughes folds his arms, closes his eyes, his jaw clenches. 'No.'

'Why?'

He breathes steadily through his nose. 'My dad ... '

'Did he stop you seeing her?' asks Archer.

Tears run down his cheeks. 'He was so cruel. How can someone you're supposed to depend on ... someone you look up to ... be like that?'

'You say "was". What happened to your father?' Archer asks.

Hughes swallows and rubs his face with his palms. 'He dug a grave for me.'

'In the garage?'

He snorts. 'You've found that, 'ave you?'

'Is your father buried there, Brynn?'

'One time he lost it. He attacked me for no real reason. None that I can put my finger on anyway. He was strong and got the better of me. He taped up my feet and hands. He wrapped my mouth with layers of tape, then threw me into that grave and left me there alone for two nights.'

Archer's own experience of being locked in a pit for two weeks surfaces to her mind but she pushes it away.

'And then he was full of remorse for his actions. He couldn't do enough to make up for his behaviour. But that soon changed, and he returned to normal. The beatings I had long gotten used to. It was the psychological stuff that tipped me over the edge. The fucking with my head. The gaslighting. The name calling. The holding me responsible for his miserable life. You name it.'

'I'm sorry you had to go through all of that,' says Archer.

Hughes rests his elbows on the table, leans over and presses his palms against his face.

'Brynn, is your father buried in the garage?'

Head down, he sighs heavily. 'Yes.'

'Did you kill your father, Brynn?'

'I had to. Or he would have killed me.'

'Brynn, just to be clear. You have admitted to killing Jason Todd, Robert Whitmore, Thomas and Lowri McKenna and your father, Ifan Hughes. You have also admitted to the attempted murder of Linda and Julian Parker?'

'Yes.'

'There's a gap of twenty-two years between the murder of your father and the murder of Jason Todd. Did you ... '

'I didn't murder anyone if that's what you're asking.'

'That's quite a long length of time.'

'I'm tired ... I didn't get much sleep.'

'We'll keep going just for a little while longer and then we'll finish up. Is that OK?'

'I just want it to end.'

'Only you can do that,' says Quinn.

'Twenty-two years passed since your father's death. Something must have set you off with Jason Todd.'

'My dad aside, in the beginning I never wanted to hurt anyone but what choice did I 'ave? I would see children being damaged and had to do something. It started small, it really did. Over the years I would go to the family homes and break their windows or scratch their cars but none of that was enough. Later, I would wait for them at night and assault them if I could but that still didn't fill the void.'

'Where did this void come from, Brynn?'

'The day Dad died, I found years of letters and gifts from Iris that he'd kept from me hidden in that grave. I was so incensed, I was. Everything changed that day ... everything. One of the gifts was jars of face paint.' He smiles at the memory. 'Iris knew of my dream about joining a circus. She was the only one that ever believed in me.'

'You must have missed her,' says Archer.

'Of course. I read all her letters. They broke me. Everything could have been so different if only ... if only Iris and I ... Anyway, when I discovered the letters, I knew what I had to do. I had to kill him. He was worthless and dangerous. He murdered me and I suppose created the Silent Man. I waited for him that night. I painted my face. I was playing my music

380

loud. He hated noise of any kind. He came home. Saw me and attacked me. I hit him with a mallet and taped his hands, his feet, his face. And then chucked him into the grave. Just like he'd done with me. I then filled it with cement.'

'You're smiling,' says Archer.

'Am I?' He shrugs. 'It's a happy memory.'

'Do you feel guilty about your father's murder?'

'He was a monster.'

'Did you see any of your father's traits in your victims?'

'I did it all to protect the children. I didn't want them to suffer what I had suffered.'

'OK, Brynn. I think we'll leave it there for the time being. The custody officer will escort you back to your cell. Get some rest, we can talk later.'

Hughes watches her with doleful eyes as she stands. 'I only wanted to protect the kids. I'm not a bad person. Truly, I'm not.'

Chapter 60

ARCHER HAD RACED FROM THE office after the interview with Hughes and driven to St Thomas's to pick up Grandad. Signing him out had gone smoothly and getting him to the car was, mercifully, easy.

Now, on the journey back in the unmarked Volvo, she glances at him through the rear-view mirror. He has a faint trace of a smile on his face as he watches the world go by.

'It's all changed so much,' he says, still with the slightest of slurs.

Archer smiles. 'You sound like you've been in hospital for twenty years rather than two weeks.'

The lights go red at the junction with the Old Vic Theatre.

'It felt that way sometimes,' he replies.

She stares at him and squeezes the steering wheel. 'I'm sure it did.'

'How long now?' he asks. In the past ten minutes he has asked this same question twice.

'We'll be home in five minutes.'

He nods his head.

'I'll make you something to eat when we get home. It's gone lunchtime,' says Archer.

Grandad continues to stare out the window. He seems not to have heard.

The car horn behind them blasts. The lights are green. Archer waves an apology, eases off the brakes and continues up Waterloo Road, turning right into Alaska Street and onto Roupell Street.

'Here we are,' says Grandad.

'This place hasn't changed much, has it?' Archer says.

'No. Not ever. You know these cottages were built in the eighteen hundreds.'

'I do. I live here too, remember.'

Grandad chuckles. 'Yes, you do.'

Archer is relieved to find a parking spot close to the house. She gets out and helps Grandad out.

'Thank you.'

'Hello, Jake. How are you feeling?' comes a voice. It's their next-door neighbour, Rita Barry, a widow in her seventies.

'Hello ... erm ... ' says Grandad, with a puzzled look.

Archer can see he is trying to put a name to the face.

'Hello, Rita,' she says.

'Yes, Rita, I'm doing just fine, thank you,' says Grandad.

Archer smiles an apology at her. Rita shakes her head and mouths a *no problem*.

'Nice to see you home again.'

Archer pulls two bags from the boot. One containing Grandad's clothes. A second containing boxes of new drugs.

'Nice to be home,' says Grandad.

'I'm just popping out. If you need help with anything, do let me know.'

'Thanks, Rita,' says Archer, unlocking the front door and pushing it open.

Inside, Grandad settles into his armchair.

'Cup of tea?' Archer asks, crossing to the kitchen.

'Yes, please.'

She drops the bags on the kitchen table and fills the kettle. She pulls off her coat and hangs it over the back of a kitchen chair. She makes them both a mug of strong hot tea and takes them into the lounge. She sets Grandad's on the side table by the armchair and sits on the sofa opposite.

'Thank you,' he says, lifting the mug. 'Cheers.'

Archer smiles. 'Cheers.'

They sit in silence for a moment, Grandad staring blankly across the room at nothing in particular.

'I can make us something to eat if you're hungry.'

He blinks and looks at her with a surprised expression as if suddenly realising she is there. 'What's that?'

'I could make us something to eat if you're hungry.'

'I'm not hungry,' he replies.

'Did you have breakfast?'

He frowns as he considers his answer. 'I think so.'

'It's no problem to make something. The doctor did say you should eat more. He said you've lost a lot of weight.'

'I'm not hungry.'

She regards him for a moment. 'You will tell me if you're feeling OK, won't you?'

It's as if he hasn't heard her. He looks beyond her, his eyes scanning the living room. 'So many memories here ... so many ghosts.'

Archer bites her lip.

He meets her gaze. 'Don't worry about me, dear. I'll be fine.' He takes a sip of tea and wraps his hands around the mug.

Archer's phone rings: Klara. 'Just going to take this call. It's work.'

Grandad smiles. Archer takes the call in the kitchen.

'Hey, Klara.'

'Hi, Grace. Sorry, I know you're working from home this afternoon ... '

'That's OK. What's up?'

'I just noticed your laptop is on your desk.'

'Oh shit! How did I forget that?'

'Easy. The interview ran over, and you had to rush out and pick up Jake.'

Archer glances through the kitchen at Grandad. She is hesitant to leave him.

'Harry's gone home. His head was pounding. I have a bunch of meetings but could bring it over later, after work, if you like,' says Klara.

'No, that's OK. I'll pop over now. I need to get a head start with reports and all that fun stuff.'

'No worries. How's Jake doing?'

'He seems a little spaced out. Still getting used to being home, I think.'

'I bet. Give him my love.'

'I will. Be in the office in fifteen minutes.'

'See you later.'

Archer grabs her coat, pulls it on and enters the living room. 'Grandad, I left my laptop at work. I'm going to race over to the office now and pick it up.'

'OK.'

'I'll be back in around thirty minutes. Call me if you need anything.'

He takes out his mobile phone from his trouser pocket. 'I always keep it close.'

She smiles and arches her brows. 'Please tell me it's charged.'

He shows her the screen. Fully charged. She bends down and kisses him on the forehead. 'I'll pick up something for dinner.'

'That'd be nice.'

'Bye, Grandad.'

'Bye, darling.'

The drive to Charing Cross Police Station takes twenty minutes, but it would have been quicker to walk, Archer thinks, as she remote locks the car and hurries inside. On the third floor, she sees Klara wave at her from her office.

'I picked it up from your desk,' says Klara, handing her the laptop. 'Can't be too careful round here.' She chuckles.

'Thanks, Klara.'

'Don't work too late. You need a break.'

'We all do. Talk later.'

Archer rushes out of the building and jumps into the car. She considers walking home but decides the drive back might not be as bad as the drive here was. How wrong she is. It takes a frustrating twenty minutes to get from Charing Cross and across a gnarled-up Waterloo Bridge. Add a further ten minutes to Roupell Street and a parking spot.

Laptop in hand, she enters the front door suddenly conscious that she never picked up food. *Shit! What is wrong with me?*

'I'm home!' she calls.

She hears the TV. Sounds like he's watching a daytime gameshow.

'Guess what? I forgot to get dinner. How about I order in a Deliveroo?'

Archer walks into the living room. The armchair is vacant. She sets the laptop onto the sofa and switches off the television.

'Grandad?' she calls, peering into the kitchen.

She freezes, her heart sinking.

Grandad is lying on the floor, eyes open, staring at the ceiling, arm outstretched, clutching his mobile phone.

'Grandad,' she says, quietly.

He does not respond.

She runs to him. 'Grandad! Grandad! Can you hear me?' She takes his hand. It's warm. 'Oh God!' Archer takes out her phone and dials 999.

'What's your emergency?' asks the operator.

Archer's head is swirling. 'My grandad . . . '

'I'm sorry?'

'My grandad . . . he's fallen over.'

'Do you need an ambulance?'

'Yes . . . Yes.'

'Can you give me your address, please?'

'Fifty-two Roupell Street.'

Archer leans close to his mouth. She can't hear or feel his breath.

'What's your name, please?'

'Grace Archer. He's not breathing!'

'My name's Vicky, Grace. I'm here to help. The ambulance is on the way.'

'How long . . . How long will it be?'

'Just checking for you.'

'Do you know how to check his pulse, Grace?'

Archer's fingers are already on Grandad's neck. She tries to calm herself. 'There's no pulse.'

'Does your grandad have any health problems?'

'He had a stroke . . . two weeks ago. He just got out of hospital, today.'

'I see . . . Grace, the ambulance will be there in minutes.'

Archer can hear the siren approaching. She rushes to the front door and waves at them. In moments the paramedics, one male, one female, are inside, tending to Grandad.

'Hello. You must be Grace. My name is Paul. This is Adriana. Can you tell us what happened?'

Archer is wringing her hands, unable to take her eyes from Grandad. 'I just came home, and he was lying here. He got out of hospital today. He had a stroke . . . two weeks ago.'

The two paramedics exchange a grave look. They tend to him for several moments, but it seems like forever. Eventually, the medic called Paul stands and gives her *that* look. The *I'm-so-sorry* look.

'Please . . . don't say it.'

'I'm afraid he's gone, Grace,' says Paul. 'It looks like he might have had another stroke.'

Archer chokes back a sob. 'The doctor said he was fine! He can't have had another stroke. They wouldn't have let him out of hospital.'

'Grace . . . '

'No!' Archer feels her pulse quicken. She tries to gather her thoughts, her blood pounding in her ears. 'Someone came here when I left. They came here to our house and got to him. Frankie White's people. Oh God!' She looks to the kitchen table and scans the worktops, searching for a Death Card, Frankie White's signature and final act of revenge. There's nothing. Taking out her phone, she calls Quinn as she searches the living room.

'Hi,' says Quinn.

'Harry, they got him. Grandad. He's gone, Harry. He's dead. Oh God! They got to him.'

'What? Grace, slow down. What's happened?'

'I went out and came back. I found him lying on the kitchen floor. He's dead, Harry. They killed him. White . . . his people.'

'But they're all dead or inside, Grace.'

'We don't know that for sure!'

He sighs. 'Who's with you now?'

'The paramedics.'

'I'm on my way. Let me speak to the paramedics, Grace.'

'Why?'

'Grace, just let me talk to them.'

Archer has never felt so uncertain, so confused in her life. She hands the phone to Paul. He talks to Quinn. Archer looks at Grandad lying peacefully on the floor. She hugs her arms to her chest, her emotions in turmoil, her adrenaline pumping. Paul hands the phone back to her. 'He's on his way.'

Archer nods.

'He said he's calling the police. They will arrange for the funeral directors to come and see to your grandfather. I'm so very sorry, Grace.'

It takes a moment for Archer to reply, 'Thank you.'

'We can stay with you until Mr Quinn gets here.'

'That won't be necessary.'

'Maybe we should.'

'Go. Please.'

'OK. We're so sorry.'

The paramedics leave. Archer is alone with Grandad. There's an unsettling ethereal feel to the silence. She shudders and leaves the kitchen, exiting onto the street. She knocks on their neighbour Mrs Barry's door.

'Grace. Hello again. I saw the ambulance . . . '

'Mrs Barry . . . Rita . . . I need to know if today or any other day you've seen anyone you don't recognise hanging around the street, watching our house.'

'Oh,' she replies, eyes wide, hand on her chest. She considers this and says, 'No, dear, I can't say that I have.'

'Are you positive?'

'Yes, I'm sure.'

'Please think. There must have been someone. They're not that clever.'

'Who's not that clever? I'm sorry, I don't understand. Is everything OK? You seem upset.'

Archer is unable to answer. She walks away and tries another neighbour and gets the same answer. She knocks on house after house, demanding to know what they saw. She does not see the time pass. A police vehicle arrives. A second car pulls into a space at the top of the street. Quinn gets out and looks her way. He is speaking, but she can't hear. Her head is spinning. The neighbours are gathered around her. What's happening? *Grandad.* Quinn is at her side, arm around her guiding her back to the house.

'Come and sit in the living room,' he says.

Archer allows him to take her. She sits on the armchair.

'I'm just going to talk with the police.'

She hears them talking and closes her eyes. Tears well up and stream down her face.

'Hey,' says Quinn, crouching in front of her, his voice gentle. He takes her hand. 'I called Charlie. He said all of White's people are inside. There's no one left, Grace.'

Archer takes three calming breaths.

'The funeral directors are on their way,' says Quinn.

'I left him alone. It was forty minutes. I shouldn't have done it. I shouldn't have left him. It's my fault.'

'It's not your fault. The paramedic said the stroke . . . well . . . it was more than likely quick is what he said.'

Archer drops her head and sobs, 'I should have been with him.'

'I'm sorry, Grace.' Quinn pulls her to him and hugs her gently. 'I'm so very sorry.'

Acknowledgements

First up, thank you to my agent and rock David H Headley. This book would not have been possible without you.

Thanks also to the team at Zaffre: my publisher Ben Willis, Isabella Boyne and designers Nick Stearn and Dominic Forbes for the haunting and beautiful cover.

As always, a big shout out to all the readers, bloggers and reviewers who have supported me and continue to do so.

If you enjoyed *The Silent Man*,
why not join the
DAVID FENNELL READERS' CLUB?

When you sign up you'll receive an exclusive deleted scene,
plus news about upcoming books and exclusive behind the-
scenes-material. To join, simply visit:
bit.ly/DavidFennellClub

Keep reading for a letter from the author . . .

Hello!

Thank you so much for picking up *The Silent Man*.

There's much to say about this book and the inspirations behind it, yet to talk about them here and now would reveal spoilers that would give too much away. And who wants that? What I would say is there are three important story lines spanning a four-part structure. Each of these stories weave into the denouement, which, in case you're wondering, is just a fancy name for the finale. As you'll discover, Grace Archer is going to have a tough time, and once again, there's a high body count yet out of the three books, I believe this is the most emotional read. I hope you agree.

The Silent Man marks the end of a trilogy that began with *The Art of Death* and was followed up with *See No Evil*. To be clear though, this is not the end of Grace Archer. She will return. Who is by her side is another matter.

If you would like to hear more about my books, you can visit www.bit.ly/DavidFennellClub where you can become part of the David Fennell Readers' Club. It only takes a few moments to sign up, there are no catches or costs.

Bonnier Zaffre will keep your data private and confidential, and it will never be passed on to a third party. We won't spam you with loads of emails, just get in touch now and again with news about my books, and you can unsubscribe any time you want.

And if you would like to get involved in a wider conversation about my books, please do review *The Silent Man* on Amazon, on Goodreads, on any other e-store, on your own blog and social media accounts, or talk about it with friends, family or reader groups! Sharing your thoughts helps other readers, and I always enjoy hearing about what people experience from my writing.

Thank you again for reading *The Silent Man*.
All my best,

David Fennell

Don't miss out on Grace Archer's first case . . .

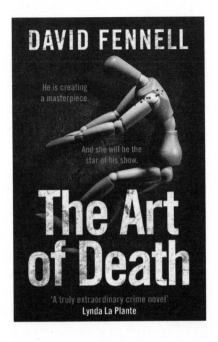

London's latest art installation is a real killer . . .

An underground artist leaves three glass cabinets in Trafalgar Square that contain a gruesome installation: the corpses of three homeless men.

With the artist promising more to follow, newly-promoted Detective Inspector Grace Archer and her caustic DS, Harry Quinn, must race against time to follow what few clues have been left by a savvy killer.

As more bodies are exhibited at London landmarks and live streamed on social media, Archer and Quinn's pursuit of the elusive killer becomes a desperate search.

But when Archer discovers that the killer might be closer than she originally thought – she realises that he has his sights set firmly on her . . .

He is creating a masterpiece. And she will be the star of his show.

AVAILABLE NOW

Don't miss out on Grace Archer's second case . . .

Two men are found dead in London's Battersea Park. One of the bodies has been laid out like a crucifix – with his eyes removed and placed on his open palms.

Detective Inspector Grace Archer and her caustic DS, Harry Quinn, lead the investigation. But when more bodies turn up in a similar fashion, they find themselves in a race against time to find the sadistic killer.

The hunt leads them to Ladywell Playtower in Southeast London, the home to a religious commune lead by the enigmatic Aaron Cronin. Archer and Quinn suspect Cronin's involvement but his alibis are watertight, and the truth seemingly buried. If Archer is to find the killer, she must first battle her way through religious fanatics, London gangsters – and her own demons . . .

AVAILABLE NOW